REVIEWERS QUOTES FOR CAROLEE JOY

Midwest Book Review's Aimee E. McLeod says "Carolee Joy is [a] treasure . . .I sincerely hope to see more written by her in the future."

BY AN ELDRITCH SEA:

"Carolee Joy has captured the otherworldly atmosphere of the Orkneys in BY AN ELDRITCH SEA. You can almost smell the sea air, feel the brisk winds . . . and sense the mysteries waiting to unfold. With an intriguing premise and an appealing, vulnerable shape-shifter hero, BY AN ELDRITCH SEA adds a modern page to the ancient Selkie legends."
~Susan Krinard, Author of TOUCH OF THE WOLF

BY AN ELDRITCH SEA is a captivating tale that centers on relationships and Selkies, a mix that works because author Carolee Joy never loses sight of her prime plot. Paranormal romantic suspense readers will obtain much joy from this well written novel.
~Harriet Klausner, AMAZON.COM

WILD ANGEL:

"If you are a fan of contemporary romance -- buy this book! This was one of the most enjoyable contemporary romances I've read in years! With enough plot twists to keep Alfred Hitchcock himself busy, this one is a real winner!"
~Vykki Hine, GenrEZONE

"A passionate love story." Three stars
~Susan Mobley, ROMANTIC TIMES

WILD FIRE AND ICE CREAM

"I read this superb book in one sitting. The light-hearted moments were just as satisfying as the more serious ones." Four stars
~Kathy Boswell, ROMANTIC TIMES

DETECTIVE NICHOLSON SNORTED. "Your husband was a fence, Mrs. Lanier. Furs and jewelry his specialty. Then he began smuggling contraband. Canada's a pretty hot market for sending and receiving stolen merchandise right now, especially bootlegged cigarettes. That may have been his fatal mistake."

His words riveted Breanna to her chair, and she couldn't look away. "Who would want to kill him?"

"I'd guess it's a pretty extensive list. An irate 'client', the local shipping competition. You."

His words slammed like a physical blow into her calm facade. Her knuckles turned white as she gripped her glass. "You can't be serious."

"Why not? You obviously had the opportunity. Three quarters of a million dollars is one hell of a lot of motive."

Breanna took a deep breath and tried to rally her thoughts. From widow to accused. The idea shocked her so badly she couldn't even find the anger to hurl back a retort for his degrading allegations. "That's ridiculous," she murmured.

Nicholson's green eyes harpooned her with another narrowed gaze. "Is it?"

A Kiss
Before Dark

By Carolee Joy

Dreamstreet Prose
Bedford, Texas

ISBN-10: 1-928704-25-5
ISBN-13: 978-1-928704-25-6

No persons or places in this book are real. All situations, characters, and concepts are the sole invention of the author.

Published March, 2007 in the United States of America

First electronically published in the United States of America by Moon Shadow Books, Starlight Writer Publications, A Division of Romance Foretold, Inc. Copyright © 2000 by Carolee Joy Jacobson
ISBN 1-58697-062-3

Dreamstreet Prose
P.O. Box 1114
Bedford, TX 76095
www.dreamstreetprose.com

Dedication

For my mother, who always encouraged me to dream and always worried about where it led me.

Prologue

They died because of her.

Breanna Alden Lanier stood at the family reception at the funeral home and clutched a lace handkerchief embroidered with her mother's initials. She wound the delicate linen around her fingers, over and over again.

Unable to meet the gazes of the other mourners, she returned to the semi-circle of closed caskets. If only she could see their faces one last time, but even that chance had been destroyed.

She should cry. Maybe if she did, the expressions of cousins and family friends would be sympathetic instead of accusing, but she had no tears left. Just a hollowed out, empty feeling she would carry with her forever. Mother, Father, her brother Brett, dead.

All because of her.

Leaning down, she pressed her cheek against the cold mahogany that entombed her father and closed her eyes. "I'm sorry, Daddy. So sorry," she whispered.

Uncle Murray came up beside her, circled her shoulders with his arm and led her back to the front row of chairs.

Looking only slightly better than a shipwreck survivor, he collapsed into the chair next to her and ran a hand through disheveled hair. "How are you holding up, sweetie?"

"Fine," she murmured and gripped his hand. How could he bear to speak to her when she was responsible for the death of his only sister? "This should be a wedding reception, not a wake," she whispered.

Murray's expression darkened. "You're the one who eloped. Where is Marc?" He surveyed the room, as if he expected her husband to also be hovering near one of the caskets.

Not likely. Marc sympathized but in no way shared her

loss. How could he? He hadn't been allowed to be a part of the family before they were taken from her.

Her fault, again. Why hadn't she waited? Given time, her family could have grown to love Marc, or at least accept him. Once they saw how charming he could be, how happy he made her, everything would have been fine.

Her father would have come around, he always did, except that other time long ago when she'd rebelled, but even that no longer mattered. Eventually, Daddy would have seen how much Marc was like him: ambitious, hard-working, trying to create his own empire for her and the family of their own she longed to have someday.

"He probably went outside for a cigarette," she whispered.

As if on cue, Marc crossed the room and sat down beside her, the smell of smoke hovering around him, making the small, overheated room even stuffier. He nodded a greeting at Murray but didn't offer his hand. Just as well. Murray probably wouldn't have shaken it, anyway.

After a long, endless moment of awkward silence, Murray made his excuses and left. Breanna again felt cut off. Marc's arm around her shoulders should have made her feel loved and protected. She'd made her choice, let herself be swept away with good looks, pretty words and promises, and he was here, beside her. But instead of comfort, his touch only reminded her of what it had cost.

"You'll feel better once the estate is settled, and you know where you stand."

Thankfully, no one else was near enough to overhear his crass observation. "I don't care about the money. I want my family back."

"Well, it's not going to happen. And $75 million is a hell of a lot of consolation."

If she'd thought she couldn't feel any worse, she'd been wrong. "Nothing can make me feel any better, Marc. My family is lost to me forever. And it's my fault!"

He made a disparaging sound. "As if you asked them to follow us? Like you conjured that early winter storm and made their plane crash?" He shook his head. "If they hadn't fought you every step of the way, if they would have wished you well, we wouldn't have had to sneak off to get married, and you'd be dancing at our wedding right now instead of sitting here choking on guilt."

His hand rested against the back of her neck, heavy and possessive. She wished she could move away but couldn't afford to risk his rejection, too. He was all she had left.

He leaned close to her ear. "They made their choice, Breanna. You made yours. And till death do us part."

Chapter 1

Duluth, Minnesota
Six Months Later

Scott Edwards glanced at the Duluth ship canal, then at his watch. Evening shadows loomed over the *Liquid Asset*, moored at Edwards and Sons Fishing Enterprises bayside pier. The lift span of the Aerial Bridge had just been partially raised to enable the Alden's private yacht, the *Breanna Colleen*, to leave the harbor and enter Lake Superior. *Six-thirty. Right on schedule.*

With a little luck, he'd be right behind her. He loaded equipment into the thirty-two foot fishing boat, threw a blue duffel bag jammed with his weekend gear inside the small deck cabin and climbed back onto the dock.

A hand gripped his shoulder. Scott turned to look down into his older brother's hazel eyes.

"Just where the hell do you think you're going so early on a Friday?"

"Early?" Scott shrugged off Derek's hand and assumed a noncommittal expression. "I told you I've got a charter out of Knife River early tomorrow morning. Since I don't share your taste for late night cruising, I'd like to get there before dark and get the boat prepped."

"Tough." Derek raised an eyebrow in what Scott assumed was intended to be an intimidating gesture.

Scott smothered a laugh. Derek used authority like a graduate from the Nazi school of management. Must be from too much time spent under maximum security. Five years in the army. Two in prison. Probably where he met Marc Lanier, but Scott had no way of knowing what had gone on with his brother while he'd been away from Duluth himself.

"So, what's your point, Adolf?"

"You can't leave until those trawlers are checked in."

"The crew foreman's supposed to do that. Where's Kowalski, anyway? Did you give out paychecks at noon again and he's still drinking his lunch?"

Derek scowled and jabbed a finger into Scott's chest. "You've been away from the business for five years, but you sure think you know how to run it, don't you, smart ass. Kowalski's been out sick all day. I can't have one of the crew check the boats in and risk pissing off the union. I'm meeting some buyers. That leaves you, and I don't give a damn if you've got ten charters this weekend. Get those trawlers checked in!"

Scott bit back a retort. Must be legitimate customers Derek was meeting or he wouldn't mention it. He shrugged to hide his irritation. Let Derek think of him as the complacent dolt. It made it easier to keep an eye on things. The charters were incidental, anyway. At least Derek understood the concept of making cash on the side.

Maybe too well.

By the time the last trawler unloaded the day's catch, dusk hung over the harbor. City lights glittered across the smoky gray hillside like fallen stars as Scott steered the *Liquid Asset* northeast from Duluth. Despite Derek and all the problems with the business, he was glad he was back. Minneapolis was too much big city to ever feel like home. A breeze rattled the rigging. Face it. He liked being back near Breanna, even if she didn't know he was there.

Breanna sighed and watched the wake from the yacht send shimmery waves across the dark blue water. Reflected stars danced in the ripples. Why couldn't she remember what had happened two months ago at the Gooseberry River?

The few details she had floated like inconsequential ghosts beside Marc's dramatic story. It probably didn't help that he never missed an opportunity to act the self-sacrificing hero to her guilty child. They had been smelt fishing. Wearing waders several sizes too big, she had lost her balance, slipped and fallen on the slick rocks in the river bottom. Marc had rescued her from the icy current.

He'd saved her life, and now she owed it to him.

"You've got that funny little frown again." Brushing her hair from her temple, Marc's fingers traced the two inch scar, her souvenir from the accident. "You never answered my question. Don't you wish we'd have waited a few more months to get married? Then you could have had it all, instead of just this money gobbling boat."

Breanna shivered from the cool June breeze ruffling her shoulder length black hair. Uneasiness surged through her at the too familiar conversation. "No." She hid the lie behind a smile and zipped her white windbreaker up to her chin. Of course she wished they had waited, but how could she admit it out loud? To him?

So much had happened over the past six months. So much of it she didn't remember clearly, her despair and regret turning her into Marc's puppet as he led her through one wild escapade after another. She couldn't decide if he cared about her at all or if she was just a toy to him. A trophy he'd won that cemented his respectability with the businessmen in town.

Or maybe she was a means to some end she couldn't visualize and didn't understand.

One thing she wished she could forget: her guilt and grief over the loss of her parents and younger brother. If she hadn't been so determined, so headstrong, if she hadn't married Marc, they'd still be alive.

If, if, if. The word whined through her mind, as unceasing as a hungry mosquito.

If only she hadn't lost their baby. But even the details of that night blurred under the weight of depression she'd been fighting for six months.

The tiny moons and stars dangling from her crescent earrings sang in the breezy silence. Marc leaned close and lightly touched a fingertip to them.

"Why do you like this junk? You should wear the jewelry you got from your mother, instead of hiding it away. I don't even know where you keep it."

"At the bank," she murmured, her gaze sliding away from his again. "Why does it matter?"

He shrugged. "If you can't force yourself to wear diamonds and opals, maybe you should sell them and help pay for the upkeep on this god-damn boat."

"You told me last week that your business is taking off. And my photography studio is finally showing a nice profit. I thought we were managing very well. Besides, my father said money problems were the true test of a marriage."

"I suppose you think he did us a favor by disinheriting you." Marc's voice held an unfamiliar edge.

"Well, sometimes I think you married the money and not me," she retorted.

Marc shot her a quick, annoyed glance. "Give me a break. I knew the old man had cut you off before we got married."

She drew in a startled breath. He'd never said that before, how could he have known? Daddy hadn't even told her that, although he had threatened it.

He sighed. "I'm sorry. I didn't mean to drop that on you. Your father came to see me about two days before we left to get married. Gave me the low-down on what life would be like when one defies the Food King. Said if you wouldn't listen to reason, he'd change his will."

She twirled the ties of the windbreaker and tried not to sound defensive. "And?"

"And here we are. See? It didn't matter. It's been six months, Breanna. How long are you going to grieve for a family who didn't give a damn about what you wanted? Watching you brood constantly isn't what I had in mind when we got married."

What did you have in mind, she wanted to ask, but the words refused to budge past the lump in her throat. She sighed and forced herself to meet his gaze. "I'm sorry, Marc. I know my family hurt you, but I can't help feeling responsible after that last horrible argument. I wish we could have shown them they were wrong about you."

He held her next to his side and pressed a kiss to her temple. "Me, too, Princess. But it doesn't matter. You'll be twenty-five next week. I just think it's time for you to stop being daddy's little girl."

Probably. But it was what she'd been all of her life. How could she change without her family to guide her through the transition? How could she stand on her own when she'd chosen a husband as formidable and domineering as her father had been at times?

"It's getting late," he whispered against her ear. "Go on down below and get ready. I'll secure the boat and be with you in a few minutes. Have some more wine and loosen up a little." He refilled her glass and patted her on the behind in dismissal.

Chastised, Breanna nodded, gripped the goblet so tight she feared the stem would snap and went down through the cockpit to the luxuriously appointed stateroom. She drained her glass and set it on the nightstand beside the king size bed.

Something glittered against the plush carpet between the bed and nightstand. She bent to pick it up, the movement making her inexplicably dizzy, and landed on her knees. Her diamond necklace, the one she'd lost at Christmas time. How had it gotten here? It was the only piece of jewelry she'd allowed herself to take home from the safety deposit box at the bank, and it had disappeared.

Marc must have found it and was waiting until later to surprise her. She fastened it around her neck and staggered to her feet.

Okay, he wanted her to relax, she'd try. She shed her jeans and shirt, hung them in the cedar lined closet and slipped into the white satin and lace teddy she found on the bed with a romantic birthday card. The words blurred, but she smiled at the manufactured sentiment. He could be really sweet when he wanted to.

Part of their problems, she realized, stemmed from his mercurial temperament. That kept her off balance, but maybe she needed to accept part of the blame. Dealing with the tragedies of the past six months and her resulting depression couldn't be easy to live with, either.

She pulled a brush through her thick hair and sank to the bed as the room started to spin. Her stomach churned. She shouldn't have let Marc talk her out of fixing a late supper. She raced to the bathroom, overcome with nausea.

A ghost of a woman peered back from the mirror, sapphire blue eyes unnaturally bright. Two splotches of red color stood out on her high cheekbones. Marc would never let up on the teasing if he realized she'd been sick. She opened the medicine cabinet and pulled out a bottle of mouthwash, displacing a smaller container. The small bottle of tranquilizers her doctor had prescribed several months ago to help her sleep clattered into the sink. Several capsules rolled out.

Breanna absently scooped pills back into the container. Funny, she rarely took them, but the bottle was nearly empty.

She rinsed her mouth, removed her contact lenses and crawled to the bed. Impossible, she thought, falling face first against the flowered quilt. Two glasses of wine, or even three, wouldn't do this. Four might, and her mind blanked as she tried to recount her consumption. She sank into a drunken pool of dreams.

Scott stared intently over the midnight blue water searching for the *Breanna Colleen*. Damn Derek, anyway. He punched the steering wheel, grabbed the binoculars and scanned the dark horizon. Useless. Might as well try to find a single ripple of water as one not so small boat. He knew the yacht was headed for Isle Royale. Maybe Lanier wouldn't travel far tonight.

Then what? He needed a plan, although he'd given up trying to understand the sense of urgency he felt and only knew he had to find that yacht, had to find Breanna. Still, right now all he could do was wait for dawn. Twenty miles out, he killed the engine and dropped anchor near the outcrop of rocks at Stony Point.

He thought about Derek's business dealings with Breanna's husband as he secured the boat, then checked fuel supplies and the generator. It didn't make sense. What possible legitimate connections could a fishing company have with Lanier's Fine Furs?

Legitimate. Lanier probably couldn't even spell the word. Neither could Derek.

As for his brother, Derek always rushed into money schemes, reckless to consequences, or legalities. His insistence that Scott relearn the business "from the trawlers up" must result from a need to keep the company paperwork, or lack of it, from Scott's probing questions. Which meant Dad was right. Derek was in up to his buggy eyes again. Scott just hoped he could keep him out of jail this time.

Then there was Derek's obstinate determination about personally handling all charters to Isle Royale. Lanier's weekend trip appeared to be at odds with their usual arrangements, but if he planned to drop something off, a cozy weekend trip with Breanna to celebrate her birthday gave him the perfect cover up.

Breanna. Scott's mind stubbornly returned to familiar thoughts. Nine years ago, he and Breanna had been kids, groping at first love. Nothing like an enraged father protecting a precious daughter to douse a hot romance. Funny how even after all this time, remembering William Alden's rage at finding him and Breanna alone at their Lake Vermilion estate sent a chill snaking up his spine. He'd been lucky to escape with all his body parts intact.

Poor Breanna, too rebellious to accept the status quo. Too much in awe of her father to break free. Still too trusting of the husband from hell. Scott had seen her several times at Murray's Piano Bar since he'd fished her out of the Gooseberry River, but she'd been deep in conversation with her uncle, and he hadn't approached her.

Why had she bought Lanier's bullshit that he'd saved her?

Which left him in the role of distant bodyguard, but maybe it was better this way. Much easier to never try and explain the hopelessness and powerlessness that had forced them apart nine years ago. They had been too young, their worlds too different.

Scott dug a bottle of Canadian beer from the cooler and fished a church key out of the tackle box. At first the news of Breanna's marriage to Lanier made Scott perversely glad she'd shown spunk and defied her father. Until he returned to Duluth and discovered the lie behind Lanier's respectable reputation. Before he'd overhead him talk about his wife to Derek. Insulting comments totally at odds with the way Lanier pawed at her and treated her like some prized possession.

His hand closed around the metal bottle opener. Sharp edges dug into his palm as his imagination mocked him with pictures of Lanier fondling Breanna. *Fool.* She married the guy. Her choice.

Even if it was a bad one.

Chapter 2

Someone spoke soothingly to her, carried her, protected her. She struggled to see his face, but it twisted into a contortion of Marc. Dark eyes glowed fire. His hands clenched her hair, held her underwater. She fought for air, tried to scream. Dragging herself from heavy sleep, she opened her eyes and stared into Marc's lust-drenched gaze. His fingers twined in her hair.

"Happy birthday, Princess," he said, his voice a silky whisper. He shifted her onto her back, fingertips tracing the little scar on her temple, the line of her jaw, her throat. "You're all wrapped up like a party favor. Feeling mellow?"

A sense of having slept for hours paralyzed her with confusion. Her head pounded, and her throat felt thick and murky. She shook her head, wincing with the effort. Weakly, she pressed her hands against his bare chest, the thick mat of dark hair scratchy on her palms. Oh, God, no. He'd already undressed. He nudged her leg meaningfully, and she wondered why he seemed to be the most persistently aroused when her desire slumbered. Why her refusal intensified his excitement. "Marc, please, not tonight."

His hand roamed carelessly over her breasts, past her stomach to the tiny snaps on the teddy. She tried to wriggle away from his prying fingers, but he flung one leg across her thighs and pinned her arms above her head.

His eyes glittered with a look she knew all too well. "If you don't want to play, you shouldn't dress for it, Princess."

Although his voice was velvety, the edginess in it filled her with dread. Making love with Marc had never fulfilled the romantic fantasies she'd enjoyed long ago with her first love but the closeness had been nice at first.

Until his desires strayed into a mix of pain and pleasure as if that would create a passionate response in her.

But maybe he was right. She was cold, repressed, or trying to ease her guilt by shutting him out. Or maybe he knew that in the secret places of her heart, she still longed for someone else.

He trailed a crimson scarf across her face, down her breasts. Over her throat. "Remember the fun we had with this?"

A cold knot formed in her stomach. Oh, she remembered all right, although she tried hard not to. Wasn't making love supposed to be just that and not some game of power and domination?

Gripping the scarf in one hand, he shoved the silky teddy above her waist with the other. "If I could find a way to stop you from pretending you're still sweet sixteen, I would. But, with a little help, you've been delightfully compliant at times. Do it again tonight, babe. Be a good girl and cooperate. One last time," he whispered.

One last time? Maybe she'd finally driven him beyond endurance. Maybe he knew how close to the edge she was. That she wanted out of this charade.

"Marc...please..."

He hovered over her, bent his head and nipped her neck. She stiffened, tried to move from under him.

He laughed. "That's right, make me fight for it."

Enough. She had to stop pretending. She didn't want this.

She didn't want *him.*

"No, Marc. *No.*" She rocked to one side, knocking him partially off balance.

His expression turned thunderous as he drew back and slapped her. She sank against the mattress.

"Yeah, you pretend to fight, but you like it rough, don't you."

His fingers bit into her skin as he used the scarf to lash her wrists to the bedpost.

She stifled a cry of pain and tasted blood, then closed her eyes to shut out the feverish look on his face. How had everything turned out so wrong?

She couldn't go on this way, dreading his touch,

mistrusting her feelings, wishing for what she could never have.

As soon as they got back to Duluth, she would leave him. For good this time if he refused to understand how she hated the games he played.

She'd married Marc because she thought she loved him. Now she just wanted to shut out the sight of him.

He gripped her chin. Hard. "Open your eyes, Breanna. Stop pretending you don't want this."

She met his gaze, horrified at the flash of loathing she saw in his eyes before his mouth covered hers in a mockery of a kiss. "No," she gasped. "No!"

Something thumped overhead just as he began pushing past her ineffective struggles.

"Son of a *bitch*." Marc took a deep breath and rolled off her.

"Don't worry, babe, I'll finish you later." He shrugged into jeans and a tee-shirt. Leaning over her, he pinched her neck, then headed out of the stateroom.

Hands still bound above her head, aching and humiliated, she tugged futilely at her bonds but only made the slip knots tighter. She scooted under the covers and tried to formulate a plan.

She struggled to remain alert, but her eyes fell shut and consciousness started to slide away.

An unfamiliar voice followed her into troubled sleep.

"Why the hell is she here?"

Scott's ears buzzed, and he huddled further into the sleeping bag. Damn mosquitoes. Couldn't even escape them out on the water. The buzzing increased to an engine-like drone. Scott dragged himself awake and sat up. Mist floated over the water as faint light flashed and chased wispy clouds. Thunder answered lightning. He searched the sky with sleep-clogged eyes but saw only the pale blue of early morning.

Another rumble drew his attention north. A tiny white speck emerged from the fog and wallowed in a cloud of black smoke and brilliant orange. The cloud billowed skyward as an explosion ripped the quiet air.

For a moment he remained motionless. Someone in trouble. He'd have to postpone his own plans and help. Scott raised the anchor, started the engine and radioed the Coast Guard.

In her dream, someone scooped her from the river, dried her tears, spoke comfortingly. She knew him, she was certain she did. Why couldn't she see his face?

Breathing became an effort as if iron bands wrapped her chest. Cold seeped through her, making her bones ache. Gurgling sounds pressed against her ears. Her eyelids heavy, Breanna opened them from fearful dreams to horrible reality.

Pink and red streaks of early morning sky reflected against the dark water and sent panic coursing through her drugged senses. She struggled to sit. Icy water sloshed around her ankles and edged toward her knees. The rubber raft wobbled.

The *Breanna Colleen* drifted a thousand yards to her right, a cottony looking splotch on blue velvet. Breanna squinted, tried to focus, tried to shout, but her voice rasped, frozen and useless. She drew her knees up and clutched the oar lock on the side of the dinghy. More water bubbled in.

An explosion ripped the quiet and the yacht burst into a mass of red and yellow flames. Water and fiberglass shot skyward. Waves hit the half-submerged raft. Numb from shock, cold and disbelief, Breanna curled against the side. Another twist in a life turned upside down. Marc couldn't have survived the explosion, but she felt no grief. Just an emptiness as cold as the frigid water.

Grogginess crept over her as her mind shut out pain and cold. She knew she'd die of exposure before much time passed. The thought seemed somehow far removed, as if she specu-lated on the ending of a movie. But it didn't matter. She'd lost everything else worth living for when she married Marc Lanier.

Now she'd lost him, too.

The fishing boat chugged closer to the glowing blob of smoke. Scott's apprehension returned. It couldn't be Breanna's boat, but an icy knot formed in his stomach.

Frustrated with fury and alarm, he circled the burning yacht as close as he dared. The flying bridge and afterdeck of the *Breanna Colleen* wore a fiery canopy. Too late for there to be any life on board. A blue life vest bobbed emptily several feet away. Sick at heart, Scott twisted the steering wheel and backed off from the intense heat as another explosion shattered fiberglass into deadly missiles. Incandescent rain pounded in front of him until the lake swallowed the last morsel.

Scott searched the area, desperately hoping Breanna had escaped. She had to survive. *She had to.*

Each minute felt like sixty, yet his watch stubbornly marched forward. Doggedly, he aimed the boat's searchlight. Yellow light reflected back in the fog. He strained to see, fighting gloomy panic at the edges of his mind. After only ten minutes in the fifty-degree water, hypothermia would set in. Her survival time would be less than an hour. He cursed the mist, the early morning light, then himself for ever letting her go.

Half a mile from the explosion site, he saw a patch of yellow through the haze. He trolled closer, relief rushing through him at the sight of Breanna, eyes closed, curled on her side in a life raft. He saw no sign of Lanier.

"Breanna," he shouted.

Despite his caution, waves swamped the rubber raft supporting her head. Scott cut the engine, frozen with horror as Breanna rolled face down. He stripped off his sweatshirt and dove, gasping from the cold water. Gritting his teeth, he reached her in a few swift strokes, shifted her onto her back, and swam back to the boat. After easing her onto the aft platform, he scrambled up. "Breanna. Breathe! Don't give up!"

He bent his head and felt slow, shallow breathing. Fingers automatically searched for a pulse and found a faint heartbeat. He lifted her into the boat and yanked off the life jacket.

She looked blue and puffy, as if she'd been on the water awhile or something else contributed to her condition. Alcohol for sure. He smelled the faint fruitiness of wine. A white satin teddy hugged every curve of her body but shredded like wet tissue as he ripped it off. She was so beautiful. So cold. God, how he wished it could have been different. Damn their age, damn William Alden.

He wrapped her in a thermal blanket, covered her head with an old knit cap and tucked her into his down sleeping bag. Then he hurriedly pulled on a gray sweat suit. The Coast Guard lifeboat would take an hour to arrive from Duluth, but Breanna wouldn't last if he didn't re-warm her immediately. She remained icily unconscious, her pulse faint.

He had only one option. He stripped and climbed inside Breanna's blanket cocoon.

He embraced an ice sculpture and resisted the impulse to rub her cold skin, knowing that would worsen her condition. "Isn't this just about where we left off nine years ago, Breena?" he whispered. "We should have faced your father together. So what if I'd ended up in traction? Broken bones would have healed better than we did."

He thought about her marriage and jealousy of the man who didn't deserve to change the oil in her car filled him with rage. "Why did you marry him?"

At least he was dead. Why else would an empty life vest have been bobbing in the waves if it hadn't been Lanier's? He hoped the bastard had been hurtled into hell.

Which would set Breanna free. The discouragement of the past two months melted. Hope took its place. Dangerous thoughts, considering he was sandwiched together with the woman whose memory still warmed his blood. He forced himself to consider possible causes of the explosion. Another accident? Not likely. Breanna had far too many in the past six months. How had she ended up in the raft? Had she been trying to get away from Lanier? Had he put her there? Maybe someone was after Lanier.

Derek would know. He'd just have to hammer some answers out of his brother. Only then could he give Breanna some serious explanations without implicating himself.

He wished she'd wake up but was relieved she remained

quiet and sheltered. Memories of their last time together and what might have been overloaded his senses. He searched for a distraction, but there was only Breanna, skin smooth and cool against his heat. Breanna, in his mind. In his heart.

"Breena, I was an immature jerk," he murmured against her ear. "I'm sorry for what happened, but I'm even sorrier for what didn't. Give us a chance to find what we lost."

Chapter 3

Why is she here?

The voice followed Breanna through her dreams. She wondered who he was, what he'd meant. Why was she there? Where? Where was she? Darkness became gray light, but the fog inside her mind persisted. Another voice called to her, coaxing, pleading. Lost in an endless eddy of sleep, she couldn't reach the man beyond the mist.

"Breanna....Can you hear me? Wake up, sweetheart."

His voice caressed her with warmth, overpowering the pain of recognition. *Scott.* She struggled to call his name. Ever since the night at the Gooseberry River when she'd nearly drowned, he'd tormented her dreams and teased the edges of her mind. She saw his familiar face, his warm smile, felt strong arms sheltering her.

Scott, sunshine hair streaked with white from summers spent on his father's fishing boats. Chestnut brown eyes danced with mischief, gave her hope, and motivated her back to reality. To wakefulness.

To disappointment and confusion as Uncle Murray's concerned eyes and red stubbles of beard greeted her instead. His black hair looked like he'd spent the night wired to an electric shock machine. Anticipation crashed.

Just a dream. Why had she expected the man who had deserted her nine years before?

Murray squeezed her hand. "Thank God, you're finally awake. You scared the life out of me again, kid, and I hope to hell it's the last time. I'm too old for this kind of stress."

Uncle Murray. How could she have made it through the past months without him?

She wet her lips. Her throat felt like raw hamburger, her body weak and lethargic. "You're not decrepit, Murray." She struggled to sit and threw her arms around her uncle. "But I am so glad to see you." The sudden movement made the white-on-white room tilt crazily. Another hospital. The third one in six months and each time Murray had been with her when she awoke.

He released her with a pat and handed her a glass of room temperature water. "You sound like the fog horn. Do you remember what happened?"

She could remember things, but nothing she would want to tell Murray. Nothing about what had led to her being here. Disoriented, she shook her head. "Not much. Not really anything. How did I get here?"

"Coast Guard. Want to tell me what happened?"

She took a sip of water and evaded Murray Sullivan's gaze as her last encounter with Marc flooded her with anger and humiliation. He was her husband. How could he do those things to her? How could he look at her as if he hated her? And where was he now?

"I'm not sure. I fell asleep early. Woke up on a raft. Saw the yacht explode. Then nothing." The familiar voice. Being held. A long ago love song. 'Wouldn't It Be Nice,' but it was just a dream. She sank back against the pillows and closed her eyes, trying to block out hazy, troubling memories. If Murray knew the full extent of Marc's behavior, her uncle would most certainly want to kill him.

"Poor little kid," Murray muttered.

She didn't feel like an innocent, she felt like the biggest naïve fool who ever walked the planet. Sighing, she opened her eyes. "What day is it? Where's Marc?"

Murray's brow creased with anger and fatigue. "It's Sunday. You've been out since they brought you in early yesterday morning. I damn near lost you." His voice caught and for a moment he was silent.

"Marc didn't survive, sweetie. Coast Guard found his life vest, then your raft. Said it was punctured, but couldn't tell how. They think the fuel line on the yacht exploded. Sheriff's office is handling the investigation for the Coast Guard. One of the deputies has been around asking after you."

A chill stole through her but no grief. Marc was dead. That much, at least, wasn't a dream. A picture of his empty life vest bobbing in the lake swam before her.

Breanna's face warmed as guilt crowded out an over-whelming sense of relief. Marc was gone, along with any love or obligation that had bound her to him. She squeezed her eyes shut, but a warm tear trickled down her cheek. Why hadn't she seen past his charming smile? How had he convinced her that what she found abhorrent was acceptable?

Not wanting her uncle to guess her tortured thoughts, she kept her eyes closed. Murray's casual hold on her arm slackened as he turned her hand over. Breanna's gaze flew open to the bandage on her wrist.

"What the hell happened here?"

"I...I don't know. I must have scratched myself."

Murray scowled. "I saw it when they brought you in. It's too clean for a scratch. Looked more like a wound from something sharp. You didn't try to do anything, did you?" He grabbed her other arm and examined it, his finger rubbing over a faint rough patch.

"How can you even ask me that?"

"Maybe because you haven't acted like your headstrong little self for months? Like since you married that bastard?"

She felt compelled to explain, although the words rang hollow in her mind. "I was just trying to make my marriage work. And Marc could be a prince when he wanted to be. I thought we would be happy together if we could just get past all the things that have happened since we married."

She squeezed his hand and eased herself from the bed, ignoring his attempt to help her by clutching the metal bed rail when her knees buckled.

"Breanna," his voice was full of worry.

"I'm okay. I need to move around a little." When the dizziness passed, she put on the glasses that Gayle must have dropped off from the studio and reached for a white robe quilted with roses. The smell of fabric sizing tickled her nose, and she noticed her matching nightgown for the first time.

Knowing how she hated hospital gowns, he'd even

managed to get her a new robe and gown. Tears stung her eyes. "Thanks, Murray," she whispered, her fingers stroking the soft flannel.

"That's okay. Spencer's been taking care of the bar. Pretty robe. Hospital stuff has improved since the last time you were here."

She hesitated, confused by his answer, then shuffled to the window. Fog, as cold and gray as her spirit, shrouded the city, obscuring the lake she knew lay a few blocks beyond the hospital. If Murray hadn't brought the robe and gown, then who had? Gayle?

"Breanna, do you forgive me?"

Startled at the anguish in his voice, she glanced over her shoulder. "For what?"

Murray spread his hands. "No matter what I said before, that you had to live with your choices, how I could have bought into Marc's bullshit like the rest of this town—"He shook his head. "You should have left him after that business at the river. No, you should have left him before that, when you lost the baby. Hell, I should have made you leave him."

"It's not your fault. It was my decision." Easy going Uncle Murray. How could he have guessed how difficult Marc was to live with at times? How her own stubbornness prevented her from admitting the depth of the mistake she'd made?

Overwhelmed by Marc's air of authority, she'd lacked the conviction to tell her uncle, exactly, what kind of desperation had sent her to his house on more than one occasion. How could she have known that the strong personality she found similar to her father's wasn't tempered by her father's kind and caring heart?

She blinked back fresh tears. Time to stop pretending she'd been happy since she met Marc. Going forward had to be better than the past months with their tormented memories.

Flowers lined the windowsill. She was lucky to have Murray and friends who cared about her. Gayle, her assistant from the studio, had sent a pot of carnations. Her fingers trailed idly over pots of daisies and English ivy from other friends.

Blue forget-me-nots nestled in a straw basket. She drew in her breath as another memory jolted through her.

A card sat half-hidden among the tiny flowers.

"Breena, Picture Hartley's Field carpeted with these. I remember saying your eyes are a prettier blue. What do you remember? Scott."

Breanna closed her eyes. Scott. *Oh my God.*

He wasn't just a dream after all. But she couldn't tell for certain where dreams ended and reality started. Glancing up, she caught Murray's apprehensive expression. "Was he here?"

"Who?"

A smile tugged at the corners of her mouth as Breanna motioned with the card toward the flowers. "Give it up, Murray. You've always been a terrible liar."

"Aw, hell." His gaze rested intently on her face. "Yes, Scott was here. Most of last night. Somehow, he convinced the nurses he was family while I crashed on the couch in the lounge. I threw him out this morning."

"Why?"

Murray strode to the window, put an arm around her shoulders and gave her a gentle shake. "Because you need protecting, kid, and the last thing you need is another fortune hunter. Your father was right about Marc. Edwards is bad news, too."

Her pride already in tatters, Breanna felt a surge of defiance and shrugged away from his arm. "You liked him. He was my friend."

"Maybe. But that was nine years ago. And after everything you've been through.... Besides, your mother would expect me to look out for you, and I've failed miserably. Guess I didn't realize it would be a full time job."

Her face flamed as his words stung. "And I've always counted on you as my friend, not my keeper!" Why did everyone think she needed protecting? Her anger quickly faded.

Maybe she did. She certainly had been making bad decisions since she'd returned to Duluth after she finished college. Starting, of course, with becoming involved with Marc.

Murray meant well, and she loved him. Overwhelmed with

fatigue, she covered her face with her hands and sobbed.

Murray put his arms around her. "Breanna. I'm your friend, always. It's just that you're the only family I have left."

She gulped, struggled to regain control. "I know. I know you have good intentions, Murray. But I have to decide for myself. I can't spend my life letting other people make my decisions any more."

She leaned against his shoulder. "Right now I just want to go home. To my family," she whispered, although she knew there was no going back.

He sighed. "You're exhausted. You need a couple more days here, okay?"

"Please, Murray. I can't stand being here."

He shook his head, and his voice became stern. "You almost died. The doctor said two more days. Then you'll stay with me until we get this mess behind you." He patted her hair, as if she were still six to his sixteen. "Now, I'll get out of here so you can rest."

Emotionally spent, Breanna let him lead her back to the bed, but as soon as the door clicked shut behind her uncle, her mind raced with the thought of leaving. But how could she? Her car was parked at the pier. She had no clothes, no keys. The muted stillness pressed against her, suffocating her, numbing her senses.

She forced herself to relax. Patience, that's what she needed. If she let her mind drift, a plan would come to her. She could call Gayle. After awhile, mid-afternoon street noises drifted up and coaxed her back to sleep.

Dreams closed in. Through heavy mist, Marc's fierce gaze bore into her, and she tried to move, tried to evade him. Images of January's argument burned into a nightmare.

Marc's anger intense, eyes the color of coal. His hand around her throat, her back against the wall. "Stupid, stupid woman, that's the last thing I wanted!"

Dark fear escalating into Technicolor horror. She had to get away or he'd...The sense of falling into nothingness.

The emptiness of losing the small life growing inside her. The grief she felt, even in sleep.

Another voice penetrated her consciousness, swept her back ten years to American literature class. *A Dream Within a Dream*. Warm breath tickled the back of her neck as Scott leaned forward and whispered a mockery of the Edgar Allen Poe poem.

"Coward," she screamed in her dream. He'd run off and left her! She swung wildly. Her fists struck a man's chin, then his arms closed around her. Jolted into wakefulness, Breanna stared into familiar brown eyes and a face framed by tousled blond hair. She wanted to scream, but it lodged in her throat.

Scott smiled, a gentle smile full of concern and tenderness. "It's okay, baby," he whispered and loosened his embrace. "Just a dream."

She almost relaxed until memories raced back. He'd abandoned her. She'd needed him to face her father with her, and he'd run off like a coward without even a backward glance.

"What are you doing here? Get your hands off me. I'm not your baby." She struggled away and bolted from the bed. Too late, she realized her damp gown clung to every curve. Her face flaming, she yanked the blanket off the bed and wrapped it around herself.

He rubbed his chin. "I'd forgotten about that nasty left hook I taught you. And that you're such a determined grudge holder. I'd hoped saving your life might make it a little easier for you to forgive me."

Despite a glimmer of remembrance, Breanna regarded him suspiciously. "Murray said the Coast Guard rescued me."

"Half true. I found you. They brought you in. Will that help you forgive me for what happened at Lake Vermillion?"

She ignored his winsome smile and glared back. Unbelievable. After all this time, after she'd accepted that she would never see him again, here he was. "No, because I don't believe you. Get out of here, or I'll call the nurses and have you thrown out."

"Your uncle tried that, but I bounced back." Scott shrugged, his eyes alight with sympathy and mischief. "Breanna, why would I lie about this?"

She shook her head, unable to come up with a reason, but

that didn't give him the right to sit here like they should just pick up where they left off all those years ago. "Prove it."

"Okay." He was silent for a moment. "You have a pretty deep scratch on your right wrist and your left was chafed a little raw. Do you remember what caused it?"

Breanna gasped as pain and humiliation flooded through her. She closed her eyes. The scarf. Why couldn't that part have just been a nightmare? Had Marc struggled to remove it trying to get her off the boat in time?

"Scott..." she turned away. "It's not..."

"It's okay," he whispered. "You don't owe anyone any explanations."

Several long moments passed before she could look at him again.

"Remember the last time we were together?" He gazed intently at her.

Unable to look away, Breanna nodded slowly, wondering if she would ever truly forget. Lake Vermilion, a passionate afternoon that had almost... She remembered every detail. Scott's heated gaze devouring her. Hard flesh pressing against hers. Doors slamming, her father bellowing. The warmth in her face crystallized into a cold knot around her heart.

"You left me to face him. Alone."

He buried his face in his hands, as if ashamed to meet her gaze. Finally, he looked up, his expression somber. "I don't blame you for still being angry. But I was scared stupid, and I've never been sorrier."

Silence stretched between them.

"I wanted you to forget me because I never wanted to come between you and your family, and as more time passed, I didn't think I had the right to try and see you again."

"How does that prove anything?"

"I brought you that robe and the gown you're wearing to make up for the white one that shredded when I had to take it off you. To warm you up."

"Oh," she gasped and covered her mouth with her hand. He'd undressed her. How humiliating. But then, it wasn't as if she'd had much on, anyway, and he hadn't seen her naked before, even if it had been a long time ago.

His smile gentled. "Do you remember?"

"No." What she remembered more than anything was all the tears and heartache she wasn't sure she had completely recovered from. She couldn't afford to let those feelings loose again. Turning away in a dismissive gesture, she flinched as Scott's arms closed around her again.

Her shriek of protest died in her throat with the words he whispered against her ear. A long ago love song, the song she'd heard in her dream. 'Wouldn't It Be Nice.'

Wispy memories tickled her mind. A campfire at the Gooseberry River the night Marc said he'd rescued her.

But it wasn't Marc she remembered. Someone's fingers brushing her hair away from her face. "Poor baby," he'd whispered. Frozen with lost hope on the lake. Someone holding her with tenderness instead of victorious vindictiveness. Smooth skin against hers. Scott, always Scott, the only man she'd ever known who found her family's wealth boring.

"I never forgot you, Breanna," he murmured. "I just didn't know the way back at first. Then I didn't think you'd want me messing up your life. I only wanted you to be happy."

Her eyes filled with tears, but she relaxed and Scott released her. "You were at the river. You saved me, not Marc."

He nodded.

"Were you following us?"

"Not that time. Friday night, yes, but I didn't get there soon enough."

"For what? What do you want, Scott?"

He sighed. "Who taught you to be so suspicious?"

Marc Lanier, but she refused to say his name as if it might conjure him back from whatever hell he'd landed in. She tipped her head back, brushed away a tear and stubbornly met his gaze. "You did."

"Ouch."

For several moments neither spoke.

Scott cleared his throat. "Look, I deserve that, but there are a lot of things you don't understand. We need to talk about them. Later, when you're up to it. For right now, I just want to help you get through this. See you get back on your feet."

"Then go away. And this time stay gone."

"I can't do that," he said softly. "You're always there, in my mind, and I can't pretend differently."

A bond of understanding held her gaze to his. She knew exactly what he meant. How many times had Marc tried to purge the shadows from her mind?

"Thank you for saving me," she whispered. "I can never repay that. But what we had was a long time ago. I can't deal with this, with you, right now."

He shrugged. "I'm here as a friend. So you had better let me help you. I'm going to hang around and drive you crazy otherwise. Is there something I can get to help you survive the next couple of days? Flowers, a magazine, a Sammy's shrimp and onion pizza?"

She tapped her fingers on the windowsill, stalling. She wanted a reason for him to stay nearly as much as she needed to erase the past year spent under Marc's dark spell. Scott had saved her. Twice. And he still wanted to help her. Maybe she should let him, providing she could keep her wobbly feelings under control. They had been such good friends once. And so much more. She turned from the window. "Clothes."

Scott raised his eyebrow doubtfully. "What for?"

She moved next to him and looked up, a little smile springing unexpectedly to her lips. Having Scott here brought a measure of comfort she would never have expected.

"I want to go home. Please. I can't bear to be here with nothing to do but think about everything that's happened. You said you want to help, then get me out of here."

An hour later, Breanna frowned at her reflection in the wall mirror of her hospital room. A Minnesota *Wild* tee shirt hung loosely to mid thigh, nearly concealing the baggy white boxer shorts beneath. She rolled the sleeves up to her forearms. "What kind of outfit do you call this?"

"Hospital get away apparel. It's the best I could do without making the trek all the way to my house." He hesitated. "Breanna, I really don't think you should do this. At least wait until your doctor sees you tomorrow morning."

She shuddered. "You don't understand. I have to get out of here. Now."

"I realize hospitals aren't exactly fun places to be, but what's the rush?"

The anguish of again being near the nursery was still too personal, too painful to share, and then there was the growing fear about the deputy sheriff's planned visit. How could she answer police questions when her memory remained so cloudy? When the thought of her husband's death brought guilty relief and not grief?

Avoiding his eyes, she glanced away. "I hate hospitals. They don't let you sleep at night, and they're full of sick people."

Scott frowned, started to speak, then shrugged, captured her arm and snipped off the identification bracelet. His fingers lingered on the oversized sleeve.

She felt a flutter in her stomach, then a rush of heat from his fingertips and pulled away from his intense perusal as hastily as if from the edge of an inferno. *Careful.* It would be all too easy to let herself be swept away by familiar feelings and take comfort in his arms. "Let's just go."

She moved to the door and quickly scanned the hospital corridor. The nurse on duty was at the nurses' station, her back turned. A few patients strolled the hall and the room next door buzzed with voices, the perfect cover up for her hasty departure. But they had to hurry. Murray had said the deputy would be back that afternoon during visiting hours.

She motioned to Scott. "Come on. I won't be able to breathe until I'm sitting in your car."

Swinging a small duffel bag, he gave her a half-guilty look as he followed her down the hallway. "I guess I should have mentioned it before. My jeep's out of commission. But don't worry. We've got wheels."

At the elevator, she half-ducked behind Scott as a uniformed man stepped off and headed for the nurses' station. Grabbing Scott's hand, she pulled him inside and frantically pressed the ground floor button. When the doors slid shut, she slumped against the wall. "I don't care what you're driving, as long as it gets me away from here."

He studied her face. "What's the matter?"

"I just want to go home." Her gaze slid from his.

"Like hell. Afraid that deputy was going to visit you?"

She froze. "Why would you think that?"

"Makes sense they'd have to investigate. Yacht explosions don't just happen. And there's a lot at stake, isn't there?"

"Yes," she said softly. "A lot." Exactly what, she wasn't sure, she just knew she was not ready to answer questions for which she had no explanations.

He didn't push, and she breathed a sigh of relief. Outside in the parking lot Scott handed her a shiny blue metal flake helmet from the handlebars of a blue and black Suzuki motorcycle.

"I haven't been on a motorcycle in years." At least it wasn't raining. This whole idea about leaving just seemed to get crazier. Maybe she should have listened to Murray. But then she'd be sitting in the hospital under the perusal of Officer Whomever.

"Remember when we used to cruise around in Hartley's field on the dirt bike?"

Did she remember? Memories as intoxicating as Grandmother Lillian's homemade plum wine flowed through her, squeezing her heart to a painful rhythm. Hartley's Field, a moonlight picnic, she and Scott as giddy with each other as from the wine. Testing limits, so many times on the brink of something she'd never even gotten close to with Marc.

Breanna stared past his shoulder as she fastened the helmet strap under her chin and forced the memories away. "No, not really," she said but her voice was unsteady.

"Liar," he said softly.

Smile fading, she felt his gaze linger on her face as she stared past him. A few strands of ebony hair straggled across her cheek, and she tucked them inside. "Can we go now, please?"

"Absolutely." He straddled the motorcycle and revved it up, motioning for Breanna to climb up behind him. "I hope you at least remember and have the strength to hold on tight."

After she got settled, putting her hands on his waist and scooting up against him, he pulled out of the parking lot and the bike roared up the avenue.

She gave out a startled whoop, then shouted above the noise. "Wait. I forgot to tell you—"

"1210 Skyline Parkway, second floor apartment. We'll be there before you know it."

She momentarily wondered how Scott already knew where she lived, but the thought slipped away as she rested her cheek against his back, too weary to acknowledge the ease with which she accepted his presence. She couldn't wait to get home, take a hot bath, and put on real clothes.

While Scott parked the bike in the street, Breanna hurried up the sidewalk into the duplex foyer and climbed the stairs to the second floor apartment. She tipped the newel post and retrieved her extra door key. He strode up beside her as she fit the key into the lock. It refused to turn. Breanna pulled the key out and examined it.

"It won't work."

Scott reached for the silver key. "Let me."

His sudden movement made her recoil, and she jerked her arm away, hoping he wouldn't notice. "I know how to unlock a door. Why do men always assume women are incompetent?" She slid the key back into the lock and twisted it. Nothing happened.

"I never have." Scott folded his arms. "But you sure are touchy. I'd hoped getting you out of that stuffy hospital would improve your mood. Now what?"

Not wanting to admit her dread at having to confront her landlady, she brushed past him and thumped down the stairs, Scott's too-big sandals slapping the steps. "I'll get another key. I've never used this one before so I'm sure it's just a misfit."

Ina Kilpela answered the door of the downstairs apartment on the second knock. Eyes the color and warmth of March slush traveled speculatively from Breanna to Scott. She patted her coifed gray hair and smoothed the hem of her black suit jacket.

"What are you doing here?"

"I live here, remember?" Breanna held up the key. "But there seems to be a problem with my key."

"I was sorry to read about your husband, Mrs. Lanier. Such an attentive, hardworking man." She shook her head and gave Breanna a frigid look. "The locks were changed after you left Friday afternoon, just like he requested. He said you weren't coming back this time."

Chapter 4

This couldn't be happening. The landlady had always fawned over Marc while treating Breanna with an indifference bordering on rudeness, but this was too much.

Breanna shook her head, her face hot with embarrassment. "I beg your pardon?"

Mrs. Kilpela's usually somber expression seemed almost gleeful. "I can't help you, Mrs. Lanier. Your husband gave specific instructions not to allow access to anyone and it's his name on the lease."

"But he's—"

"If there's anything in that apartment you wanted, you should have taken it with you on Friday. I can't allow you to swoop through there like a pair of vultures." Mrs. Kilpela's icy gaze impaled Breanna, then shifted to include Scott.

"But I am, was, his wife! Certainly I'm entitled to have access to our home!"

"I'm going to let the probate court decide that. Good day, Mrs. Lanier." She shut the door in Breanna's face.

Breanna's mind whirled as she spun around and slammed out of the building. *'He said you wouldn't be back this time.' 'Be a good girl and cooperate. One last time.'*

Why had he told their landlady she wasn't coming back?

"Breena," Scott's hand brushed her arm. "It's okay. We'll figure something out."

She supposed she could ask Murray for help and a place to stay. He'd simply insist she check back into the hospital. And she couldn't. She just couldn't face it. She crossed her arms and looked down. How had her life become a murky pool of quicksand, pulling on her, dragging her down? When would the nightmare end?

"I have nowhere to go," she said finally.

"Sure you do."

When he paused, she looked up at him. It would be too easy to lose herself in the depths of his gaze and the confidence he radiated, except for the fact that she no longer trusted her emotions, or her reactions. As for instincts....

"I'd say you have three choices. Go to Murray's to spend the night and end up in the hospital; join the homeless on a bench in Leif Ericson Park. Or spend the night, week, or month, at my house." His eyes twinkled. "It's not much, but at least the walls aren't white."

Breanna sighed and searched his face. "Sounds like a choice among three evils."

Scott gently took her hand. "I may be a lot of things, doll, but evil isn't one of them."

She used to like it when he called her that. But she was no longer sixteen. She pulled away from his familiarity even though she wanted more than anything to lean against him and let him take care of her, if only until she could get past the overwhelming fatigue.

"Then don't call me doll or baby or anything except Breanna. What do you expect in return?"

Scott hesitated. "Expect? Nothing. Want? Everything. Now."

She sucked in a breath, startled at his bluntness. "Scott..."

He paused, as if searching for the right words to reassure her. "Friendship. I know I can't ever change what happened, and even if we could wouldn't that make us different people than we are now?"

She shrugged and said nothing.

"Can't we at least be friends again?"

"Just friends? Do you think that's even possible?"

His gaze caressed her face, and he brushed a wispy ebony strand of hair from her cheek. "God, I hope not, but I think it's a damn good place to start over."

Starting over. She sighed, wishing it were possible, although she'd rather just erase the past six months. But since that wasn't going to happen, she needed to careful as she made her way through the maze of decisions she now faced.

For now, her choices were limited, and Scott could be gently persuasive when he set his mind to it, sometimes with disastrous results.

His hand closed around hers. "Let's get out of here. Your kind-hearted landlady has enough fuel to generate three weeks worth of gossip without us standing here feeding her curiosity. I promise, I'll sleep on the couch. Besides, you can always call Murray from my house if you change your mind."

Fifteen minutes later, Breanna trudged up the sidewalk of a house barely larger than the garage set back beside it. Physically weary and emotionally exhausted, she felt as if she'd spent the day as a speed bump. She could barely put one foot in front of the other. Porch steps loomed before her like Spirit Mountain. She closed her eyes, not realizing she was falling until Scott caught her and pulled her close against his chest.

Scents of scrubbed cotton and sunlit trees enveloped her as she slipped her arms around his waist and held on, waiting for the world to stop shaking. Her lungs contracted, and she struggled for breath, fluttering her eyes open in panic.

Scott swore, scooped her up and carried her through the enclosed porch, through a small living room, into a minuscule bedroom dominated by a king size bed.

He set her down on the bed, rubbed her back with a circular motion and covered her mouth with his other hand. "I should have known better than to let you talk me into helping you out of that hospital, lady. You haven't recovered from the accident yet, and now you're hyperventilating. Close your eyes and breathe. Slowly, not like a hooked fish."

Gradually, the pressure against her chest eased, and Breanna let herself settle into the warmth of Scott's side.

"A flounder. What a flattering image," she murmured. Despite her determination, Breanna let her eyes drift shut and felt herself sink onto the bed. She could rest here, just for a little bit, that's all she needed. "Why didn't you answer my letters?" she mumbled as exhaustion closed around her.

"I did. Fifty times until I couldn't stand knowing you never got them." He muttered a curse as he realized she hadn't heard him. Oh well. They could deal with all of that later. He removed her shoes and covered her with a blue and yellow afghan.

"I never wanted to let your father win, Breena," he said, gently brushing her hair from her face. "And I'll never let anyone stand between us again."

Thunder. She heard a distant whistle and the house began to tremble. Breanna sat up with a startled shriek, threw off the blanket and stumbled into the living room.

Empty.

A kitchen the size of a closet was also barren. She called out, but her words were lost beneath the rumble and shake of a passing train. She peered out the small window to the well-kept back yard. A light glowed from the detached garage. She left the house and went in search of Scott.

She found him in the garage. He looked up from beneath the hood of a familiar looking red Jeep Cherokee as she approached.

"The evening train startle you?"

Breanna circled the jeep and watched as he went back to work on the engine. She rubbed her eyes. "Yes. You didn't tell me you had an adjoining lot with Burlington Northern."

Scott chuckled. "Wait until morning. The five a.m. wheezes up that hill below us like it's taking its last breath. I never need to set an alarm clock. Want to help, or just watch?"

She laughed. "If I help, your car would become a permanent fixture in this garage. Actually, I'd like to take a bath and put on some decent clothes."

Scott gave her a wide grin. "What you've got on looks fine to me."

"You're either desperate or blind."

"Nope. I just know what I like."

She did too, and resisted an impulse to wipe away the faint grease smudge on his smooth jaw. She tentatively rolled the hem of the shirt between her fingers. Long days ago, feelings could be relied on, and she wondered if she'd ever trust herself again, let alone anyone else. She watched him from beneath lowered lashes. "What am I going to do?"

"About what?"

She held her arms out in exasperation. "Nothing major, just my entire life, which suddenly seems to be headed for the sewer."

"Guess that depends on how sensible you want to be."

"Sensible! And I suppose someone who drags nets around with other addicted sportsmen is just the person to show me how to do that." Uncertainty flared into anger fueled by deeply buried hurt. She glared at him.

"Interesting description for a commercial fisherman." Scott struggled to conceal his amusement. "I'd almost forgotten about your easy-going Irish temperament. Don't worry about me. I've picked up a few other skills besides fishing in the past nine years."

"What have you been doing all this time?" She couldn't help but be curious. Back in high school, he'd been nearly a genius at science and math. She had often wondered if he had stayed in Duluth to work in the family business or had found his own way at something better suited for his abilities.

"Finished high school. Moved to Minneapolis and went to school. Trained to be a paramedic."

"Why did you come back here?"

He shrugged. "Got a little weary of living in a constant crisis. Dad needed me. Besides, fishing is an honest living."

She thought she caught a glimpse of uncertainty in his eyes, but it was gone before she could be sure. "I suppose it would have to be."

"What's it going to take for you to stop being mad at me, anyway?"

Breanna momentarily lost herself in contemplating the possibilities. She remembered a time when all he had to do was flash his charming grin, and she'd forgive him anything. Golden hair tumbled across his tanned forehead. Biceps bulged below the rolled up sleeves of his white tee shirt. He had been cute at sixteen. At twenty-five, he was devastating. Chocolate brown eyes twinkled as he caught her contemplation of him.

Breanna turned away and shrugged off the momentary

feeling of intimacy. Time to be sensible. Long past time to return from romantic flights of fancy and magic carpet rides that had crash-landed into reality.

One day at a time, first things first and all that. She had to find a way back into her apartment, short of hiring a lawyer, or securing Murray's help.

"Scott," she said in a burst of inspiration. "I've got an idea, but I need your help."

He looked doubtful. "What for?"

"We'll wait until midnight, then sneak into my apartment. We could easily jimmy open the door onto the balcony, I could get some clothes, and Mrs. Compassionate would never know."

Scott shook his head. "Hopeless situations make even calm people hatch wild-eyed schemes."

"I'm not wild-eyed, just desperate. I don't have any clothes or any way to get any. Unless I want to run like a helpless baby to Murray again." She gave him an imploring look. "Please? Or I'll just have to go myself."

Scott set the tools down and slammed the hood of the jeep. "You will not, if I have to tie you up and stow you in the closet. You think you've got troubles now, just imagine having to spend time in the county jail."

"At least I wouldn't have to worry about what to wear or where I'd sleep," she grumbled and followed him back inside the house. "I can't even get into my studio or get my car until I can get back into that damned apartment."

The necklace. Much as it would hurt to give up her mother's necklace, she could pawn it. What had happened to her necklace? "Was I wearing a necklace when you found me? A big diamond one?"

He gave her a puzzled look as he washed his hands at a chipped porcelain sink. "I already told you everything you had on. Do you usually wear your jewelry to bed?"

"Of course not." She stopped as a memory burned her mind. Marc rolling off her, the diamond clenched in his fist. 'You won't be needing this.' The smug satisfaction on his face, the bite of the necklace against her skin before the chain broke. She automatically rubbed a small chafed spot on her neck.

"It looked abraded when I picked you up. Maybe the necklace got caught—"

"Forget it." She felt the humiliation rising in her cheeks. Not only had her husband practically raped her, he'd stolen her necklace. "I made a mistake." His compassionate look simultaneously touched and infuriated her, and she turned away. "Has the Sheriff called you about your part in all this?"

"No. I don't think they've put a name to the fisherman yet, so you should be okay here. Why don't you read the funnies while I shower. Then I'll go pick up a pizza. Somehow I have the feeling you'd rather not go out tonight, right?"

That was just the beginning of it. She still had tomorrow to worry about. No money. No clothes.

Nobody.

A funeral to arrange, Marc's family to call. She wasn't even sure how to find them, wasn't sure she wanted to try.

She nodded and bit her lower lip to keep it from trembling, wishing she could return Scott's brilliant smile. She held her breath as he moved closer, the sun in the midst of black storm clouds, but exhaled in a rush of relieved disappointment when he kissed the top of her head and strode from the room.

Monday morning Breanna finally reached her receptionist/ assistant, Gayle Montclair, and rode with her to the photography studio where she changed into the extra clothes she kept there and picked up her spare car keys. At least these necessities kept her from having to rely on Uncle Murray. As upset as he was about her leaving the hospital, she couldn't ask for his help.

Gayle agreed to reschedule the day's appointments while Breanna went to the bank.

In the office of Albert Warren, her trust officer at North Shore National Bank, Breanna shifted in her chair and tried to ignore the scrape of linen against bare skin. She felt half-naked, in a plain white blouse, dark slacks, no makeup, no jewelry. No underwear. She stifled a shudder at the actions the outfit would have provoked Marc into and imagined the ideas fogging the wire-rimmed glasses of the over-starched Mr. Warren.

A bland man, thirty-five going on fifty, he probably had as much imagination as the leather chairs standing at attention in the dark paneled office. But at least that would be easier to live with than Marc's dark fantasies.

She breathed a sigh of guilty relief. He was gone. Forever, and that part of her life could be buried.

Mr. Warren looked up. "I'm sorry, Mrs. Lanier. All your joint accounts show a zero balance. Except for the small balance in the studio account, you are completely without funds."

Bankerese for dead broke. Breanna swallowed the knot of panic welling up in her throat. What had Marc done with all their money? Although it had been months since she'd been put on an allowance and denied access to the bank accounts, Marc bitingly assured her he knew how to handle finances.

Mr. Warren cleared his throat, sounding like a tractor starting up. "Then there are the loans. Several are already past due. Two others require balloon payments in a few weeks."

The words made no sense. Marc repeatedly bragged about how good his wholesale business was doing. "What loans? Surely I'm not responsible for Marc's business obligations?"

Mr. Warren handed her a pile of promissory notes. "You must know you co-signed these?"

Breanna stared at the swirly curlicues of her own signature, her mind transported to her kitchen. "Can't I at least look these over before I sign them, Marc?"

He had scowled, brows drawn together like black snakes. "Of course, you can, but what's the problem, Princess? Don't you trust me? You can't deny I handle money better than you do." His calm words barely screened simmering anger. She hesitated, then scribbled her name. Anything to avoid another confrontation. Anything to prove she trusted him with every-thing.

Now she had nothing.

Breanna folded her hands atop the papers and gave the banker a shaky smile. "I need your advice, Mr. Warren. I don't have a place to live, clothes, anything. My landlady has locked me out of my apartment. Now I don't even have enough money to hire a lawyer to fight her. What are my options?"

He looked shocked, patted her hand in an awkward gesture, reached for the phone and made a call. "Someone from the legal department will handle that right away so you can get your belongings. But why don't you call her bluff and move into your grandmother's house? You've told me before you wished to do so but your husband preferred the apartment. We can advance some money from your trust to cover your living expenses until you're back on your feet. As for the loans—"

Breanna leaned forward. "The boat was insured. Once that's settled, I'll have your money."

Warren nodded. "Of course, we can offer a temporary extension of them pending settlement of your husband's estate."

She gave him a blank look. Estate. The man had just established that Marc was a penniless liar. How could there be an estate? "Thank you. Could I please have the key to my safe deposit box?"

A few minutes later, Breanna sat in the quiet sterility of the bank vault and held the antique earrings against her ear. Mr. Warren's words echoed in her mind. Strange, how even in death Marc's actions affected her life. What a fool she'd been.

At least she'd had the sense to leave the jewelry at the bank. Losing grandmother's antique gold and diamond earrings would be almost like losing another family member. Reverently, she clipped the heavy earrings on and watched the ceiling spotlights send a rainbow of color dancing in the tiny alcove.

Closing her eyes she could picture her mother, Fiona, dressed for the Junior League Christmas ball in a purple silk dress. The deeper hue of the marquis cut stones in the heavy gold setting reflected off the round, full carat white diamonds in the center and on the ear clips.

Breanna had worn them only once outside the bank. Marc fixed a look of such malicious greed on her she'd hurriedly replaced them in the vault the next day. He'd hounded her mercilessly about them since, offering to get them appraised and insured. Luckily, she'd sensed the lie.

She sighed and returned the jewels to their secured place. Maybe someday she'd find the courage and the opportunity to wear them again. Maybe they'd even bring her the good fortune they'd brought her grandparents.

Later that afternoon, she stood at the door of her apartment and tried to ignore Ina Kilpela's hostile attitude as she worried the key in the lock.

"Should have known you'd bring in your hired guns before your poor husband was even found. You rich people think you own this town. And lawyers. What do they know about honoring agreements? You still have four months left on your lease, you know."

"His lease. Not mine." Hands on her hips, Breanna turned to look at her and caught Mrs. Kilpela's jaw working like an elephant chewing peanuts as the door swung wide.

Breanna gasped and stepped into a trashed world. The stylish contemporary apartment she'd worked hard to keep in the well organized manner Marc demanded looked like the aftermath of a vindictive tornado.

Slashed couches and chairs lay overturned. Stuffing from feather pillows covered the floor like snow. Breanna waded ankle deep through papers in the bedroom that served as a small office and dazedly moved through the apartment. Contents of closets and drawers from toiletries to lingerie littered the rooms.

Overwhelmed by a sense of personal violation, her footsteps took her into the breakfast room. Five five-inch by six-inch glossy color photographs marched meticulously across the kitchen counter. Breanna stared, horrified. Five. There should be six. Marc had promised to get rid of them after the only argument she'd won.

He'd sworn he destroyed them. A conciliatory gesture for her mortified anger about the wild night the diamond pendant had first disappeared, the night she'd been so strung out from drowning her grief her memories were hazy to non-existent.

Scarlet satin and lace, each pose more revealing than the one before.

Breanna squeezed her eyes shut, but the image of the missing picture burned. A crimson flowered silk scarf.... She flinched. How could she have let him take those pictures? How could he have kept them? And how could she endure knowing a stranger possessed the most degrading one of all?

Chapter 5

The murmur of strangers' voices accompanying Mrs. Kilpela's high-pitched tones jerked Breanna back to reality. The pictures. She couldn't let anyone see them.

Seizing the photos, she scanned the room for a hiding place and stuffed them into the microwave oven just as the landlady and two uniformed policemen entered the apartment. The oven door closed with a click that sounded like an explosion. Breanna jumped guiltily.

"Don't touch anything until we dust for prints." The sergeants' cool gaze rested briefly on her before he followed the other officer to the broken balcony door.

Later, the officer asked Breanna for what felt like the hundredth time if anything was missing. "Sure you don't know what they were after? Or if anything was taken?"

She shook her head and took a deep breath. "No." She swallowed the sticky taste of the lie and forced a tiny smile. Marc could have kept the sixth picture somewhere else. His office, for instance. "I'll let you know if I discover anything different."

"Yeah, do that." The officer's assessing gaze swept over her again as he and his partner left.

Breanna breathed a sigh of relief. He knew she was lying about something, she felt certain of it. Scott had always kidded her about having a glass head. Apparently, time spent with Marc hadn't improved her skill as a liar. But how would anyone have known to look for the pictures? She must be wrong, jumping to conclusions again. After all, no one would have vandalized the apartment for the type of photos they could easily find on the Internet.

"I hope you don't blame me for this, Mrs. Lanier." Ina Kilpela turned a challenging look on Breanna. "The apartment was fine, just fine, Friday evening when I had the locks changed. Now back to your lease."

"My lease? Yesterday you wouldn't even let me in long enough to get a change of clothes! I know you've never liked me. I don't know why, nor do I care. I think we'd both be happier if I just moved out. I'll have everything out by tomorrow night." She rested a hand on her hip and returned the older woman's cold stare without flinching.

Mrs. Kilpela muttered a response and left, slamming the door behind her. Breanna shook her head. Her father had always said being the wealthiest family in a small town created animosity. She'd attended public school until her junior year when her father had sent her away, but being the daughter of the food king had stirred up envy and made it difficult to form lasting friendships.

Except for Scott. He'd never cared that her family lived in the biggest house in town or been impressed that her father's car cost more money than most families earned in a year. He'd been her best friend.

Until the afternoon at Lake Vermilion. Before he ran off. Before her world crashed in and she ended up in an exclusive private school in Dallas. Alone.

Breanna surveyed the wrecked apartment, struggling against the hopelessness threatening to overwhelm her.

Maybe she should have stayed in Texas. At least then she wouldn't have met Marc.

She moved toward the patio door. Watching the harbor always soothed her, but she found no peace in it today. English ivy in a large brass pot hung from a hook in the ceiling and moved slightly in the breeze from the open door, transporting Breanna six months back in time. The missing picture sprang to life in a hazy, nightmarish, remembrance.

Her face burned, her arms and back ached with the memory of total submission. The plant had arrived two days later, Marc's pretense of an apology gift. In reality a constant reminder of her shame. Rage flooded through her. Anger at Marc's lewd behavior, disgust at her weakness.

Breanna grasped the pot, ripping the ceiling in a shower of

plaster. She hurled the reminder across the cluttered room. A brass floor lamp crashed as the plant thunked against the wall.

Never again would she allow herself to be so submissive, so victimized. Never.

She moved to the bedroom and began picking clothes up off the floor, sorting them into piles of his and hers.

How odd. Although Marc had been an extremely good dresser with a pricey wardrobe, hardly any of his things were in the heap that had once been the contents of the master bedroom closet. She went to the closet and surveyed what was left. Nothing on her side, everything had been thrown onto the bedroom floor.

Empty hangers crowded against the wall on his side. Where were all of his belongings? How had she missed noticing that earlier?

Two hours later, she flung half empty bottles of toiletries into a trash bag in frustration. Amazing how much of Marc's things were gone. Why would someone take only Marc's possessions? Unless he had done it?

Marc had been the last one in the apartment on Friday. She'd gone straight from work to the pier. Which meant anything could have happened after she left for the studio early Friday morning.

It was only supposed to be a weekend trip, yet Marc must have packed as if he didn't plan to return.

Maybe he hadn't. *"Be a good girl and cooperate, one last time."*

She shuddered and lugged the trash bag down to the dumpster and tossed it in.

Returning to the apartment, she surveyed the mess that remained. She sighed. It was going to take a bulldozer to clean up the debris and still no address book, phone numbers, nothing in what was left of Marc's personal belongings offered a clue as to where she could find his family. She'd always assumed Marc's defensive secrecy about his family was because they lacked money and social standing, two things she never considered important, anyway.

Maybe he'd been hiding more serious things. Had he been

trying to run from something, someone?

He might have kept records in his office at the warehouse, but she didn't want to go over there alone. The idea of asking Murray for help stung after his early morning interrogatory call. Scott might help, but she still felt angry from their argument about her uncle. Finally, the desecrated apartment closed in, suffocating and threatening, but she showered and changed clothes, trying futilely to ignore invisible demons.

She grabbed the keys to her car and fled.

Edwards and Sons Fishing Enterprises, a familiar landmark on Lake Avenue, looked untouched by time since her last visit with Scott ten years ago despite the new and renovated buildings surrounding it.

Breanna ignored the wolfish stares from the fishermen and tapped her foot against the dirty, gray floorboards on the loading dock. As soon as she saw Scott, a look of exasperation on his face, she wished she'd called first, but it was too late to turn back.

He stalked down the loading dock toward her. "Damn it. You don't belong here." Irritation apparent in his voice, he gripped her elbow and guided her toward the alley door.

Startled, Breanna jerked her arm away. "Get your gritty hands off me. You smell like a fishhouse."

"So will you unless you get out. And that would be a shame, since you smell even better than you look." His gaze traveled over her in an appreciative survey, from the deep blue cropped top skimming the waistband of her clingy white slacks to red painted toes exposed by narrow straps of white leather sandals.

Breanna watched Scott's expression and tried to fathom the reason for his annoyance. He probably expected her to apologize for this morning. She squared her shoulders and returned his gaze. Well, she wouldn't. He couldn't drop back into her life after nine years and think he had the right to dictate to her.

Blond hair tumbled over Scott's forehead, partially obscuring dirt smudges. She watched warily for several moments until Scott blew out a slow breath and grinned.

"I'm sorry. But what *are* you doing here? Not that I mind. It's just no place for a lady."

Breanna relaxed. He wasn't angry, just concerned like a friend would be. "I need you to go somewhere with me."

"Now? I don't finish work until six."

She shrugged. "You're the boss. Can't you leave early?"

Scott laughed. "Doesn't work that way here, doll. Besides, we wouldn't want to ruin Derek's illusions about who's in charge. I'd be scrubbing out the trawlers tomorrow just to offset the freedom. And as bad as smoking fish is, that would be worse."

Breanna wrinkled her nose. "Are you sure about that? And I'm not your doll. I told you not to call me that, remember? I just need your help, that's all."

"With what? You gave me the definite impression this morning that you'd skinny dip in Lake Superior before you'd take my help again."

She let out a long sigh. "I'm sorry, Scott. You still know how to make me so damn mad. And I don't like being ordered around."

She'd had enough of that, but it wasn't going to be easy to find the middle ground between pushy and pushover. She paused. "Look, I hate to drag you into the muddle my life's become, but I found the key to Marc's warehouse, and I feel uneasy going there alone after everything that's happened. Please?"

Scott gazed down into eyes so blue, he felt as if he were drowning, but what a way to go. He stuffed his hands into his coverall pockets to stifle the overpowering urge to circle the tiny strip of skin revealed above the waistband of her slacks as she shifted her weight. "If you can wait until I get through here, I'll pick you up at your apartment."

Breanna stiffened. "No, no. That's okay. I'll come back."

"Here?" Scott's brows shot up. "Nope. I need to clean up. Meet me at my house at seven." He steered her toward a crimson Mercedes convertible.

Derek was due back any time. Seeing Breanna at the Fishery would arouse all kinds of unwanted speculation from him, along with certain crude remarks. "The warehouse is closer to my place, anyway. Go set things right with your uncle." He closed the car door and waved her away.

Feeling dismissed, Breanna tapped the accelerator. Gravel spewed as she charged out onto Lake Avenue. To hell with seeing Murray. He might be all the family she had left, but he was acting unbelievably aggravating. She'd go to the warehouse herself.

But watching Scott in the rearview mirror strangely dissipated her irritation. She couldn't find the strength of purpose to go to the West End, and she was perplexed by why Scott already knew where the warehouse was for Lanier's Fine Furs. She sighed.

Might as well go check out Grandmother's house and make arrangements to start moving. She needed a place to spend the night and hoped the house wasn't too musty and dusty. Her pride refused to ask Murray for help, while spending another night with Scott was asking for trouble.

Scott watched Breanna spin out of the parking lot, hair blue black in the sunshine, a mesmerizing contrast to the late model red convertible. Whistling, he trudged up the wooden steps and into the narrow back door. Into the dark odorous fishery and Derek's sarcastic scowl.

"Look who's trying to score with the wintry widow."

Scott shrugged and started to step around his older brother. "What's it to you?"

Derek's paw on his sleeve stopped him. "Just trying to save you some trouble, little brother. From what I've heard, and I've heard a lot, that woman makes a glacier seem warm and inviting."

"Buzz off, Derek, and mind your own business while you've still got a business to mind."

A livid flush crept up Derek's neck. "Yeah right, hotshot. But you mind what I'm telling you or you just might end up with frostbite on your—"

Derek's words died into a strangled curse as Scott grabbed his shirt collar, lifted him two feet off the floor and slammed him against the brick wall of the smoker.

"I don't give a damn what kind of garbage you've heard about Breanna Alden, you low-life scum. Keep your nasty comments to yourself."

Derek struggled. Scott tightened his grip. "One more word, Derek. That's all it will take for me to rip your tongue out and stuff it down your throat. You get the picture—partner?"

Derek's eyes narrowed. His face twisted with hostility and rage. "Yeah."

Scott lowered him to the floor and strode away, shrugging off Derek's hostile chuckle and a rude remark that made little sense.

"Yeah, the proof is in the picture. And it suits me just fine if you want to end up as fish bait, little brother."

Satisfied to have settled a few things into Lillian's old house, Breanna paced the small distance from Scott's living room couch to the kitchen. She surveyed the minuscule room. Shiny white mini blinds contrasted starkly with faded yellow walls, dingy white cupboards, torn vinyl flooring.

Whatever else the past nine years had brought Scott, financial security obviously wasn't among them. Still, the cleanliness of the tiny house reflected pride of ownership. She poured the remainder of her coffee down the drain and rinsed out the mug. The sound of running water stopped and an ear-piercing yell broke the silence.

Breanna rushed toward the living room as Scott, towel wrapped around his middle, emerged from the bedroom dripping water onto the worn carpet.

He scowled. "Didn't I tell you not to turn on the water in the kitchen?"

Breanna smothered a smile behind her hand. "Maybe I just

thought you could use a cold shower."

"Is that right?" Scott grinned as he stepped past her and headed for the kitchen. "Need some more coffee?"

"No thanks." She followed him, half wishing he'd retreat back into the bedroom. Water droplets slid in fascinating rivulets across his deeply tanned shoulders and down his back, leading Breanna's eyes on a long remembered journey to the top edge of the precariously fastened towel.

She turned away and gazed into the back yard. "I wish you'd get dressed so we can get over to the warehouse before dark."

Scott studied her, apparently amused at her refusal to meet his eyes. "You're just as patient as you always were."

Obviously, he enjoyed making her uneasy. The thought goaded her temper. "Patient! I've been waiting for you for over two hours. I could have been to the warehouse fifteen times by now."

Scott sipped slowly from a beat-up looking mug. "So why didn't you? Not that I mind going, but what's the problem?"

Breanna tried to shrug off a persistent sense of dread. "I don't know really. Maybe it's just because Marc was insistent I stay out of his business affairs. I went over there once to surprise him with lunch and instead started an argument that lasted for two days." Wrapped up in unpleasant memories, Breanna sharply drew in a breath as Scott's arm slid around her shoulders. She let herself be gently drawn into his warmth, closed her eyes and rested her cheek against his damp skin.

"It's okay, Breena," he murmured. "I've heard plenty of stories about your husband. None of them good. You don't have to pretend to me that you're sorry he's gone."

She nodded, trying to bask in the comforting words, but the sense of dread persisted.

Twilight hovered around the edges of the city, shrouding the Grand Avenue warehouse district with duskiness. Breanna took a deep breath and turned the key in the locked door of Lanier's Fine Furs, Wholesalers. Yellow yard lights cast elongated shadows and shimmered against the glass inset.

Scott shifted his weight impatiently until the lock clicked, then he pulled the door open.

Breanna fumbled for the light switch near the door, hesitating as Scott covered her hand with his.

"Don't."

She turned and tried to see the expression in his dark brown eyes, but couldn't keep the peevish edge from her voice. "I suppose that makes a lot of sense, to stumble around here in the dark. What's the matter with you?"

"Breanna, wait," he protested as she flipped the switch and flooded the small reception area with light.

She waved her hand at the sterile-looking room. "What's the big deal? If Marc really had much of value here, he'd hire a security guard. And we didn't need to park out back, either. I told you, I've been here before, months ago. Marc's office is upstairs at the back of the warehouse, although I wasn't allowed to venture past that door." She inclined her head toward a white painted door marked Employees Only. She pushed past Scott and tugged open the door onto a fathomless black cavern.

"Breanna," Scott laid a hand on her arm. "Take the flashlight. I'll cut off those other lights."

"Why are you so paranoid? Why should we skulk around here in the dark? I have every right to be here, and you're acting like a cat burglar."

"After what happened with your landlady, you shouldn't take anything for granted."

She hadn't thought about that. But who would be watching the warehouse? She twirled the flashlight like a baton and waited in the darkness for Scott to rejoin her. He stepped inside and closed the door, and the darkness became as suffocating as a locked closet. She felt his breathing near her. Fingers curled over her hand. A knot of panic exploded inside her, and she jerked away.

Scott grabbed at her. His foot slid across a slick spot, then he lost his balance and crashed against a stack of cartons.

Breanna found the overhead light switch. Scott sprawled amidst overturned boxes.

"What the hell is the matter with you? I only wanted the flashlight."

She crouched and touched his shoulder, laughter bubbling forth. "I'm sorry. You startled me, that's all." Probably because his caution made her nervous and twitchy, but she kept the thought to herself.

He scrambled to his feet. Breanna followed, surveyed the room and rubbed her arms in defense against the cool air. Fuzzy fluorescent light flickered across a meager assortment of fur coats hanging from a freestanding rack. More cardboard boxes towered against one wall.

Scott shook his head. "Not much of an inventory. Did an animal rights activist get hold of him?"

"You're assuming he had an ounce of sensitivity."

"Good point." He was silent for a moment, then nudged a carton with the toe of a well-worn Nike. "Any idea what's in the rest of these boxes? They don't seem heavy."

Her eyes focused on the far corner of the warehouse, shadowy in the puny light. "More furs, I guess. He said he was expecting a shipment the night we were on the boat. Look, I'll have to figure something out about the business, but right now I just want to check out the office."

Scott reached for the overturned crate and moved another aside as if to make a path to the source of the wetness coating the floor and pooling in a shallow puddle where he'd slipped. "Go ahead. I'll check this out."

"Not now. Besides, whatever is in there is none of your business, and I'm not sure I want to know." She grabbed his arm and tugged him over to the stairway at the rear of the building. "The office is back this way, and that's all I'm ready to deal with tonight. Come on."

Her sandaled feet clattered up the metal staircase to the office that overlooked the rest of the warehouse.

Breanna tried the door. Locked. She sorted through the remaining keys on the ring, and after three false tries, turned the lock. Inside, Marc's desk looked compulsively neat, an expensive leather blotter and desk set Breanna had given him for Christmas precisely arranged. *A place for everything and everything in its place.* The words swirled through her mind, echoes of the hundreds of times he'd said them to her.

She hurried over to the desk and futilely yanked on one of the drawers. Obviously Marc's obsessive secrecy carried into his business as well. None of the keys remaining on the key ring were small enough for the round lock. She surveyed the desktop for a letter opener, anything to open the drawers.

Scott lounged against the doorjamb, prepared to wait, but her increasing impatience proved contagious. "You'd make a lousy burglar, you know that?" He strode over, groped under the drawer and produced a small key. A bit of scotch tape remained on the end. He peeled it off and opened the drawer. "There you go."

Breanna rested her hands on her hips, frowned, and looked him over. "I'm really starting to worry about how you've been spending your time, Edwards. Any reason why this place seems familiar to you?"

Scott laughed. "Nah, that's just the oldest trick in the world. Your problem is you never liked those old mystery movies."

Breanna's face warmed as memories of wintry nights spent huddled in front of the television set in the Alden's cozy rec room resurfaced. She and Scott, munching popcorn. Nibbling each other. No wonder she couldn't remember the movies.

Scott leaned over her shoulder, his breath tickling her neck as she rifled through documents in the desk drawer. "Just what is it that you're looking for?"

"Names, addresses. Have you forgotten I have a funeral to arrange?"

He touched her shoulder. "I'm sorry, Breena. Guess all that falls to you."

Breanna pulled a slim, burgundy journal from amidst a sheaf of insurance papers. Flipping it open revealed Marc's immaculate script. "Looks like a log book," she answered Scott's unspoken question. Intrigued, she scanned a page, her curiosity instantly replaced by a gnawing sense of dismay. She stuffed the insurance papers and the book into a purse the size of a tote bag.

"I have to see what's in those boxes downstairs."

She flew down the stairs behind him and gave in to his insistence to open the first box. Clenching and unclenching her hands, she watched as Scott slit cardboard with a pocketknife. Cigarettes. Cartons and cartons of cigarettes. The tote bag slid to the floor. "This makes no sense. What's in that one?"

Scott sliced open another crate, revealing more red and black Marlboro cartons. "Looks like his shipment came in."

Breanna let out an uneasy breath. Whatever she had been expecting, hundreds of cigarettes wasn't it.

He raised a brow. "Do you want me to open all of them?"

She guessed there was no avoiding it. Shrugging, she pulled an ivory handled nail file from her purse. "If that's what it takes. I'll start over here." She moved to the area where Scott had slipped earlier from the puddle.

She tried to move the box behind the one he'd tripped into, but it barely budged. "This one's heavier. It looks like it's been wet." A nasty order assailed her. She wrinkled her nose. "Phew. Do you smell something weird?"

Scott glanced up as the nail file clattered on the concrete floor and a foul smell poured out of the crate she'd opened.

Breanna backed away from the open box, her stomach roiling. She clutched her throat. "Oh, God no. No!"

Soggy cardboard gave way and a woman's body spilled out onto the floor. Stringy brown hair hung around her face. Purple splotches circled her neck.

Breanna screamed again, partially muffling the sound of splintering glass from the outer office. Scott scooped up the tote bag, grabbed Breanna's arm and propelled her to the far side of the warehouse and the door to the loading dock.

"I sure hope that door isn't padlocked." He pushed the heavy door open and shoved her ahead. The back warehouse door crashed open. A shot echoed hollowly behind them.

"Damn it, Breanna. Run. RUN!"

Chapter 6

Breanna stumbled down metal stairs. Footsteps pounded the warehouse floor as she and Scott ran to the jeep. She yanked the door open and fell into the passenger's seat. Scott grabbed her by the shoulder and shoved as the jeep squealed out of the parking lot.

"Get down!"

She did, too terrified to argue. Scott ducked. A bullet shattered the rear window, creating a glass snowstorm. The jeep veered sharply. Breanna gripped the seat, dizzy and feeling like her insides had turned into scrambled eggs. After several tense moments, she edged up and peered out the side window as the vehicle darted up the exit to Interstate 35.

"Are you crazy? You're going the wrong way up the ramp!"

"I was hoping you wouldn't notice."

"Obviously. Are they following?"

"Not yet." Scott checked the rearview mirrors, hit the brakes and maneuvered a sharp turn onto the freeway.

Breanna landed in a heap on the floor. She climbed into the seat as tires squealed and the jeep picked up speed again.

Scott shot her a glance. "What do you think you're doing?"

"It's either sit here and risk death or stay on the floor and guarantee carsickness."

"Okay, okay." He squeezed her hand. "You gonna make it?"

She nodded and looked around. Over a hundred feet below, the bay water shimmered blackly as the jeep sped along the Bong Bridge toward Wisconsin. "Why are we heading for Superior? We need to go to the police. In Minnesota, not Wisconsin."

Scott looked over at her. "We will, as soon as I'm positive we can make it without an escort. Watch out behind us."

But he felt certain they weren't being followed and didn't

like the only possible reason why.

Breanna shifted in the seat and searched the road behind them. Duluth's West End warehouse district merged into glittery lights. A few cars trailed far behind them on the four-lane highway over the bay. "Looks clear."

"So who was that?"

"I don't know. I didn't see them."

"I mean the dead woman. Did you know her?"

A knot of nausea swelled in her throat. She twisted her gold wedding band. "Nina Rogers. She worked for Marc. I wondered if they were having an affair. He was so insistent I stay away from the warehouse. Sometimes he'd get calls late at night and leave. After the first few times, I didn't dare ask where he was going. It wasn't worth the arguments."

She bit her lip remembering Marc's rage the last time she'd dared question him about where he'd been and what his phone calls were about. None of it mattered any longer, despite the revelations in the burgundy journal. She intended to bury him, complete with all his nasty secrets. Her wide gold wedding band scraped skin off as she twisted and pulled to remove the constant reminder. "Stop the car."

"In the middle of the bridge? Are you sick?"

Breanna had the door open before the jeep jerked to a complete halt. Scott put the flashers on and leapt out as she scrambled over the guardrail to the bicycle path.

"What the hell are you doing?"

Breanna hesitated, and clutched her hands together. An image of Marc's taunting smile provided the final stimulus. "Bastard," she shouted, swung her arm and sent the ring sailing toward the inky water below.

Turning, she found Scott watching from beside the jeep. "Are you all right?"

"Starting to be." She climbed back into the jeep and took a cleansing breath as Scott resumed driving. A floating sensation crept over her, dizzying, liberating. She wondered if newly released prison inmates had the same feeling.

Scott picked up her hand and kissed the scraped knuckle. "I think you'll make it."

Her eyes met his, and she managed a smile.

Scott drove through Superior's business district, periodically checking the rearview mirrors. Nothing. Probably better to go back to Duluth and the police station. He turned onto Hammond Avenue and the Blatnik Bridge. Breanna had been silent since they'd stopped on the Bong Bridge and he'd left her alone, knowing she needed time. Lots of time to put everything into perspective.

Soon he'd have to tell Breanna about Derek's involvement with her husband, but not yet. He had to have more time. Time to regain her trust. Time for her to discover on her own the true nature of Lanier's "wholesale" business and who else was involved in it.

"Did you fix things with Murray?"

Breanna stared out the side window. "No."

"I hope you're not planning to stay at the condo."

She gave him a cautious look. "I suppose you think I'm safer with you?"

"You're safer anywhere other than your apartment. Murray is your best bet."

"Stop telling me what to do. I wasn't going back to my apartment, anyway."

Scott arched an eyebrow. "Why not?"

Breanna shifted uneasily, hesitated, then rushed on. "It's been ransacked. I couldn't feel safe there even if we hadn't gone to the warehouse."

"What? When did all this happen?" Scott's voice sharpened.

"The police aren't sure. Sometime between when Mrs. Kilpela changed the locks and this morning."

Scott angrily slapped the steering wheel. "Why the hell didn't you tell me this afternoon?"

She bristled. "Why should I? The police are investigating. What could you have done about it, troll for suspects?"

Scott flushed. "Could have kept you from going to that warehouse and nearly getting us killed, that's what."

She shivered and rubbed her arms against the chill that his words, coupled with the scene at the warehouse and the missing picture gave her. "I thought I was a random victim of an ordinary burglary."

He sighed. "And tonight, victims of a random warehouse shootout? Breena, didn't you ever notice anything weird about your husband's business?"

Stung by the implications in his voice, she clenched her hands in her lap. "I had nothing to judge it against. Daddy never kept Mother informed about business, but then she never asked, either. I think that's an ordinary enough situation between husband and wife, but then how would you know that?"

He flinched as the mark bit deeply, her words recalling his own mother's desertion when he was nine. "Breena, nothing about you is ordinary. Never has been, so don't think you have to remind me I'm not good enough for you. Your father thoroughly drilled that into me nine years ago."

Breanna pressed her palms against her warm face. "I'm sorry. You know I never felt that way. But there's a lot of things you wouldn't understand."

"Then enlighten me." Scott took her hand and linked his fingers through hers. "Look, if we're going to be friends, you've got to trust me. I know it's tough after the hell you've been through."

"With Lucifer's partner," she mumbled. Silently, she studied the slope of Spirit Mountain as they drew nearer to Minnesota, the outlined ski area looped across the dark hills like artfully arranged necklaces. The West End stretched out at the foot of the hills, a glimmering crystal ribbon. One of the points of light expanded into a red glow. An orangish ball billowed skyward. A diffused boom cracked the night air.

Breanna tightened her fingers in Scott's. "Oh, my God. It's coming from the warehouse district. What if the warehouse is on fire?"

Scott sucked in a breath. "Random victim, huh? You're a walking doomsday, lady."

Breanna was silent. He was right, and she wondered how she could expect him to stay around when her life was a time bomb. Scott parked the jeep and they pushed their way through the small crowd gathered in front of the blazing warehouse. Breanna hugged her arms to her chest and watched firefighters hose down the smoldering outline of the warehouse for Lanier's Fine Furs. Numb, she closed her eyes as a body bag was trundled past and lost herself in a return to the horror of her last night on the yacht. Marc dead. Her miserable life turning into a nightmare.

She felt Scott's warmth beside her, his arm around her shoulders. "There goes your inheritance. Up in smoke. But don't feel too badly. Those things could kill you."

Breanna gave him a withering look. "This is no time for stupid jokes."

"Maybe not. But stupid's the best I could do."

At the Police Station, afraid to admit she and Scott had been at the warehouse minutes before it was torched, Breanna tried to evade endless questions about Marc's business.

Finally allowed to leave, Scott silently escorted her back to the jeep. She folded her arms and gazed out the window as Scott eased from a parking space in the Civic Center.

"Where to now? Want to get something to eat?"

Breanna shuddered, images of the dead woman and the incinerated warehouse making her stomach convulse. "No way. Drive me home, please. I'll get my car from your place tomorrow. Somehow."

"I'll bring you over there in the morning. After breakfast."

She turned a cool gaze on him. "Wait a minute. You can't stay with me."

"I'm afraid I can't not." He gave her a devilish grin and eased the clutch out as the vehicle trudged up the steep incline of Mesaba Avenue. "Besides, I figure you owe me a night."

"Based on what?"

"Other than this friend stuff has turned into a full time job, there's the possibility of midnight visitors at my house that I'd like to avoid."

Breanna bit her lip, reluctant to admit what she had already guessed. "You mean, they didn't follow us from the warehouse because they know where to find us later."

He nodded. "Right. Except if you don't go back to the

condo or my house, they're stuck. For a while anyway."

She sighed. "You win."

Scott chuckled. "Don't sound so enthused. Now tell me where I'm going."

"The wrong way. Go back down the hill. To London Road. I've moved into Grandmother Lillian's house. There's a big comfortable couch, so don't get any funny ideas, and I don't want to hear any griping about the mess, either."

"Fair enough." He gave her a cheerful smile.

Scott parked the jeep in the street level garage. With only the roof visible from London Road, Lillian's quaint house appeared dark and undisturbed as he followed Breanna down the steps to the sloping lawn and the home that rested on the black rocks lining Lake Superior. A buttercup moon shone off the water, throwing elongated tree shadows along the house. A branch scraped against the shingles.

The lock clinked, then Breanna pushed on the heavy oak. The door screeched open. A crash resounded. Scott pressed Breanna against the brick walled porch, blocking her vision, muffling her startled protest.

"Who knew you were staying here?"

Chapter 7

Scott edged forward, peering into the darkness. Footsteps thundered down a staircase, clattered across a wood floor. A darker shape burst from the shadows, hit him in the chest and knocked him backwards.

Scott cursed, losing his balance and pinning Breanna against the porch railing. She shrieked and pushed on his back as 70 pounds of Irish Setter planted huge paws on his shoulders and proceeded to lick his face.

"What the...Hello, Flannaghan. Long time no see."

"I thought you were here to protect me, not suffocate me." Breanna pounded a fist on his shoulder.

"I did. I've saved you from this savage beast loving you to death." Scott tousled Flannaghan's fur and pushed the dog away as Breanna squeezed out from between his back and the railing.

Her voice shifted the dog's attention. Flannaghan fussed and begged to be petted. "I wasn't sure he'd remember you."

Scott stroked the dog's silky ears. "Why not? I bet no one else brings him fish every night for supper."

"You didn't, either," she teased and led the way into the house. "Just smelled like supper some nights."

Scott grinned ruefully, but joined in her laughter at the shared memory of the night he'd stopped at the Alden's straight from the fishery with a package of smoked herring for Fiona. "I'd hoped you'd forgotten that."

"Not a chance. The image of you and Flannaghan rolling around in the snow will stay with me forever." Along with snow tag, a first kiss and the smoky mustiness of Scott's clothes.

Breanna turned away and flipped on the lights in the entry hall. Ivory woodwork on the walls and curved newel post sparkled in a tangle of prisms from a crystal chandelier.

Flannaghan danced along beside her as she walked into the living room. Moonlight streamed through a wall of glass overlooking Lake Superior, illuminating shrouded furniture lurking like misshapen ghosts.

She turned on a floor lamp and pulled a dust cover off a cushioned sofa, feeling Scott's gaze while she removed the remaining sheets and wadded them into a ball. She flicked a speck of dust off the rose damask upholstery and straightened the pillows. Lillian's house still reflected her eclectic style, a combination of traditional and avant-garde. Antique furniture boasted contemporary fabrics and competed for attention with art deco accessories, ginger jar lamps and a coffee table shaped like a three-hundred-pound encyclopedia.

"You always loved this house." Scott's voice was low.

Unable to continue the mindless busywork under his intense perusal, she glanced up. "Umm. Especially this room. Always gave me the feeling the house was floating at the edge of the water."

"So why live at the condo when this was yours?"

She shrugged. "Marc's idea. He hated this place. Too small and close to the lake. Besides, the apartment gave him a good excuse not to let me keep Flannaghan."

"Then where has he been?"

"With Murray. I just reclaimed him this afternoon."

"I thought you said you hadn't talked to him yet."

Breanna headed for the bedroom. "I didn't. Just picked up the dog and left a note saying I'd call him later."

Scott followed and accepted the blanket and pillow she scavenged from the linen closet. "Breanna," he began.

She stood on tiptoe and kissed his cheek, anxious to hide away before the temptation to throw herself into his arms and seek comfort proved overwhelming. "Thanks, Edwards. Hope the couch isn't too uncomfortable. I'd offer to fix you something to eat, but I haven't had a chance to buy groceries. See you in the morning."

The next instant Scott found himself staring at the closed bedroom door, his well intentioned suggestions unspoken on how she could make amends with her uncle. He shook his head and moved away. It was nearly midnight, anyway. After a good night's sleep, she'd realize he was right. At least he hoped so. Murray could give her the sense of security and reassurance he suspected she needed now. He wondered how long it would be before she could accept that from him.

Sometime later, Breanna awoke, startled by her surroundings. Gradually the four-poster bed and antique dresser became familiar in the fading moonlight. She lay quietly for several moments, half asleep, unsure of what had awakened her. She touched her cheek, and all the pain of the past six months washed over her.

She'd lost everyone she cared about, but worst of all, lost herself in a futile attempt at happiness with Marc.

What a fool she'd been.

Overwhelmed by emptiness, she buried her wet face against the pillow to hide the anguish pouring out.

Scott bolted upright, his palm cold and damp from Flannaghan's insistent nuzzling. The house rested, quiet except for the rhythmic ticking of the grandfather clock in the foyer.

And another softer sound.

He followed Flannaghan to Breanna's bedroom and listened at the partially open door. He hesitated, but her muffled sobs wrenched his heart.

She gasped when his weight settled on the mattress and his arms went around her. "It's okay, Breena," he murmured against her hair.

She pushed half-heartedly against his bare chest. "Go away."

"Can't, not as long as there's the slightest chance you need me." He wouldn't abandon her again. He intended to be there for her, no matter what.

She threw her arms around his neck and sobbed harder. "I don't need you. I wish you hadn't come back."

"I know, I know," he whispered. "But I had to. I'd give anything to change what happened but since I can't, let me hold you, sweetheart. At least trust me that much."

She wanted to. More than she'd ever realized, she still wanted Scott. His laughter, his smile, his arms around her.

Like before, when every day felt created just for them.

When she'd trusted him, and he was always there. Until that last day at Lake Vermilion, and the time she'd needed him the most.

Tuesday morning, fog hung like wet gray sheets over the lake. Breanna awoke to the aroma of bacon and coffee and found Scott in the kitchen. Flannaghan stood wagging his tail, following Scott's movements expectantly.

"Don't spoil my dog," she cautioned.

He slipped a sliver of bacon to the Irish Setter. "Too late. Besides, I suspect someone else has already done that to *our* dog."

Breanna frowned and accepted the mug of coffee he handed her, the steam momentarily clouding the glasses she favored over her contact lenses first thing in the morning. She decided to ignore his proprietary remark. "Must have been the year spent with Murray. When did you get groceries?"

"Oh, I always wake up with the birds. Even though today the birds had the sense to sleep in. I thought you could use a good night's sleep and a hot meal."

"I guess so," she murmured. Yesterday seemed like a twenty-four hour bad dream, and she tried to remember if she'd even had lunch. Maybe eating would chase away the exhaustion that still clung to her despite the late morning hour. She sat down in the wooden captain's chair and tucked her bare feet under the knee length sleep shirt. "Don't you have to work?"

He gestured toward the window. "This ain't fishing weather, and I've had all I can stand of the smoker for awhile. I took the day off. Thought maybe you could use some help getting settled, although things look okay. Like Lillian just left and went out for a stroll."

"I kept the place more or less cleaned up in hopes of renting it." Breanna studied him over the rim of her coffee mug, fascinated with the flexing muscles in his upper arms as he stretched and opened cupboards searching out tableware. She wished he would hug her, touch her, but he moved about the kitchen, apparently oblivious to the warmth in her face and the distressing flutters she felt remembering his midnight visit. She wondered if he'd left her room as soon as she fell asleep. If he'd slept at all on the couch.

"Will you help me move some stuff from the condo?"

He smiled and tousled her hair like her brother Brett used to do. "Sure. Just call on Edwards' Easy Movers."

Scott flung open a cabinet door. A water glass tottered, and he made a desperate attempt to rescue it, but the glass shattered on the granite counter top. Breanna smothered a smile at his chagrined look.

"The movers who handle your valuables with casual disregard?"

He grinned. "That's right. You know our motto: We sweat. You fret."

Later, Scott glanced around the kitchen of Breanna's high-tech apartment. He wondered if the condo reflected Marc's personality or Breanna's. Must have been Lanier's influence. It sure didn't look like the Breanna he remembered.

Stark white European style counters matched the cabinets and contained only the barest essentials. The whole apartment was a sterile world compared to Lillian's house of antiques and interesting collectibles. Surely she hadn't changed that much in nine years.

He wiped a black streak of fingerprint powder from the cabinet, a rude reminder of the vandalism. Might as well get started while he waited for Breanna to return from her landlady's apartment. He opened cabinets and drawers and stacked utensils and cookware in boxes.

He glanced up as she entered the room and watched him close a container. "Get things squared with Lady Bountiful?"

"Close enough. I never understood why she seemed to hate me so much."

"You mean besides the fact that you're young, beautiful and rich, and she looks like a rusting freighter?" He grinned.

Breanna laughed, pushed glasses framed in the palest blue up on the bridge of her nose and looked down at her faded jeans and navy Chanel T shirt. "I'd believe the young part. The rest doesn't seem to be true." She sighed and looked around the apartment, apparently anxious to finish up and get out.

"I'm not going to miss her or this place. Why don't you start carrying stuff out? I can do the packing."

Scott opened another cabinet, wrapped a glass and placed it in the box. "I don't mind. There's not much left. This is a pretty classy place. Fully equipped, too. Sure you won't miss it?" He paused, surveyed the room and turned a quizzical look on her as he opened the microwave oven and picked up several five by six pictures. "Is it some neat photographer's trick to store photos in the oven?"

Breanna practically leaped across the small space and tried to yank the pictures from his grasp. "Don't!"

He glimpsed a nearly naked woman and couldn't resist holding the photos just above her head to get a better look. He whistled. "Maybe these should have been stored in the freezer."

He glanced again at the glossy pictures, amusement shif-ing to shock as the hazy woman became Breanna. A strip of crimson bound her wrists. Dark hair half obscured her anguished face, but there was no mistaking her creamy skin, her... He swallowed and relaxed his grip.

Breanna yanked the pictures away and began tearing them into dozens of tiny pieces. Two bright spots of color flared on her cheekbones. "Damn you!"

The tears in her eyes made questions impossible. He reached out to touch her shoulder, but she jerked away, and he dropped his hand. "I'm sorry. I didn't mean to snoop."

She refused to meet his eyes and moved stiffly toward the living room. "Let's finish and get out of here."

Scott watched her leave. Lanier and his nasty games. Good thing the lying bastard was already dead or he doubted he'd be able to resist pounding the cruel smile off his face.

Yet even as he felt the anger ignite, the question of why Breanna allowed it to happen insinuated itself into his mind.

Chapter 8

Wednesday morning, back at work in the studio, Breanna rechecked the lighting and peered through the camera lens. It should feel good to be doing something real, something she loved. And Tiffany was the sweetest little girl. She forced herself to concentrate.

"Okay, Tiffany, show us a pretty smile." The six-year-old stared back with timid solemnity until Breanna tickled her chin with a pink stuffed bear. "Say, 'my mom sleeps in the bathtub.'" Tiffany dissolved into giggles. The shutter clicked in a staccato rhythm.

Breanna rubbed her fist into the small of her back. Usually the studio offered solace and satisfaction, no matter what other problems hung over her. Not today.

She shrugged off a backache and watched Mrs. Hennessey fuss and arrange her daughter's curls. She couldn't shake the weariness that had enveloped her since waking in the hospital Sunday. Scott had warned her about going back to work too soon, but she had to. She needed the distraction. She desperately needed the money. Breanna returned her attention to her tiny client.

The studio door opened and Gayle Montclair stuck her head in. "Excuse me, Breanna. There's a Mr. Nicholson here to see you from the insurance company. I asked him to come back this afternoon, but he insisted he needed to see you now."

Breanna adjusted the frothy trim on Tiffany's satin dress and pulled down a background of spring flowers behind her. "He'll have to have a time out until I finish this sitting. I will not make a six-year-old wait."

Tiffany giggled. "Time out means you've been naughty."

Gayle rolled her eyes. "I'll tell him, but the gentleman seems to have less patience than most of our clients." She shut the door, muffling her voice as she relayed the message.

Twenty minutes later Tiffany and her mother left the studio. Breanna shook hands with Mr. Nicholson and sat down in her shoebox-sized office. She reread his business card. *N. J. Nicholson, Providential Security Company, Minneapolis.*

"What can I do for you, Mr. Nicholson?"

Thirty-ish, he appeared to study her in methodical detail, gray-green eyes regarding her coolly from her face down to her shoes.

Breanna crossed her arms, wishing he'd finish his scrutiny and get to the point.

"I'm sorry about your husband, Mrs. Lanier, and I'm sure this is rough for you, but I need a little more information than the police reports show."

"You spoke with the police?"

He spread his hands. "Routine procedure. As you know, you carry several policies with my company."

She tossed the card into the heap of mail on her desk. Policies. She hadn't had a chance to look through all the papers she'd taken from the warehouse Monday night.

"Actually, I don't know. My husband handled our financial matters. Do you mean the insurance on the yacht?"

"Marine insurance is handled through an affiliated company. So is the warehouse. We can't settle those claims until the investigations are wrapped up, and that's where I come in. Then there's the life insurance you and your husband carried. We've already received an inquiry from the secondary beneficiary."

Breanna straightened. She'd listed Murray as the secondary beneficiary on her policy and Marc had listed—she didn't know. Why would Murray have called? "Secondary beneficiary? Who? From where?"

He gave her a speculative look. "Gregory Lanier, your husband's brother in Montreal. I explained to him about the delay in issuing a death certificate since your husband's body hasn't been recovered."

Breanna shuddered as she again saw the yacht burst into red and white flames. "He won't be. I saw the explosion."

His split second hesitation and interrogatory glance gave her a tremor of uneasiness before he said, "You're probably right. So far the Coast Guard hasn't recovered much of the boat. Which leads to my questions." He produced a small notebook and pen from his suit pocket.

Breanna's desk phone buzzed. She picked up the phone and spoke briefly with Gayle, then turned to the insurance man. "I'm sorry, Mr. Nicholson. But my next appointment has arrived, and I have a meeting after that. Could you come back this afternoon?"

"I'm afraid not, but we do need to talk as soon as possible. Are you free this evening? I could stop by your apartment."

Breanna started but detected only professional interest in his eyes. Still, something in his attitude instilled her with caution. "Why don't we meet at the Pickwick? Seven thirty?"

He smiled in agreement and nodded. Trying to hide her tension, she stood. "Great."

As she watched him drive away in a tan Chevrolet, she realized what it was that disturbed her. Despite his conservative navy suit and burgundy tie, he looked more the Porsche type, and she doubted his choice was based on financial considerations. Something about him just didn't ring true.

Breanna handed his business card to Gayle. "Call Providential and check this guy out for me, please."

That evening, Breanna closed her eyes and applied a final spritz of hair spray. All this damp weather made her hair droop into strands straight enough to belong to an Indian princess.

Princess. Marc's taunting pet name gave her a twinge of humiliated anger. Breanna stared out the window at the black rocks below. Now there would be Gregory Lanier to deal with once she got the information she needed from Nicholson.

Marc had never spoken of his family, and had retreated behind a wall of dark silence when she had tried to ask. She had almost convinced herself Marc was an orphan. It would have been easier, but life with Marc never was. Why should she expect his death to be?

Then there was the Mt. Everest of debt he'd left behind. She wished she hadn't had to cancel her appointment at the bank, but her afternoon photography session with a tyrannical two-year-old had gone badly, and Elliott Stenberg had been in other meetings when she finally finished. Usually she dealt only with Albert Warren and again wondered why one of the senior vice-presidents had requested a conference.

The portable CD player blared with the Moody Blues and "Your Wildest Dreams". Wondering if Scott's thoughts of her during the past nine years had been more than fleeting, she moved away from the bedroom window, switched off the rock music and walked into the living room. Flannaghan padded along beside her, then took off in a streak of burnished red toward the dimly lit kitchen.

Shadows shifted. Breanna drew a sharp intake of breath and pressed a hand against her chest. A man emerged from the gloom, the Irish Setter dancing alongside him, and she relaxed. "Scott! Why didn't you let me know you were here? You scared the life out of me."

He gave her a friendly kiss on the temple and grinned. "You should have asked Flannaghan. He greeted me at the door."

Breanna moved away, disturbed at the way his slightest touch jump-started her heart. This wasn't right, besides not being fair. He seemed totally unaffected, overly platonic. She turned on the light in the kitchen. A small feast was arranged on the table, complete with wine in Lillian's Waterford goblets.

She felt a pang of regret. "This looks very inviting, but I was just leaving. If you're still worried about going back to your house, you can stay here. I shouldn't be gone long."

Scott frowned, as if noticing her teal blue silk jumpsuit for the first time. His eyes smoldered an invitation and longing flared between them.

He shook his head. "You can't go when I brought your favorite."

"My favorite what?"

"Junk food. Smoked ciscoes, Triscuits and cheap wine." He picked up a cracker and held the tidbit against her lips, letting his fingertips lightly brush her mouth. His other hand slid down her arm as he moved closer.

Breanna munched the cracker and tried to swallow past a throat suddenly gone dry. The intensity of Scott's gaze branded her skin. "You should have told me."

"But then it wouldn't have been a surprise." He handed her a goblet, crystal clinked, and he raised his glass. "Here's to your new home. You don't really have to leave, do you?"

Breanna sipped the white Zinfandel and tried to dismiss the jitteriness that made her tighten her grip on the wine glass. "Thanks. Look, you're very sweet and I really appreciate this, but I have to go. I'm meeting someone in ten minutes."

"Who?"

Breanna straightened, her chin tilting defiantly. She didn't like feeling as if she were being interrogated. "Not that it's any of your business, but the insurance adjuster. He came by the studio this morning."

"Are you sure?"

"Sure of what?" Impatience swept over her.

"That he's who he says he is."

Breanna set her glass down so hard wine sloshed onto the snowy tablecloth. "Why do men have to act like they've cornered the market on intelligence? After everything that's happened to me during the past few days how can you think for even a second that I wouldn't check him out?"

He gave her an apologetic smile. "Sorry. It doesn't hurt to ask, does it?"

"Sometimes." Breanna looped her purse strap over one shoulder and took a deep breath. "Will you be here when I get back?"

He tipped the goblet, watching the wine tilt from side to side. "Is that a request?"

"Yes."

"Then I will be." He flashed the grin that could still make her insides flutter. "But don't be surprised if the wine's gone."

N. J. Nicholson was sitting at a corner table in the bar

when Breanna arrived. He stood as the waiter held her chair out and again she wondered how he managed to make an intense perusal seem so innocuous, despite giving her the uncanny feeling he could have guessed even her shoe size.

She ordered a Dr. Pepper and listened politely to genial observations about the weather. He motioned to his green knit sweater the same shade of jade as his eyes.

"Guess you don't ever put away your winter woolies here. How did you survive out on the Lake?"

Breanna started at the abruptness and the unanswered question that had haunted her for days after Scott's description about recovering Marc's life jacket. "I thought you said you'd read the Coast Guard reports."

He stabbed the olive in his drink. "I did, but I'd like a first-hand account."

"Then you'll need to talk to the fisherman who rescued me since I was unconscious at the time."

His scrutiny softened a bit. "I plan to. Look, I know this is pretty unpleasant, but there must be something you remember about last Friday night. Anything you can tell me will only help get the insurance claims settled faster."

Breanna sighed. He was right and certainly had good reason to be asking questions. The yacht had been insured for half a million dollars. The warehouse for a quarter million. Payoff would mean Elliott Stenberg would have his money, and she'd be off the hook for all Marc's business loans.

Life could go on.

She pressed her fingers against her temples and concentrated. "We were celebrating my birthday with a trip to Isle Royale. Marc insisted on piloting the boat. I'm afraid I drank nearly an entire bottle of wine. We talked, I left the bridge to get ready for bed, and fell asleep." She paused. So many blanks, yet the memory of Marc's bedtime visit remained vivid enough to make her cringe. But nothing had happened, really, and it was no one's business but hers. "I awoke, freezing cold, sitting in the life raft. I screamed for Marc."

"Where was the yacht?"

"About a hundred yards away."

"Could you see your husband?"

Breanna shook her head. "Mr. Nicholson, I could barely make out the boat. I'm very nearsighted. One moment it drifted quietly, the next it was entirely in flames. Then I lost consciousness."

He tapped his fingers on the table. "And you don't remember getting into the raft."

"No."

"How long have you been on sleeping pills?"

"Who said I was?" Breanna curled the edges of the paper napkin beneath her glass, and waited with the calmness of the innocent despite a look from N. J. Nicholson that would have made a saint squirm.

"We have your medical records on file. I rechecked because the hospital blood tests showed a high concentration of sleep inducers after the Coast Guard brought you in. How many did you take Friday night?"

"None." Breanna edged back in her chair. Now she remembered. The bottle falling into the sink, capsules spilling everywhere, the sense of some missing. "I didn't take any. I told you, I drank too much wine. Why does it matter?"

He leaned forward. "Because, Mrs. Lanier, there's just an awful lot you can't remember. I want to know why. I want to know everything that happened that night. Because unless we recover more of the boat, or your husband's body, we can't ignore the likelihood of suicide. Or murder."

MURDER! Breanna knew her lips formed the word, but it refused to dislodge from her throat.

N. J. Nicholson's green eyes harpooned her with another narrowed gaze before he continued. "Which brings me to some other questions. What do you know about your husband's business? What was taken from your apartment? And why were you and Scott Edwards at the warehouse minutes before it was torched?"

Chapter 9

Several minutes passed before Breanna found enough composure to answer. She tapped her red polished fingernails on the table and returned Nicholson's stare. "You ask pretty strange questions for an insurance adjuster. But I suppose that's because you don't really work for Providential Security, do you, Mr. Nicholson? I know what you are—a private investigator." She dug his business card from her pocket and flipped it across the table. "I could accuse you of misrepresenting yourself."

His green eyes held a flicker of surprise and admiration, and he laughed. "Almost, but not quite. My company does a lot of consulting work for Providential."

"I know. Finding out about you was easy. Unraveling my husband's life is something entirely different." Breanna leaned forward, determined to lay her cards on the table in the hope of erasing the accusatory look his eyes held.

"Marc was very secretive about business matters, but many husbands are. Unfortunately, the intense privacy extended to his entire life. I let it go, assuming that he didn't want me to draw comparisons between my family and his. Monday night I went to the warehouse in the hopes of finding an address book, letters, anything that would help me locate his relatives. It was the first time I ever ventured past the reception area. I knew nothing about his furrier business."

Nicholson snorted. "That's because it was pure fiction. Your husband was a fence, Mrs. Lanier. Furs and jewelry his specialty. Then he began smuggling contraband. Canada's a pretty hot market for sending and receiving stolen merchandise right now, especially bootlegged cigarettes. That may have been his fatal mistake."

His words riveted Breanna to her chair, and she couldn't

look away. "Who would want to kill him?"

"I'd guess it's a pretty extensive list. An irate 'client', the local shipping competition. You."

His words slammed like a physical blow into her calm facade. Her knuckles turned white as she gripped her glass. "You can't be serious."

"Why not? You obviously had the opportunity. Three quarters of a million dollars is one hell of a lot of motive."

Breanna took a deep breath and tried to rally her thoughts. From widow to accused. The idea shocked her so badly she couldn't even find the anger to hurl back a retort for his degrading allegations. "That's ridiculous," she murmured.

"Is it?"

She bit her lip to stop the trembling and although his eyes remained hard as jade, his expression softened.

"I have to recognize the possibility, Mrs. Lanier," he said quietly. "But, after meeting you it's tough to imagine you as a killer. Or a fire bug. And after reviewing the police and the Coast Guard reports, I'd say whoever set the charges on the yacht and torched the warehouse knew exactly what they were doing."

"What do you want me to do?"

"Think. Try to remember everything that happened Friday night. During the week before. See if you can recall phone conversations your husband had. Anything." He scribbled a phone number on the back of the business card on the table and handed it back to her. "I'm staying at the Edgewater. Call me if you think of anything, no matter how insignificant it seems."

Breanna pushed her chair back, the need to get away overwhelming. "I will."

"Oh yeah, one more thing. What was taken from your apartment?"

Breanna felt a traitorous heat creep into her face. She bent to retrieve her purse from the floor and straightened, brushing her hair away from her cheek. "Nothing."

He nodded slowly. "So you've said. But let me know if anything comes up missing."

Breanna nibbled on her lower lip, contemplated her conversation with N. J. Nicholson and battled a sense of hopelessness as she drove home. He didn't trust her. She could feel it despite his efforts to set her at ease.

There had to be a way to dispel the doubts. She needed to look over those papers, needed to find out how Gregory Lanier could be contacted. She wondered how Scott had spent the evening, if he had stayed, and breathed a sigh of thanks at the sight of his jeep parked in the garage. Why it mattered so much, why his presence gave her a sense of security, she dismissed with only a moment's thought as she pulled the Mercedes alongside the red four-wheel-drive vehicle.

Yard lights glowed invitingly against the darkened house. Flannaghan pranced up to meet her at the door, nuzzled her hand, then raced back upstairs. His footsteps echoed like a galloping buffalo. Breanna followed to the second floor dormer room Lillian had used as her study. Scott sat behind the desk, studying papers, blond hair partially obscuring the scowl creased in his brow.

She watched him for a few moments before she spoke. "What are you doing up here?"

He looked up and gestured at the burgundy notebook and the insurance policies spread out on the desk. "Checking out Monday's spoils."

Breanna plunked down on the window seat and kicked her Italian sandals off. She tucked her legs up and stared out at the lake, too tired to resent his prying. In the distance the Aerial Bridge marked the harbor entrance in silvery lights. "Find anything interesting?"

"You might say so. What's the matter?" His voice concerned, Scott took a seat next to her and touched her hand.

She turned and looked searchingly into his brown eyes. "Did you ever consider the possibility that I might have killed Marc?"

"Hell, no." The desperate look on her face made him choke back a laugh at the ludicrous idea. He gently took her hand. "Lady, I was there, and I know you."

She shook her head. "Knew. People change."

"Give me a break. Where'd that question come from, any-way? Mr. Good Neighbor give you a tough time?"

"You might say that." She wiped an errant tear with the back of her hand. "He's a private investigator for the insurance company."

"Great. Just what you wanted, some nosy old goat asking stupid questions. When did you file a claim?"

Breanna studied his face and stifled the impulse to trace the light salting of evening beard with her fingertip. "I didn't, my banker did. Nicoholson's okay. He had a lot of questions, that's all. Simply routine."

Scott raised an eyebrow. "Accusing you of bumping off your husband is routine?"

Breanna lifted her shoulders slightly. "Just covering all possibilities, I guess. Tell me what you found."

"Some kind of log of shipping transactions, but it's hard to decipher." Scott paused and his gaze searched her face. "Why did you and Marc have so much life insurance?"

She rested her chin on her knees. "A hundred thousand isn't that much."

"Yeah, just pocket change. But you're way off. A cool million. On each of you."

"Oh, no. That's not right. He told me—"Breanna jumped up and grabbed the papers from the desk. Examining them confirmed Scott's words. The photocopied application at the back of her policy bore her signature. The terms were what Marc had told her. Except the amount had one more zero. Ditto for Marc's policy. Just what she needed. More motives.

Motives. Sleeping pills. Too much wine. The lustful glint in Marc's eyes. Be a good girl and cooperate. *One last time.*

One last time, one last time.

Breanna pressed her hands over her ears but couldn't drown out Marc's final words. He'd wanted her dead. He'd planned it. The papers fluttered to the floor as the realization shook the very foundation of all that she'd wanted to believe.

She'd wanted to believe that despite everything else, he'd given up his life saving hers. Fire was always a possibility on a large boat and so far the Coast Guard reports listed the explosion as accidental. A careless match, faulty wiring, improperly stored fuel supplies.

Ugly memories crowded in. The satin teddy. Her resistance, his insistence. The bite of the necklace chain breaking. Cold. The leaky raft. He'd *wanted* her dead! Fool!

She felt Scott's hand on her shoulder, felt his presence, but all she could see was Marc. All she heard were Marc's words. *Time to return from Iceland, babe. Be a good girl. One last time.* Iciness pressed closer. Her chest constricted. She screamed, struggled to breathe and pounded her fists against Scott's chest.

"Let go of me!"

He shook her. "Geesh, Breanna, snap out of it."

Gradually the room returned and memories retreated to the dark part of her mind. She wrapped her arms around his waist and buried her face against Scott's shirt. "Oh, God, why did he hate me so? He tried to kill me, didn't he," she whispered.

He stroked her hair, wishing he could lie, knowing it wouldn't help. "Yes." More than once, he wanted to say, but held back.

"The river, too?" The anguish in her voice dug a knife into his gut and again he wished for a lie, but couldn't go through with one.

"I think so. But it's over and you're going to be okay."

She shook her head. "I feel..."

"What?"

"Stupid. Deaf, and blind. Like a complete idiot."

"Stop beating yourself up. Sometimes people can only see what they need to see. It doesn't matter. He's history."

"How can you be sure?"

He leaned back and studied her face. "Breanna, you know nobody, nobody could survive in that forty-degree water. I found his life jacket, remember?

"My guess is that he planned to leave you stranded, knowing you'd die from exposure within an hour. No one would have found you on that huge lake till long after it was too late. He probably planned to abandon the yacht and the explosion took him by surprise, but it doesn't matter. He's dead."

Breanna tightened her grasp, desperate for reassurance, but engulfed with fear so powerful, a bitter taste rose in her throat. "What if he's not?"

Chapter 10

He needed to explain about Derek.

Several hours and glasses of wine later, Scott tossed another log on the fire, then sat on the couch and stretched his legs out. Although weary, his mind wouldn't rest and his body argued about the sense in spending another night on Breanna's slippery damask couch while she slept peacefully in the bedroom.

Sense! If he had half an ounce of sense, he'd hit the road. Give her time to sort out the past week, hell, the past year. If he had any sense, he'd never have let her go the first time.

Damn their age and William Alden. He should have found a way to stop her marriage to Lanier. He should have told her about Derek right from the start. Now how could he do it without implicating himself? He should have...

Flannaghan's footsteps pattered across the hardwood hall floor, and he landed with a thump on the cushion next to Scott. Breanna, clad in a cherry red sleep shirt, plunked down on his other side. She tucked her legs under, bumping her shoulder against his upper arm and gave him a distracted smile.

Scott stifled the urge to put his arm around her and cuddle her into his side. "You okay?"

"Couldn't sleep." She stared toward the fire, her forehead tensed with a tiny frown. Absently, he brushed a dark strand of hair from her cheek, wishing he could as easily dismiss the demons that pursued her in slumber.

A presumably dead demon, he corrected himself. Although gone, Lanier still had a strangle hold on her life. "Want some more wine?"

Breanna shook her head. "Thanks, but no."

"A double shot of Drambuie, then. Guaranteed to either make you sleep, or keep you from caring when you don't."

"Murray claims Irish Whisky does that, but no. There's really only one drink that goes with a fire—hot cocoa. With marshmallows."

"If you'll settle for instant, I'll go get some. Eastside Market's probably still open."

Breanna hopped up and walked to the kitchen. "That's okay. Maybe I'm a limited cook, but I still remember sophomore family living class."

Scott followed and gave her a wry grin. "So do I. Complete with scorched milk and burnt cinnamon toast."

She wrinkled her nose and took milk from the refrigerator. "You were supposed to watch the broiler."

"You distracted me." Which still didn't take much, he thought, watching Breanna glide around the kitchen, scouting out sugar, cocoa and cups, her shirt shifting up past mid thigh as she reached for a box high on the pantry shelf.

When she bent over to remove a pan from the drawer beneath the stove, Scott left the room before reality outdid memory and imagination. He absently stirred the glowing wood in the rock fireplace and tossed another piece of driftwood on the embers. Better to concentrate on solving the mystery of Breanna's life than on Breanna herself, who was one minute a flirty sixteen-year-old tease, the next a reserved remote woman.

The fire hissed and popped. Again he saw the yacht burst into flames, remembered the sick feeling that Breanna was on board. Lanier had to be dead, although his plan didn't make sense. The setup on the yacht was as complex as a double-sided jigsaw puzzle.

He reviewed the information over and over and again decided the explosion must have caught Lanier by surprise. An explosion that someone else rigged, or why send Breanna out on the raft to die of exposure.

Someone else—but who?

His attention stubbornly refocused on Breanna as she entered the living room, set a tray with two mugs on the coffee table and plopped on the couch. He sat down next to her, picked up a cup and inhaled the chocolaty steam.

"Too bad Miss Peterson can't see you now. Maybe she'd take back that F."

Breanna swatted his arm with a flowered pillow, sloshing drops of hot cocoa onto her shirt and his arm. "That was your fault, and you didn't do any better."

Scott set the mug down and wiped a speck of chocolate from his hand and dabbed at the hem of her shirt. Impulsively, he leaned over and placed a kiss on her warm mouth. "So it was, and I'm still not sorry."

Breanna looked momentarily surprised. He started to make another light remark when her arms slid around his neck and her lips sought his, stopping words, terminating rational thoughts. She shifted onto her knees so that she was slightly above him, kissing him until he could barely breathe.

He tasted like sweet chocolate. Breanna lingered in a kiss that was at once brand new and yet hauntingly familiar. Her hand cradled his cheek, imploring him to rediscover a long remembered path. One kiss melted into another. Then another. Scott's arm encircled her waist. His hand smoothed over the satin curve of her bottom, slipped beneath lacy panties to bare skin with a touch so light, she couldn't find a reason to protest.

The fire popped, the crackle resounding like gunshot. Flannaghan barked. Breanna wriggled free and leapt up, as startled by the smoldering ember on the braided rug in front of the fireplace as she was shaken by her runaway feelings. Scott jumped up and stomped on the rug. Flannaghan raced to the French doors on the far side of the room, barking furiously.

Her thoughts tangled in fear, hesitation, and desire, Breanna watched the elongated shadows thrown against the walls of the dimly lit room. One shadow too many.

She whirled and ran to the doors, but Scott was right beside her. He grabbed her arm and pulled her behind him. Frozen with terror, she waited, listening to tree branches rub together, waves crashing on the rocks. Flannaghan's barks dwindled to growls, then silence.

Scott released her and peered out the windows overlooking the patio, then motioned to the telephone on the secretary in the opposite corner. "Call the police. Either we have a garden variety peeper or someone has figured out where you are."

"And just what are you going to do?"

Scott scanned the room and seized the fireplace poker. "Play caveman. I don't suppose you have a gun around here?"

"Racks of them. All locked up. Grandmother was a collector but never let anyone know where she kept the cabinet keys."

"That's no good. Lock the door behind me." He opened the patio doors. Flannaghan wriggled through the narrow opening and raced off, a throaty growl increasing to sporadic woofing. Scott followed.

Prickles of fear stabbing her, Breanna called 911, pacing within the limits of the telephone cord while the operator asked questions. She glanced at the mantle clock. Finally, she hung up, moved to the window and searched the darkness.

Scott and Flannaghan had disappeared beyond the yard lights' golden pool. Each shifting shadow sent a shiver down her spine. She glanced at her bare legs, then ran to the bedroom and pulled on jeans and a sweatshirt.

Still no sign of Scott when she returned to the glass doors. Breanna twisted the pleated shade cord around her hand. The string bit into her skin. Where were they?

Long moments later Scott and Flannaghan returned, and she breathed a sigh of relief.

He shook his head at her unspoken question. "Guess the dog scared him off. Flannaghan headed straight for that patch of woods between you and the next house but stopped at the fence. Maybe the police will find footprints."

He reached for her but Breanna shook her head and sat down in a wingback chair, leaving Scott to sit alone on the couch. She couldn't sit by him, didn't dare look at him or she would rush into the safe haven, from fear and overwhelming loneliness, he could give her. Heeding the wary voices inside her mind, she picked up her hot chocolate and took a slow sip. "I'm sorry."

"What does that mean?" He watched her for a moment, then grabbed his own cup. "Sorry for starting, sorry for stopping, sorry for the interruption, sorry for what?"

She waved her hand. "Just sorry. I told you Monday I wish you hadn't become involved in this mess."

He watched her over the rim of the mug and took a long drink. "My choice."

She glanced briefly at him, then her gaze shifted away. "I really meant I'm sorry, for you know, forgetting the friends part. We're friends. Nothing more. I didn't mean to start anything."

Neither had he, but it was too late now. Memories rekindled, hot and exhilarating, making the air in the cozy room hard to breathe. "No problem." He searched for a different topic and found it in other unanswered questions. "Who is Gregory Lanier?"

"Good question. Marc never mentioned him."

"Didn't you know he was named on the insurance policies?"

She shook her head. "I listed my Uncle Murray. At least I thought I did."

"Add insurance fraud to the ever increasing crime list. What are you going to do?"

She sat back in the chair. "I don't know for sure. I suppose I'll have to get in touch with him. Invite him to the memorial service."

Scott slammed the mug down on the acrylic tray. "Wait a minute. Two hours ago, you were worried that Marc's still alive. Now you're trying to tell me you want to have a service for him? You're not going to pretend to grieve for that bastard."

"I have to put him to rest. A service is the only way. Besides, it wouldn't look right not to."

"Wouldn't look right? Breanna, no matter what the official reports say, he tried to kill you!"

She stared down at her lap and looked up angrily. "I know that, you know that, I'll be damned if I want everyone in this town to know it! Poor, stupid little rich girl, daddy cuts her off, husband cuts her throat."

Scott shook his head, trying to clear it. "All right, enough. But you can't do it until he's legally declared dead. Which under the circumstances could take quite awhile." He became silent, thinking. "How long do you think that investigator creep will hang around? Maybe he can speed up the process."

"Maybe he can. He didn't say how long he'd be here."

"Breanna," Scott hesitated, "do you remember anything else about Friday night? Besides what you've already told me? How'd you end up in the raft? When was the last time you checked the safety equipment on the yacht?"

Breanna rubbed her forehead. "Marc said he checked it before we left." She closed her eyes. Something pulled at the edges of her mind like a fish nibbling on a line. "I thought I heard voices. Marc's, another man. Two sided, like on the radio, but it might have been a dream."

Scott leaned forward, resting his elbows on his thighs. "What was the last thing he said to you?"

Breanna's eyes flew open, and her expression became a mixture of fear, panic and dread. "I don't remember!"

Flannaghan barked. The doorbell rang. Breanna jumped up and ran to the door, obviously desperate to hide the lie. Making Scott equally determined to discover what was so horrible she couldn't tell him. Somehow, he'd have to find a way to get her to confide in him. Her answers might hold the only solution to the puzzle Marc had left behind.

Several hours later, Breanna lay on her back in bed and decided she hated the color blue. Particularly the faded navy of policemen.

Two officers had made an exhaustive search of the woods bordering her property and spent another hour on interminable inquiries. Queries about her apartment break in, the warehouse fire. Questions, questions, questions.

All for nothing.

The officers regarded Scott's presence with cool curiosity. Thank God, she'd had the presence of mind to put clothes on before the police arrived.

She rolled onto her side and tried to shut out other memories. Scott's hand sliding beneath her shirt. His mouth warm on hers. Flickers of excitement exploding into mind-numbing desire.

Loneliness. That's all it was. The thought lasted only a moment.

Liar.

She'd never lost the insatiable curiosity she'd had about being one with Scott. Never stopped caring. Neither had he, apparently. Nine years should be long enough to eradicate someone from your system, or so she'd believed. If only she could be sure enough of his feelings to trust her own, but she doubted it would ever happen.

The door creaked open. Breanna squeezed her eyes shut and breathed quietly despite the wild racing of her heart. He whispered her name, a velvety caress from the shadows. She heard the soft thump Flannaghan made settling down on the bedside rug. Then the door clicked shut. Scott's footsteps faded down the hall.

Breanna awoke to daylight and a quiet house. Sunshine poured through the living room windows and spilled into the empty kitchen. A note in Scott's clipped handwriting leaned against the thermal coffee carafe.

Breena, Wish fisherman and photographers kept more compatible hours, but fish need catching earlier than pictures need snapping. Want me to barbecue supper tonight? I'll be gone most of the day, but will try to 'catch' you at the studio later. Scott.

Breanna smiled and poured a cup of coffee. He seemed willing to continue with the idea of friendship, and she valued it. Most of the friends she'd had in high school had moved away by the time she'd returned from photography school in Dallas, and work tended to isolate her, except for clients. She needed Scott's friendship even if it meant stifling deeper feelings.

Before she left for the studio she tried again to contact Elliott Stenberg at North Shore National Bank.

More meetings. Didn't the man ever just sit in his office?

She left a message and slammed the phone down.

The Mercedes purred to life. Breanna backed out of the garage onto London Road, accelerated and adjusted the rear-view mirrors. From out of nowhere a plain white sedan appeared behind her. She eased off the gas pedal to thirty miles an hour. Another quota-happy policeman setting a trap along the North Shore Highway. The way her life had been going lately, it would be just her luck to get zapped by an un-marked squad car.

Sun sparkled off Lake Superior and warmed her wind-tossed hair as she headed toward downtown Duluth. Perfect convertible weather but remembering that the car had been her present from her parents on her eighteenth birthday brought sadness.

Another reason not to like her birthday. Between last year's tense family party and Friday's early 'celebration' on the yacht, she never wanted to think of her birthday again. Ever. Fortunately, being on the outs with Murray made it unlikely anyone would remember what today was.

At the studio, she greeted Gayle. In her own office, she sat at the jumbled desk and sorted through the morning mail and messages. Two from Mr. Nicholson. Not a word from Murray. A chatty letter from Mariette Marcel, owner of Mariette's Moments, a gallery in Montreal, who'd scheduled a showing of Breanna's landscape photographs. She glanced at the date and checked her calendar. Next week!

She couldn't possibly be ready, especially since a promised shot of Split Rock Lighthouse hadn't been satisfactorily com-pleted yet. Breanna tapped her fingers on the desk and reread the letter. Mariette explained that another artist's cancellation meant Breanna's showing had been bumped ahead a month. She'd included two plane tickets as compensation for the change in schedule. One for Breanna. One for Marc Lanier, although he'd never actually agreed to accompany her.

She could delay the trip by a week or two, but it might be weeks, perhaps months before the investigations were con-cluded and the insurance claims settled. In the meantime, she couldn't afford to ignore her work or cancel a trip that could add new dimensions to her career.

Montreal. Where the mysterious Gregory Lanier lived. She stared at the papers in her hand, felt a mist of perspiration on her forehead and knew she had to go. Had to find some answers to the tangled mess Marc left behind. The gallery showing provided a perfect opportunity to get away. She'd spend a few extra days in Montreal doing a little detective work on her own. Maybe uncover enough of Marc's secrets to at least assure herself that he wasn't going to come back.

Satisfied with her decision, she called Mariette and confirmed the showing. She tossed the itinerary aside and checked her appointment book. Gayle had scheduled a full day. Time to get back to business.

"So where did you meet this Mr. Right?" Later that morning, Breanna stacked props against the wall, straightened up the studio and glanced over her shoulder at her assistant.

Gayle blushed. "I didn't say it was serious. Yet."

Breanna laughed. "You just did."

"We met over in Superior at the Cove. He's in shipping. I wish you'd stick around. He's picking me up for lunch."

"Can't. I'm going to grab a Mainburger, then tackle that mountain of paperwork on my desk before our one o'clock shows up. I hate to interfere with new love, but I'll need you to be back by then, okay?"

Gayle nodded.

Breanna picked up her purse and opened the entrance door onto First Street. Nicholson's brown Chevy idled at the corner, waiting for the light to turn green. Breanna drew back and took another cautious look. Just what she needed in the middle of a hectic day, another interrogation.

She stepped back inside and decided to use the alley exit. After asking Gayle to plead ignorance to the detective about her whereabouts, Breanna hurried down the narrow alley to Third Avenue West.

The Main boasted the best burgers in downtown Duluth. Decorated in cheap Mediterranean style, the restaurant and

bar crowded red and black vinyl booths and tables into a small
dining room. Still smiling about her escape, Breanna found a
seat at the bar and ordered a hamburger and ginger ale. She
swirled the ice with a swizzle stick and took a sip.

"Isn't it a little early in the day for that?"

Nicholson's voice made her choke on an ice cube. Breanna
looked up at his serious expression reflected in the mirror
behind the bar. "Not really. After all, it must be five o'clock
somewhere."

He smiled and straddled a stool. "Mind if I join you, Mrs.
Lanier?" He motioned to the bartender before she could
answer.

"Actually I do mind. I told you I'd call you if I remembered
anything else."

Nicholson ordered a draft beer. "That's not why I'm here."

"Then why?"

He shrugged. "Just wanted to talk. I was downtown anyway, drove by your office and saw you sneaking down the alley.
Thought I'd buy you lunch, since you wouldn't stick around for
dinner last night."

Breanna looked him over warily. She knew better. This was
not an impulsive man. Everything about him seemed too
deliberate, right down to the casual clothes he wore today
instead of yesterday's nondescript business suit. A tan sweater
the same honey color as his hair. Dockers khaki jeans. Dark
brown loafers. His taste in clothes was certainly better than his
taste in cars. A nice looking man, she decided. Minus the
moustache, of course. He looked about the same age as Marc,
too.

"Please call me Breanna. And I feel silly calling anyone
under the age of forty by their last name. Any chance you'll tell
me what your first name is?"

He smiled and green eyes twinkled. "None whatsoever. I
don't intend to have *that* much to drink. But you can call me
Nick."

"All right, Nick. How long are you planning to be in town?"

The waiter delivered two gigantic hamburgers. Breanna cut
hers in half and took a bite.

His expression sharpened. "As long as it takes. Why? Anxious to get your money?"

Breanna returned his analytical stare. For all of two seconds, she could have sworn he was trying to be friendly. But he had a better knack for swamping her with guilt. "Only to satisfy the sharks."

"Sharks?"

Breanna swallowed a laugh at his reaction, intent and assessing, as if his radar screen had suddenly filled with blips. "My bankers. Maybe you can't take it with you, but my husband made sure he left nothing behind, either. Nothing but a mountain of debt."

"What about your parents' money? North Woods Foods was a multi-million-dollar company."

"My father put everything in charitable trusts. I got the yacht. I also have a small inheritance from my grandmother, but the way things are going, I'll be lucky if I have grocery money next week."

"Interesting," he murmured. "All that money, and you on food stamps."

Breanna flushed at the implication. This guy could find motives in Flannaghan. She wiped her fingers on a napkin and swiveled her stool. "I can see the wheels in your mind churning like over-greased gears, but I haven't spent years of training and poured every cent I have into my business because I want to live off someone else's money. That includes your company's. So pay off the bankers and keep the rest. And I'll tell you something else, since you practically accused me last night. I did not kill my husband. I didn't hire someone to do it, either."

Without waiting for a response, she slid off the stool. "I'm going back to my studio. I have to make a living."

Breanna glanced angrily over her shoulder as she left the bar. Nick reached for his wallet and laid several bills on the counter. She strode up the avenue toward First Street, turned the corner and saw him break into a run behind her. Great. Now he was following. He caught up in front of the studio.

Breanna took a deep breath and turned to face him.

"What's really on your agenda?"

His expression was completely unreadable. Scott would tell her she should take lessons.

"I told you, lunch." The slight change in his tone of voice put her on guard.

"And then?" She glanced over her shoulder as a maroon and white patrol car stopped at the curb and a deputy sheriff climbed out.

"Mrs. Lanier? I've been trying to reach you. I need you to come over to headquarters and answer a few questions. The Coast Guard recovered a body earlier this morning. Washed ashore south of Knife River. Fits the description of your husband, but we want you to make a positive ID."

Chapter 11

Marc's body found? Breanna glanced at Captain Belcastro's identification and tried to listen to his explanations beyond the words criminal investigator, St. Louis County Sheriff's Department.

Oh my God, what next. She drew a shaky breath and met Nick's eyes. His gaze flickered over her, probably gauging her reaction. He must have known about this, the fuss about buying her lunch a ploy to hang around until the investigator showed up.

"Are you sure it's my husband?"

"No ma'am. We're not. That's why I need to ask you a few questions, look over some photos."

She motioned at Nick. "Will he be in on this, too?"

Belcastro shook his head. "No, we'll need to speak with you alone."

Breanna wavered between relief and regret. The thought of Nick being present bothered her, but even worse was the thought of being alone at the station, then having to answer the questions all over again. Nick at least had already become a familiar face, though not a particularly friendly one. For an instant, she wished Murray was there to lean on.

Or Scott.

She straightened. "I have to check in at my office first."

Belcastro nodded. "Go ahead."

Nick and the captain followed her into the studio's reception area. Breanna glanced at her watch. Twelve thirty. Gayle wouldn't return from lunch in time to cancel the one o'clock appointment. She'd have to do it herself.

Inside her private office, she picked up the phone and rescheduled the sitting, then dialed Murray's number. No answer at home. He wasn't at the bar either. She started to leave a message, but worried about what his reaction would be to this latest event. He'd probably storm down to the sheriff's office and be more trouble than help. She nibbled on her fingernail.

Nick lounged in the doorway. "Calling your lawyer?"

Breanna narrowed her eyes to hide the apprehension his words gave her. "Think I need to?"

He shrugged. "Isn't that what rich people always do?"

"I thought I explained that at lunch. I'm not rich." She wouldn't even hit middle class either, if she had to continually cancel appointments. Or ended up in jail while the sheriff conducted an investigation. She pushed paranoid thoughts away and focused on business concerns.

The entire afternoon needed to be rescheduled, but she stalled. She couldn't afford to do that, yet felt trapped and scribbled a noncommittal note for Gayle. "I'm just taking care of business. I doubt I'll be in any kind of shape to deal with reluctant toddlers after this."

"As long as you're honest, you have nothing to worry about, do you? I'll be in touch." Nick left, his last remark hanging in the air like an imminent storm.

Breanna shivered and went out to meet the captain.

St. Louis County Sheriff's Headquarters was on Second Street, behind the other buildings in the Civic Center Plaza. Belcastro and a deputy escorted her into a small, windowless room in the gray, granite structure. Apprehension mingled with claustrophobia until Breanna felt as if she were suffocating.

Sitting on a straight back wooden chair at a scuffed oak table, she glanced nervously from Belcastro to the deputy. This was not a simple questioning. Nick's bizarre accusations glinted in Captain Belcastro's eyes despite his controlled congeniality.

She clasped her hands together in her lap. "Do I need to call a lawyer?"

"I don't know, ma'am. If you feel like you need to have one present, of course, you do have that right. However, we just have a few questions and can handle it more quickly this way."

He crossed his arms, a picture of patience while Breanna considered her choices.

Refusing to answer his questions would only increase his suspicions. So would insisting on calling her attorney. She felt damned either way, but finally decided compliance would be the safest response. After all, she had nothing to hide. "That's okay, Captain. I'll be glad to help."

Belcastro nodded. "Good." He began with a thousand questions that reminded Breanna of how little she had really known about her husband. Had he ever broken any bones? Had major dental work done? Distinguishing characteristics. Did he drink heavily, smoke? Had he been drinking the night of the accident?

Breanna buried her face in her hands and tried to remember. Marc had been insistently sober that night, but she knew now it was because he'd drugged the wine. "He drank a cola." That in itself had been odd. Marc claimed anything that could remove rust from metal had to be toxic.

"Could someone else have been on the yacht?"

Belcastro's watchful intensity was as bad as being wired to a lie detector. She focused on hazy memories and recalled hearing voices just before she had fallen into troubled asleep.

Why the hell is she here?

The two way radio, probably. Marc had mentioned he needed to check on a shipment. A dozen strange things half remembered about Friday night tangled together in her mind. A vivid recollection of Marc's midnight abuse blotted everything else out.

Breanna struggled to maintain her composure. She didn't have to tell anyone about that. It couldn't possibly have any bearing on the investigation. What had happened, or not happened, between her and Marc was no one else's business.

"Impossible. We didn't make any stops after we left Duluth."

"Okay. How did he receive the head injury?"

She gave him a blank look. "What do you mean?"

"He suffered a severe blow to the back of the head. Here, maybe this will jog your memory." Belcastro thrust the photographs in front of her. Frozen, Breanna couldn't touch them, couldn't bear to look, until Belcastro impatiently flipped through them, one by one. Finally, she stared at the mutilated body in the digital photos and tried to disassociate her mind from her senses. Tried to stifle the nausea welling in her throat.

Belcastro dropped the pictures to the table. Morbidly curious, she couldn't stop herself from sifting through the grotesque images one more time. Charred skin and pale flesh glared against a white background. She shuddered. How unlike a human being it looked. She couldn't relate the image with Marc.

"Looks worse than you thought, doesn't he? Face horribly burned, no hands. Tough to reconcile memories of a loving husband with a nasty looking corpse, isn't it?"

Breanna shuddered and closed her eyes. "Yes," she whispered.

"Is that your husband, Mrs. Lanier?"

"I don't know."

"What kind of relationship did you have?"

Her eyes flew open. "What?"

"I said, did you have a good relationship. After all, you were married less than a year. Still newlyweds by most people's definition. Did you argue?"

Breanna stared at the scratches on the oak table. "Yes, of course. But nothing serious."

"How about Friday night? Did you fight? Maybe he provoked you and you pushed him. He hit his head, got knocked out."

What was he getting at? She forced herself to look up and speak calmly. "No. I told you, I drank too much wine and went to bed early. He was fine the last time I saw him." No matter how hard she tried, she couldn't banish the memory of Marc's last words, the hateful lust in his eyes. She dropped her gaze back to the table. "I've told you everything I remember."

Belcastro planted his hands on the table compelling Breanna to raise her eyes level with his.

"Really? No one would blame you. It must have been hell,

knowing you lost millions because of him. Most people would resent that, especially when times got tough."

"What are you accusing me of, Captain?"

His eyes bored into her. "Nothing. Yet you seem to have a lot of guilt about an evening you claim you can't remember."

She gasped. "He died, and I survived. Wouldn't you feel terrible to have cost someone else their life?"

He shrugged. "Mrs. Lanier, you are either unbelievably naive, or you think I am. What kind of gun did you carry on board?"

"Gun?" As far as Breanna knew, Marc didn't own a gun. Of course, that didn't mean anything, given all the other things about his life of which she was ignorant.

Belcastro looked impatient. "The life raft that fisherman found you in. Care to explain how it got punctured?"

She drew in a breath, laced her fingers together and put her hands back in her lap. "I have no idea what you're talking about."

"Then I'll remind you. Someone put a bullet through it. Maybe someone who'd been unconscious and awakened at a most inconvenient time. Someone who didn't want you to get away. Now look at those pictures again, Mrs. Lanier and tell me. Is that your husband?" He shoved the pictures at her again.

"I don't know!" She stood up so fast the wooden chair crashed to the floor. "I've told you what I remember. You've checked everything else, haven't you seen the hospital reports? I was drugged!"

Belcastro and the deputy exchanged glances. "Care to explain the significance of that?"

Breanna tried to find the words. She wet her lips, and looked at Belcastro. As impassive as stone, he waited. She couldn't tell him about Marc. Couldn't voice the realizations that her husband had been trying to kill her. Had nearly raped her. It sounded like a far-fetched defense, even in her own mind. Husbands didn't rape their wives.

She looked away. "I'm not sure. My doctor gave me a prescription for sleeping pills several months ago. I don't remember taking any, but Dr. Allen told me it showed up in my blood tests."

Belcastro casually paced in the tiny room. Breanna shifted her weight from foot to foot. God, would this never end?

"Not unusual for someone to overdose after drinking. And you've told us repeatedly you had too much wine." He gave a sarcastic emphasis to the last words. "That's all for now, Mrs. Lanier. We've already contacted the Canadian authorities. Hopefully we'll have some dental records to match up after the autopsy is completed."

An autopsy. Marc carved up like last year's Thanksgiving turkey. She had to get away from here before she lost lunch.

"I haven't finished going through his personal papers. If I find anything, I'll let you know. Can I please leave?"

Belcastro's hesitation made her heart stop. He nodded. "Hanson will drive you back to work, or home, if you'd prefer."

The hell he would. Breanna grabbed her purse and strode toward the door. "No thanks, I'd rather walk."

She made it out to the hallway and the water cooler. Icy water splashed onto her face and she drank, the liquid fresh and cleansing. She whirled around, realizing Belcastro had followed and watched her like a cat over a mouse.

"Mrs. Lanier, I hope you'll keep me posted on where you can be reached."

She straightened. "Don't worry, Captain. I want this settled even more than you do."

Three o'clock. Still in a daze after two hours of Belcastro's harassing questions, Breanna walked to North Shore National Bank. She got the safe deposit box key from the Trust Department secretary and headed for the vault. But the windowless room stole her shaky composure. She grabbed the velvet pouch containing the antique earrings and stuffed it into her purse. Fresh air, lots of it, that's what she needed. And wide open spaces.

"Miss Alden! Excuse me, I mean Mrs. Lanier." Breanna turned away from the escalator as Elliott Stenberg's executive secretary hurried toward her. "I'm glad I caught you. Mr. Stenberg's been trying to call you all afternoon. Could you come with me, please?"

Breanna followed into the Senior Vice-President's office. Soft grays and blue-greens gave an expansive, soothing feeling to the plush interior. She sank down into an overstuffed chair and gratefully accepted a cup of coffee. Too bad she couldn't ask for a shot of something stronger.

A few minutes later, Mr. Stenberg wedged himself into a chair opposite her, reached over, patted her hand and offered sympathy about Marc's death. As William Alden's friend and banker for years, he was as familiar to Breanna as if he'd been family, but she wondered what business he had to discuss with her that couldn't be taken care of with a brief telephone call.

"I'm so glad Charlotte was able to catch you. I have some news that will be just what you need at a time like this."

Breanna waited, mystified. What could Stenberg possibly say that could soothe away not only the horrors of the afternoon, but those she'd have to deal with in the days to come? Her life had gone from unhappy to desperation in just a matter of days.

"First, let me say that your mother wasn't initially in favor of William's financial arrangements, nor his insistence on confidentiality. However, he was very determined not only to protect his privacy, but to do the right thing by you and eventually he convinced Fiona."

His words made no sense. "Mr. Stenberg, I don't have the vaguest idea what you're talking about. I thought my parents' estate had been settled already."

"For the most part, yes, but only the assets that had to be probated. Nearly all of your father's holdings, including North Woods Foods, went into what's called a living trust a month before he died. At his death, the trust became irrevocable. "

"I see," she murmured, although she didn't. What had her father been trying to accomplish?

"Several charities are the contingent beneficiaries. The principal isn't distributed, just the interest and dividends provided certain conditions are met. With the sale of the company, the trust approximates $75 million. Thus, the earnings are substantial."

Breanna rubbed her forehead. "But what does all this mean?"

Stenberg smoothed his maroon silk tie over his rounded stomach. "It means that once certain conditions are satisfied, all of the trust income, and the entire principal, reverts to a designated beneficiary. Your father insisted these terms be kept confidential."

"Terms? What terms?" Breanna shifted in her chair, wishing he'd get to the point so she could leave, not sure she wanted to hear about her father's legal machinations.

"A stipulation that if you married Marc Lanier, several charities would receive the income during your life. However, should your marriage end, either by death or divorce, you become the beneficiary and all the income is paid to you. Along with one third of the principal when you reach 25 years of age. The remaining two thirds will be distributed half in five years, on your 30th birthday, with the balance paid in ten years, on your 35th birthday. Had your brother lived, the two of you would have shared equally, but since he did not, you are the sole beneficiary."

Breanna felt as if she had just received a blow to the temple. Dizzy, she briefly closed her eyes, hoping the room would stop spinning. The headache that had been threatening since morning pounded at her brain. "In other words, I get a reward for the death of my marriage."

Stenberg shifted in his chair and looked distinctly uncomfortable. "My dear, I understand this is a shock, but please remember your father's concern was only for your welfare. In any event, your share of the entire trust would have reverted to you on your 40th birthday. William hoped that if he was wrong, time would prove it."

She had no idea how to respond to that.

Stenberg brightened. "I'm sure that after you've had a chance to think about it, you'll find some comfort. I feel particularly pleased to be able to share this with you today."

Breanna's confusion deepened. "Today?"

"Why yes. Today is your birthday, isn't it? I hope this will give you a reason to celebrate, despite what's happened."

Celebrate! The word tasted worse than sour milk. Remembering the celebration aboard the yacht one week ago, Breanna pressed the accelerator on the Mercedes and sped along the Blatnik Bridge back to Duluth. She glanced at the digital clock, startled to find that she'd been driving aimlessly for four hours and still anger at her father made her slam her fist against the steering wheel.

Damn him! She didn't want the money, never had. Why couldn't he have forgiven her before it was too late?

Breanna brushed away a tear, took a deep breath and turned the cell phone back on. She was immediately rewarded by an irritating chirp and pressed the hands free button.

"Where the hell are you?" Scott sounded more worried than angry.

"In my car, obviously. Where the hell are you?"

"The bottom of a well. Please pick up the phone so I can hear you."

She seized the tiny phone and plucked the hands-free device off. "What do you want?"

"You. Here. Pronto. I thought we had plans."

Irritated to distraction, Breanna slammed on the brakes to avoid making a Honda a permanent hood ornament. "So who made you the social chairman?"

"Geesh, woman, who overloaded your fuses? I've just been worried about you, that's all. According to Gayle, you should have been home hours ago. I told you I'd barbecue tonight."

"You don't need to worry. I can take care of myself."

Scott sighed. "Maybe. But considering you've nearly been killed several times during the past week, not to mention threatened and burglarized, I think worrying is an appropriate response to your disappearing. So where are you?"

The line popped and crackled. Breanna switched lanes onto the North Shore Highway section of Interstate 35. "Would you believe halfway to the Canadian border?"

"Nah. You left your makeup bag here."

She felt a surge of irrational anger and tried to stay calm. Surely Marc was the only man who'd stoop to raking through a woman's personal things, but she couldn't stop from blurting an accusation. "Playing amateur detective, Edwards? Think you can go through my stuff, just because I let you stay at my house?"

Scott's voice became as frigid as the lake. "Breanna, I'm going to pretend you're not acting like a twenty-four carat bitch and start the grill. It was a joke. You remember what those are, don't you? If you're not here by the time the hamburgers are done, I'll shove off."

Breanna bit her lip and swiped at the strand of hair blowing across her face. She should apologize. Her trashed life wasn't his fault. But the words lodged in her throat. "I'll be there in about fifteen minutes."

"Fine. Hope you like charburgers." The line beeped and went silent.

Cruising along London Road, Breanna switched on the radio. Instead of providing a diversion, DJ chatter and news increased her aggravation. Frustrated, she leaned over and flipped through the stereo's compact disc catalog.

Nothing.

Marc had apparently pilfered, then alphabetized and categorized all her CDs for the Isle Royale trip. Straightening, she glanced in the rearview mirror. Shivering with apprehension, she held her breath. But the white sedan signaled a turn and pulled into PJ's Quick Mart.

She berated herself for the paranoia attack but didn't stop watching the rearview mirror until the Mercedes was secured in the garage.

Breanna took several calming breaths. If she didn't get her feelings under control, she'd no doubt be in for another interrogation, only from Scott this time. And of course, Nick was likely to show up with his list of questions at any moment.

She pushed open the front door into a dusky interior, wondering why Scott hadn't bothered to at least turn on a lamp for her. Her skin prickled with alarm.

The room exploded with light before she found the wall switch. Shadows became people. Breanna screamed, then covered her face with her hands when she realized who was standing, singing and throwing confetti at her.

Gayle. Murray with Spencer, his assistant at the bar. A tall, blond body builder she assumed was Gayle's new boyfriend. Flannaghan wriggled, jumped and licked Breanna's face.

Scott grinned and pulled her into a bear hug. "Happy Birthday, Breena."

Chapter 12

"I'll get you for this," she whispered against his ear. "Your sense of timing is as nonexistent as your sensitivity."

"You're welcome," he whispered back as she slipped from his arms. She turned to greet Murray, grateful for the chance for a reconciliation, but feeling more like battle lines were being drawn.

Maybe he knew about the money, and that's why he was so paranoid about her friendship with Scott. Fiona had often confided in her younger brother, knowing he could be trusted.

Murray's apprehension showed in the way he rubbed his chin, and hesitated. Finally, he grinned and Breanna's speculations vanished.

"If you'll forgive me for being an overbearing old goat, I'll forgive you for acting like an Alden."

Breanna playfully punched his arm and shrieked when he swept her into his customary birthday hug, lifting her off the floor and swinging her around as if she were five instead of twenty-five.

He released her. "Happy birthday, sweetie. Hope this marks the beginning of happier times for you."

Gayle and Spencer chimed in with agreement. Then Gayle introduced Lucas Brogan. He clasped Breanna's hand in a lingering handshake that inexplicably made her want to yank her hand back. Nerves. She could implode from them.

Forcing a smile, she ushered everyone into the living room, then followed Scott over to the bar. Oak paneled bi-fold doors that usually concealed the serving area between the built in bookcases had been pushed open. Tiered glass shelves displayed leaded glass tumblers, goblets and several bottles of expensive liquor.

Breanna motioned to the set up. "Did you do all this?"

He shook his head and dropped several cubes of ice into a highball glass. "Not all. Murray stocked up. There's even some Irish Mist." He waited, but Breanna was silent, her mind still reeling from the disasters of her day. Her life. Of all the nights to have a house full of people, this had to be the worst.

What kind of crazy impulse had made Scott do this?

He touched the back of her hand, and she jumped. "Are you on drugs or something? Cause if you're not, a little Valium might do wonders for you. Or maybe a drink."

She doubted all the liquor in Murray's bar would be enough to wash away the torment of anger, frustration and fear that was tying her insides in knots. Might as well have one for the sake of her guests, however. "Give me a double shot of Drambuie. On the rocks." Breanna ignored his raised eyebrows, accepted the glass and stalked off to join her friends.

Scott watched her retreat to the other side of the living room. She'd always had a temper, but something else was wrong tonight. Fidgety and overwound, she twisted her pink ice necklace until he became certain the chain would snap.

She repeatedly deflected questions about her afternoon activities with one evasive answer after another. Finally, Murray put his arm around her shoulders and gave her an exasperated squeeze. The necklace clattered to the floor.

Breanna looked momentarily pained, but flashed another plastic smile, shrugged away from her uncle and stuffed the chain into the pocket of her turquoise slacks.

Glancing at the group, Scott noticed Lucas' inattentive expression as Gayle entertained the group with a funny story about the studio. Lucas' gaze followed Breanna as she wandered over to the window and back, but apparently feeling observed, he focused on Gayle as Scott walked up in time to catch her punch line. Lucas' laugh sounded forced, a little too loud, a little too quick. He must feel out of place, and Scott wished Gayle had shown some sense and not dragged a stranger to what was intended to be a family gathering.

Spencer was a different case. Scott knew from his visits to

Murray's bar that Breanna practically regarded Murray's assistant as another uncle. Tonight she seemed oblivious to everything and everyone. Her eyes bright sapphires against pale skin, she pointedly ignored Scott, downed the Drambuie and drifted back to the bar.

Spencer requested a refresher, but Breanna didn't seem to hear as she refilled her own glass and disappeared down the hall. Scott supplied another round and turned to find she was still gone. After steering everyone else to the kitchen for appetizers, Scott decided to try a more direct approach to find out what was wrong.

She wasn't downstairs. Scott rechecked the bedroom, put Gayle and Murray in charge of dinner and headed up the stairs. He found her on the window seat in the darkened study, resting her chin on drawn up knees.

"Are you okay?"

She started, one slender hand clutching her throat, then released her breath and turned back to the window. Heavy earrings gleamed dull gold in the dusky light and flashed like a shooting star as she shifted on the cushion. "Don't you have a party to tend?"

"Sure, but I need a guest of honor."

"Honor! My family has a distorted concept of the word." Breanna swirled her glass and downed half the contents.

"What do you mean?"

"You knew my father. You, of all people, should remember just what an honorable man he was. Please just go back to the party." She turned her back.

Puzzled, Scott hesitated but decided to let it go. "After all you've been through, I think you need major league cheering up. I was worried at first you'd be upset about having a party, but Murray thought it was a great idea, so don't disappoint him. Come on. Snap to it, party girl."

"Just like that?" Breanna turned around and snapped her fingers, but they didn't quite click.

Scott sighed. "This isn't a conspiracy against you."

She widened her eyes. "Of course not. Everyone's concerned for my welfare, just like dear old dad."

He leaned against the doorframe. "I suppose you think you'd rather mope around alone, but you've got four guests who are going to wonder why they bothered to show up if you don't shift out of hostile."

Her eyes reflected remorse but still the bitterness spilled out. "You invited them—feed them, serve another round of Chivas, and they'll stop wondering."

He crossed his arms, wishing he knew the reason for her angry expression. She looked mad enough to start throwing furniture. "What happened today?"

Breanna finished the Drambuie and shrugged. "Nothing."

He narrowed his eyes. "Right. You've got a chip the size of a redwood on your shoulder and friends aren't allowed to ask questions? I'm not the butler, Princess."

He bit his lip. He'd hoped to shake her from brooding, but so many times, Scott had overheard Lanier's sneering nickname for Breanna, it slipped out unbidden.

Breanna leaped up. Her crystal glass shattered against the wall next to his shoulder. "How can you say that to me?"

"Maybe it fits the way you're acting tonight. But I'm still sorry I said it." Out of patience and disgusted with himself, Scott turned away, half expecting her to throw something else, stunned by the words she hurled after him instead.

"Those awful pictures. They already think I killed him. What will happen when they find out about the money?"

He strode over and gripped her shoulder. "What the hell are you babbling about? Who will? Tell me what happened!"

She unclenched her hands and shoved him, but Scott wrapped his arms around her, pinning her hands against her sides. "Lady, I can't tell if you're drunk, or what. But I know something is terribly wrong. Talk to me, Breanna. Tell me what happened!"

Breathing in short gasps, she trembled, her words an incoherent jumble of names and places. Insistently, he rubbed her back and stroked her hair. "Take your time, Breena. Calm down. Then tell me what happened. I'm here now and nothing's going to change that."

Breanna closed her eyes and held him so tightly her arms began to ache. His warmth dispelled the cold tightness in her chest and gradually the trembling subsided. She relaxed. And hiccupped. "Oh, Scott. I'm so scared."

Scott chuckled. "I don't think anybody's ever died of hiccups."

Hysteria edged her laugh, and she hiccupped again.

He tipped her head back and rubbed away a tear with his fingertips. "I thought all that booze was a bad idea. Gayle said the last time she saw you was right lunch. Where'd you go?"

"To the Main with Nick—Mr. Nicholson, from the insurance company. But then I got sick in Patterson Park. Too much grease and all the driving around, I guess."

Nick? Scott dismissed a jealous twinge. The guy was probably balding and fifty. "You drove around with Nicholson?"

Breanna shook her head. "No, alone. After I left the Sheriff's office. After the bank. I needed time to think."

Scott led her over to the window seat and sat next to her. "Wait a minute. One place at a time. What did the Sheriff want?"

She took a deep breath, gripped his hand and stumbled through a recap of the interrogation.

Scott was silent for several moments. "Are they sure, are you sure it's Lanier?"

Breanna closed her eyes. The memory of the digital pictures burned in her mind. Her stomach lurched. She hiccupped and met Scott's gaze. "No."

His brow wrinkled. "But logically, who else could it be?"

"I don't know. None of it makes sense. If Marc wanted to kill me, why did he put me in a raft, and then put a hole in it?"

Scott shrugged. All the scenarios he'd come up with were full of holes. "Beats me. Unless he wanted to make sure your body was found, make it easier to collect the insurance money. He knew the cold would have killed you faster if you were in the water. Stop getting all tangled up with worry. The Sheriff just has to cover all possibilities. You didn't know about the amount of insurance, and even if you had, that's not much motive."

Breanna rested her forehead against his shoulder. "No, but $75 million is."

Scott swallowed and waited, sure he heard wrong.

"Even from the grave, my father has to pull the strings on his puppets. After he and mother died, I thought everything except the yacht had gone to charity. Today I found out the truth. With Marc dead, I get it all."

"How is that possible?"

Breanna raised her head and gazed out the window. "It is what's called a living trust—meaning that until he died, he could change it all. After he died, the terms become irrevocable. But it will destroy my life. Who's going to believe that I didn't know about it?"

Scott took both of her hands in his. "Me."

Breanna managed a smile and met his eyes. "That's worth a lot. But what are the chances anyone else in this town will believe me? More important, what are the chances Belcastro will believe me?"

Scott rubbed his chin. "I think there are two chances. Slim and none."

Chapter 13

Gayle's voice drifted up the staircase. "Lucas! Where are you going? I thought you heard me say the bathroom is down the hall past the living room."

Heels clicked on the hardwood floor below. Breanna and Scott left the study and stepped into the upstairs hallway. Lucas stood on the bottom step, one hand resting on the banister.

He looked up, a foolish grin on his face. "Sorry. Didn't mean to disturb anything."

"There you are," Gayle said before Breanna could respond. "We're ready to eat. Murray said the hamburgers are done." She led him away.

Breanna put a hand on Scott's arm and spoke in a low voice. "Murray? You asked Murray to barbecue?"

"Yeah. Anything wrong with that?" Scott looked surprised.

She groaned. "Nothing. That is, if you like burnt offerings."

"Don't worry about it. Everybody is probably so loaded you could serve one of those black rocks from the beach."

"They'd probably be less dried out." She managed a smile and rubbed her forehead. "I'm sorry for behaving like such a brat. I just...," her voice trailed off.

"It's okay, Breanna. I understand." He squeezed her arm.

"I don't want Murray to know about this afternoon. He'll rush down to the Sheriff's office and make a mess of things. You know how he gets when he's angry."

Scott grinned. "Must be a family trait."

"Very funny."

He grinned. "You think that's a joke? How about the thought of four people sharing the living room with me to-night? I'm not sure we have a designated driver among them. These people really like to party."

Breanna hung back and avoided his eyes as they walked

downstairs. "Does Murray know you're staying here?"

A muscle tensed in his jaw. "Ashamed of the fisherman, Breena? But no, he doesn't know. At least I haven't said anything."

She grabbed his hand and stopped on the bottom step. Taking a deep breath, she met his eyes. "Don't do this to me."

"Do what?"

"Don't make me feel guilty for what my father did. You're the only one I halfway trust right now. I just don't think Murray would understand that we're only friends."

Scott was sure he wouldn't, especially since he didn't understand it himself. "Halfway trust, eh? Does that mean you're not upset about the party?"

Breanna kissed his cheek. "I'm sorry about the way I acted. But don't worry. You'll get yours."

His eyes darkened, became intense with yearning, but she hurriedly moved away. "I keep hoping," he muttered and followed her to the kitchen.

"About time you showed up!" Murray's wiry, black hair haloed around his head. He waved a spatula toward a huge oval platter covered with what Breanna assumed had once actually been ground round. "Grab a burger and fixings. Everybody else is out on the patio, swatting mosquitoes and eating."

Breanna picked up a hamburger. How did Murray manage it? she wondered. Charred on the outside, uncooked meat glared bright pink when she cut the burger in half. The digital pictures replayed in her mind. Distorted images of a human being, skin charred into an unrecognizable mass. Her stomach rolled. She slapped the hamburger back onto the serving platter. "I think I'll just have a salad. Thanks anyway, Murray."

Scott quickly picked up on her distress and distracted Murray by thrusting a plate at him and insisting he check on Spencer, Lucas and Gayle outside. Then he followed Breanna toward the side patio off the living room. Flannaghan barked as the doorbell chimed. Breanna hesitated, placing her hand on the knob of the French doors, then moved aside.

"It's okay, Scott. Go on outside. I'll get it." Still carrying her plate, she hurried to the foyer and swung the oak door open.

Nick stood on the porch. He surveyed the balloon filled entryway, then took in every inch of her. Heat flared in Breanna's face. Stretching out a hand, he removed a piece of hot pink confetti from her hair. "Glad to see you're taking the bad news so well, Mrs. Lanier."

Rather than explain the events of the past few days in front of everyone, Breanna introduced Nick as a business acquaintance and invited him to stay for supper. Although her shaky calm fizzled under Nick's scrutiny, she kept everyone focused on food, drinks and the Twins chances for the pennant until she thought she'd scream from Nicholson's casual assessment of the evening.

Scott's scowl didn't ease tensions. Gayle and Lucas left shortly after supper was over. Spencer and Murray insisted on staying to help clean up and finally left at ten p.m.

Breanna closed the door behind her uncle and Spencer with a sigh of relief. All she needed now was to temporarily get Scott out of the way. Apparently, Nick was intent on having his chance to interrogate her even if it meant hanging around all night.

She found Scott and Nick in the kitchen, Nick casually leaning against the counter drinking a bourbon and water and Scott finishing up the dishes, trying without much success not to glower at the detective. His earnest attempts to protect her alternately infuriated and warmed her. The conflicting emotions deepened the tension in the small room.

Breanna laid her hand on Scott's arm as he dried the last tumbler. "Thanks for everything, Scott, but I understand if you need to be going."

He gave her an inscrutable look, then a slow smile. "Right. Dawn comes awfully early."

She followed him to the door. Nick lingered at the living room windows, probably with all senses on red alert, but Breanna knew he wasn't close enough to catch their conversation. "Thanks for everything. See you soon?" she whispered, hoping he realized the reason she needed him to leave.

Scott kissed her cheek. "Anytime, Breena. But don't forget about the dust clods."

She stared at the door after he left.

Dust clods.

The words tickled her mind but before she had time to recapture the memory, Nick spoke up.

"Thanks for agreeing to talk with me tonight, Breanna. I suppose I put a damper on the celebration."

She walked back into the living room, took his glass and refilled it. "Do you have a family?"

"Why do you ask?"

She gave him her sweetest smile. "Because unless you crawled out from under a rock, you know that families have a strange way of helping during a crisis. Besides, through no fault of mine, today is my birthday and no one here knows about Marc's body being found."

He studied her for a moment. "Why didn't you tell them?"

She shrugged. "It didn't seem like proper dinner table conversation. And even the Sheriff's not sure it's Marc."

"Well, I apologize for my remarks earlier. Seeing you partying just hit me wrong."

Breanna sat in the wingback chair while Nicholson settled into the couch. "Multiply that by a trillion and you'll have a hint of how I felt when I got home tonight. But they meant well."

He set his glass on the coffee table. "How does Edwards fit into the family?"

Breanna poured a cup of coffee from the thermal carafe on the table and stirred a spoonful of sugar into it. "Scott and I were friends in high school, which I'm sure you've discovered, but we hadn't seen each other for years until last week."

"When he just happened to find you in the middle of Lake Superior. Lucky coincidence, wasn't it?" Nick's jade eyes darkened to emerald as he looked her over.

"I'd say so, since I'd be dead now if he hadn't." Breanna sipped the coffee and considered all the shades of gray the truth came in. If she was open with Nicholson, maybe he'd be on her side, help her find some answers. "Because I'm hoping you can speed up solving this mess, I'm going to level with you. Scott finding me wasn't a coincidence. He says he'd been following me, or as he put it, keeping an eye on me since last April."

Nick leaned forward, his interest intensified. "Really. Why?"

She set the cup down and clasped her hands together. "Because last April, Scott happened along when Marc and I were smelt fishing in the Gooseberry River." She paused and her eyes locked with his. "My husband tried to drown me, Nick, and Scott saved my life."

Nick's brows raised in surprise before he quickly resumed his look of casual interest. "Why don't you start from there, Breanna, and tell me everything that's happened."

A thousand questions later, Breanna thought Nick would never leave. But as his queries moved in ever-wider circles around her life, she caught a glimmer of understanding in his eyes. At least the piercing accusations were absent.

The grandfather clock tolled midnight when, blurry with exhaustion, Breanna dead bolted the front door and switched off the lights. She missed Scott, and the emptiness of the house echoed inside her. Confident that he'd find a way to wait and return after Nicholson left, Breanna had lost hope in the face of Nicholson's interminable curiosity and nearly two hours of questions and conversation.

She sat down on the four-poster bed to remove her shoes, dropping them one at a time to the floor. Her blood froze and she screamed when a hand grabbed her ankle. She stood, hopping on one leg, swatting at the hand.

Flannaghan bolted in, wagged his tail and dove under the bed. Scott yelped and rolled out from under the dust ruffle. Breanna fell on top of him, swinging her fists and cursing. Flannaghan barked.

Breanna rubbed the Irish Setter's nose, tried to catch her breath and struggle away. "You're about five minutes late, traitor."

Scott flipped her onto her back and held her wrists together. "You mean me, or the dog?"

Her heart beat furiously as she fought the panic welling up inside. She tried to free herself and failed. "Both of you. Let go of me! What are you trying to do? Scare me into a heart attack?"

Scott leaned his head down to her chest and went very still for a moment. "Yes, you do have one, after all. For a while tonight, I wasn't quite sure."

Breanna released her breath with a gasp. Scott touched his free hand to her cheek. "If I didn't know better, I'd say you were terminally terrified right now."

She moistened her lips. "Don't be ridiculous. I knew it was you all along."

Scott shook his head. "Liar. And you're still scared. Why? Are you afraid I now have proof you're a casual housekeeper because you could play soccer with the dust balls under the bed?"

She wrinkled her nose and blew at a curl of dust on his shirt to hide her alarm. "Dust clods. All I see is one big tow-headed clod."

Scott sighed. "I know it's been nine years, but I thought for sure you'd remember. Maybe you need another clue."

His lips brushed hers in a teasing invitation. Breanna's arms instinctively circled his neck as he released her wrists and embraced her. Past merged with present as the warmth of his mouth recalled a night long ago, Scott leaving her house, returning through her bedroom window and hiding under the bed until after the Aldens had retired for the night.

"Now do you remember, Breena," he murmured, kissing her face, her throat, overcoming her fear, drowning her senses. Her nose tickled, and she sneezed. Once, twice, three times. Breanna dissolved into giggles against his chest.

Scott chuckled. "Seems to me that's what happened last time." He scrambled to his feet and extended a hand to pull her up. Grasping her wrist, he pulled her against him and bent his head to kiss her, but Breanna eased away from him and stood at the window.

"How did you get in here? Think I need to install burglar bars?"

He walked over to the window and fiddled with the latch. "Maybe. The lock's broken. I'm surprised you haven't had problems before considering how long the house has been empty."

Dismayed, Breanna jiggled the metal. "When did this happen? I checked everything before I decided to start living here."

"Are you sure? You could have overlooked one."

Breanna put her hands on her hips and gave him an exasperated look. "Yes, I'm sure. And I double checked after we had the prowler last night."

Scott rested his hands on her shoulders and gently but insistently drew her closer. "Don't worry about it. I'll pick up a replacement at the hardware store tomorrow." He cupped her face with his hands and kissed the tip of her nose, then her face until Breanna's lips tingled with anticipation.

She clasped his wrists, unable to ignore the longing welling up inside, but afraid to let him continue. "Don't," she whispered.

"Give me one good reason why not." His mouth descended to hers and for a moment, she was lost, caught up in an unreal place between what might have been and what was.

She pressed her hands against his chest and broke away, her breath caught in her throat, shaky and uneven. "You promised you only wanted to be friends."

His voice husky, he held her and searched her face. "I said it was a good place to start. What are you afraid of?"

She feared everything that went with the kind of intimacy Marc had taught her. The pain, the disappointment, the emptiness she knew would follow.

Breanna looked away. "Nothing."

For a moment he looked hurt, but he released her and jammed his hands in his pockets. "Right. What did Nicholson want to know?"

Breanna crossed her arms and rubbed her hands up and down her chilled skin. "My favorite color."

He gave her a probing look and frowned. "What did you tell him?"

"Turquoise."

"Give me a break."

"Okay, I told him that Marc was trying to kill me. That you finding me on the Lake was not a coincidence. That you've saved my life twice."

"That's terrific, Breanna. What else did you tell him so that he can decide I'm an accomplice, that the whole thing was a set up? Did you tell him about the money?"

She tossed her head and glared at him. "No. But I've been around the man enough to know that if I don't tell him, he'll find out we've known each other for years, anyway. I'm hoping he'll be able to help. Find out what really happened before the Sheriff jumps to the wrong conclusions. He just wants to settle the case, that's all."

Scott shook his head and headed for the door. "I hate to be the one to shatter your innocent illusions, but I don't think that's all he wants. See you in the morning."

Chapter 14

Scott pulled his pillow and blanket off the shelf in the hall linen closet. What a stupid jerk he was. Nothing like a few strong-arm tactics to win a woman over.

He wanted to believe she needed him tonight, needed the closeness of someone she trusted and hadn't intended anything more than holding her.

Instead he'd behaved like a hormonally deranged teenager.

He flung the bedding on the living room floor and placed several pieces of driftwood in the fireplace. Typical weather for June, the warmth of the day had turned into a damp and chilly evening. Still, sleeping on the floor had to be better than the narrow couch. After arranging the quilts and blankets, he lay on his side and stared into the flames.

Thinking of Nicholson's ill-timed arrival brought an unexpected surge of anger. Pretty foolish to have assumed the detective was an older man, but for some reason Breanna hadn't discouraged his remarks. She must have thought he was jealous.

Maybe he was.

That possibility made him feel even worse.

He had to tell her about Derek. With Nicholson prowling around looking for suspects, Scott was amazed he hadn't discovered that already. He had to tell her himself. Hearing about his brother's ties to Lanier from someone else might make it impossible for her to believe he wasn't involved, too.

Tomorrow night. He'd make sure they had time alone so he could explain everything. Together they could find the answers.

He thought about Breanna's other mysteries. The erotic photos he'd discovered in her apartment, her embarrassment and anger at him. Her refusal to tell him what happened Friday night on the yacht. Her blue eyes wide with fear as he teased her about the dust under the bed. How could she have married someone as sadistic as Lanier? And exactly what he had done to her that paralyzed her with fear even now?

Breanna couldn't sleep. Her gaze kept drifting back to the unlocked window and despite Flannaghan's comforting presence at the foot of the bed, she couldn't relax. The heavy gold earrings clunked against her neck every time she moved, but the broken lock bothered her so badly she couldn't make herself remove the antique jewelry.

The hall clock tolled one. Breanna grabbed her pillow, reassured Flannaghan and crept into the hallway. Scott lay on his side by the fireplace, eyes closed, golden light reflected in his hair.

She tiptoed closer.

His bare chest, gleamed bronze in the firelight, rose and fell with even breaths. A pewter chain trailed around his neck, the medallion partially hidden beneath the covers. She placed the pillow down, stretched out on the quilt and covered herself with her robe.

Lying on her back, she removed the heavy earrings and held them up to catch the firelight. A thousand prisms of light scattered from the purplish stones as if captive moonbeams danced across the silent room. Sighing, she tucked the earrings beneath the pillow and curled onto her side.

"Took you long enough," Scott whispered grumpily. "Get under the covers, woman. You're almost as cold as the morning I found you." He pulled the quilt out from beneath her and tucked it up around her shoulders. His arm curved over her and snuggled her close.

Breanna tensed. "Scott—"

He kissed her temple and sighed. "Go to sleep, Breanna."

Realizing he already had, she relaxed into his warmth and dreamed of Lake Vermilion. And what might have been.

Friday morning at her studio, Breanna glanced for the

dozenth time at the headlines in the *Duluth News Tribune*. "Businessman's Body Washes Ashore at Knife River. Wife Questioned."

No wonder the phone had been ringing off the hook. One cancellation after another, but it was just as well. She doubted she'd have the necessary patience for her diminutive clientele.

Sighing, she hoped the showing in Montreal would bring her the attention she needed to branch out of the portrait business. Maybe she'd even get an occasional freelance job for a national magazine.

Much as she loved the children she photographed, the pay didn't equate to the effort it required.

She switched on the radio and checked the weather forecast. Sunny with no chance of rain. Sounded like the kind of weather she'd been waiting for to get some great shots of Split Rock Lighthouse. Although she had enough of her best work to make the gallery showing in Montreal worthwhile, she'd been determined to capture a truly unique photo of the historic lighthouse.

She called Gayle into her office. Her assistant brought in the coffee pot, poured Breanna more coffee and plopped down in the side chair.

"What kind of fireworks did Lucas and I miss last night?"

Breanna looked up. What an odd remark. "What are you talking about?"

Gayle sipped her coffee, the mug only partially concealing her smile. "Mr. Nicholson and Scott. Don't tell me you didn't notice brown eyes turning green and green eyes shooting off sparks."

Breanna tapped her pencil against the desk. Scott had hinted the same thing. "That's ridiculous. Just because you're floating doesn't mean the rest of the world's in love, too. Scott and I are friends from a long time ago, and Nick is just morbidly snooping."

"Nick? When did you get on a casual basis with this guy? That just proves he likes you more than you'll admit."

"It means he must have a very peculiar first name." Breanna frowned. "Most of the time he watches me as if I were a black widow." She hesitated, reluctant to spoil Gayle's sunny mood but took a deep breath and filled her in about the Sheriff's questioning.

Gayle paled and stared into her coffee cup. "But it was Marc, right?"

"I don't know. It must be, but I wish I could be sure. All this uncertainty, I can't make plans when I'm stuck in neutral." Breanna's eyes stung, and she bit her lip.

Gayle looked up. "I'm sorry, Breanna. You've been so stressed since your parents died, almost like a ghost, and then Marc weirded out. It's easy to forget you once cared about him. I was just kidding about Scott."

"I know. It's truly bizarre, isn't it?" She paused, concerned about her friend but not wanting to pry. "How well do you know Lucas? He's not much of a talker."

Gayle smiled. "I guess that's why I like being with him. He never interrupts."

"Uh, huh. The blue eyes and bulging biceps have nothing to do with it."

Gayle blushed. "Enough. What's on the agenda for today?"

Breanna sighed. "Looks like a good day for me to get out to Split Rock and finish my portfolio for the gallery showing next week. I was going to ask you to go with me, but I think it's best if you stay here and mind the store. Call next week's appointments and reschedule."

Gayle sat forward, her fingers tightening on the coffee mug. "You're actually going to Montreal? Think you'll get a chance to look up Marc's brother?"

Breanna shuddered. "I'm not looking forward to it, but yes, I thought I'd try. So far no one, not Nick, or the Sheriff has turned up an address for my mysterious brother-in-law. I've decided you should go with me. Maybe the two of us can turn up something. If not, at least it will be a change of scene. Don't you have some family of your own there, too?"

Gayle sat back, momentarily speechless. "Some cousins," she finally stammered.

Breanna sorted through several papers and handed her the itinerary. "Great. Family reunion time. Call and get the extra ticket changed. Then I'd like your help getting my equipment together for today so I can get out of here before the sunshine has a chance to change its mind."

At noon, Breanna pulled the Mercedes into the parking lot next to Scott's red jeep at Edwards and Sons Fishing Enterprises. She hoped he was working at the warehouse and not out on the lake. Scott had been insistent she meet him after work and she'd agreed, but since it had taken her most of the morning to get her gear together, they'd have to make other plans. The lighthouse was a two-hour drive from Duluth, and she knew she couldn't make it back by 6:30. Not if she wanted to catch the lighthouse in afternoon splendor, anyway.

She'd been at the fishery many times in the old days, but her skin dimpled with a sudden chill as she walked up the wooden steps to the loading dock.

No wonder. A man dressed in greenish gray overalls had stopped his work and watched her from the moment she stuck her foot out of the car. What was his problem?

He blew out a cloud of smoke and crushed his cigarette on the concrete floor. "He's not here. Anything I can do for you?"

Something about his tone of voice made the innocuous words sound like a lewd proposition. Breanna hesitated. "Do you mean Scott?"

"Like you'd be here looking for anyone else?"

"Can you tell me when he'll be back?"

"Nope." The man removed his cap and stuck it in the back pocket of the overalls. "He's out on the lake today. Might be back around five. Then again it might not be until dark."

Without his hat, the shape of his face, the line of his jaw struck a familiar chord, despite the light brown hair cropped in military style.

"You're Derek, Scott's brother, right? I don't believe we've met. I'm Breanna Alden." Breanna held out her hand and looked into eyes the murky color of a mixed paint palette. Not green, not brown. Not pleasant enough to be hazel.

"I know who you are, babe. Too bad about your old man."

He took her hand and held it, barely stroking the back in an insinuating gesture.

"Thank you," she murmured and took a step back, easing her fingers away from him.

Her uneasiness seemed to amuse him. He smiled, pulled a pack of Marlboros from his pocket and offered her one. She shook her head.

He looked her over again, his gaze lingering in places it had no business being. "How long have you known Scott?"

"We went to high school together." She remembered being at the Edwards home. Derek's picture on the bookcase. "You were in the Army, or something like that."

Derek chuckled. "Yeah. Something like that."

"Will you give him a message for me?"

"I doubt I'll see him." He inhaled and blew the smoke out slowly. "Tell you what. Why don't you come on inside? Write out your message, and I'll leave it with his gear. That way, if I have to leave before he gets back, he'll know you were here."

Breanna hesitated. Something about the way he acted made her very uneasy, but after all, he was Scott's brother. Funny, he never talked about him.

She forced her misgivings away. The past week had her looking at everybody suspiciously. "Okay."

She followed him into the gloomy building and up a short flight of stairs to a small office. Derek handed her a yellow pad and ballpoint pen.

Breanna sat carefully on the edge of a grimy steel desk chair, thought for a moment, and started writing. The pen skipped. She shook it and glanced up. Derek had been standing near the door when she sat down. He'd moved and stood so close to the desk her arm brushed his pants leg.

Nerves jangling, she scribbled a message, tore the sheet from the note pad, and folded it in thirds. She rose, hoping he'd move back. Instead, he stood way too far into her personal space.

Derek held out his hand. She had an impulse to stuff the paper in her slacks pocket and run, but took a deep breath and gave the note to him.

"You won't forget?"

He must have noticed her trembling fingers, because he smiled, not bothering to disguise the leer this time. "Forget you? Not a chance, babe. And I'd be glad to fill in for him if he doesn't get back."

In your dreams, Derek. Breanna gave him an icy look, shoved past him, hurried down the stairs and strode out to her car. She glanced over her shoulder.

Derek stood on the loading dock, laughing, and she realized with sudden clarity why he disturbed her with his leering expressions, his too familiar attitude.

Scott's brother gave her the skin-crawling feeling he knew things about her it should have been impossible for a stranger to know.

Chapter 15

Shaken from her encounter with Derek, Breanna decided to go home before she headed up the North Shore Highway to Split Rock Lighthouse. She walked through the house, checking windows and doors, but everything seemed to be in order. Murray had been in and repaired the broken window latch, returned the spare key to the turtle planter on the front porch and left a note on the kitchen table, asking her to stop by the bar that evening.

Sighing, she tossed the note inside. He intended to talk her out of the Montreal trip, she could tell, and her only defense would be to avoid him and his paranoid logic between now and Sunday.

She slapped a sandwich together and changed into sky blue denim shorts and a knit pullover. Flannaghan watched while she grabbed a blue and pink windbreaker from the hall closet. He sat up and begged, holding out a paw as if pleading.

She had to smile at his pitiful expression. She hesitated, but only for a moment. Might as well take him and let him have a chance for some fresh air, too. Besides, she needed company even if she had to settle for the four-legged kind.

"Okay, Flanny. You win." Flannaghan pushed past her, bounded across the yard, than ran back and nudged her along.

"All right already, I'm hurrying." She patted his head and opened the car door. Flannaghan leapt into the passenger seat as if it were his throne.

Reaching the outskirts of town, she relaxed and let the splendor of the day override the misery of the past week. Lake Superior sparkled like the green and purple fire in Grandmother Lillian's alexandrite and diamond earrings.

She clapped a hand to her forehead. The earrings. At Scott's insistence, she'd left them at Herzberg Jewelers that morning. Murray had severely lectured her for wearing them at the party last night, and although she knew their value was high, to her knowledge, they'd never been appraised.

She punched in the number for the jewelry store, but Mr. Herzberg was out. It might be Monday before they had an answer, but she supposed the earrings were as safe in the jeweler's vault as locked away at the bank. Once she had them insured, maybe she'd dare wear them occasionally. Marc had been right about one thing, at least. It seemed a waste to have something so spectacular and keep it hidden from the world.

The highway wound close to the rocky shore, climbing and twisting along the cliff. Pine trees mingled with birch along the woods on the opposite side of the road and rose along the hillside in varying intensities of green. Momentarily reminded of Nick's green eyes, Breanna checked the rearview mirror for the dozenth time.

Nothing.

Despite the uneasiness that followed her everywhere lately, she'd managed to elude Nick and whoever else might be trailing her. She luxuriated in the freedom. Gayle better not allow anyone, especially Nick, to coerce her into revealing where Breanna was spending the day.

Flannaghan sniffed the breeze, tongue lolling, and she reached over and ruffled his fur, shimmery copper in the sunshine. He sprawled across the console and tried to climb in her lap, crowding between her thighs and the steering wheel.

Laughing, she pushed him away. "Just like a man, aren't you, Flanny. The tiniest bit of encouragement, and you want to take over."

Scott crept back into her mind. His behavior this morning had been decidedly cooler than last night but he'd gone through his daily ritual of how she needed to continue being careful. Don't go anywhere alone, make sure you're not being followed, lock doors, on and on and on.

She worried about him just as much. As far as she knew, he hadn't been back to his house since Monday night except to grab a change of clothes. She hoped creepy Derek would at least leave her message. If she didn't show up to meet Scott as planned, he'd be calling out search parties.

The twinge of annoyance his over-protectiveness gave her melted under warmer memories as her thoughts wove a different ending to the afternoon nine years ago at Lake Vermilion.

Feeling her skin burn under the heat of what ifs, she pressed the accelerator and turned up the volume on the stereo. *Idiot.* What might have been should no longer matter in the aftermath of what was.

But it did, and she couldn't stop the fantasies as they played through her mind like a slow motion video.

The drive along the winding highway passed quickly, two hours fusing into miles melted beneath the convertible's tires. She pulled off the highway into the State Park and drove up the road to the lighthouse. With a permit purchased at the expense of warnings from the attendant about Flannaghan, she reached the parking lot. Two tour buses. Just what she needed, half of northern Minnesota and southern Ontario looking on and getting in the way.

She tied Flannaghan's leash to the door handle inside the car and followed the path to the lighthouse. Cool air blew against heated skin, and she shivered, zipped the windbreaker and leaned against the fence. White water shot upward as waves crashed against the rocks 170 feet below.

"Treacherous, eh?"

Breanna jumped at the distinctly Canadian accent in the man's voice and looked up. Tall, and fortyish, he stood at her elbow, a Bluefin Bay cap pulled down low over gray eyes.

"Yes," she murmured and edged away. A prickle of apprehension traveled down her spine.

He stepped closer, pushed the cap back and gave her a friendly smile. "Been in the museum yet? Really fascinating, how they built this all those years ago." He gestured to the lighthouse looming behind them and launched into a monologue about the hazardous shoreline, shipwrecks, and the resulting construction of the lighthouse in 1910.

"Wayne!" A woman whined from the lighthouse steps. "You're going to miss the bus again."

Breanna breathed a sigh of relief as the man said goodbye and hurried after the stout woman and the rest of a tour group. Just a harmless tourist. How long could she live like this before her nerves shattered, when everyone she saw was suspect, every motive was questioned, every noise threatened.

She climbed the steep stairs inside the lighthouse, careful not to look straight down. Through the glass, the Lake stretched out like shiny blue satin, and she had a moment's vision of herself adrift on the vast surface only six days ago.

So much lost and still she had no answers for the things that had happened the past week. Not even about Nina Rogers' death. Although the police had confirmed her identity, they also said she might have been strangled before being dumped at the warehouse.

No suspects yet, not even for the fire.

Breanna suppressed a shudder. At least she hadn't been accused of that, too, but probably only because Captain Belcastro hadn't yet compared notes with the Duluth Police Department.

After exploring the lighthouse area and surveying the rocky beach to the west, Breanna sought out the Park Ranger. The park closed at five p.m. If she could get permission to stay, there'd still be plenty of good light for another two hours without dozens of sightseers cluttering the scenery.

By six o'clock, the late afternoon sun at her back, Breanna had filled up most of the memory card but still didn't have the shot she wanted. Finding secure footing for the tripod on the rocks wasn't easy, but she moved the camera back and refocused.

Last Friday, she'd had hopes of getting some pictures from the deck of the *Breanna Colleen*, although the area near the lighthouse was filled with dangerous rocks. Still, with calm water and the right lens...

Maybe tomorrow she'd wheedle Scott into a trip on his charter boat. The thought lasted only a moment. Probably not a good idea to face the vastness of the lake again this soon after her ordeal.

Besides, all he needed, all she needed, was several hours

alone in the small space of his boat for feelings to spin out of control.

She stood back from the camera and frowned. Puffy clouds kept drifting over the sun, casting a shadow across the massive cliff over which the lighthouse stood sentinel. Another hour passed while she waited for her chance.

The southeast wind turned cooler, whipping her hair back. Her leg stung and she jumped, startled, only to discover the windbreaker's ties flapping against her thigh. Much as she hated to make the quarter mile trek back to the car, she needed another memory card, and it wasn't in the camera bag. She trudged up the hill, gave a dozing Flannaghan a reassuring pat, and retrieved the filter.

Returning down the narrow path to the isolated shore, she glanced repeatedly over her shoulder as the snap and rustle along the quiet wooded path filled her with unease. A squirrel darted across the trail.

Breanna let her breath out in a rush. Varmints. The woods were full of them, like her life lately.

Shadows deepened where the trail ended at the rocks.

Breanna hauled tripod and gear across boulders and outcrops and selected a different angle. She shivered. She should have asked Gayle to come with her. They'd be headed for home by now. Finally, with the first hint of dusk, she packed her gear and started up the winding path through piney scented woods.

Thick undergrowth blocked gusts along the trail, and the wind tickled only the treetops and murmured through the lower branches. Silence hung heavily, broken only by rustling leaves and the crunch of pinecones beneath her feet. A twig snapped behind her.

Breanna glanced over her shoulder and quickened her pace despite being loaded down with equipment. No squirrels this time, and the dread of being followed that had plagued her all week returned full force. Something, someone stalked through the bushes. The muted thrashing halted, then came closer and closer.

Breanna dropped the tripod, a scream frozen in her throat.

In a blur of burnished copper, Flannaghan rocketed out of

the thicket and knocked Breanna on her backside. His large pink tongue swiped at her face. She scrambled to her feet, and he fenced with his paws, attempting to encourage a game of chase.

She rumpled his fur, almost shaking with relief. "Lunatic dog. What am I going to do with you?"

He barked and shook his head. The leather leash dangled from his neck, a good two feet shorter than earlier, apparently snapped off near the handle. He barked again and prodded the back of her leg with his nose. Breanna sighed and picked up the camera gear, alternately scolding and petting him.

She trudged up the rest of the hill to the parking lot and stowed the equipment in the trunk. Flannaghan politely waited for her to open the door, then leaped back into his place on the passenger seat.

"Okay, now you have to have me open the door. It sure didn't hold you back from escaping, did it?"

Perched on his throne, Flannaghan thumped his tail.

After thanking the ranger for letting her stay, she sank into the Mercedes' leather upholstery and leaned her forehead on the wheel for several moments before starting the engine and heading southwest toward Duluth.

Flannaghan's antics had drained her, and she felt as wilted as yesterday's salad. How much longer before she recovered from this bone-jarring exhaustion?

A mile later, she pulled into the parking lot of a wayside rest and convenience store. Large signs proclaimed the best view of the Lighthouse from the adjacent lookout tower, but all she wanted was to get a soft drink and head back to town.

Although a white Ford was parked in the far corner of the lot, the store was empty and the clerk was placing the closed sign in the window when Breanna walked up. She purchased a Coke, exchanged pleasantries with the woman and climbed back into the Mercedes.

As she backed out of the lot, a sudden movement from the front seat of the Ford caught her eye, but the car looked unoccupied in the early evening shadows. Something about it seemed vaguely familiar.

She puzzled over it as she pressed the accelerator but dismissed paranoid thoughts. There had to be hundreds of white cars on the highway, each one looking like the last.

The sun disappeared into a dark bank of clouds. Breanna wished she'd put the top up before she left the lighthouse. Now there was nowhere safe to stop until she reached Gooseberry Falls.

She wondered if she'd ever again cross the Gooseberry Park bridge without remembering last April and how, according to Scott and her own hazy memory, Marc had tried to drown her in the river. She pulled into the parking lot and hurriedly unsnapped the leather boot covering the folded canvas. A press of a button and the top locked into place.

A white sedan loomed through the wisps of fog drifting over the bridge, slowed, and passed. Breanna pulled out onto the highway behind him and let enough distance build between them that she lost sight of his taillights. Relaxing, she switched on the radio, then tried to call Scott. The cell phone refused to work, no matter how many buttons she pushed. Rounding a curve she looked up and again saw the white car, this time pulled over to the side of the road, the hood raised.

As she passed, she glimpsed a man, blond hair partially covered by a white hat. She hesitated, reluctant to ignore someone stranded on the lonely highway, but even more unwilling to take a chance and stop. The idea of helping fled and her stomach curled into a knot as she watched the rearview mirror and saw the car pull out onto the highway behind her just before she rounded another bend.

A coincidence, nothing more.

The car stayed some distance back, but Breanna's panic increased with each curve of the winding, climbing road. She took a deep breath and tried to subdue her fear with logical explanations. With few signs of civilization until Two Harbors, it seemed reasonable that the white Ford kept reappearing. But the man stayed relentlessly behind her, despite her efforts to vary her speed and let the sedan overtake her or drop behind.

For several days, she'd had the ominous sensation of being watched, a kind of prickling on the back of her neck but hadn't found any basis to the suspicions.

Until yesterday morning when she'd imagined a white car followed her from London Road to downtown. Then again in the afternoon, she remembered having the sensation of an uninvited escort just before she got home.

Who was it and what did he want?

Past Castle Danger, Highway 61 climbed higher. A wall of rock loomed above the road's north edge. Far to her left, the cliff dropped 125 feet to treacherous rocks and Lake Superior. Breanna eased back on the gas. A yellow diamond shaped sign appeared under the swath of headlamps. The tunnel through Silver Cliff.

Wind buffeted the car. She slammed on the brakes, yanked the wheel to the left and back, tires squealing, narrowly avoiding the rockslide that covered half of her lane just as she reached the tunnel entrance. Flannaghan slunk to the floor and covered his nose with his paws. A flash of blinding light ricocheted off the rearview mirror.

Chapter 16

Breanna tore her gaze from the mirror and crushed the gas pedal to the floor. The Mercedes responded with a roar of power and hugged the asphalt. She checked the mirror again. Nothing but velvety darkness behind her.

Twin beams of light appeared from behind. Heart pounding, she gripped the steering wheel and pushed the convertible to the limits, blasting from the tunnel and down Highway 61 the rest of the way to Two Harbors. Relief crept over her. She lost him, but for how long?

In town, she found herself in the midst of the annual summer carnival. Great. Local police had traffic rerouted for the parade.

She collected her composure from the slower pace and thought quickly. Whoever was following would have no problem catching up. Her only hope was to get lost in the confusion of detours, and illegally parked cars, and somehow make a Mercedes convertible inconspicuous.

Scott drummed his fingers on the bar and earned an irritated glare from Murray. He glanced toward the door, wishing for Breanna, dreading the appearance of N. J. Nicholson. Nosy scum. He looked forward to spending another evening with the man as much as he welcomed the idea of scaling fish with Derek.

Derek! Maybe Breanna had gone by the fishery, and he knew something about her whereabouts.

Ridiculous. Scott immediately dismissed the idea.

Derek had apparently left work around noon to meet with buyers. Besides, Scott had warned Breanna about going to the fishery and putting herself through the scrutiny of the dockworkers. To his surprise, she'd agreed. But thinking about his brother reminded him of what he needed to tell her.

Before someone else did.

The phone rang. At the far end of the bar, Spencer nodded to Murray and covered the mouthpiece with his hand. "It's your missing person."

Scott and Murray almost collided, but Murray snatched up the receiver first.

"Breanna! Where the hell are you?" He motioned impatiently at Scott. "Yeah, well he's only been sitting here for the past two hours. You going to square up his tab?"

Scott rolled his eyes. As if he expected Breanna to fund his beer. *Thanks a lot, Murray*, he mouthed to her uncle.

Finally Murray relinquished the phone to Scott. "Hope you have better luck. She's talking as fast as a wind surfer in east winds, and I can't make any sense out of it."

Scott held the receiver and covered his other ear to block out the noise from the piano. "And just where did you run off to this time, with my dog?" Breanna sounded incoherent, like she'd been crying. He listened to her account of the drive to Two Harbors, trying to make sense out of it.

"Stay where you are. Wait for me inside. I'll be there as fast as I can." He hung up.

Murray gave him a questioning look. "Well?"

"She's at Oscar's. In Two Harbors."

Murray looked astounded. "What the hell is she doing in that two bit diner?"

Scott shrugged. "Said she had a craving for a rare hamburger. Probably because of last night. I'm going to meet her."

Murray bristled. "Those burgers were the best I've ever barbecued. And hold on a minute, I'm going with you. Spencer can take care of things here, even if it is Friday night." He whipped off his apron and stuffed it under the counter.

"Wait a minute, Murray. Both of us don't need to go."

"Then you stay here and wait for Nicholson." Murray stood his ground, and Scott gave in, reflecting it was probably better after all. If they took Murray's car, Scott would be free to drive the convertible back to Duluth with Breanna.

The Mercedes was parked behind Oscar's Grill, squeezed between the dumpster and a cargo van. Scott reached in through the partially open window and patted Flannaghan soothingly. "Good boy. Don't worry, we'll be out of here soon."

He and Murray walked inside the cafe and found Breanna at the counter, sipping a cup of coffee as calmly as if at the neighborhood donut shop. Scott took the stool next to her.

She set the cup down in the saucer and brushed a lock of hair away from her face with a shaky hand.

"Thanks, Edwards, but you really didn't need to do this." She leaned closer and spoke in an almost imperceptible whisper. "Did you have to bring him, too?"

Scott took her hand in his and was surprised to find it icy cold despite the hot coffee cup she'd been gripping. He nodded. "He drove. That means I can take you back in you car, okay?"

Breanna nodded and eyed her uncle. "Hi, Murray. You guys didn't both need to drive all this way on account of my jittery nerves. Shouldn't you be tending the bar to make sure Spencer isn't watering the drinks?" Her smile seemed forced but grateful.

Murray scowled and squeezed her shoulder. "Let him. All I see is one scared woman, trying to water down a story. Let's hear it. From the beginning. As in, what in God's name did you think you were doing roaming the countryside alone after everything that's happened? And why in the hell didn't you tell me last night about Marc's body being found?"

Breanna stood and hugged her uncle. "I'm sorry, Murray. I just hated to see you worry more." She shuddered. "And it isn't easy to talk about." She gestured toward an empty booth. "We'll have a little bit of privacy over there, okay?"

Thirty minutes later, Scott walked Breanna to the Mercedes. He held out his hand for the car key.

She frowned, caught Murray watching from two cars over and dropped the key ring into his palm.

"All right, I know when I'm outnumbered." Waving goodbye to Murray, she got in and sank into the passenger's seat. Flannaghan rested his head on her leg.

Scott eased the car out into the unusually heavy flow of traffic. "Lucky for you, Two Harbors was having their annual carnival this weekend. Please tell me you didn't intend to drive the rest of this gloomy highway with someone after you."

"I suspect I ended up with that, anyway." She paused and gave him a tired smile. "Murray took it better than I imagined, the idea of you staying with me."

Scott grinned. "I think he's just relieved that he's not the one who has to sleep on that concrete slab you call a couch." He glanced in the rearview mirror. "You're sure someone was following?"

Breanna stared out the opposite window into the dark woods. Birch trees loomed like ghosts among the spruce and poplars under the flicker of headlights.

"No, of course not. I told you on the phone. But it scared me." She sighed and her head dropped against the headrest. "Didn't Derek give you my message?"

"No. About my brother," he paused, knowing this was the opening he needed to start the explanations.

Apparently misreading his hesitation, Breanna launched into a detailed account of the afternoon's shoot at the lighthouse as if anxious to divert a lecture like the one she'd already received from Murray.

She talked nonstop during the twenty-minute drive to Duluth. Recognizing the monologue as an outlet for pent up nerves, Scott let her ramble, figuring he'd have his chance for explanations later. He pulled the car into the garage. Flannaghan bounded out across the lawn while they walked up to the front door.

"A hot buttered rum and a bath, that's all I want right now, Scott." Breanna turned the key in the lock and glanced over one shoulder at him.

He couldn't resist giving her a wicked grin and leaned close until his breath stroked her cheek. "Okay by me, just let me know when you want your back scrubbed."

Her stomach fluttered, and she readied a retort, but it died as she looked past his shoulder to the figure striding down the front sidewalk. Flannaghan gave a half-hearted growl.

N. J. Nicholson glanced from Breanna to Scott and frowned. "Hello, Breanna, Edwards. Glad I caught you."

Breanna's face warmed and she fought a sudden urge to clutch the windbreaker closer. "Hi, Nick. What brings you here tonight?"

Nick frowned. "Had a few things I wanted to talk to you about. Are you okay?"

Breanna shoved the heavy oak door open. "Fine, just fine." Scott and Nick followed her inside, but no sooner were they standing in the foyer, than she turned toward the detective with an angry gesture. "I've put up with your nasty insinuations, your million and one questions about things that are none of your business, but I want to know why you're having me followed. What do you think I'm going to do? Lead you to buried treasure? Or maybe you've decided Marc's not dead and he's hidden away somewhere, just waiting for me to collect the insurance money?" She planted her hands on her hips and glared at him.

Nick regarded her with a cool gaze. "Interesting concept. Maybe I should check that out."

Breanna stared back. "So who do you have trailing me?"

"No one. And I spent the day with the Duluth PD and the St. Louis County Sheriff's Department. Ask Edwards. He called me this evening wanting help finding you. I missed him and Murray by about five minutes, but I'm glad at least that mystery has been cleared up."

She glanced uncertainly from Nick to Scott. "You called him?"

Scott nodded slowly. "When I didn't hear from you, I started to get desperate."

Momentarily taken aback, Breanna moved into the living room and switched on a brass floor lamp. She threw herself into an overstuffed chair, flung her bare leg over the armrest and chewed on a polished fingernail. "Then who was it?"

Scott sat on the edge of the couch. "Wait a minute. Not ten

minutes ago you told me you weren't sure someone was after you. Now all of a sudden you are?"

She straightened, placed her feet on the floor and clasped her hands in her lap, looking from Scott to Nick. Both men sat on the couch, furtively eyeing each other with hostility. "I could be wrong. And nothing happened."

Nick spoke up quickly. "Let's hear the whole story."

Again, Breanna recounted her afternoon at the lighthouse, ending with Scott and Murray's arrival at Oscar's Grill.

Nick looked thoughtful for several moments. "Did you get the license number?"

She shook her head.

"Why didn't you notify the police in Two Harbors?"

"Are you trying to be funny? I'd rather have just stopped and asked the mystery man who he is and what he wants. Besides, Two Harbors finest were busy directing traffic."

She pushed herself out of the lethargic-inducing comfort of the overstuffed chair. "Anybody besides me need a drink?"

Scott and Nick spoke simultaneously, then glanced irritably at each other. Breanna turned her back to hide a smile and went to the kitchen to fill the ice bucket.

Maybe a couple of drinks would dispel the tension between the two men. Of course, Nick looked at everybody like a suspect, and Scott considered himself her personal bodyguard. It didn't make for a relaxing environment.

She closed her eyes and rubbed the back of her neck, jumping when she felt Scott's warm hands on her shoulder. She cast a guilty look toward the living room. "What about Nick?" she whispered.

"What about him?" Scott's thumbs expertly massaged the taut muscles between her shoulder blades, compelling her to relax into his fingertips.

She glanced up at him. "I don't want him getting the wrong idea about us, that's all."

Scott scowled, but his voice was light. "He asked to use the phone, so I sent him upstairs. But don't worry," he added at her quick intake of breath. "Flannaghan's keeping an eye on him."

Breanna turned and tugged his earlobe. "If I didn't know better, Edwards, I'd think you were jealous."

"Of that prying gumshoe? He's old enough to be your— uncle, at least."

"He's thirty-seven. Same age as Marc. Was." Breanna filled the ice bucket and handed it to Scott. "Mind taking this and fixing the drinks? I'll settle for something cold and get some pretzels." She lowered her voice. "I don't want him staying any more than you do, but I can't tell him to buzz off."

"I can. Want me to?"

"No." Breanna cast a nervous glance at the door as Flannaghan bounded in beside Nick.

His glance swept the room and came to rest on Breanna. "Can I help?"

Realizing Nick could be a good source of information, she subdued her apprehensions, thrust the bowl of pretzels into his hands and steered him back to the living room. "I hope so, Nick. I'm leaving for Montreal Sunday and was wondering if you'd talked to Gregory Lanier yet. I want his address and phone number."

"Montreal!" Scott and Nick responded simultaneously, and again glared at each other. Since Scott was fixing drinks at the bar, Nick caught her attention first. "What for? Have you told Belcastro you're leaving town?"

Breanna sighed. "It's a business trip. And yes, I called the Sheriff's office this morning. They're still waiting to hear from the Canadian authorities to try and identify the body. That might take at least two weeks. In the meantime, Belcastro's not concerned I'm going to flee. Why are you?"

A smile played around his mouth. "I'm not. But if you did, we'd just have to say we were looking for a blue eyed brunette who wears chandeliers in her ears to birthday parties."

Breanna laughed and touched her ears where blue and white beaded earrings dangled to her shoulders. "You mean the pair I wore last night. They belonged to my grandmother, an anniversary present from my mother's father. His father won them in a private poker match in Monte Carlo. Or so the story goes. They've been in the Sullivan family long enough that no one really knows where they came from."

"The Original Christmas Store," Scott said. "If you get tired of lead weights on your ears, you can always use them as tree ornaments."

Breanna wrinkled her nose and sipped her rum and coke. "Laugh now, but wait until I get the appraisal back from Herzberg."

"And they will collect dust in the bank vault forever." Scott shook his head. "I bet you'd have more fun with Austrian crystals, Breena. At least you wouldn't have to worry about someone ripping your earlobes off."

Nick leaned forward. "You don't mean to say those are real diamonds, do you?"

Breanna shrugged. "Supposedly, and alexandrites, too, although that's hard to believe given the size of those stones. Back to my question, Nick. Where can I find Gregory Lanier?"

"Montreal, although the address Providential has is no good. Can't get a phone listing, either, but I'm working on it. Still, I don't want you doing anything on your own. What if he was involved in the smuggling? He'd be the last person you'd be safe with."

Scott busied himself laying kindling in the rock fireplace. Could be his guilty imagination, but Nicholson's sidelong glances made him want to punch his lights out. He took a stick match from the brass holder on the mantel and watched the dry wood spark and flare into small, hungry flames. When was this clown going to leave so he and Breanna could have some time alone?

Not anytime soon, Scott realized as Nick stood, took Breanna's glass and fixed another bourbon and water for himself and a rum and Coke for her. Pushy bastard, making himself at home.

"How about you, Edwards? Ready for a refill?"

Reluctantly, Scott walked over to the bar and handed Nick his glass. "Sure, although Breanna looks like she's ready to crash."

Her legs tucked beneath her, Breanna was staring at the fire through half closed eyes. What an insensitive clod

Nicholson was. Couldn't he see how tired she was and get the hell out?

"Breanna," Nick sat on the edge of the couch. "How long have you known Gayle Montclair and where did you first meet her?"

Breanna jerked her head around and met a gaze as sharp as pine needles. She frowned. "She's been working for me for about six months. I advertised for an assistant in the newspaper. A week later she applied for the job and we hit it off. Why?"

"I had the feeling she wasn't from Duluth."

Breanna swung her legs to the floor and reached for her glass. "That's because she's originally from Quebec and spent several years working in Minneapolis before she decided she's a small town girl. What do you need to know?"

Nick swirled the ice in his drink and took a sip. "Nothing in particular. Just doing my best to check out everyone and everything."

Dismayed, Scott sank into the couch pillows. No doubt about it, he needed to tell Breanna about Derek tonight. Time was running out. Nicholson fired off several more queries about Gayle, then talked about the progress, or lack of it, the police had made into their investigation of the warehouse fire.

Nick emptied his glass and stood. "Well, Edwards, should we shove off and give Breanna a chance to get some sleep? I didn't see your jeep. Need a lift home or back to Murray's?"

His words caught Scott in a gulp, and he choked. Damn him! Now he had no choice but to leave with the detective and return later. A replay of last night. "Back to Murray's, if you don't mind."

"No problem. I'll talk to you tomorrow, Breanna." His hand lingered on her shoulder a moment, then he strode to the door.

Scott held out a hand and pulled her to her feet. "See you later. Don't forget to lock up."

Breanna dragged herself along to the foyer.

Scott winked. *Wait up. I'll be back,* his eyes implored, then he turned and followed Nicholson out the door.

The deadbolt clicked. Breanna leaned against the door and

squeezed her eyes shut. A tear rolled down her cheek. She swiped angrily at it and stalked to the bedroom, Flannaghan padding along beside her.

She had removed her contact lenses and begun to wash her face when the phone rang. Eyes stinging, she grabbed the receiver on the nightstand. It was probably Murray, and he'd have a panic attack if she didn't answer. "Hello?"

Several long moments of crackly silence greeted her. "Just checking," a man's voice whispered, not quite distinguishable, but terrifyingly familiar. Shards of fear stabbed her chest. The line buzzed in her ear.

The receiver slipped from her shaky fingers and clunked on the hardwood floor, followed by an electronic tone. She picked up the phone, fumbled it into the cradle and stumbled back to the bathroom. Icy water restored reason and relieved her stinging eyes. Breanna patted her face dry and stared at her reflection in the mirror over the sink.

It couldn't be Marc. He was dead. DEAD! But someone else wanted to play games. This time she would fight. She raced up the stairs to the study and rattled the handle on the gun cabinet. Locked. She had known it was, but couldn't it be pried open? She ran a hand down the cherry wood cabinet. Not without ruining it, and she wasn't that desperate. Yet. The key had to be here somewhere.

She began at the corner bookcase, methodically pulling down books, rifling through them. No key, but by the time she'd finished the first two shelves, a pile of $100 bills lay on the floor. What a hoarder Grandmother had been.

Several times during the past six months, Breanna had planned a workday at her house, intending to box up the books, memorabilia, and knick-knacks. Marc had wanted to "help", and knowing he'd pocket any money he found and use for his own mysterious purposes, she had stalled. As the pile of green grew, so did her gratitude that she faced the task alone.

After the third shelf, she stopped and caught her breath. This was ridiculous. The key wouldn't be randomly stashed in any old book. Grandmother had been somewhat eccentric, but always followed her own brand of logic. Searching for a clue, she recalled conversations with Lillian and remembered catching her off guard in the foyer.

'What are you doing, Grandma?'

'Nothing much, Pet. Just killing time.'

Killing time. Breanna stumbled over the stack of books and ran downstairs. In the foyer, the pendulum in the grandfather clock swept gently back and forth. She popped open the glass door, and put a hand on the brass, her fingers skimming over the back. Nothing. She ran her hands over the back and sides of the cabinet, then pressed against the bottom, hoping to discover a secret compartment, but the clock yielded no secrets.

She paused and closed her eyes. *'The clock struck twelve, the mouse ran down.'*

Breanna opened the glass door over the sun and moon face, carefully moved the hands ahead to twelve and held them for a count of twelve. A creak, a groan and a tiny compartment hidden in the woodcarvings at the top of the cabinet popped open. Standing on tiptoe, she groped until she felt metal, and dug out a small key. She gave the pendulum a gentle nudge, closed the door and bounded up the stairs.

The key clicked, the gun cabinet swung open. Breanna scanned the antique hunting rifles and then used the key to open the small drawer below. Her hand closed around a pearl handled revolver.

At the sound of movement behind her, she whirled toward the door, instinctively raising the gun and gripping it with both hands.

Chapter 17

Scott stood in the doorway, hands raised. He surveyed the mess of books and money on the floor. "What did you do while I was gone, Breena, rob a bank?"

Breanna exhaled and dropped her hands. "I swear, if you don't stop sneaking up on me, Captain Belcastro will be investigating *your* homicide."

He entered the room, took the gun from her white-knuckled fingers and turned the revolver over in his hands. "Besides the fact it's probably not loaded, I seem to remember you couldn't hit the broad side of the carriage house."

She sniffed. "That's only because I couldn't aim with your arms around my shoulders. Sometimes I think you forget I had a life after you left. The summer I was seventeen, grandmother took charge of my education. She thought a woman needed to be able to protect herself."

"You'd have been better off with karate lessons. What about all that stuff you used to spout on the dangers of hand-guns?"

"That was before, and I'd be careful with that if I were you. Lillian always said having an unloaded gun made as much sense as having a second husband.

Momentarily taken aback, Scott frowned. "Did she say that before or after you met Marc?"

Breanna reached for the gun, but he held it beyond her grasp. "She passed away before I met him. Besides, what difference does that make? My grandfather died the year I was born and, whether he was so terrific that grand-mother couldn't imagine anyone taking his place or such a tyrant she swore off men, Lillian just said she never found another man worth giving up her freedom for."

"That was a long time ago. It's different now."

Breanna shook her head. "Only on the surface. You of all people should understand. Don't you think that must be why your mother left?"

"Geesh, Breanna, I was nine at the time. How the hell would I know why she took off?" He shifted uncomfortably, and his jaw tightened.

She touched his face. "I'm sorry. It wasn't your fault, you know. You used to hear from her once in awhile. Do you still?"

"Nope, and I'm not interested." He popped open the gun, disbelief threading through him. "What the hell were you doing waving a loaded gun around, anyway?"

Breanna took the weapon and switched out the lights. "I got a very weird phone call."

Scott followed her around the small house as she rechecked doors and windows.

"Weird like what?"

Breanna clutched her neck with one hand and dropped her voice to a whisper. "I know this is impossible, but it sounded like Marc."

His eyes widened. "You're right. That's impossible. And very weird."

She wrapped her arms around her middle. "Okay, but someone wants something. I don't know what, and I intend to be ready when they come to collect." She stood on tiptoe and kissed his cheek. "I'd still like that hot buttered rum. Mind playing bartender? I'm going to take a hot bath, sip my rum and crash."

"No problem."

Again, she softly touched his face. "I'm glad you're here. Makes me feel safer."

"Yeah, real safe," he muttered. "That's why you're going to tuck a loaded pistol beneath the pillow tonight. Breanna," he said, grabbing her hand and tugging her to a stop as she headed for the bedroom. "We need to talk. I've something on my mind, and I think you need to hear it."

"I know what you're going to say."

His stomach knotted with anxiety. "You do?"

She nodded, her eyes smoky blue in the dim hall light. "It's still there, even after all these years. At least I think it is. But with everything that's happened and so much still unknown, I have to be sure I'm acting, not reacting. You do understand, don't you?"

Scott felt more and more like the rug was being pulled out beneath his feet. "No. What are you talking about?"

"Chemistry. It's still there. I just don't want it to blow up in my face this time." She turned, slid one arm around his waist, and kissed him.

The touch of her lips against his and the importance of words unspoken vanished with her soft, tentative kiss. He pulled her closer, tasting rum on her tongue. The scent of sunshine lingered in her hair and a faint essence of flowers pervaded his senses. The cold metal gun barrel pressed against his back, but he barely felt it.

Breanna disentangled herself with a lingering kiss and moved away. "Will you fix me a drink?" She asked over her shoulder as she headed for her bedroom.

Scott stood still, rooted to the floor, trying to recapture the balance she stole from him. "Lady, right now I'd do anything you asked me to."

He fixed the two hot drinks they'd wanted before Nicholson showed up. Breanna claimed hers right before she escaped into the long awaited bubble bath. He tried not to think about her stepping out of her clothes and into the tub.

Scott took Flannaghan outside, ostensibly to stretch the setter's legs and recheck the property. In reality, to let the cool night air dispel thoughts of Breanna wearing nothing but frothy suds and only an unlocked door and a persistent sense of caution keeping him away.

He had to talk to her tonight. Nicholson was too close to discovering the connection between his brother and Breanna's husband, and if Nick told her first, the small trust she'd begun to have would vanish.

By the time he'd rethought his story and explanations, the grandfather clock was tolling midnight and making a peculiar grinding sound. Flannaghan barked simultaneously with the pounding on the door. Scott glanced through the glass panels and opened the door for Murray just as Breanna emerged from the bedroom, wrapped in a royal blue terry cloth robe.

"Hi, kids. Just wanted to check and make sure everything's okay."

Breanna smothered an exasperated smile and gave her uncle a peck on the cheek. "Hi, Murray. Everything's okay. You can go close up the bar now."

He bristled and pushed past Scott and into the living room. "Nice to know you're glad to see me. I left Spencer in charge. I got concerned when I noticed Scott's jeep was gone, and I wondered if he'd made you drive him over to pick it up."

Breanna glanced at Scott and rolled her eyes. "No, actually Nick stopped by and offered to give Scott a lift."

Murray dropped a handful of ice cubes into a tumbler. His bushy eyebrows shot up. "He left you alone?"

She sighed. "Honestly, Murray. First you're upset that I might have driven him anywhere. Then you're mad that I was alone for all of about twenty minutes. Do you think I require round the clock surveillance?"

"Maybe." Murray gave her a stern look.

She returned it, glare for glare. "Everything's fine, except I'm exhausted. So if you'll excuse me, I'm going to bed. Have a drink, and I'll talk to you tomorrow. Found some money in grandmother's things. When I figure out what's there, I'll split it with you."

Murray poured Scotch into the glass until it was half full. "Oh, no you won't. She wanted you to have the house. That means everything in it as far as I'm concerned. That ought to help you right now with all the money troubles you said you were having."

Breanna shifted uncomfortably from foot to foot. "Were having. I haven't had a chance to tell you about my meeting with Stenberg."

"Bankers. What a bunch of sharks. They smell blood, they start circling and get ready to rip you to shreds." Murray took a deep draught of Scotch.

"Actually, he had good news. Of a sort." Breanna rushed on. "Seems I'm going to get my inheritance after all. Dad put everything in a trust. Once Marc's death has been established, it all reverts to me."

Murray choked and sputtered. "What the—?"

Breanna crossed her arms. "Mother always confided in you, Murray. Did you know about this?"

"Hell, no. Matter of fact, I tried to push her not to let your father cut you off in the first place. Just didn't seem right, but your dad had to make his point, like always. And now this."

Murray shook his head and took another drink of scotch. "That man had more calculated moves than a world class chess player, but at least he planned to set things straight." He set his glass down and put his arms around Breanna. "Sure am sorry, sweetie. You going to be okay?"

She nodded, finding comfort from Murray's familiar smell of smoky taverns and British Sterling cologne. "I hate the money," she whispered, tears threatening to choke her. "It can't bring them back, so what good is it?"

He patted her back awkwardly and let her move away. "You'll find good ways to use it. I've got faith in you, but you're right. Money can be a curse. Makes it tougher to sort out your friends from the blood suckers." He glanced at Scott.

Scott scowled and poured a Coke. "Thanks for the vote of confidence, Murray. I'm not Lanier, and I'll keep pestering your niece trying to prove that no matter what it takes."

Breanna rubbed her eyes. "Enough, already. You two can stand here exchanging insults if it makes you feel better, but I'm going to bed." She kissed Murray on the cheek, brushed Scott's arm with a fingertip caress and trailed off toward the bedroom. "See you tomorrow."

Scott raised an eyebrow and regarded Murray. "Care for anything else, Murray, or do you need to be going?"

Murray rubbed his hands together, walked into the kitchen and filled the coffee maker. "Coffee sounds good. Want some?"

Scott gathered up the mugs and glasses from the living room set them in the sink and turned on the water to wash up. "I'll pass. But go ahead and make yourself at home."

Saturday morning Scott called and checked in with Derek, hoping the tentative fishing charter had canceled after hearing the day's weather reports. "Didn't this bozo hear about the possible storm brewing later on in the day?"

"That bozo paid a cash deposit for a day long fishing trip, wise ass. If we canceled a charter every time the weatherman said it might rain, we'd have a two workday summer. I already told you I'm taking a group to Copper Harbor. So get your chicken shit butt down here and get ready to fish."

Scott slammed down the phone and cursed the change in plans. Having to acquiesce to Derek's orders left a bitter taste. He grimaced and dumped his coffee into the kitchen sink, ran water and stomped down his feeling of irritation. Tonight. He'd take Breanna out someplace nice for dinner.

Then they'd talk.

Breanna slept late, lulled into slumber by the sunless day. She stretched, then padded out to the kitchen in her bare feet, disappointed to find Scott's note propped against the thermal carafe. Disappointed he was gone, she sipped coffee and stared out at the day, a slate gray sky turning the lake into leaden murkiness. Looked like good fishing weather, at least. She hoped Scott's charter had a good time of it.

After breakfast, she carefully rechecked the locks, took Flannaghan and climbed into the Mercedes. She looked forward to spending a few hours "creating" with her photo software.

Since she'd hired Gayle, Breanna spent less and less time working with her pictures once she'd trained her assistant in the basic procedure. The shots of the lighthouse were something special, however, requiring experimentation and technique to get the effect she was hoping for.

She checked the rearview mirror several times on the drive to the studio, but didn't see anything suspicious. Still, having Flannaghan with her gave her a sense of comfort. She hoped being at the studio for several hours wouldn't make him stir crazy.

As if following a routine of years, Flannaghan explored the office, then curled into a ball of copper fur under Gayle's desk. Breanna went to work on the computer.

Several hours later, she finally printed out the best shot of the lighthouse to exactly the composition and color she wanted. She stretched and sighed with satisfaction. Now she could go to Montreal with a portfolio displaying the best elements of her work.

A number of pictures she'd snapped as practice shots had turned out well, too. Studying them, she decided that a collage of the best ones would make a nice addition to the other pictures displayed in the reception area, but they needed to be enlarged. She experimented with photos of varying angles of the lighthouse and park grounds and began zooming in on a shot taken from the lighthouse steps.

Her breath froze as the enlarged detail of the photo brought a white car into the foreground. Intent on the developing image, she magnified what had been insignificant background until she could make out the driver, slouched forward, a white cap partially shielding his face. Breanna gasped as his familiarity became a name.

Lucas Brogan. Why had he been at the lighthouse yesterday and what did he want?

She left the workroom and grabbed the phone off Gayle's desk, punching her number in with trembling fingers. Taking a deep breath, she managed to greet Gayle with controlled tones.

"Hi, Gayle. I know you're busy getting ready to leave tomorrow, but I'm at the studio and I've run into a bit of a problem. Could you buzz down and give me a hand?"

"What kind of a problem?" Gayle sounded cautious.

Breanna twisted the telephone cord. "It's complicated. How soon can you get here?"

"Give me fifteen minutes."

Breanna agreed and hung up the phone. Considering Gayle's constantly changing parade of boyfriends, she hadn't considered Lucas's sudden appearance in her life unusual. Now his blond handsomeness seemed menacing.

Breanna studied the picture again. It was definitely him.

Gayle wore a bewildered expression as Breanna whisked her over to the computer and explained what had led to her discovery. With the picture blown up as much as possible without losing the detail to the grain of the film, Breanna was even more convinced of the man's identity.

Gayle reluctantly agreed. "But it doesn't make sense. He told me he had to work yesterday, and you're saying he tried to follow you home last night."

"Not tried," Breanna corrected. "He followed me. I just didn't recognize him in the shadows."

They left the workroom. Breanna folded her arms and leaned against the desk. "Tell me again, how did you meet this guy, what have you told him about me, and exactly what do you know about him?"

Gayle shifted her weight and looked away. "I didn't want to tell you this. I know how you felt about Nina Rogers, so when you asked me how I met Lucas, I thought it was better to leave her out of it."

"Nina Rogers!" Breanna shook her head. "What does Marc's secretary have to do with this?"

Gayle sank down into the desk chair. "We went out for drinks. To the Cove. Last Thursday night, the night before you and Marc left for Isle Royale. Anyway, Lucas was there. He sat with us, came on really strong to Nina but she brushed him off. He got angry and left."

Gayle picked up a pencil and started doodling on the phone message pad. She looked up and met Breanna's eyes. "I think you were right about Nina. She was after Marc, but I think it was one sided. Anyway, Lucas called me the next day and took me to lunch. I like him, he's nice in an intense kind of way."

"Intense? Why do you say that?" A shiver of fear crept down Breanna's spine.

"He doesn't talk much and when he does it's usually a question about something. He really knows how to draw some-one out. I was flattered that he seemed so interested. Why does that upset you so much?" She glanced up, her expression defensive.

"Think about it Gayle." Breanna shuddered. "The man's

been following me for days. I have several narrow escapes. He knew Nina, sounds like pretty well. And now Nina is dead."

"That's crazy!" Gayle's eyes widened. "I can't believe he'd do anything like that! Why are you trying to ruin things for me?"

Breanna touched her arm. "I'm not. You're my friend, your happiness matters to me. As does your life."

Gayle looked away. Several moments passed. "He did lie about where he works." Her voice was hushed.

"What do you mean? You said he's in the shipping business."

Gayle twisted her fingers together. "In a way. I figured he was trying to impress me, make me think he was some kind of hotshot for Terminal Warehouse. He's actually a stevedore."

"Oh, Gayle." Breanna slumped back. The worst kind of scum worked the docks, all brawn, little brain and even less ethics required for the union jobs. "A dock worker?"

Before she could answer, Flannaghan barreled out from under the desk, barked and raced to the door. Breanna strode over and unlocked it for Nick.

He wore a moss colored sweater and tweed slacks that gave him a quiet professional appearance and set off his coloring of changeable green eyes and light brown hair. He looked her, Gayle and the room over with the scrutiny she'd come to expect, but this time it didn't make her as uneasy.

"Good afternoon, Breanna. Got your message and since I was downtown anyway, I thought I'd just drop by. Hello, Gayle."

Gayle mumbled a greeting and looked away.

Breanna settled into a worn velvet side chair. Nick sat opposite her. "We were discussing Lucas Brogan. Seems he hasn't been entirely honest about his occupation."

"You do seem to attract that sort."

Breanna's cheeks warmed with anger. "He's Gayle's friend, not mine. Anyway, Lucas isn't the shipping magnate he wants us to think he is. He works the docks."

"I know."

"You know." She threw her hands up in exasperation.

"Thanks for sharing the information, Nicholson. Any chance of getting some inside information from you? Or do I have to investigate on my own?"

Nick crossed his arms and gave her an exasperating smile. "I'm not in the habit of spouting off during an investigation. If you ask me about something, I'll tell you. Otherwise I'll keep you informed on a need to know basis."

Breanna narrowed her eyes. Men. Their pompous self-assurance never failed to amaze her. "The reason why I called you, Nick, is I wanted to know if the police had any more details about the fire at the warehouse."

"As a matter of fact, that's where I spent the morning. The medical examiner finished the autopsy. Nina Rogers wasn't strangled after all, but forcibly drowned, sometime last Thursday night. Her lungs were filled with water." His piercing gaze swept from Gayle to Breanna. "And she was pregnant."

Breanna gasped and caught Gayle's eye. "I think you'd better tell Nick what you just told me. Because if Nina was killed Thursday night, that means you and Lucas were probably the last ones to see her alive."

Nick insisted on calling the police. Sergeant Bergsteed arrived and questioned Gayle carefully, going over and over her chance meeting with Lucas Brogan, Nina Rogers, and every encounter she'd had with him in the past week. An hour later, he snapped his notebook closed and stood.

"If you think of anything else, let me know. In the meantime, be careful about being anywhere alone. Either of you." His glance swept from Gayle to Breanna, then he left.

Breanna retreated to her office and collapsed into the corduroy overstuffed chair. Gayle's and Nick's voices murmured from the reception area. A door banged. Feeling a moment of pique that Nick would leave without saying goodbye, she closed her eyes and gathered her thoughts. Scott was right. Nicholson had strange ways. She wished he were more open with her.

She sensed a presence and opened her eyes, expecting her assistant. Instead, Nick lounged in the doorway.

"You look beat. How about lunch?"

Breanna got up and tried to step around him. "No, thanks. I need to go home and pack for my trip. Why did Gayle leave?"

"Said something about business to take care of before tomorrow." His hand closed around her wrist, gentle but unyielding. "Look, Breanna. I'm not trying to trick you. I want to help, and right now you look worn out. Let's go eat. We can get a grease burger at that funny little drive-in you like down at the pier."

She gave him a cool look and wriggled her arm free. "I've only known you three days, Nick. How do you know where I go?"

His eyes twinkled. "Would you believe, lucky guess?" She shook her head. "Didn't think so. Grab a jacket and your pet monster, and I'll explain on the way."

Breanna picked up a deep purple windbreaker, clicked her tongue at Flannaghan and pulled the studio door shut as she and Nick stepped out on the sidewalk. "Were you a military commander in a previous life?"

Nick laughed. "Something like that." He held the door of the Chevy open for her and walked around to the other side.

She watched his face as he pulled away from the curb. "Why do you have this compulsion to know so much about me?"

He shrugged. "Endless curiosity, I guess. An occupational hazard. By the time this investigation is closed, I intend to know everything about you, Breanna."

An odd little flutter settled in her stomach. "Everything?"

He stopped for a red light and turned toward her, green eyes darkening to emerald while he scrutinized her face. "Like I told you before. Everything."

Chapter 18

At Canal Park, Breanna tossed the last piece of her hamburger bun on the ground and waited for the inevitable seagull fight. A snowy white bird with silver tipped feathers picked up a bread chunk and flapped his wings only to have his lunch ripped from his beak by a larger speckled gull.

"Kind of remind you of people, don't they?" Nick gave her a shrewd look, and rested his arms on the back of the park bench.

She flopped down next to him. "I've known a few like that."

"Like your husband?"

"That's a rather insensitive remark." Breanna reached down and petted Flannaghan, curled on the ground by her feet.

Nick shrugged. "No use pretending he was a saint if he was a sinner."

"I never said he was either of those."

"So tell me about him. Where you met, that sort of thing."

She didn't like to talk about her relationship with Marc, not even something as innocuous as how they'd met. Daddy and Brett had been relentless in their insistence that Marc had met her by design, not chance. Maybe they'd been right.

Perhaps Nick would see some clue she'd overlooked. She gestured to the pier. "Actually we bumped into each other right here."

"Here?" Nick looked surprised.

"Where did you think? A bar in Superior or something?"

He shook his head. "I don't know. He sounds more like the type to cruise the bars."

"Maybe he was. But I'm not."

He brushed the back of her hand. "Easy. I wasn't insinuating anything."

She sighed. "I love the pier, especially the boardwalk. So I was doing what I did every day at noon, I was in-line skating on the pier and lost control. Literally knocked him over."

"Did he know who you were?"

Breanna cast him a sidelong glance. Here it came, the assumptions, the questions. "What do you mean?"

Nick gave her a patient look, as if she were a rather slow child. "Your family's pretty well known. You get your picture in the paper occasionally. Did you ever consider that he might have planned a meeting?"

How dare he? Breanna leapt to her feet. "Trying to take over where my father left off? How am I supposed to know the answer to that, for sure? It's not very likely Marc would tell me he set me up, planned everything right from the start, is it?"

Nick radiated calm. "When did you start feeling like he did?"

Breanna hugged her arms, trying to hold the hurt and loss inside. She closed her eyes for a moment and took a deep breath. "When I lost the baby."

Nick's face remained impassive, but a spark of sympathy flashed in his eyes. "I'm sorry. The hospital reports said you fell."

Breanna was silent.

Nick continued. "So Marc came home and found you in the foyer after you'd fallen down the stairs."

"That's a lie!" She couldn't control the outburst. Despite her efforts to remain calm, his words resurrected the pain, the fear until she felt like she'd choke with it.

"Then what did happen? I know your uncle tried to make a case against your husband, but gave up when you stuck with Marc's story."

Breanna looked away from his prying eyes and uncomfortable sympathy. She laced her fingers together. "When I woke up in the hospital, Marc had already told everyone he wasn't there when I fell. I was too weak, too sick, too scared to argue. Eventually he convinced me I was wrong, that I slipped on the top step. That he wouldn't hurt me, wouldn't do something as horrible as push his pregnant wife down the stairs."

She closed her eyes, wishing for peace from painful

memories. Tears burned at the back of her eyes. Damn Nick's inquisitiveness. He would be an easy person to hate, at times. Opening her eyes, she met his gaze. "Whatever happened, it's not relevant now. And unless you can convince me it is, I won't talk about it anymore."

She turned and walked down the pier, Flannaghan beside her. A cold east wind sliced through her jeans, whipped her dark hair across her face. She wondered where Scott was, if he'd be back before the weather turned worse. She felt Nick's presence beside her, but he didn't speak until they reached the lighthouse.

His hand brushed her elbow. "Look, I'm sorry to have to bring up all that. But I think it's important. It establishes a basis for what's happened since. If I'm going to get this case settled, I need the facts."

She dropped her arms to her sides and clenched her hands. "Facts! What about feelings? Like what it feels like to have everyone tell you someone can't possibly be interested in you for yourself. Suspicions gnawing away at your soul that maybe they're right. Then finding out they were after it's too late to do anyone any good." She turned away, the gusty wind so strong she gasped for breath.

His hand rested lightly on her shoulder and eased her back to face him.

"Why were you going out alone that late? Where were you going that night?"

She shrugged his hand away. "Isn't it obvious? I was leaving him, and he swore he'd see me dead first."

Scott scanned the sky and re-baited a fishing line for a middle-aged man. Recreational fisherman. He couldn't quite fathom the thrill of it.

To the north, the Sawtooth Mountains appeared as a wavy, pencil line, then the shoreline disappeared into a smudge on the horizon. A slight breeze kicked up foam along the waves. He followed the blips on the radar, chasing a school of lake trout. The screen went blank. Scott slapped the dial and let the boat drift. A strike from one of the passengers captured his attention and for the next thirty minutes, the boat was filled with the activity of re-baiting and hauling in lines.

The sky remained heavy and gray, casting the lake with a leaden tint and creating the feeling of drifting inside a covered minnow bucket. Scott switched up the volume on the marine radio. Nothing. He tapped the side. Funny, he'd used it just an hour ago and spoke with another fishing boat miles away on the vast lake. He returned to the deck to check on the passengers.

With the perception that comes with years spent on the lake, Scott noticed the shift of the wind seconds before it sent a half full Coke can toppling from a bench seat. He grabbed a handful of paper towels from the deck cabin and started mopping up, waving away apologies and help from a middle-aged woman stuffed into a pink sweat suit.

He didn't mind doing it. Besides, if the pink lady had to bend over, Scott was certain the skin-tight suit wouldn't take the strain.

She touched his arm. "It feels colder than just a few minutes ago. Are we in for a storm?" She searched the sky with an anxious expression.

Scott straightened and scanned the horizon. "Haven't heard about any wind advisories, but I think it's time to head for shore, just in case. Sorry to cut the trip short, folks." The six passengers nodded in disappointed agreement and crowded inside the cabin.

He handed out life jackets, then went to work stowing fishing tackle, fish and gear, working quickly but calmly. By the time the last lines were reeled in and secured, the *Liquid Asset* wallowed between wave swells, each one looming menacingly alongside the thirty-two foot boat.

Grand Portage was the closest safe harbor, miles away. He had to make a push for it and hope for the best.

Clouds opened with a burst of icy rain, fusing the sky into the lake. Scott and the boat battled waves against a lost sense of direction. The radar screen remained ominously blank.

What was wrong with the damn radio?

Breanna braked for a red light and glanced in the Mercedes' rearview mirror. Nick remained several car length's behind. She wished he'd just go back to his hotel, but realized the wisdom of letting him see her safely home. Flannaghan sprawled on the front seat and rested his paw on her leg.

She patted his head. Good old Flanny, the one male she'd always been able to depend on.

By the time she reached the house, fat drops of rain splattered the windshield. Breanna locked the garage and hurried down the steps to the house. Nick dashed onto the porch as she unlocked the door. At his insistence, he quickly checked the house while she waited in the foyer.

Breanna adjusted the pendulum on the clock and glanced up at the detective's return.

"Everything looks fine. Just be sure to keep the doors and windows locked."

"For someone who's been halfway convinced I'm guilty of murder, you're suddenly very concerned for my welfare." She closed the door on the clock, the metal click echoing in the small foyer.

He shrugged. "That was before I had a chance to check out the situation. And you."

Breanna turned away to hide a smile and headed for the kitchen. "Does that mean I'm off your list?"

Nick followed. "One of them."

Interesting response. Just what did he mean, exactly? She rinsed out the coffee carafe and pulled a filter from the cabinet. "Would you like some coffee?"

He smiled. "I do have a few more questions, but I know you must have a lot to do to get ready for your trip tomorrow."

She readied the pot and switched it on. "I do, but it's not midnight yet."

Nick gave her a puzzled look.

She laughed and moved to the window. "I realized a long time ago that no matter when I start packing for a trip, I'm still running around at the last minute. So now I just do it all in a rush. You know, tasks expand to fill the time available."

Sheets of rain pelted the glass. Waves rose and crashed at

the foundation of the house. Nick stood next to her. "Aren't you worried about rocks breaking a window with this kind of wind? I'm surprised you don't have storm shutters."

Breanna pressed her palm against the pane. "Heavy duty plate glass. Guaranteed to stop hurtling stones. Besides, how would you get around the front and fasten shutters?" She leaned her forehead against the window and struggled to see through the gusty rain. She hoped Scott had made it back to the harbor. Any harbor. Breakers lashed at the house with frightening intensity. If something happened to him....

She started at the sound of Nick's voice.

"What's wrong?"

"Scott had a charter out of Grand Marais today. I hope he made it back safely." She walked to the built-in desk and checked the recorder. One message from Murray, indicating he planned to stop by later. Nothing from Scott. Her stomach curled with apprehension.

Nick watched her speculatively for a few minutes, then leaned closer to the window and looked down. "Pretty unusual to put a house so close to the water. Especially on this lake."

She poured coffee into black and white checked mugs and sat at the table. "Oh, but this isn't an ordinary house."

Nick raised a questioning brow, and she continued. "Used to be a water pumping station, years and years ago. Grandmother Lillian bought it after my grandfather died, completely renovated it, added the dormer room upstairs and moved in, much to my father's dismay."

Nick sat and picked up his mug. "So she moved out of the family house. Why did it matter to your father?"

"You would have had to know Daddy. He thought we should ramble around like one big, happy family in their house. It's on London Road, a few miles closer to downtown."

"I know where it is." He paused. "Who owns it now? I noticed it's vacant."

Breanna sipped her coffee and avoided his eyes. "I still have a set of keys. I'll take you over there when I get back from Montreal, if you'd like."

Nick set his cup down. "What's wrong with right now?"

In the silence, she heard the rhythmic ticking of the grandfather clock. Afraid to arouse his suspicions about her inheritance, she agreed. What could it hurt to go over and look around? But the thought of venturing into the empty house filled her with melancholy.

Fifteen minutes later, Breanna shook the rain from her red vinyl raincoat and stepped through the vestibule into the main hall. Nick closed the leaded glass and oak door, the sound resounding emptily in the two-story entry.

She glanced at the stairway, curving majestically to the second floor and was transported back two years. Her mother, elegant in purple satin and Grandmother's alexandrites and diamonds, descended the stairs to meet her father while Breanna and Brett watched from the hall. She swallowed.

Gone. The people she'd loved most. Gone forever.

Forcing memories aside, she assumed the business-like manner of a tour guide. She led Nick through the bedrooms and sitting rooms draped in dust cloths on the second and third floor. Then back downstairs, entertaining him with stories about the redecorating the house had gone through after her parents took over from Lillian when Breanna was three. Fiona's attempts to maintain the house in turn of the century splendor. The bickering with Lillian about how the gardens should be kept.

Nick ran a hand along the chestnut paneling in the den and raised a brow. "Who did this castle actually belong to?"

Breanna adjusted a covering on a camelback couch. "Grandfather Sullivan built it for his bride. Imagine returning from a honeymoon and trying to set up housekeeping in this monstrosity. Luckily Grandmother had the skills of an army general. When he died, the house went to my mother with a life estate for Lillian. That's why Dad didn't want her to move out. I guess he felt guilty. Mother seemed relieved, although she'd never admit it."

"Interesting," he murmured. "Moving into the family castle. Seems like he might have been more sympathetic toward your husband."

"That's a laugh. But Marc thought so. It really bugged him,

but the situation's not the same. My father was already very successful when he married Mother. They could have lived anywhere they wanted."

They ended the tour in the lower level and stood looking out at the weather from the enclosed winter garden. Again, Breanna worried about Scott as marble-sized hail bounced on the brick courtyard.

"Preoccupied about your friend?" Nick's voice slightly stressed the last word.

Breanna folded her arms. "Can't help it. We've known each other for years, and I know he was reluctant to take out a charter today, but his brother insisted."

"What do you know about Derek Edwards?"

Breanna could almost see Nick ticking questions off a list and chose her words carefully. She couldn't admit that Scott's brother appeared to be totally sleazy. She suppressed a shudder, remembering her last visit to the fishery. "I don't know anything about him since I've only met him once. Seems to be very different from Scott."

She moved away and switched off the lights as she walked up the stairs to the first floor. "Seen enough?"

Nick surveyed the hall again as she slipped into her rain coat. "Twenty-six rooms, a carriage house, indoor pool, miniature bowling alley in the basement. Very impressive."

Silently, she snapped her coat shut and picked up her umbrella.

"Must have been a fun place to grow up in."

She looked up and met his gaze. "It was. But only if you like museums."

During the drive back to her house, Breanna gazed out the window. Although the rain had slackened to a drizzle, fog rolled off the lake in smoky billows. She tried to shut out an image of Scott struggling with the small boat and started at the sound of Nick's voice.

"What's going to happen to it?"

"To what?" She gave him a blank look.

"The house. Will it be sold?"

"I'm not sure anyone would be able to buy it. I may have to

donate it. Maybe to the University or something." She caught her lip between her teeth.

Nick pounced on the slip. "Why do you have keys to the house, Breanna, and why is it sitting there waiting for someone to come home?"

She watched him for a moment, then turned back to the side window. "I don't think that's any of your business."

He pulled over, half jolting her from her seat. Gripping her shoulder he forced her to face him. "Damn it, Breanna. I want to believe you were the victim, that you didn't willingly participate in any of this. How can I do that when you won't level with me?"

She wrenched out of his grip. "How are you going to do that knowing Marc's death dumped everything back to me? Whether I wanted it or not?"

Nick blinked and sat back.

Breanna twisted the door handle and leapt out, afraid of blurting out more in anger. Damn him and his unending questions. Let him figure the rest out.

She darted across the street and pulled the hood of her raincoat over already damp hair. She kept telling herself he'd have found out anyway. It was just a matter of time.

A few minutes later, she was on a westbound bus with nowhere to go.

She ended up at Murray's, spilling the story out to her uncle as Spencer discreetly tended bar. Spence set another Irish coffee in front of her and went back to rearranging the pyramid of glasses lined up against the mirrored wall.

Murray shook his head and spoke, as always unmindful of Spencer's presence. "Bad move, sweetie. Now he's really going to be all over you like a bad rash. Think he'll pass the information on to Belcastro?"

Breanna rested her head against her palm and stirred the coffee. "Probably. They are working the same side of the street." She drank half the coffee, then reached for Murray's hand. "Can I have a ride home?"

"Sure. It'll be a while before the Saturday crowd arrives." Murray grabbed his overcoat, then waved to Spencer.

Wired from caffeine and anxiety, Breanna spent a sleepless night. Every rustling leaf, wind gust, and Flannaghan's nocturnal prowling made her reach beneath her mattress for the loaded pistol countless times. By five a.m., concern for Scott gnawed at her and overrode her concern for her own safety.

She took Flannaghan outside and walked up to the mailbox to get the Sunday paper. Pink clouds streaked the sky as she sat down at the breakfast table to have a revitalizing cup of coffee.

The cup crashed to the floor as she shook open the front section to check the headlines. Her college picture stared up at her from center page. *Heiress Loses Husband, Regains Fortune* screamed bold print. Sick with disbelief, she scanned the article, noting the Associated Press byline. A knot formed in her stomach. Now even Marc knew, *if* he was still alive somewhere.

How would she stop him if he decided to come back?

Chapter 19

Ten minutes later, Breanna called Murray. The telephone rang twelve times before she succeeded in rousing him.

"I promised I'd drive you to the airport, sweetie. We don't need to leave for another two hours," he mumbled, his voice thick with sleep.

"An hour, Murray. That's when the plane leaves. But I've changed my plans. I need you to pick up Gayle in fifteen minutes."

She pictured Murray, black hair jutting out like porcupine quills, struggling to emerge from the clutches of slumber.

"Fifteen minutes! What the hell's going on now?"

Briefly, she described the newspaper article. "Since I had to tell Belcastro where I was going, I can't take the chance that some hot shot reporter from the Tribune won't be at the airport waiting for a big scoop. I've decided to drive to Minneapolis and make the connections there. All I need is for you to pick up Gayle and meet me at the scenic overlook near Spirit Mountain."

He agreed, and Breanna hung up the phone. She was doubly glad now she'd insisted yesterday that Nick help her pack up the pictures for the gallery showing. At least she wouldn't need to stop by the studio before leaving town.

After taking one last look around, she picked up her bags and locked the house. Flannaghan answered her whistle and jumped into the car.

Breanna paced at the overlook, glancing at her watch every thirty seconds. Flannaghan obediently padded along beside her, stopping occasionally to sniff at the brisk air. Far below, Lake Superior shimmered in early morning light. Gray puffs curled from the smokestack of a freighter nearing the Aerial Bridge. Breanna leaned on the stone wall and took a deep breath. No matter how much turmoil beleaguered her, she loved the picture the harbor made, serenely still after last night's storm.

Murray and Gayle arrived at the overlook five minutes later.

"Sure you don't want me to drive you?" Murray insisted as Breanna handed him Flannaghan's leash.

"Positive. Just take good care of my baby."

Murray shifted the leash to his other hand. "Always have, for all the appreciation the mutt's shown. Runs off with you, first chance he gets."

Breanna kissed Murray's stubbled cheek. "He's loyal. The most redeeming quality a guy can have. At least this time he's not likely to chew up the vinyl floor in your kitchen." She hesitated, wanting something more from her uncle, not sure how to ask. "Murray, I need one more small favor."

He scowled, black eyebrows pulling together in a fierce line. "What else, besides not telling Nicholson how to reach you for the next seven days?"

She pressed a slip of paper into his hand. "Here's the number for my hotel. Call Scott's brother. Find out if Scott made it back yesterday, or where he is. Then let me know tonight. Or I'll call you when I get there. Now stop worrying about me."

He gave her a quick hug. "Can't. It's become a way of life as far as you're concerned."

Gayle was quiet during the drive, apparently drifting off to sleep shortly after Breanna waved goodbye to Murray and left the wayside rest. They'd almost reached Moose Lake when the cell phone chirped.

"Breanna!" Scott's voice faded in and out amidst a crackly connection. "Glad I caught you."

She laughed with relief. Thank goodness he was okay. "Just barely, Edwards. I've been worried sick. Where are you?"

"Grand Portage. I'll explain how I got here later. I think it's a really bad idea for you to go to Montreal. Stay put, and I'll explain when I get back."

She felt a flash of irritation. "You're too late. Gayle and I are on our way to the Minneapolis airport."

The line went silent, and Breanna hung up. It rang again. She snatched it up. "I have to go, Scott, and I really need to get out of this town for a few days."

"Listen to me for once."

"No, you listen. I have a commitment to the gallery owner, and I can't afford to screw it up because you're paranoid. We'll be staying at Les Quatres Saisons...Damn." The line crackled and sputtered, then went blank. Breanna snapped the phone shut.

"Just say The Four Seasons." Gayle's tired voice sounded patronizing. "At least you can pronounce that."

Breanna glanced over at her assistant. Her University French wasn't that bad, but she decided to let it pass. "That's why I'm glad you're coming with me. Help with the language from a native. Mariette said she's expecting a good turnout for the opening Tuesday."

Gayle continued staring out the opposite window. "Don't worry. English is perfectly acceptable, even in Old Montreal."

Breanna hesitated, considering speaking to Gayle about her attitude, but decided not to. She was probably immersed in her own concerns and the problems of seeing family left behind long ago.

Breanna understood. It was never easy going home again, but she wondered what kind of family secrets Gayle was hiding.

Les Quatres Saisons was on Sherbrooke Street, adjacent to McGill University. Breanna and Gayle checked in, enjoyed a quiet dinner in the hotel restaurant and said an early good night.

Still unable to reach Scott, she called Murray, gave him her agenda for the week and promised for the umpteenth time to be careful. "Don't worry, Murr. I'll call the Royal Mounties at the first sign of trouble."

She pictured the exasperated expression that must have accompanied his heavy sigh. "Fine. And quit fussing about your fishy friend. I'll keep trying to run him down and give him your message."

Breanna spent Monday at the gallery with Mariette Marcel and Gayle, setting up and discussing the best positioning for the work she'd brought as well as the portraits she'd shipped earlier to the gallery owner. Mariette's Moments occupied a corner location on Sherbrooke Street and housed an eclectic variety of photographs, contemporary paintings and small sculptures.

Breanna's work filled a strategic section of the first level of the gallery with the shot of Split Rock Lighthouse framed and displayed in the window facing the busy street.

Mariette adjusted the frame of a picture hanging a micron higher on one side. "That should do it for today, ladies. All set for grand opening tomorrow. You really should get out and enjoy the city. By the end of the week, it will be a mob scene."

Breanna pushed the blue frames of her glasses higher on her nose and glanced critically around the studio. Everything looked well placed. "Why is that? A convention or something?"

Mariette rested her hands on her hips and gave Breanna a surprised look. "The International Jazz Festival, of course. Concerts in the streets, jugglers, magicians, vendors. It's really something. Lasts ten days. I'm so glad you'll have a chance to experience it."

Experience it. Breanna exchanged a resigned look with Gayle. She'd hoped for a few days of peace and quiet despite the hectic schedule Mariette had planned. "Sounds interesting. If you're through with us, I guess we'll see you tomorrow morning."

Gayle was silent in the limo to the hotel, ignoring Breanna's exclamations and questions about the architecture of the buildings they passed. Again, Breanna wondered what was troubling her assistant and laid a hand on her arm. "Look, Gayle, whatever's bothering you, maybe I can help."

Gayle glanced at Breanna's hand as if wishing to dismiss an overly friendly puppy. "I doubt it. I'm not looking forward to family reunion time, that's all."

"If it would help, I'll go with you this afternoon."

"Non!" The word exploded with the force of Gayle's previously concealed Quebecois accent. She gripped her hands in her lap and met Breanna's startled gaze. "Sorry. I've been gone a long time. I'm just edgy."

Only a trace of an accent remained as Gayle took a deep breath and spoke more slowly. "All that stuff about Lucas has me looking over my shoulder and searching my memory for what I've said to him. Creep. I should have listened to Nina. Can't trust guys you meet in a place like The Cove."

Or the park. Anywhere for that matter. At least now she knew what was troubling her assistant. Gayle had been acting like someone she'd never met before ever since they'd begun this trip.

Breanna sat back and watched the city framed through the car window. Strange to think that Marc had spent most of his life here and never mentioned the city, never even shared a photograph.

Minutes later, Gayle said goodbye and hurried to her room. Puzzled, Breanna watched her enter the room halfway down the hall from hers without even a backward glance. A few minutes later, from inside her own room, she heard the door slam again.

Breanna kicked off her shoes and pulled Marc's burgundy log book from her portfolio. Flipping through the pages, she discovered a page of Marc's tight handwriting she'd overlooked before. Numbers and street names. Indecipherable instructions of some sort covered one page. No phone numbers or names, except for one. Gregory. Maybe she could find a number for Marc's mysterious brother. Somewhere in Montreal.

She flipped open the phone book, wishing for an address and phone number. A page of Laniers and nothing even close. No possibilities presented themselves from the various first names and initials. Breanna rubbed her eyes and laughed at her foolish hopefulness. As if Marc and his brother would be listed in the local directory. Lanier and Lanier, International Smugglers and Murderers, Ltd.

She paced the room, fighting the impulse to hire a taxi and go searching. Going alone in a strange place would be foolish and where would she start? If she waited for her assistant to return, at least she could count on Gayle's knowledge of the city.

Breanna turned her thoughts to business concerns and ate supper alone in her room. At nine o'clock she tried calling Gayle's room and received no answer. She continued trying until ten-thirty, then gave up and went to bed.

She awakened to see bands of sunshine sneaking around the heavy linen draperies. The bedside clock read nine and she jumped out of bed. She'd have a terrible time making it to the gallery by ten if she didn't hurry. She tried ringing Gayle again. Still no answer.

At ten she left a message for Gayle at the front desk and hurried to the gallery in a courtesy car. The day went quickly amidst the throng of people passing through the gallery, but by the six p.m. closing, she'd still not heard from Gayle.

Mariette turned the sign to closed and locked the glass doors. She glanced at Breanna and gave her a satisfied smile.

"I hope you're as pleased as I am. And just wait. Tomorrow will be even better. Worried about your assistant?"

Breanna nodded. "Actually, I alternate between irritation and concern. She's been so reliable, but over the past few days, I've realized how little I really know her."

Mariette shook her head. "I hope it's nothing important, but yesterday, I thought she acted like a wounded bird, just waiting for the big bad cat to pounce."

Cold settled around Breanna's stomach. "What an odd thing to say. Why would you think that?"

Mariette shrugged. "Every time the door opened, she jumped, then tried to hide her discomfort. Was your friend expecting a visit from someone she really didn't want to see?"

A short time later, Breanna thought about the gallery owner's observations as she stood on Sherbrooke Street and waited for the hotel courtesy car. She considered walking the few blocks to the Four Seasons, but couldn't muster the energy to find a phone and cancel the arrangements. The hotel used a silver Cadillac. Or was it a Lincoln? She tried to remember and wished she'd paid more attention that morning to the driver and the car instead of the scenery.

A pale blue Lincoln Town Car with opaque windows slowed and pulled to the curb. The driver climbed out, a navy cap covering most of his hair and shielding his face. Reflective sunglasses obscured his eyes.

Breanna hesitated and approached the vehicle when he opened the rear door and gave her a curt nod. She moved slowly, trying to gauge the overwhelming sense of unease that made her legs feel like lead weight. The driver took her hand as if offering assistance and steered her toward the car. She stiffened, sensing a shadowy presence on the far side of the back seat.

The man's grip tightened. A scream welled in her throat.

Chapter 20

"Breanna!" Nick's voice sounded urgent from somewhere behind her.

She struggled against the insistent pressure of the driver's hand on her elbow. Jerking free, she stumbled backwards and crashed into Nick. His lean fingers dug into her upper arm. The driver muttered in heavily accented French.

Nick loosened his grip and shouted a response. She wrenched free and ran, too terrified to question why Nicholson had suddenly appeared or why he would want to shove her into a strange car. Footsteps pounded behind her. She glanced back.

The blue Lincoln merged into the eddy of traffic on Sherbrooke Street and disappeared from view. Nicholson followed her a short distance behind.

"Breanna! Wait!"

Weaving between pedestrians on the crowded sidewalk, she rounded the corner of Marc Street. A bad omen. Nick reached her, grabbed her arm, his urgent expression stifling her urge to scream and break away again. Flattening herself against a building, she tried to catch her breath, tried to stop trembling.

"I didn't realize I had this effect on you." Nick's teasing words were uttered with deadly seriousness. He rested his palm on the brick, his face close to hers.

Breanna snapped. His sudden presence, the tension of the trip, the worry about Gayle, escaped like an over-wound jack-in-the-box suddenly set free. She clenched her hand and swung, punching him in the ribs. His breath escaped in a rush.

"You son of a bitch! What are you doing here, sneaking up behind me, trying to stuff me into that car!"

"The hell I was. At first I just wanted to catch your

attention, but it took all of two seconds to see what was going on back there. Getting into that Lincoln would have been the last thing you did voluntarily. Any chance you saw who was in the car?"

"No." A chill rose along her bare arms despite the late afternoon warmth. Her legs buckled, and she felt herself sink.

Nick's arm went around her shoulders, and he pulled her against him. Breanna buried her face in her hands and took several deep breaths, subduing her apprehension and distrust.

She'd checked him out, she knew she should trust him, and right now it was all she had. His cotton shirt felt cool against her hands. A musky scent filled her senses and for a few moments, she forgot her anger and longed for Scott and the smell of sunshiny woods and smoke chips.

"Why were you getting into that car anyway?" Nick's words admonished, but his voice was soft and husky.

She felt a resurgence of anger, edged away and brushed a stray lock of hair from her face. "I thought it was my ride back to the hotel until you showed up."

"In the nick of time," he said.

Breanna winced, but she smiled. "A joke, Nick. I didn't know you had one in you."

"There's a lot you don't know about me, but you must know I can be trusted."

"Do I have a choice?"

He shook his head. "What's been happening?"

She took a deep breath. "All day I've been hoping Gayle would come back. You were the last person I expected to see."

"I don't know why." Nick smiled with his usual cool professionalism, but something else burned in his eyes. "I've always liked jazz."

Breanna looked away, flustered and confused. "I know you didn't come for the Jazz Festival. What are you doing here?"

He ignored her question. "Why are you worried about Gayle? Where is she?"

She spread her hands. "That's just it. I don't know. She left yesterday afternoon to see her family, and I haven't heard from her since."

Nick cupped her elbow and steered her toward St. Catherine Street. "Montreal is filled with interesting little sidewalk cafes. Let's find one and have some coffee. Preferably one that serves it with brandy. You're going to need it after I finish telling you everything I've uncovered about Gayle Montclair Lanier."

Breanna swirled a swizzle stick in a tower of whipped cream and fought the sense of panic and outrage she felt at Nick's latest information dump. She pictured Gayle, sipping coffee in her office, trying to offer sympathy over Marc's death, all the while plotting against Breanna, wondering about the fate of her own husband.

Gregory Lanier.

She pressed her hand against her forehead. Was no one who they seemed to be?

"I haven't even found Marc's mysterious brother and now you tell me my assistant is really my sister-in-law." She sipped the cafe au lait, laced liberally with French brandy. It burned a path down her throat. "What other good news do you have for me? Found out what Lucas Brogan is up to and how he fits into the mess my life has become?"

"Can't say which side of the fence he's working. I'll let you know when I can."

She wondered if he meant he didn't know, or wouldn't tell. The air around them was filled with sounds of cars and conversations held in soft French. Light breezes ruffled her hair, flapped the green and white stripped awning overhead.

A romantic city, a romantic place, but Breanna shivered and rubbed her arms. She longed for somewhere familiar. Somewhere safe. Somewhere with Scott.

Nick leaned back in the white wrought iron chair. "Now you understand why I couldn't take the chance you'd go exploring the city with her. And knowing who she really is, there's no telling what she's capable of once she suspects the truth about the yacht explosion."

Breanna tightened her grip on the crystal coffee mug. "Tell

me, please, and get it over with. He's alive, isn't he?"

Nick tapped a finger on the glass-topped table. "Not likely. At least we still don't have any reason to believe that. I think Marc had a rendezvous with his brother. Some of the wreckage retrieved suggests that another boat went down. Given a little more time, the Coast Guard might find another body. But I came to Montreal to try and prove your husband's dead, one way or another."

She vaguely remembered hearing voices on the yacht but hesitated telling Nick. Too many questions, and he'd suspect she hadn't told him everything.

But she couldn't tell him what Marc had tried to do to her. She couldn't. "How do you plan to do that?"

"Dental records. Too bad they can't do DNA testing, but since all of Marc's personal belongings are gone, we can't even get our hands on skin or hair samples. I've got contacts with the Canadian authorities, though. A few favors owed me."

Breanna shook her head trying to dispel the sense that the digital photos Captain Belcastro had shown her were a stranger, not her husband. It had to be Marc. There was no other logical explanation.

"It was Marc," she murmured and avoided Nick's eyes. "But I have to know for sure."

She watched passersby, ladies dressed in designer fashions, businessmen hurrying with end-of-the-day hustle. People leading normal lives. Would she ever be able to do that again?

She turned her attention back to Nick. "And what about your previous life, Mr. Nicholson? You don't act like a burned out cop turned private investigator."

Green eyes twinkled, and he looked amused. "You're right. So what would you guess?"

Breanna surveyed his navy suit and blue tie. "One hundred percent government employee, right down to your conserveative socks."

He threw his head back and laughed. "Guess you can take the man out of the Bureau but you'll never take the Bureau out of the man. What's wrong with the way I dress?"

"Absolutely nothing. If you're trying to melt into a crowd or win over a grandmother. But while we're here, just for fun, I'd like to take you shopping. Mariette told me there are some great boutiques along rues St. Laurent and St. Denis."

"Whatever makes you happy. Because for the rest of the week, consider me your bodyguard. Wherever you go, I go."

Her eyes met his. The brandy curled languorously through her. "If I didn't know better, I'd say that sounds like a proposition, Nick."

His gaze flickered to the hollow of her throat and back to her face. "I already told you. There's a lot about me you don't know. Yet."

With Gayle's disappearance less than forty-eight hours old, the Montreal Police politely refused to offer any assistance, but Nick somehow convinced the hotel manager to allow them into Gayle's room. Breanna looked around the immaculate space. Not even her toothbrush remained.

Nick whistled. "Almost looks like the place has been swept clean. I'd bet there's not so much as a stray hair."

Breanna pushed aside the sheer curtains and watched the traffic several stories below. Sighing, she turned away and circled the room again. "Give me a professional opinion. What does this mean to you?"

Nick closed a drawer in the elegant cherry wood desk. "Same thing you're thinking. When she left yesterday she had no intention of coming back."

Breanna shuddered. "Or someone wants me to believe that."

"Exactly. Maybe now you understand why I think you can't be too careful. Let's get out of here and have some dinner."

"Fine." She wasn't hungry and doubted she'd be able to swallow around the tension constricting her throat, but the hotel closed around her, unfamiliar and suffocating.

Nick produced a bottle of wine and insisted on taking Breanna to a Greek restaurant on Prince Arthur Street. Since Ambrosius' was only half a mile from the Four Seasons, they decided to walk. Breanna hoped the exercise and the soft summer night would stir her appetite for dinner. At the same time she felt apprehensive about spending time with Nick. Although she needed his protection and wanted some companionship, she couldn't forget the fact that his friendly motives were bound to be double edged.

Late Tuesday afternoon, Scott dropped the wrench into the toolbox and wiped his hands on a greasy rag. Finally, after two days of tinkering and scrambling for parts, the *Liquid Asset* was ready for the trip back to Duluth. Cosmetic repairs to the hull would have to wait until he got back to town. No way did Grand Portage or even Grand Marais have the resources, and he sure didn't have the time to wait, anyway.

The generator had been deliberately sabotaged. There was no other explanation for the melted mass of wires in the fuse box. He wondered who had access to the boat. Despite the hostility between him and his older brother, he didn't want to accept the idea that Derek would want him permanently out of the way. Or was willing to kill off innocent strangers at the same time.

Fortunately, none of the passengers suffered more than inconvenience from their unplanned stop at Isle Royale Saturday after several hours spent in the worst lake storm Scott had ever experienced. He'd made arrangements for them all on the Voyageur II for Sunday morning. At dawn, he'd bummed a ride with a fisherman bound for Grand Portage twenty miles away on the Minnesota shore, hoping to call Breanna and stop her crazy trip to Canada.

He slammed the lid shut on the toolbox. Breanna and her damn stubbornness. He wished the phone connections, erratic from the storm, hadn't fizzled Sunday morning. No telling where she was when he'd called and he hadn't been able to reach her again. Even Murray was conveniently out of touch. Scott didn't know how to find her in Montreal, short of calling every hotel in the city. Or going after her.

He refueled the boat, planning to spend the night on board and depart early Wednesday morning. Engines buzzed as the

Isle Royale Seaplane Service prepared for departure from Rock Harbor. The red and gold plane lifted off, banked and turned south, headed toward Houghton, Michigan.

Memories of waking to pink streaked clouds, a misty lake and the explosion of the *Breanna Colleen* ten days before sent his mind whirling.

Something nagged at the edges of his mind. Lanier and Derek. How they got their stolen merchandise into Canada. Why Derek seemed so unconcerned about Lanier's death.

Maybe Breanna's instincts were right and Lanier wasn't dead after all. And Derek knew.

With nothing to gain and everything to lose by wasting any more time on the wilderness island, Scott unfastened the moorings, revved the engine and sped away from the marina.

Wednesday morning Breanna called Duluth and listened to the phone ring at her house. Maybe since she was gone, Scott had decided to go back to his own place. She redialed, but there was no answer at his house either. He was probably at the fishery, but no way would she take a chance on talking to Derek. Just remembering her visit with Scott's brother made her feel like she needed to take a bath and burn her clothes.

That afternoon, Breanna and Nick walked to the front desk at the Four Seasons. She rested her arms atop the marble counter. "Any messages for me?"

"One moment, Madame. I'll check." He handed her a sealed hotel envelope. "Just this."

She murmured a thank you and turned away. Nick peered over her shoulder.

"Who's it from?"

Breanna hurried to the elevators, feeling a need to open the envelope in private. "Gayle."

Nick stuck to her like a burr, following her into her room and taking a seat at the leather-topped desk. Breanna sank down on the love seat and carefully pried open the letter written in Gayle's familiar handwriting.

"Breanna, I apologize for leaving like this. I never wanted

to cause problems for you. Please believe that. The family situation is much worse than I suspected. Circumstances dictate that I not return to Duluth with you. Since I had only booked a couple of appointments for you, next week should be quiet. After that, everything could hit. Check costumes. I should have told you about tarnished stars. I regret if I put you in a tight spot. Gayle."

Silently she handed the letter over to Nick. He scanned it and handed it back. "Any idea what she means about the studio?"

Breanna folded the letter and stuffed it into her tote bag. "None."

"Does it sound like she wrote it?"

Breanna shrugged. "It's definitely her handwriting, but—"

His eyes rested intently on her face. "But, what?"

"I have the worst feeling she's trying to tell me something important, and right now, I can't see what it is."

Thursday and Friday passed uneventfully at the gallery. She still hadn't reached Scott. With the letter from Gayle, and no evidence she'd been taken against her will, The Royal Canadian Police could not offer help.

True to his promise, Nick stayed with Breanna throughout the day, somehow managing to make his constant presence at the gallery unobtrusive to everyone but her.

At night, he occupied the room next door. She had the bizarre thought that gargling would bring him smashing through the door for fear she was being strangled. His constant presence was like a wool blanket, occasionally comforting, but mostly irritating and restrictive.

By Friday evening, bustling Montreal increased its hum with the beginning of the Jazz Festival. Breanna looked down at the street below the hotel and tapped her foot impatiently. "Come on, Nick, it's been a long, frazzling week. We've done nothing except go from gallery to hotel all week. I need to get out before I implode."

Nick hesitated. "I don't think that's good idea. Too many things can happen in a crowd."

Too many things could happen due to proximity and

claustrophobia, too. Nick might get ideas she didn't want him to have, and she might choke him out of the increasing frustration she felt about being watched like a bug under glass.

"I might never get another chance to be here."

He held his hands up. "All right, all right. But we're not staying out late. And I intend to stick to you like glue."

A short time later, they stood shoulder to shoulder with the crowd along the square at rue St. Denis. She'd never been to a street concert before. The rich brass sound of saxophones and trumpets resonated against the dark stone buildings.

Breanna's spirits lifted, and she clapped her hands with the other onlookers, caught up in the tempo of an old Charlie Parker tune.

Her skin tingled. The hair rose on her nape. She glanced toward a sycamore tree on the far side of the square. A man lounged against it, a black felt hat pulled low, casting his eyes into shadow. Marc's height, similar build, but clean-shaven.

She looked away, shuddering as memories of Marc's moustache, rough as a wire scrub brush against her skin made her stomach constrict. He was dead. Dead!

She glanced back. The man was gone. She let her breath out in an uneasy rush. Apparently caught up in the music, Nick hadn't noticed. The song ended in a blaze of clarinets and sax amidst thunderous applause.

He smiled down at her. "Pretty spectacular, isn't it?"

Still caught up in the fear of a moment ago, she could only nod.

"How about some ice cream?"

"Okay."

He took her arm and guided her over to the opposite sidewalk and a street vendor's cart. "What would you like?"

"Rocky Road." She said the first flavor that came to mind, while she scanned the nearby crowd. The dark stranger was nowhere to be seen.

Nick laughed. "I imagine that's a little too American. You might have to settle for French vanilla."

"Whatever," she murmured. Chill bumps formed along her arms. The mystery-man now stood at least a room's length away, but despite the distance she could feel his gaze crawling over her.

Nick handed her a cone of vanilla. "So what do you think?"

She took a cautious bite of the ice cream but didn't notice the taste. "This is fine."

Nick gave her a searching look. "I meant the concert. Something wrong?"

Breanna tore her eyes away from the stranger and gave the detective her brightest smile. "I've never been a jazz fan, but this is interesting."

Nick took her arm, and they started walking slowly along the crowded sidewalk. A leaden sensation pressed against the back of her head. She glanced over her shoulder.

He was following, although he remained some distance behind. She nibbled on the cone, but it tasted like an old shoebox. Ice cream dribbled down her fingers until finally she pitched the cone in a nearby trashcan. She smiled apologetically at Nick. "Sorry, I guess I'm really not hungry."

He stopped. "All right. Out with it. What's wrong?"

Seeking security, she laced her arm through his and darted a look behind. From several yards away, the man's dark eyes snapped like hot coals. Summoning every reason Nick had given to trust him, she moved closer and whispered, "I have the strongest feeling we're being followed."

"Are you sure? It's quite a crush of people here."

She wet her lips. "He...he looks a lot like Marc."

"Where?" Nick turned slightly and surveyed the street behind him, though his actions seemed to indicate his interest focused on Breanna.

"The man in the dark hat." She turned. The stranger was gone. She shrugged and laughed nervously. "I don't see him now. My mistake, but he looked like I imagine Marc would have without his moustache."

Nick smiled tenderly down at her and touched her chandelier-style earrings. "Breanna, he's dead. I've checked out every port he could have gone to, if it had been possible for him to get off the yacht."

"He was staring at me."

"I imagine that happens more often than you're aware of. You're a very attractive lady. But if you're uncomfortable, we can go back to the hotel now."

She murmured acquiescence, and they walked several streets over to hail a cab. Nick talked about different jazz artists and learning to like the music when he'd done a long assignment in New Orleans some years back.

Once in the cab, she stifled the impulse to watch the traffic behind them, and if Nick did, she couldn't tell. At the Four Seasons, a valet held the door of the cab open.

Nick paid the cabby. One of the heavy turquoise and purple shoulder duster earrings she wore caught on her purse strap. She jerked the leather band, yanking the clip free and sending the earring splattering to the ground. She bent to retrieve it.

Straightening, she glanced across the broad street. The man stood on the other side. The light evening breeze ruffled black hair before he jammed a hat over it. Breanna's insides turned to ice, but before she could catch Nick's attention, the man walked away and disappeared around the corner. Without looking back, she hurried into the hotel.

Chapter 21

Scott spent Tuesday evening at Murray's Bar, trying to coerce, beg, and bargain Breanna's hotel number from her uncle. To no avail.

"And I'm telling you, she's fine." Murray refused to say anything else and moved off to wait on the back booth section of the bar.

Scott caught Spencer's sympathetic gaze on him, but Murray kept his assistant hustling until the bar closed, ruining any chance Scott might have had of getting information from him.

At two a.m. Murray ushered Scott out and started to close the door behind him. Scott wedged his foot into the opening. "One last time, Murray. Why won't you tell me where she's staying?"

"Because I know you won't give her a moment's peace. She needs some time alone. Some space to get herself back together."

"Did she say that?"

Murray scowled. "Not exactly. But I think it's best. And it's no use asking Spencer where she is. He doesn't know, either. Why don't you try Nicholson?" Murray practically chortled as Scott withdrew his foot and turned away.

He had to leave before Murray's misplaced over-protectiveness pushed his temper over the edge.

Nicholson. The idea of having to ask him about Breanna's whereabouts made Scott want to punch his suspicious face in, then drive to Montreal and shake answers from Breanna.

Why she left. Why she didn't leave word on where she was. Why she hadn't called.

Wednesday morning he arrived at the fishery ready to do battle with Derek only to discover his brother had left early

Tuesday for a three day trip to Copper Harbor. With the crews needing instructions, and a day's worth of work for the smoker, Scott had no time to use the opportunity presented by Derek's absence to go through the papers and books in his private office. His locked private office.

Night came before he finally had the warehouse to himself. After picking the padlock on the small room Derek had commandeered as his office, Scott rifled through the unorganized mass of papers atop the scratched metal desk and jammed into drawers. No wonder Derek had arrogantly declared the financial aspects of the business off limits to Scott. But their father had quietly urged his youngest son to discover what Derek was up to, no matter what methods he had to employ. At the very least, Derek was guilty of mismanagement. At the worst...Scott shrugged.

He picked up the heavy adding machine and almost dropped it on his foot. There, mixed in with scraps of paper containing scrawled phone numbers and names, was a picture of Breanna. The picture that must conclude the five photos Scott had found in the microwave oven at her apartment.

What the hell was Derek doing with it?

He swallowed and wondered how Breanna had stayed with a man as twisted as Marc Lanier. Gazing at her dressed up in silk and lace like Christmas at the Marquis de Sade's made him feel like the worst kind of peeper. Torn between shock and fascination, he slid the five by six picture in his jacket pocket. No way was he going to let his brother continue to hold it.

He rechecked the desk drawers. Crammed between a sheaf of papers was a bound book similar to the one he and Breanna had found at Lanier's warehouse the night of the fire. He sat down and riffled through the pages. Numbers, some sort of code. Handwriting that didn't match Derek's, other scrawled notes in his brother's hand.

The notes forced another memory. Returning early from fishing one day. Finding Derek scrambling around the brick wall behind the smoker. Scott jumped up, and took the stairs down two at a time. On the back wall, he ran his fingers over the bricks. Counting, trying to remember. His fingers scraped across a small crack. He wiggled the brick, so intent on his task he didn't hear sounds behind him until it was too late.

He started to turn. Pain exploded in the back of his head and the room turned black.

Breanna snapped the lock shut and latched the security chain. Despite Nick's presence in the next room, she couldn't shake her cold fear of the stranger across the street.

Coincidence, that was all. Besides, she couldn't be certain it was the same man. In a city with such a rich French heritage, probably half the male population had dark eyes and hair.

She was paranoid, overreacting to Gayle's disappearance, and all the bizarre events of the past two weeks.

She tried calling Scott again at her own house. No answer, and she'd disconnected the answering machine before she left, concerned about receiving either more threatening calls or hearing from nosy reporters.

The hotel had left a complimentary bottle of wine on the coffee table. Breanna retrieved a cork screw from the mini-bar, pried the seal and cork from the bottle, poured a glass and drank half of it, then refilled it while she drew a bath.

She lay back in the tub, bubbles up to her neck, and closed her eyes. Tired beyond reason, she wished she could relax and reached for the wine glass. Without her glasses on, she misjudged and brushed the goblet stem. The glass teetered, then smashed against the white tile floor. Burgundy seeped across the floor and saturated the snowy monogrammed bath mat.

Great. So much for relaxation. She stepped gingerly from the tub, wrapped herself in a terry cloth robe and began cleaning up the mess. Shards of glass and sand lay in a cranberry puddle. Carefully picking up the broken glass, she dabbed a finger in the wine and rubbed the grains against her palm. The grit dissolved.

Breanna tensed. It wasn't sand. Even if it was, how would it have gotten on her bathroom floor? What was it?

She leapt up, memories of Marc's favorite Cabernet and his insistence she drink it on the yacht filling her with alarm.

Using a napkin, she picked up the wine bottle. Dark hued glass made it impossible to discern anything wrong. Grabbing another goblet, she poured and held it to the light. The wine sparkled like garnets.

She considered dialing Nick's room and getting a professional opinion and finally discarded the idea. He'd say she was hysterical, and he'd be right. She'd tell him in the morning. She dialed housekeeping instead.

Breanna relocked the door behind the maid and set the safety chain in place. It wasn't enough.

It would take fifteen locks and a Bengal tiger standing watch to make her feel safe, but every little bit helped.

She dragged a heavy wingback chair over and placed it against the door.

She got in bed and turned off the light, but the room was too dark, too eerily shadowy without her glasses on. She snapped on the bathroom light and left the door ajar, then opened the draperies on the balcony door. Soft light glowed through the sheer curtains, partially illuminating the room. Once settled in bed, she tried to relax and keep her eyes closed and away from the door.

Finally, she drifted into a twilight sleep.

She awakened sometime later to a soft click, like a lock being painstakingly turned. Her senses hummed, trying to discern sounds in the quiet. The bedside clock glowed in fuzzy digits. She reached for her glasses and knocked them off the nightstand.

A slice of light banded the door. She grabbed the phone and pressed zero. Metal snapped. Grayish light grew larger. With no time to wait for a response from the operator, she dropped the receiver and scrambled off the bed.

The door thudded against the chair. She heard a muffled curse.

She had to find a way out. She darted to the sliding glass door, fumbled with the latch, and yanked it open just as the wing back chair scraped across the carpet. A cool breeze billowed the sheer curtains as she shrank behind the heavy linen draperies.

Footsteps resounded faintly on the tiled bathroom floor, then the room darkened. Someone moved across the carpet, paused near the bed. She tried to slow her breathing and the furious pounding of her heart. A man's voice murmured an apology in French. The telephone clattered on the nightstand.

Breanna held her breath as footsteps came closer, hesitated. The curtains slid back and a figure stepped through to the balcony. She quickly shoved the door shut. The man whirled around as the lock clicked.

Inches away and yet she couldn't see his face, only a black shape with hollowed out eyes. Metal glinted in the dim light as he raised his arm. She turned to run as the door exploded in a shower of glass from the force of his blow.

Hit by flying glass, she screamed. Her legs stung.

He lunged through the door opening, caught a fistful of her sleep shirt and fell. Fabric tore with a hiss. She sprawled headlong, then scrambled to her knees. Glass bit into her palms as she scooted away from his cruel grasp and backed into the coffee table.

A spicy citrus scent assailed her nostrils. White teeth flashed a terrifying grin.

Dear God, no. It couldn't be.

Breanna's fingers closed around the wine bottle and smashed it against the side of his head.

He grunted and collapsed on top of her, pinning her legs to the floor. In renewed panic, she wriggled away, crunched over broken glass with her bare feet and ran out into the hallway.

The lights nearest her room were out, and she stumbled down the dimly lit hall, leaving a trail of glass and blood on her way to the elevator. As she rounded the hall corner, she squinted over her shoulder. The intruder staggered from her room. His face, covered with a ski mask, looked so grotesque, she screamed again.

She ran to the stairway. On the opposite wall an enormous burled walnut armoire used for storing fresh linens and towels rose nearly to the ceiling. After slamming the stairwell door shut, she hurriedly slipped inside the half empty linen cabinet and held her breath.

Footsteps approached, hesitated. She heard the elevator ping through the blood pounding in her ears. Voices came closer. A door slammed shut nearby. She prayed it was the stairwell. Footsteps faded.

She waited, straining her ears for sounds of the man's return, hoping someone, anyone would discover her room a shambles. Where was Nick? Her hands and feet throbbed. Glass prickled her neck. The dark enclosure pressed in. Hot tears pooled in her eyes, but she swallowed hard and fought hysteria.

Home. She wanted to go home. The thought only brought more despair when she realized she no longer had one, no longer had a family except for Murray.

If only she'd never met Marc Lanier. If only she hadn't been so stubborn, so selfish. If only she hadn't chosen him over everything and everyone else, she wouldn't be bleeding and hiding in a closet in a strange hotel, in a strange city.

And maybe her mother, her father and Brett would still be alive.

She wasn't sure how long she huddled inside the cabinet, but the need to get out became stronger than her fear. The need to escape the hotel overwhelmed reason. She had no idea how much time had passed, but she returned to the wreckage of her room, and groped near the bed until she found her glasses. She hurriedly put on shoes, pulled a turquoise raincoat over her torn gown, threw a few loose items in her bags and left.

Nick certainly had proven himself less than useful. Where in the world was he when she needed him the most?

The elevator door opened on the lobby and a uniformed security guard. His hands clutching a cup of coffee, he gaped at her.

"Mademoiselle Alden! You're not leaving!"

She gave him a cold look and glanced at his name tag. Police and security. Mutually exclusive words. "Any reason why that's a problem?"

"But it's three a.m. Mr. Nicholson will be back soon and I promised to look out for you."

She brushed past him. "So meet him in my room and you can show him what a fine job you did, Ducette. And then tell him I'm not coming back."

The valet hailed a cab for her. Breanna climbed inside and gave the driver the address of the only person she knew in Montreal, Mariette Marcel.

A short time later, Mariette opened the door of a granite row house in a quaint residential section of the city near Old Montreal. She brushed a wedge of dark hair away from her cheek and regarded Breanna with a sleepy look.

"Must have been quite a night, eh? Your friend try to show you all the joie de vivre in the city?"

Breanna set her garment bag down on the stone step. "Mariette, I'm so sorry to bother you like this. But I have to leave on the first flight out to Minneapolis, or Chicago. Whatever I can get. And I have nowhere to go until then."

Mariette bent and picked up the bag, straightened and linked her arm through Breanna's. "Poor thing," she murmured and made sympathetic sounds as she guided her inside. "Of course, you can stay with me. And then I can talk you out of this foolishness. If you and Monsieur Nick had a fight, he will apologize, I am certain."

"It's much more complicated than that, I'm afraid." Breanna searched for a reasonable explanation for her middle of the night appearance. She limped across the hallway and winced as she set down the small suitcase.

Mariette glanced down at her feet and seized her wrist. "Mon Dieu! What on earth did you do to your hands?"

Breanna flushed, but met the gallery owner's gaze as Mariette surveyed her disheveled appearance. "I guess you could say I killed a bottle of wine."

Scott woke to a pounding pain in his head and Kowalski's gin-laced breath in his face.

The middle-aged foreman gripped his shoulder and shook. "Scott, wake up. Wake up!"

Red lights swirled, zipped past. Scott rubbed his eyes, and

gingerly felt the back of his head. "What the hell is going on?"

Kowalski sat back in the driver's seat of his rusted pickup and rested rough hands on his knees. "Gas leak. Fire department hasn't got it sealed off yet. Lucky I happened to show up when I did. Found you passed out near the smoker. Guess the fumes got to you before you even knew it."

Scott grimaced. "Not unless they hit like a lead pipe. Any chance you saw someone else here?"

"Don't think so." The foreman glanced away.

"Why are you here?" Scott glanced at his watch. Midnight A good four hours since the last fisherman had left for the day.

Kowalski shifted in his seat. "I, ah, left my lunch bucket. Wife would give me no end of hell if I showed up at home without it."

Scott reached under the pickup seat and pulled out a paper bag wrapped bottle. "If you say so, Ernie. Now, why don't you search that well preserved brain of yours and tell me what you saw, and then we'll see what we can do about your domestic problems."

Chapter 22

Kowalski pounded his fists on the steering wheel. "Damn it, Mr. Edwards, I haven't done nothing illegal." Obviously defensive and sullen, he sank lower into the seat.

Scott considered the man. Ernie Kowalski had been an employee of Edwards and Sons Fishing Enterprises for as long as Scott could remember. When Scott had returned to the business four months ago, the man's drinking problem caught his immediate attention. But his father insisted that Ernie was "good people" and urged his son to cut the man some slack, so long as the business wasn't jeopardized.

And it hadn't been until the past few weeks when Kowalski had become increasingly unreliable. Especially on payday when he'd disappear late morning and be gone the remainder of the day. Oddly enough, Derek ignored it all.

"Take it easy, Ernie. Tell you what. My head feels as battered as a hockey puck, and I never did eat supper. Looks like it'll be a while before the fire department will let me back in that building. Let's go grab a bite. But I'll drive."

A short time later, Scott slid into a cracked red vinyl booth at West End Truck Stop and ordered two coffees. The waitress tucked a scraggly strand of blonde hair behind one ear and scribbled their breakfast order. Kowalski gripped his coffee cup as if it held a formula for eternal life and gulped. Under the harsh lights of the cafe, he looked at least fifteen years older than his fifty-five years.

After the food arrived, satisfied that the foreman had sobered up somewhat, Scott scooped up a mouthful of half cooked eggs and grimaced. "What's Derek got on you, Ernie?" he asked quietly.

Kowalski's eyes glistened with tears, and he held his hands

out. "At my age, with my record, I'd never be able to get another job. I've still got one kid at home, another drifts through when she's between husbands, leaving us with the grandbaby. Your brother found out I like to have a drink now and again. Said he'd can me if I didn't make myself useful."

"Just how useful have you been?"

"You have to know, I'd never hurt anyone. Don't matter what it cost me. Derek just said we'd scare her off, that's all. I didn't set that fire, didn't know the police would find a body there. Come to think of it, don't think Derek knew about her, either. I don't think he's got the stomach for murder."

Gutless in every way, Scott thought. Even in crime, fortunately. "You mean it was you and Derek shooting at us at Lanier's warehouse?"

"Just Derek." Kowalski tore off a hunk of toast. He chewed for a few moments. "I thought Derek was going to shoot his foot off before he got a shot close enough to keep you running without looking back. Whatever your brother was hunting for, he didn't find. So he sent me home and took care no one else would find it either."

Kowalski rested his elbows on the table and leaned forward. "I want out of this mess. Whatever your brother's into, I want out. I told him that, too, when I followed Miss Alden around for a couple of days and caught someone else doing the same thing."

Scott set his cup down. Suddenly the air in the diner was leaden and hard to breathe. "Any chance you know who it was?"

"You bet. Same guy I saw leaving the fishery tonight. I dozed off, woke up and saw a white Ford sedan driving away. He works the docks. I seen him there a few times. His name is Lucas Brogan."

Scott lay on his back on the lumpy mattress in his father's spare bedroom and stared at a dark circle on the ceiling. He believed Kowalski had told him the truth. At least as much as he knew of it.

Scott had a lot of experience lately with half truths, and wished he'd taken a chance and told Breanna about Derek. The story he'd given his father had been carefully edited, containing just Derek's indiscretions and disinterest in paperwork at the fishery. He couldn't accuse his brother of arson and maybe murder until he had more proof than Kowalski's earnest wish to save his own skin.

He rolled onto his side. Somehow sleeping on Breanna's damask sofa was a lot more comfortable. And the fantasies were better, fueled by possibilities when she was only a few urgent footsteps away.

Breanna. The curve of her face. Her silken skin.

He loved her, had for years, probably always would.

To be near her and be only her friend was driving him crazy. Half aroused, his thoughts drifted to what he wanted to happen when she returned from Montreal.

Other thoughts intruded. Her dark life married to Lanier. He rolled off the couch and dug into his jacket pocket. Alarmed, he checked the other pocket. Then rechecked.

The picture of Breanna was gone.

Thursday was a headache from start to finish. Scott had a knot on the back of his head, a nagging pain between his brows, and total chaos at the fishery. Per their agreement, Ernie Kowalski was on sick leave.

Which meant the union rep acted like a pregnant woman on her third day of labor. Scott finally had to take the crew out himself, leaving their nineteen year old receptionist in charge of deliveries and telephone calls.

Despite good weather conditions on the lake, they made a light haul and came back late. Scott found a stack of messages on his desk. Suppliers demanding payment. Customers demanding delivery. The IRS demanding money. Digging through the mess of papers on Derek's desk, he frowned.

Business had been good since spring. What was his brother doing with their cash flow?

Scott secured the doors and again tackled the job of finding a hiding place in the brick wall of the smoker. After an hour's careful search, he finally found the niche. Empty.

He spent that night at his father's as well, certain that Derek wouldn't want anything to happen to Harvey. Besides, it gave Scott a chance to keep an eye on his dad himself. He scowled as Harvey, permanently disabled from lung cancer, lit yet another Marlboro.

"You told me you'd quit."

Harvey looked sheepish. "I gave it a shot, but Derek dumped a whole case on me last week as a Father's Day present." His expression turned defensive. "Hell, at least he appreciates the fact that I've got few pleasures left in this life."

Scott picked up the pack and examined it. A whole case. How unlike Derek. "Where did you store them?" He bounded off the couch and headed toward the basement of the small frame house.

"Hall closet," his father hollered. "Basement's too damp."

The closet overflowed with red and black cartons of Marlboros. Scott carefully checked the cartons. Couldn't be a coincidence that it was the same brand of cigarettes he and Breanna had found at the warehouse last Monday night. Leave it to Derek not to pass up the opportunity for freebies.

Harvey switched channels to the Twins game, and Scott nodded off, his head thrown back against the worn upholstery of the ancient couch. He awakened to hear his father hanging up the telephone.

"Pretty late for a phone call, Dad. One of those wild widows wanting to tuck you in?"

His dad grinned and shuffled to his recliner. "Laugh if you want to, but that one was for you. Didn't know if you wanted anyone to know you were here, and I hated to wake you, you looked so tuckered out."

Suddenly wide awake, Scott's fingers dug into the arms of the couch. "So who was it?"

Harvey Edwards gave his son a quizzical look. "Don't you look like someone just pressed your on button. It was the Alden girl. What in the devil is she wanting from you after all this time?"

Scott spent a restless night, alternating between elation and exasperation. Breanna wanted to talk, but not enough to leave a number, and she didn't call back. He arrived at the Fishery shortly after dawn. Men clustered together in small groups in the parking lot.

Strange, the assistant foreman had a key and usually everyone was on their second cup of coffee by the time he or Derek handed out the day's schedules. He climbed from the jeep and strode up the steps. Men followed, and formed a silent knot at the bottom of the stairs leading to the loading dock.

Scott stared at the padlocks securing the doors. Bright stickers plastered peeling green doors. Property of U.S. Government.

Mountains of untouched paperwork on Derek's desk tumbled through his mind. The IRS. Government at its worst.

When Derek screwed up, he didn't fool around about it.

He had no choice but to tell his father before a Treasury Agent showed up at Harvey's house. After dismissing the workers with what he knew sounded like empty promises, he drove back to his father's small house on Water Street.

A white Ford sat out front. Scott bounded up the steps and found Lucas Brogan inside.

Brogan flashed a government ID and a counterfeit smile. "As I was telling Mr. Edwards, I need to get in touch with your brother."

"Derek's out of town. I'm not sure when he'll be back." Scott surveyed Brogan. "How about presenting that ID again? This time so I can really see it."

He examined the picture and identification card. Looked real, so why did he doubt Brogan's story? What rock had he crawled out from under? Why was he also interested enough in Breanna to be following her around? He handed the wallet back. "My father hasn't been involved in the business for nearly two years. Anything I can help you with?"

Brogan's eyes were as cold and hard as Lake Superior in January. "You better hope not or we'll have to book you a real nice room downtown, too. Your brother's been exceptionally uncooperative. I've put a tax lien on all the assets of Edwards and Sons Fishing Enterprises. I don't think you'll be fishing anytime soon."

After a round of probing questions for which Scott had few answers, Brogan finally left. Hoping for the relief of fresh air, Scott opened the living room windows.

Harvey stared into space, his forehead creased. "How come you didn't tell me things were this bad?"

He sat down across from his dad. "I didn't know. Derek's kept everything under locks."

His dad looked up. Smoky gray eyes snapped with a familiar fire. "Find him. And when you've finished kicking his ass from one side of town to the other, let Brogan have him."

By an oversight, probably because of the fact that the fishing boat was dry docked for hull repairs, the *Liquid Asset* had escaped the levy. With the work completed late Friday morning, Scott re-launched the boat and headed for Copper Harbor.

Derek was nowhere to be found. The tour operators he'd supposedly been subcontracting for hadn't seen him in weeks. By the time Scott returned to Duluth, darkness shrouded the harbor. He berthed the boat in the Alden's empty slip that had once housed the *Breanna Colleen* and headed straight to Murray's bar.

Scott drummed his fingers on the wood rail and waited for Murray to take a break. He eluded Scott's questions until time for the bar to close, then refilled Scott's beer schooner and took one himself. Settling onto the next stool, Murray took a long draught of Old Style and sighed.

"So what kind of sad story are you going to give me tonight, Edwards?"

Scott scowled. "If I tell you who Lucas Brogan really is, will you give me Breanna's phone number so I can call her and tell her not to worry when she gets back here Sunday?"

Murray shrugged. "I'll be glad to pass along a message."

Scott slammed a fist on the bar. "Damn it, Murray. What's with you? If she really didn't want to talk to me, then why did she try to reach me at my dad's last night?"

For the first time that week, a look of uncertainty flashed in

Murray's eyes. "She called you?"

"Yeah, so lighten up and give me a break."

Murray sighed and went behind the bar to the cash register. He returned with a slip of paper and handed it to Scott. "Nicholson's been there since Tuesday. They're at the Four Seasons. Here's the number."

Breanna and Nicholson. Scott swallowed an angry retort and felt it settle like a hot coal in his gut. Snatching the note from Murray, he hurried to the phone and made the call even though he knew it was 2 a.m. in Montreal. The hotel operator came back on the line.

"I am sorry, Monsieur, that line is busy. Would you like to hold?"

He said no and hung up. Trying again a few minutes later yielded the same results. Who the hell could she be talking to at 2 o'clock in the morning? He gave up and left the bar. Back at his father's he called again. This time there was no answer.

Where was she? If she were someplace with that smart ass detective.... He reminded himself that Breanna had repeatedly said Nicholson made her uneasy. Maybe something was wrong. He asked the operator to connect him with the desk clerk and waited on hold. Interminable moments later, the man came back.

"I'm sorry, Monsiuer. Mademoiselle Alden has checked out and left the hotel."

Chapter 23

Although Mariette skillfully fielded Nick's phone calls, Breanna knew he'd soon be on his way over. No doubt to convince her to stay in Montreal till Sunday. She shuddered.

One more day would be three too many. She left for the airport as soon as the morning clouds turned pink with early light.

Nick caught up just before Breanna boarded a flight to Chicago. She yanked her arm from the insistent pressure of his hand on her elbow. Trust him to get through security.

"Breanna, you can't leave now. Alone."

She straightened. "You think I'm safer here with you?"

Nick flushed. "Ducette's an idiot. I'm sorry I didn't see that sooner. Tell me what happened last night. I'll make sure it doesn't happen again."

"Forgive me if I don't find that especially comforting." She edged away. "I have a plane to catch."

"I got a fax from Belcastro last night."

Breanna stopped. Cold dread clutched her heart. "So?"

"So they've positively identified the body as Marc's. I went out last night to get some more information, but I'm convinced he's right."

She laughed, and it sounded as bitter and hollow in her ears as she felt. "How trusting you are. Belcastro's wrong. Marc was in my room last night."

Nick stood before the skyway, blocking her path. He frowned. "Impossible. I don't doubt it had something to do with your late husband. But it wasn't him. Be reasonable."

Reasonable. She narrowed her eyes. Nick expected proof and all she had was instinct and every cell in her body screaming out it was her husband who'd tried to kill her.

Again.

"You didn't actually see him did you?"

"I don't need to. No, I couldn't see very well, but his eyes, the way he moved. Something else."

"Breanna, think about how nearsighted you are. You were probably terrified last night and overreacted."

"NO!" She clenched her hands into fists. "Yes, I was terrified, but no, I did not overreact."

"Breanna,"

She hugged herself and swallowed the taste of fear that went all the way to her soul. "His scent. No one else could possibly smell like that."

Nick looked startled and paused, apparently holding back his next argument. "What do you mean? Lots of people use the same cologne."

"They don't *bathe* in it. You want to help me, then find a way to prove Belcastro's wrong. Because I know my husband attacked me last night. Just like I know he'll be back. I'm not going to sit here and give him another chance. See you in Duluth." She pushed past him, handed her ticket to the stewardess and hurried down the skyway to the plane.

She changed planes in Chicago and by early afternoon reached Minneapolis. Leaving her sunglasses on, she hurried through the airport. Warned by Murray her life story had been front-page news the past few days, she didn't enjoy the thought of being recognized, but luckily, she apparently looked like just another frazzled traveler.

At last, she sat in the Mercedes in the parking garage and thought about where to go.

Home. She wanted to go home, but the likelihood of Murray's gentle interference and the real possibility of a surprise visit from Belcastro made the prospect less appealing.

Not ready to face them, she called Murray and told her uncle she'd decided to spend the night in Minneapolis. He didn't mention Scott, and she decided not to ask. Concern for him mingled with hurt.

Despite her instructions to her uncle, he hadn't called. Not once, and after she couldn't even reach him at his father's she'd given up.

She really intended to check into a hotel near the airport and get some sleep, but wired from the previous night and needing time alone, she got on the freeway and started driving instead. Interstate 35 North was lightly traveled on Saturday afternoons and the miles melted away beneath the convertible.

She needed somewhere safe and quiet to think things through. Get some much-needed sleep. Half an hour from home, she turned off the freeway on State Highway 33 near Carlton. It would take another couple of hours to reach Lake Vermilion, but at least no one, especially Murray, would think to look for her there.

Two hours later, gravel spewed out from under the Mercedes as Breanna negotiated the narrow, private road leading to the Alden's summer home. Atop a thirty-foot bluff overlooking the lake and sloping gently down to a quarter mile of shoreline, the house looked different in the late afternoon sun. Empty. Void of her father's dynamic presence. Drapes covered the floor-to-ceiling windows like shuttered eyes.

She'd always preferred the lake house to the elegant estate in Duluth and after their meeting at the bank, Stenberg had told her that the house was hers to do with as she pleased. She got out of the car, took the For Sale sign and stashed it behind the garage.

Breanna climbed onto the redwood railing of the wide porch that wrapped the front and south side of the house. Fiona's hidden key rested in its usual place on one of the granite columns supporting the overhanging roof.

Opening the drapes revealed the impressive view of the water and opposite shore that the house commanded. Sensing William Alden's constant disapproval, she hadn't been here at all in the year since she'd met Marc. She had missed it, the quiet woods, the sense of home.

Moving through vaulted-ceiling rooms, she touched knick-knacks, saw visions of her family gathered near the fire. Although she knew small planes often had fatal mishaps, the recurring thought that Marc might have caused their deaths stabbed her with guilt and regrets. She tried to shake off the feeling and hurried outside.

Down at the boathouse, she stood on the dock and watched the deep blue of the water, remembering Brett's patient efforts to teach her how to water-ski; her father's teasing when she decided at age twelve that stabbing minnows with a fishhook was gross.

Inside the small upstairs apartment, she saw her brother in the hockey trophies and pin ups that marked Brett's private retreat.

Dampness and musty odors hung in the air and tickled her nose. Breanna sneezed, then threw open the windows and walked back to the main house. Memories pressed in as she roamed aimlessly through the bedroom wing and picked up a bottle of Fiona's white ginger cologne. Clothes hung neatly in cedar closets. In her own room, she found jeans and an old East High School tee shirt that had been Scott's. She changed out of her silk jumpsuit and put on the jeans and tee shirt.

Continuing her wanderings, she browsed through the kitchen and living area. The cottage, though rustic with knotty pine paneling and massive stone fireplace, still held her mother's meticulous touch, right down to the carefully arranged pillows on the day bed in the loft.

Too many memories. Running away from the London Road house for a secret rendezvous. Sweet sixteen and lost in love with Scott. His hands on her skin. Trembling with sensations she'd never felt again. Breanna squeezed her eyes shut against the painful reality of shattered dreams.

No going back, too much had changed to start over.

Terminally alone.

Curling onto her side on the bed, she wept, wrenching sobs that made her chest ache. Finally, she drifted into an exhausted sleep.

Jagged yellow light illuminated the loft like a flash camera gone berserk. Eyes burning, disoriented and groggy, she dragged herself from bed. Dark clouds collided with fading sunlight across the lake. Lightening streaked the sky.

Storms came fast across the huge lake, expanses of blue water turning leaden under a heavy sky. She hauled in a load of driftwood and lit a fire as fat raindrops clattered on the wood shingled roof. Brass wind chimes on the deck changed their sultry dance to a writhing, twisting clatter of sound.

Wind chimes, flirting with a breeze
tremble, anticipating
Stormy winds ripple across the water,
whisper round the eaves,
and bring you to me.

Breanna leaned her forehead against the cool pane and yearned for Scott, and what might have been. What would it take to ease the craving?

Being with Marc had only made it worse. He must have sensed the shadow of someone else in their marriage bed, even if she had been too naive to realize it at the time. Her inability to truly respond. His increasing impatience, then cruel games and rages.

She'd written the poem nine years ago and wondered if Scott ever received it. She imagined his reaction. Rain spattered against the glass, broke through her fantasy. The boathouse. She'd left the windows open in Brett's bedroom.

Darting down the stone sidewalk, her bare feet slipped, and she almost lost her balance. Rain and wind plastered her hair and clothes to her skin. She emerged from the boathouse as a bolt of lightning cracked and exploded a transformer half a mile away. Flames shot up and sizzled, then the lights went out, plunging the house and yard into darkness.

Bursts of lightening illuminated the path. She made her way carefully back to the house. A figure hovered by the porch. Nearly choking on fear, she hung back under the birches. No, it couldn't be. No one could expect that she would come *here*.

"Breena!" Scott shouted at the top of his lungs, cursing the booming thunder, the blackness, her absence.

She rushed forward from beneath a stand of birch trees, throwing her arms around him, drenching him with her wet hair and clothes.

He wrapped his arms around her. "You just go running off and never call. You have anything to say for yourself, lady of the lake?"

Half laughing, half crying as he swept her off her feet and swung her around, she blinked the rain from her eyes and hugged him. "How did you know I'd be here?"

"I seem to remember this being a favorite hideaway."

Inside the house, Scott shed his jacket and brushed the rain from his hair. He couldn't take his eyes off her.

Breanna shivered, obviously cold despite the heat rising in her face and the warmth from the fireplace.

"You're soaked. Don't you think you should get out of those wet clothes?" he murmured and gently rubbed the back of his hand along her face. "I'll get a blanket." He bounded up the curving stairway and returned a moment later with the quilts from the bed.

Breanna huddled near the fire as if frozen in time. Her hair gleamed blackly next to her face. The tee shirt clung to her breasts, hugged her waist and hips. Her skin shimmered through the translucency of the cloth.

Like a dam bursting, desire coursed through him, but he knew they needed to talk before anything else could happen between them. He dropped the blankets and turned away. "You need some towels," he said gruffly, "and some dry clothes. Maybe a keeper."

Breanna caught his hand and held it against her cheek. "Oh, really," she whispered. "Know anyone who might be interested in the position?"

"Maybe. Now, I'm going to go in the other room and let you change, before I do something really crazy."

Her gaze held his in an electrifying bond. His breath caught.

"Like what?"

"Lick the raindrops off you, that's what," he growled and pulled her close. His mouth pressed against her neck, trailed up her face and captured her lips. Her mouth warmed under his, became pliant and seeking. A soft sigh escaped her. Her kiss was feverish and demanding. Scott felt caught in an inevitable whirlpool from which he had no will to escape. Groaning, he held his cheek against hers and closed his eyes. "Breena, tell me to stop while I still can."

"I can't." She laced her fingers behind his neck, stood on tiptoe and pressed her body along the length of his.

Present merged into long ago. "Deja vu, Scott. You can't leave this time. I have to know."

Overwhelmed with a desperate need, she slowly peeled her clothes off and kicked them aside.

Her fingers struggled with buttons, his belt and zipper. Then his cotton shirt and jeans joined hers in a heap. She sank to the quilt and pulled him down beside her before the fire.

Golden light danced across his tanned skin, flickered like sunshine on his hair. Tentatively, she brushed a lock of hair off his forehead.

"You're sure," he asked, searching her face.

Shaky with want and cold, she nodded, lay back and held out her arms. Scott pulled a blanket over them and gathered her close, kissing her face, her neck and teasing her ear with his tongue.

"Then what's your hurry, sweetheart," he murmured. "Don't we have forever?" His hands moved with agonizing slowness, cupping her breasts, down her stomach, over the curve of her hips. His fingers slipped inside.

She moaned an answer, as his mouth followed the path, savoring her skin, devouring the essence of her until she dug her nails into his shoulders and cried out.

He entered her slowly, then shifted their bodies until she lay on top of him. Hands roaming over her back, he moved leisurely. She watched him through half closed eyes and kissed him, tasting muskiness on his tongue.

Exquisite sensations fluttered through her. She moved her hips faster. His breathing quickened, and he clasped her buttocks, rising into her again. And again. The fire snapped and flared. She gasped as pleasure exploded inside her, and Scott cried out her name.

Rain battered the windows as the storm outside raged. Breanna heated vegetable soup on the gas stove. They drank from ceramic mugs and munched butter crackers on the floor before the fireplace.

"Not bad," Scott mumbled, nibbling on her shoulder, bare above the blanket she'd wrapped around herself, "but not nearly as delicious as your incredible skin."

Breanna ran her hands down sleek biceps, across the smooth expanse of his chest. "I wrote a poem about us, in our other lifetime. I never knew if it reached you."

"Joyfully we shelter together, seeking warmth, finding love." He reached across her for his pants and pulled a worn, brown wallet from the pocket. Carefully unfolding a yellowed square of paper, he held it out to her.

Surprised, she felt a renewed sense of wonder. "You kept that all these years?"

He nodded. "Along with every letter. When are you going to believe that I never stopped caring?"

Tantalizing her with kisses, he captured her breast in his mouth and teased the nipple with his tongue until her scalp tingled. "All right, already. I'm convinced. Don't you ever want to sleep?" she gasped.

He gave her a wicked grin and kissed the tip of her nose. "I've been doing that for nine years, but it's not on my list at the moment."

She studied his face for several moments, half afraid he'd vanish like so many dreams. "When Dad sent me away, I was so lonely I thought I wouldn't survive to be seventeen. I still think he was wrong."

Scott was silent and all the things she needed to say tumbled out. How she met Marc, why she'd married him to defy her father. "We ran off to South Dakota despite an early winter storm warning. Dad's plane crashed when he, Mother and Brett tried to follow us. I've had a hard time believing it was an accident." Choking back a sob, she closed her eyes and shook her head.

Scott listened and held her hand, his fingers intertwined with hers, making little circles in her palm, over and over. He knew he needed to tell her about Derek, now more than ever, but his own revelations had to wait. "Why did you stay with him?"

Breanna pulled the blanket around her drawn up knees. A tear rolled down her cheek. "The pictures you found at my apartment, I don't even remember what happened that night. Then he promised he'd destroy them, said we'd gotten drunk and crazy. That something was wrong with me for making a big deal out of it. And one way or another he'd find my hot spots. I tried to leave, but after I lost the baby, I was too afraid."

Scott's heart paused, then began thumping painfully. Anger flared as he pictured the argument between them. Breanna's eyes flashing defiance, Marc's volcanic rage, her fall down the stairs. "I didn't know about your baby. I'm sorry."

She shivered and continued. "Then I finally found the courage to try again to leave. I had papers served on him the Friday afternoon before Gayle and I went smelt fishing at the Gooseberry River. You know the rest. When I woke up in the hospital, Marc was there, all sweetness and concern. I thought I owed him my life. And Gayle backed him up."

"Damn her." He held her tightly against his chest. Damp hair smelled like rain-drenched flowers. "Now I understand why you believed him. You don't have to say any more."

"Yes, I do," she sobbed. "You wanted me to tell you what happened on the yacht, and I couldn't. I felt guilty about everything—actually kept thinking there was something wrong with me. That night. I think he had drugged the wine. He kept pushing it on me, yet didn't have any at all. I got sick and fell asleep. Later he..." she drew a ragged breath. "How could I expect you to believe that my husband tried to rape me?"

"Oh Christ, Breanna." Images of Breanna the day he'd found her on Lake Superior, skin chalky white with cold, only partially dressed in a satin teddy. If Lanier wasn't dead, he swore he'd kill him. "I'm so sorry."

She fell asleep curled against his side, her head resting on his chest. He watched her face. Black lashes cast shadows against her pearly skin. The need for her ran hot through his blood, but he contented himself with holding her, picturing a life together. There would be other nights. There had to be.

The storm outside abated. Thunder ceased, and only an occasional bolt of lightening brightened the night sky. Raindrops slithered down the window in slow motion, caught in the glow from the fire.

Breanna stirred, gave him a lingering kiss and snuggled down again. Her hands trailed lazily across his stomach, down his leg. Stroked him. She smiled when he drew in a breath. "I'm sorry, Scott."

Resting on one elbow, he gazed down at her. "For what?"

"It should have been you. First. Last. Only."

He stretched out above her and entered her slowly, watching her eyes flutter, her fingers curl as she became his again. "Sweetheart, in the only way that matters, I believe I am."

Breanna awoke to the far away sound of chain saws. Faint light glowed at the windows. Scott stirred beside her. She kissed his ear. "Go back to sleep," she whispered. "The caretaker must be clearing the road from the storm."

She slid from the warm blanket cocoon and roamed restlessly around the living room, checking the locks on doors and windows. Finally, she sat on the hearth and watched Scott, his face peaceful in slumber. She was glad she hadn't told him the worst yet.

That Marc was still alive.

She feared for Scott as much as for herself. His hand groped the empty space next to him, and she slid back under the covers, snuggling on his arm and curling her backside against him.

"Missed you," he murmured. "Whatever happens, Breena, always remember how much I love you. I'd protect you with my life."

Feeling safe and secure, she drifted into wishful dreams.

Startled awake by rapping on the door, Breanna scrambled into her half dry shirt and jeans. Scott rolled onto his back and mumbled something.

Must be the caretaker. Who else would come here? Brushing her hair from her face, she hurried to the door, threw it open and blinked at two uniformed deputies.

"Are you Breanna Alden Lanier?" The man asked.

She nodded and glanced at his name. Jukich. Officer Carlson, a woman, stood beside him and returned her hesitant smile with an impassive expression.

A knot of fear formed in her stomach. She glanced over her shoulder. Scott, still shirtless, walked up behind her.

"What's the problem?"

Ignoring his question, the deputy kept his hand near his gun, somehow conveying the impression of watching them simultaneously. "We have a warrant for your arrest, ma'am. For the murder of your husband, Marc Joseph Lanier."

Chapter 24

This couldn't be happening. Scott raised his arms above his head as the deputy nudged him around to face the stone porch wall. Deputy Jukich searched him for weapons, patting the pockets and legs of his jeans while Carlson performed the same humiliating procedure on Breanna.

"But he's not dead," she murmured over and over.

Jukich raised an eyebrow. "And the corpse that washed ashore just happens to have the same set of teeth."

"You're making a mistake."

The deputy raised an eyebrow. "You mean we should include your friend in this outing?"

"No! He didn't even know my husband. You can't do this to me!" Breanna's voice rose.

"Afraid I can, Mrs. Lanier." He intoned Breanna's legal rights, then clamped handcuffs around her wrists. Metal clicked with sickening finality.

"Please don't. It's a mistake. I saw him two days ago in Montreal." Breanna gave Scott a panic-stricken look as the deputies led her to the waiting car.

"I'll call Murray," he shouted, jolted from initial shock at her last statement. She'd seen Marc? What the hell was she talking about?

"No! Call Nick. He should still be at the Four Seasons." Carlson none too gently assisted her into the back seat before Scott had a chance to respond.

Her request filled him with a curious mixture of jealousy and anger. "Nick? What the hell is he going to do?" But it was too late for an answer.

He watched helplessly as the squad car took off slowly along the gravel drive.

Breanna was gone.

Scott shivered and went back into the house. After shrugging into a shirt, he stirred the ashes in the fireplace. A solitary spark lingered among the cold, gray embers. He poked at it, raking the coals over carefully.

He had to hold on to the warmth of last night. Breanna beside him, in his arms. His, at last.

They had to get through this. He'd make sure they did. He snuffed out the fire, closed up the house and headed for town.

Breanna hunched her shoulders and tried to ease the ache that had settled in the middle of her back from the pressure of her arms locked behind her. Forest raced past the window. The two-and-a-half hour drive to Duluth was the shortest and at the same time most interminable she'd ever endured.

The handcuffs weighed heavily on her small wrists. She blinked back tears. *Stop it!* It wouldn't do any good to cry now, and she'd rather choke before she asked Carlson for a tissue. Besides, how would she use it?

Immediately after arrival at the St. Louis County Sheriff's Headquarters, she was searched again and led to the same windowless room where Captain Belcastro had questioned her a week and a half ago.

Breanna sat at the narrow table and longed for freedom, but at least Carlson removed the handcuffs. She shook her hands to ease the stiffness in her wrists.

Deputy Carlson provided stony silence. Minutes dragged past, Breanna's apprehension increasing while she waited for Captain Belcastro to appear. She shifted uncomfortably on the straight back chair, crossed and uncrossed her arms, then her ankles.

"Good morning, Mrs. Lanier." The door slammed shut. Belcastro pulled out a chair across from her at the scratched oak table, his casual glance giving the impression that he'd already been watching her for several minutes.

Breanna brushed back a strand of tangled hair and tried to stifle panic and self-consciousness. "I think I have a right to know why I'm being held."

"Is that so?" Belcastro's voice held barely concealed sarcasm. "I think you'll be astonished at how few rights one has after they've committed murder."

"He's not dead!"

"It'll be interesting to hear you explain that before the grand jury when the coroner has made an identification of his body. Why don't you save yourself a lot of trouble and tell me now? You can make it easier on yourself if you cooperate with me."

Breanna leaned forward and narrowed her eyes. "Marc's in Montreal. He attacked me in my room at the Four Seasons Friday night. Call Mr. Nicholson. He'll confirm that."

Belcastro studied his nails. "Oh, he'll confirm that you were attacked. But not that it was by your husband."

Uneasy, Breanna glanced at the Captain and forced herself to sit quietly. After all the things he'd said, surely Nick would back her up. He'd had enough time since she left to check out what had happened Friday night. "What do you mean?"

Belcastro stood and planted his hands on the table in an explosive motion that made Breanna shrink back against the wooden chair. His face inches from hers, his dark eyes flashed menace. "I suspected you from the first. And the more I look, the more motives I find. We know your husband was smuggling stolen goods to Canada and generally making himself a nuisance to you. We know about his life insurance. Then there's the matter of a $75 million inheritance being restored. And of course, we can't forget Scott Edwards."

Breanna hugged her arms to stop the trembling and forced herself to meet Belcastro's intimidating gaze. "I hadn't seen Scott Edwards since I was sixteen until he rescued me from the explosion."

"Then you admit that you've known him for ten years."

"Yes."

"And that the two of you are very, very good friends." His voice paused on the last word.

"Yes."

Belcastro stood back and inclined his head toward Deputy Carlson. "Edwards was with you at Lake Vermilion at the time of your arrest."

A vision of the appearance she and Scott must have made to the deputies surfaced. Two sleepy lovers, obviously fresh from bed.

Despite an increasing sense of doom, Breanna felt forced to speak. "Yes."

"Your friend must be a pretty kinky guy."

She waited, afraid to breathe, to move. Carlson stepped forward and dropped a five by six picture onto the table. The photo missing when her apartment had been burglarized.

Horrified, Breanna stared at the glossy image of herself. Hands raised over her head, bound with a crimson flowered scarf, she hung, in suspended animation. Naked. Her face burned. "Where did you get this?" The words emerged as a croak.

Belcastro chuckled. "Edwards' office. Taped inside his desk. Funny how for some guys, they need a picture."

Scott spent the drive to Duluth arguing with himself about honoring Breanna's request to call Nicholson. The thought of them in Montreal for nearly a week, alone, made his blood boil. But she must have a good reason to want his help. It wasn't until he'd watched the squad car drive away that he realized he still didn't know what had happened in Canada to make her flee two days early. And where was Gayle?

Back at his own house to get a change of clothes, Scott managed to put aside his distrust of Nicholson long enough to dial the number for the Four Seasons only to be told the detective had checked out. He slammed the phone down. He'd have to catch him as soon as he got into town.

Scott threw extra clothes into a duffel bag and headed for Breanna's house.

He'd barely had time to check the house when the doorbell chimed. Nicholson stood scowling at the front door.

"Hey, Nick..."

"Edwards. Where's Breanna? I've been trying to reach her for two days."

Scott's dislike returned full force at the detective's condescending tones. "She's not here."

Nicholson raised an eyebrow and brushed past him into the house. "Really? Then what the hell are you doing here?"

Finding no reason to tell the detective they'd been sharing the house for the past two weeks, Scott ignored his question. "Listen, I tried calling you earlier at her request. For some peculiar reason, she thinks you might be able to help."

"What's wrong?" Nick glanced around the entry. His hurried manner intensified Scott's aggravation.

"Breanna insists Lanier attacked her Friday night and that you'll confirm this. I'd appreciate knowing what the hell she was talking about."

"Stay out of it, Edwards. And get the hell out of her house. You'll only make more trouble for her."

Scott clenched his jaw. "While you waffle back and forth between accuser and white knight? What's on your agenda, Nicholson, as if I couldn't guess?"

Nick's face tightened with anger. "Told her yet about your charming brother?"

"She's met Derek." Scott kept his voice expressionless. What had this nosy detective found out? He wondered if he knew Derek had been Lanier's partner and had disappeared. Or that the family business was now in the hands of the U. S. Treasury Department.

Nicholson stepped closer and shouted in his face. "Does she know he's been working for her husband? Or maybe you're afraid that if she knew, she'd suspect you helped set her up? Did you, Edwards? Gonna let her take the rap while you and your brother skip the country?"

Scott grabbed the lapels of Nicholson's leather jacket. "Listen here, asshole. If you were even half as smart as you think you are, you wouldn't make such a stupid accusation—"

Nick's arms flew up and knocked Scott's hands away. He landed a solid punch on Scott's jaw, stealing his balance on the slippery hardwood floor. Scott staggered back into the grandfather clock. Recovering, he lunged at the detective, knocking Nick to the floor. Fist raised to slam into Nick's face, Scott hesitated as the clock bonged.

Sanity returned. What in the world was he doing, letting his emotions rule over his intellect?

He pulled his arm back. "Wait a minute. Much as I'd like to shove your nose to the back of your head, this isn't going to get Breanna out of jail. You know I never helped Lanier, or Derek. Don't you."

Nicholson gave him a stony look but didn't answer.

Warily, Scott stood and stepped back as Nick got up.

"Breanna's in jail? What happened?" Nick's speed shift into concern sent a fresh wave of irritation down Scott's spine.

"Belcastro arrested her this morning."

"Shit."

"Funny, that's about what I said. Did *you* see Lanier?"

Nick sighed. "There was a break-in at the hotel Friday night. She was frightened, and at first thought the intruder might be her husband. But you and I know that's impossible."

"Is it?" He wasn't nearly as sure as he would like to be.

Nicholson cleared his throat in what sounded like a growl. "You saw the explosion, Edwards. Very conveniently, I might add. Thought about how you're going to explain that coincidence to the Sheriff?"

Scott's gut tightened with apprehension. He'd saved her from the lake, true, but how could he save her if Belcastro misconstrued the situation?

Nicholson continued. "Now, since you were there, could Lanier have possibly gotten away without you seeing something? Or did your brother use Nina Rogers as an example to convince you to keep your mouth shut?"

Scott narrowed his eyes. "I don't think Derek killed her. And I don't believe you think so either."

Nicholson chuckled softly. "You're right. Your brother is a greedy scumbag, but too gutless to be a killer. But you know what Derek and Lanier were up to, don't you?"

"Maybe. I might even have figured out how Lanier got off the yacht. Which he must have done. Because if Breanna says that piece of trash was in her room Friday night, I believe her. And since we both want to see her cleared, why don't you get off your arrogant ass and figure out who that dead guy is? For starters, you can help me get her out of jail."

Breanna stared at Captain Belcastro. "No. No. You're wrong. It's not like that at all. We aren't, weren't lovers. I didn't know he'd be there. I didn't know Scott was following me." She clapped her hand over her mouth as words tumbled out, each one fueling the triumph in Belcastro's eyes.

"Then you admit that Edwards didn't just happen along."

Breanna shook her head. "I don't have to answer that. I don't have to tell you anything. I want to call my lawyer."

"Nobody'd blame you for wanting Marc Lanier out of your life." His voice became deceptively soothing. "As for Edwards, maybe he used you to get rid of a bad business partner. Maybe you didn't plan any of this. Forget about saving his worthless skin. He's obviously not worried about yours." He glanced down at the picture.

Heat burned her face again.

"Cooperate with me, Breanna. Make it easy on yourself."

His sudden change in tactics sparked her temper. "If you're so certain Scott Edwards is my accomplice, why haven't you arrested him?"

"Because, Mrs. Lanier, we have a chance to clean house here. Or more accurately, the harbor. Lanier's gone, but we really want Derek Edwards, too. Scott can lead us to his brother, but not if he's in jail."

"Why do you want Derek?"

He hesitated until she felt her nerves would snap like too thin ice.

"We suspect Derek killed Nina Rogers, probably on your husband's orders."

Wary, she studied the Captain's scowling expression. "Why would Derek do that? They didn't even know each other."

Belcastro's laugh was without humor. "Why, Mrs. Lanier. Didn't your lover tell you everything? Derek Edwards didn't shit without permission from your late husband. Apparently, they met a few years ago at the Federal prison in Stillwater. They've been fencing and smuggling through Lanier's Wholesale Furriers. With Edwards and Sons Fishing Enterprises providing transportation. But now your husband is dead.

"And the question you should be asking is who Scott Edwards is double crossing. His brother? Or you?"

Chapter 25

Breanna slumped against the chair. Lies. Belcastro had to be lying. He was digging for answers and counting on a hysterical reaction from her to provide them. She wouldn't allow herself to be used. Ever again.

Hugging her arms, she retreated to a far away corner of her mind.

Belcastro droned on, his voice buzzing indistinctly while she conjured a summer day and drifted on a raft, sun warm on her back, the mirrored stillness of Lake Vermilion reflecting a few puffy clouds.

Finally, the door slammed and shattered her trance. Deputy Carlson jerked her to her feet and escorted her from the suffocating room.

"You can make your call now."

She called Murray and instantly regretted her decision to ask her uncle to "help".

"Don't worry, sweetie. I'll call Grady, and we'll be right down to straighten this thing out."

"Grady O'Neal couldn't settle a dog fight, Murray. I'm being charged with murder, not a leash law violation." She pulled her fingers through the tangled mess of her hair and glanced up. Officer Carlson signaled time's up. "I have to go now. Please call Daddy's attorney and find a defense lawyer for me. Someone with experience."

"I told you not to worry. I'll take care of everything."

Which was exactly why she worried. Murray always had the best intentions, but possessed a misdirected sense of loyalty to the various regulars that frequented his bar. Grady O'Neal enjoyed happy hour too much to be anything more than a traffic ticket fixer. Murray, loyal to a fault, couldn't see beyond O'Neal's arrogance.

She went through booking. Pictures, fingerprints. Delousing. Dressed in a faded green cotton uniform, Breanna huddled on a cot and buried her face against a scratchy gray blanket, wishing she could blot out the humiliation. Bed covers smelled of strong soap but at least filtered out the lingering musty cell odors of mildew, pine cleaner and urine.

How had her dreams become nightmares? A year ago, she'd thought Marc Lanier handsome and intriguing. How could he be an ex-con? He'd even been named independent businessman of the year by Duluth's Chamber of Commerce.

But if Belcastro was right, Marc had been fencing and smuggling since he moved to Duluth, before she met and married him. How could he have deceived everyone? Everyone except her father and Scott.

When Murray showed up with Grady O'Neal during mid-afternoon visiting hours, she refused to talk to him, afraid the dime store lawyer would antagonize the judge so badly she'd never make bail. Or that she'd inadvertently blurt something that would implicate Scott.

Scott.

She stirred tepid vegetable soup and considered Belcastro's statements about him and Derek Edwards. She'd believe anything evil about Scott's brother. But after all the caring Scott had shown during the past two weeks, the initial shock and anger she'd felt had dissipated.

In her heart, she couldn't believe he'd lied to her, tricked her, seduced her for purposes as twisted as Marc's.

She bit into a dry baloney sandwich and forced herself to chew. Scott either didn't know what his brother was doing, or had been afraid to tell her. She had to believe that. And she hadn't given him much opportunity to tell her, either.

Face it, the past two weeks had pretty much been about her and her problems. How could it not have been when she'd been thrown one twist and turn after another? But she still felt a pang of guilt that she hadn't looked outside herself more.

She gave the tray of half eaten food to the trustee and returned to her cot. Closing her eyes, she imagined herself in Scott's arms, heard his voice.

No matter what happens, Breena, always remember how much I love you.

Scott paced the lobby of the St. Louis County Sheriff's Headquarters and waited for Murray to return from his visit to the jail. Nick remained glued to his cell phone and turned away in a dismissive gesture.

Scott scowled at the detective's back and threw his hands up in exasperation. If this was a sample of working with Nick, he'd be better off on his own.

Murray entered the waiting area with a man Scott vaguely remembered seeing somewhere.

"Did you see her? Is she okay?"

"She's as contrary as ever." Murray introduced Grady O'Neal. "No point in hanging around here, Scott. My niece doesn't want to see you."

Scott raised an eyebrow. "Did she say that, Murray, or are you lying to me again?"

Murray flushed. "She even refused to see me and Grady."

Scott took in O'Neal's lime green plaid slacks and thought Breanna had made a good decision, and he knew the reason why. Then he remembered seeing the attorney at Murray's bar. Participating in a chug-a-lug contest St. Patrick's Day.

Murray and Breanna. Loyal to a fault. Must be a family trait. He hoped her loyalty would include him once he had a chance to explain about Derek.

Nick sauntered over and nodded at Grady. "No offense, O'Neal, but Breanna already has a lawyer. He's flying in from Chicago in the morning."

"Since when?" Scott and Murray spoke simultaneously. Each glared suspiciously at the detective.

Murray spoke up. "My niece needs someone who can get her out of here today."

"She needs the best. Wade Crandall can't get here until tomorrow, but Belcastro won't make it easy to get her out before then, anyway. Today is Sunday, remember?"

Murray sighed deeply. "So what's the plan?"

Frustrated and uneasy, Scott shrugged. "Guess I'll head back to Breanna's and finish sorting through the papers we found at the warehouse."

Nick nodded. "Good idea. Catch you later, Murray. Let's go, Edwards."

"I'm right behind you," he growled.

"I'll meet you at Breanna's," Murray shouted after them.

Back at Breanna's house, Scott surveyed the wet bar while Nick roamed the living room, inspecting windows and locks. Maybe a drink would settle everyone's jangled nerves. He put a splash of water in a glass of Chivas and ice. "I checked everything before you got here."

"Can't be too cautious." Nick picked up the drink and took an appreciative sip. "Thanks. You know, Edwards, the way you act, I'd almost think you lived here, not Breanna."

Scott refused the bait but returned his hard stare. "If I had a first name like yours Nicholson, I'd probably prefer using my initials or last name, too. But since I don't, you can call me Scott."

They stood glaring at each other until Murray broke the silence.

"Thought we were going to have a strategy meeting, not a cold war. Anyone have an idea?"

Nick set his glass on the bar. "Scott is going to spend some time taking care of family business. I'll be checking out things here."

The phone rang. Scott grabbed the receiver from beneath Nick's fingers. "Hello?"

"Breanna. Hurry, please."

He strained to place the woman's whispery voice. "Sorry, Breanna's not here right now."

"Is she still in Montreal?"

"No, she got back yesterday. Who's calling?" He turned away from Nick's furious gesture.

"Is this Scott?"

"Yes."

"Thank God she left. It's Gayle. I need to tell her—" The line clicked and buzzed in his ear.

Puzzled, he hung up the phone. "Why wouldn't Gayle know Breanna left Montreal yesterday?"

"Damn it, you should have let me answer." Nick grabbed the phone and punched in several numbers. "Because she disappeared last Monday. Christ, didn't Breanna tell you anything?"

Scott shrugged, remembering Breanna cuddled against his side, firelight casting shadows on her pale skin. Warmth curled through him, and he stifled a smile. "Sure. But not about her trip to Canada."

Nick hesitated, his narrowed gaze piercing, then turned away and spoke into the phone.

Incredulous, Scott listened as Nick had Gayle's phone call traced. "You had Breanna's phone tapped? Did she know?"

Nick's voice was cool. "She told me about the call she suspected was from Marc. So after last Friday night, I thought it would be a good precaution. I've been having all her calls recorded."

"But does she know?" Torn between grudging admiration and outrage, Scott stifled the impulse to shake an answer from him.

"I planned on telling her when she gets home. If I'm not here, I'll leave a message with Crandall."

"I'll be here."

Nicholson tapped his arm. "No, you won't. Find your brother. Whatever it takes. Maybe Lucas Brogan has a few ideas on where he might have gone. I've got a few things to follow up on. Then maybe I'll be able to track down Gayle."

Scott clenched his jaw. Brogan. He'd just as soon ask for help from Belcastro as that snake.

Breanna watched dawn lighten the tiny window nearest her cell. *Please, please let me get out of this hole today.* If she could just get in touch with Elliott Stenberg at North Shore National Bank. He'd know who could get her out of this hell.

The morning dragged as she tried to use her five-minute phone calls to track down Stenberg at the bank. Mid morning, she finally made it through three transfers to his personal secretary. But Stenberg was spending a week on Isle Royale and couldn't be reached. She succeeded in getting the name of her father's lawyer in Minneapolis, only to find he was in New York for an SEC hearing.

Dismayed, she hung up the phone as the deputy motioned her back to the cellblock. Grady O'Neal was starting to look like a good prospect and the thought alarmed her.

Early afternoon, a guard summoned her from her cell.

"Must be nice to be able to hire a hot-shot lawyer from Chicago." Stocky and gray haired, the woman looked disgruntled as she escorted her to the visitor's room.

"Yes, I suppose it would be," Breanna said coolly, expecting to see Grady with her uncle. Instead, a man in his late thirties, dressed in a charcoal gray pin stripped suit, stood and extended his hand.

"Miss Alden, my name's Wade Crandall. I'll be representing you if you go to trial. Meanwhile, bail will be arranged as soon as you answer a few questions."

Crandall and Crandall, the most prestigious law firm in the Midwest. And Wade Crandall, the lawyer who could make a determined prosecutor look like a kindergarten teacher.

Dazed, Breanna sat and waited until they were alone before speaking.

"Why are you here?"

"You'd rather spend the next several months in jail?"

"Of course not. What I meant is who called you? I haven't been allowed to use the phone long enough to get past the receptionists."

Crandall smiled, showing perfect teeth as white as his starched cotton shirt. "Nick called me yesterday. Asked me to take the case. That is, if you have no objection."

"No, of course not," she murmured. "Nick called you?"

"Old college buddies," he said. "Now I have a few questions to ask, then we'll get you out of here. You've been charged with killing your husband—"

"I didn't kill him!"

"Miss Alden, you don't—"

Breanna sat forward in her chair. "If you are going to represent me, then you need to be crystal clear on this. I didn't kill him, or try to," she repeated. "And he's not dead. He's somewhere in Montreal."

Crandall nodded. "Nick said you think you saw him."

"I don't think I saw him, I know I did."

"The Sheriff is convinced his body is lying in the morgue, but we don't have to prove it's not him to get the case dropped. Belcastro's theories are as leaky as that raft you ended up in."

"I appreciate your saying so." She hesitated. "But the best way to prove I'm innocent is for Marc to reappear."

Crandall tapped his finger on the tabletop. "Assuming he's alive, why would he do that?"

"Because he can't stand to lose." Remembering Friday night and the overpowering scent of him, she shuddered. "Marc may be in Montreal now, but not for long. He'll wait until I'm out of here. Then he'll be back. I can feel it."

Despite Crandall's efforts, the judge set bail at half a million dollars. Breanna knew Murray didn't have the cash to cover it and with Stenberg gone, she was trapped in a tiny cell with a multi-million dollar inheritance beyond her reach.

Tuesday morning, she sat with her uncle trying to ignore the panic that threatened to engulf her. Another night locked up might destroy the thin shield she'd managed to hide her feelings behind. Scott hadn't even tried to see her and as time elapsed, more doubt crept in, chipping away at her certainty that Belcastro was wrong.

"I'm about ready to rob that bank." Murray drummed his fingers on the table. "Wait a minute. What did you do with those earrings?"

Breanna massaged her forehead, trying to ease an unrelenting ache. "Left them at the jewelers to get an appraisal." She looked up and clasped his hand. "Murray, that's brilliant. They must be worth enough so I can borrow the money to get out of here. Call Herzberg. And please, bring me clean clothes to go home in."

Several hours later, Murray walked her up to the front door of her house. "I'll stay, if you want me to."

She shook her head and bent to pet Flannaghan. "I'm going to spend an hour in the shower. Then go to bed. I feel as if I haven't slept for days." In truth, she hadn't done much more than doze since Saturday night at Lake Vermilion. With Scott.

Memories of his arms around her, her sense of safety again allayed the doubts that crept insistently around the edges of her mind.

"If you're sure." Murray's voice was filled with doubt, but he turned to go. "Oh, almost forgot. Here's the appraisal on those earrings. Albert Warren said they'd keep them in the vault as collateral until Stenberg gets back. But I think you should leave them there permanently. See you later, sweetie. Call me if you need anything."

"Thanks, Murray." She threw her arms around his neck. "I love you."

"Me, too, you." He kissed her cheek and left.

Flannaghan pranced on his hind legs, then swatted her with his tail until she threw her arms around him and let the Irish Setter lick her face. "Hi, Flanny. Sure is good to see you."

She sank into a wingback chair in the living room, unfolded the jeweler's stationery and caught her breath. 'Ladies antique earrings. Each earring contains six marquis cut four-carat alexandrites, two brilliant four-carat white diamonds, ten half-carat white diamonds set in eighteen-carat gold. Estimated value: one million dollars.' Her breath escaped in a rush.

She'd always known the earrings were special, but not once had her mother or grandmother ever given any indication they were worth a fortune. No wonder Marc had been so interested, so insistent she bring them home from the vault.

Like he had Friday night on the yacht after he'd harassed her about her pewter earrings. His voice echoed in her mind. *You should wear the jewelry you got from your mother, instead of hiding it. I don't even know where you keep it.*

Marc's midnight visit. 'Where are the earrings, Princess? Be a good girl and cooperate, one last time.' *One last time. One last time.*

She squeezed her eyes shut and pressed her hands against her ears. Other images intruded. The sense of personal violation as his groping hands had shoved the satin teddy above her waist. Marc's weight on her before he'd suddenly rolled off an instant before he'd made her shame complete.

Being carried. Voices. Whispering. *She wasn't supposed to be here.* Her eyes flew open. Hazy images vanished but Marc's face haunted her as badly as a physical presence.

Shuddering, she rose and went to take a shower. It might take more water than Lake Superior held to wash away the memory of Marc's degrading use of her body, but at least she could rid herself of the lingering odors of jail.

Reluctant to stop scrubbing, she stayed in the shower until her skin glowed pink, and the water turned cold. The phone rang. Hesitating, she wrapped a towel around herself and dashed into the kitchen to cut off the answering machine. Too late, she heard Scott sign off. The machine clicked and announced the time. She pressed replay. Nothing. The tape ejected. Murray must have reconnected the machine, and fast-forwarded the tape instead of rewinding it.

She flipped the tape over to the blank side and inserted it into the player.

"Princess." Marc's voice filled the room, and she recoiled.

Chapter 26

Flannaghan barked furiously and raced to the front door as the bell chimed. Not thinking about being clad in only a towel, Breanna ran to the entry, checked the peephole and threw herself into Nick's arms.

"He's back. Now I know for sure he's back."

He held her, one hand cradling her damp hair, the other patting her back. "Take it easy, Breanna," he murmured. "I won't let anything happen to you."

She pressed her face against his sandalwood scented sports coat and took comfort from his reassuring voice and calm strength. Then she remembered she wasn't dressed. Her face flamed with embarrassment, and she slipped from his embrace.

"The answering machine. Listen to the message. I'll get dressed." Clutching the towel's top edge, she hurried into the bedroom and shut the door.

After drying her hair, she pulled on a purple tee shirt and shiny purple warm-up slacks. All the toiletry items she'd had with her in Montreal had been neatly placed on the dressing table. Car keys rested in a green and white 1930's style glass dish. Murray must have gone to Lake Vermilion and brought all of her things back, although his usual style would be to throw everything on the bed.

Half afraid and embarrassed to return to the living room, Breanna dawdled, lining up the perfume bottles on the dresser, moving the comb and brush an even distance from each other and the table edge.

Sighing, she left the quiet sanctuary and found Nick in the kitchen. He handed her a cup of coffee.

"Here, drink this. Then listen to the message again."

Her eyes stung as hot coffee and brandy hit the back of her throat. Nick pressed the replay button on the answering machine. "Princess." Breanna shuddered at the sound of Marc's voice. Nick caught her as she collapsed against him.

"Don't go off the deep end. Notice anything unusual about the way this message was recorded?"

"You mean other than that it was made by a dead man?" She moved away, sank into a chair and buried her face in her hands.

"It's not time and date stamped. Which means it's just an old tape that's been sitting in the machine for months."

Breanna shook her head and took another gulp of coffee. "I don't think—" but she realized Nick's words made sense. It probably was an old message.

"Okay, I see your point, but I still swear that was him in Montreal." She stared out the kitchen window to avoid meeting his eyes, wishing he'd believe her.

Scott would. If only she'd had time to tell him before she was taken away. Lake Superior shimmered in dusky twilight, deceptively peaceful. She took another sip of coffee and let the calmness of the lake seep into her along with the brandy.

Nick pulled out the chair across from her. "I know you do, and I did everything I could to find whoever was in your room last Friday night. But I don't see how it's possible it was your husband. I think we've got something else to worry about."

Breanna jerked her gaze away from the rippled water and met his eyes. "Belcastro?"

Nick set his cup on the table. "Of course, but Wade will handle that. Don't you wonder why that message isn't dated?"

She nodded, not sure she wanted to consider other possibilities nearly as frightening as Marc's return.

"It's been edited. The question is by whom?"

Breanna hugged her arms as hopes of a restful night galloped away on her fear. "Any ideas?"

Nick shook his head. "I don't trust Edwards."

She gasped. "I don't believe this. He saved my life! Twice."

Nick narrowed his eyes. "I don't believe in coincidences. And you haven't seen him for years. People change."

Both she and Scott had changed in the past nine years, she knew, but one thing remained constant. He loved her. He'd sworn he'd protect her with his life and had proven it.

Or had he, a small doubting voice nagged at the edges of her mind.

Abruptly, she pushed her chair away from the table. Coffee sloshed onto the blue gingham tablecloth. "Scott wouldn't do anything dishonest. I trust him."

Nick stood and took her arm. "I don't want to hurt you," he said softly, "but you have to be realistic. He knew his brother was involved with Lanier. Why didn't he tell you? At the very beginning? Surely he had plenty of opportunities."

She stared at the floor. "Maybe he was afraid to."

Nick snorted. "Exactly. If he had nothing to hide, why would he act like a coward?"

"He's not a coward!" Hot tears stung her eyes, and she pulled angrily away.

"Did he try to see you while you were in jail? Do you know where he is now?"

Miserable, she shook her head. "He called while I was in the shower. That's why I rushed out here in a towel."

"And?"

"There was no message. The tape hadn't been rewound."

Nick placed an arm around her shoulders and guided her to the sofa. "He said he was going to look for his brother. That was two days ago, and I haven't heard a word. Are you going to take steps to protect yourself, or are you just going to sit around, hoping, waiting to see if he comes back?"

Breanna forced herself to listen as Nick gave his account of how Derek and Marc had been smuggling to Canada, and how Scott had eventually become just as involved. Like Derek, taking the boats out on nonexistent charters while Marc lined up customers and merchandise.

"I don't believe it," she insisted stubbornly.

Nick took her hand. "If Edwards wasn't involved in something illegal, why did the IRS seize his business?"

Startled, Breanna sat up straighter. "When?"

"While we were in Montreal. You didn't know?"

She shook her head. "That can't be true. Scott would have told me."

"Are you sure?" Nick spoke softly, yet insistently, and Breanna was forced to think about the hours she and Scott had spent together the past two weeks. She had tried to blame herself for the reasons Scott hadn't told her, but there must have been dozens of opportunities to tell her whatever he knew about Derek and Marc.

Scott had chosen to ignore them.

At first, the night she'd spent at his house, then the next night at Marc's warehouse. Plus all the nights he'd spent sleeping on her sofa.

Lake Vermilion. Thinking about Saturday night, the storm, and Scott's gentle lovemaking brought a rush of remembered pleasure that left her shaky and even more uncertain. She edged away from Nick.

"I brought something for you I'm hoping you won't need." He stood and strode to the kitchen, returning with a handgun. Sitting next to her, he placed the gun in her palm. "Know how to fire one?"

Irritated, she tried to hand the heavy pistol back to him. "Yes, thank you. And I have two cabinets of these things upstairs."

He shook his head. "Antiques. Good for collectors, but not very useful. This is a 9mm Beretta. Tomorrow, I'll take you to a gun range, show you how to use it."

She ran her fingers over the black plastic stock. Grandmother's ivory handled Smith and Wesson was lighter, but the Beretta looked a lot more deadly. She shivered and jumped up. "That's not necessary. Let's go outside, and I'll show you."

"You'll rouse the police using firearms in the city limits."

Breanna laughed. "When you've been arrested for murder, a petty misdemeanor doesn't seem worth worrying about. Besides, I've got a terrific lawyer." Seeing him frown, she turned the gun over in her hands, checked the safety and pretended to aim. "I'm kidding, okay? We'll forget the demonstration. Today or tomorrow."

He took a deep breath as if he planned to argue. Breanna bent and kissed his cheek. "Thanks, Nick. And don't worry. I can handle a gun if I have to."

He looked momentarily satisfied with her acceptance, but patiently pulled her down to the couch. "No deal. I'll pick you up in the morning. Not too early, I promise, but I can't give this to you without taking the time to make sure you really know how to use it. Each one is different. I've had your phone tapped, too."

Taken aback, Breanna searched his face. "Why?"

"To find out who's been making those weird calls. It's already paid off. Gayle called. We were able to trace the call to a Montreal bus station, but of course she was long gone."

Breanna was silent. An odd feeling of compassion welled up for her assistant. Gayle had been the closest to a friend she'd had since returning to Duluth. Whatever she was involved in, Breanna wondered if she'd survive. If she was with Gregory Lanier, did he, unlike his brother, have a shred of decency?

Nick insisted on staying and cooking dinner.

"I don't really have any groceries," Breanna protested, knowing by the emerald glint in his eyes he wouldn't take no for an answer.

"I didn't expect you would, so I picked up some steaks at Eastside Market. You need to eat. After three days on jail food, barbecuing will seem like a gourmet feast."

"Are you kidding?" she said, following him back into the kitchen. "Even shoe leather would taste better than the dried out baloney they serve."

Nick laughed and pulled ingredients for a salad from the refrigerator. "I started the grill and put potatoes on while you were getting dressed."

"Glad you feel at home here, Nick." She gave him a wry smile and got Lillian's hand-carved wooden salad bowl and spoons from the cupboard. While she tore lettuce leaves, Nick chopped celery, green peppers and fresh mushrooms, then cooked the steaks.

Breanna replaced the coffee-stained tablecloth with a pink gingham one from Lillian's seemingly bottomless linen drawer and set the table. Being involved in such domestic pursuits with the man who'd accused her of murdering her husband felt strange, and she tried not to think about their first meeting. So much had changed in such a short time.

Over dinner, Nick entertained her with stories about other cases he'd resolved in the two years since he'd left the FBI. But when she tried to ask questions about his work as a Federal agent and why'd he left, he froze up and began clearing the dishes away.

Afterwards, she curled up in a corner of the couch with a cordial glass of Irish Mist while Nick sipped Chivas and water, resting his arms along the back of the couch.

She wished he'd leave, but he seemed content to share her silence. Her eyelids drooped, and she suppressed a yawn. He stood and brought his glass to the kitchen. "You're worn out. Looks like I'd better be going."

She trailed along behind him to the front door. "Good night, Nick. Thanks for everything."

He leaned down as if to kiss her, but she quickly turned her face. His mouth grazed her cheek. Stifling a shudder at the feel of his moustache, she folded her arms and took a step back.

"Breanna," he began and stopped. His fingers brushed her cheek, and she looked up, startled by the momentary warmth that flickered in his eyes. "I'll see you tomorrow. Call me if you need anything."

She closed and locked the door behind him. Seemed like Nick could be a friend after all, although friend wasn't quite the right word. Two weeks ago, she'd never guessed it possible.

In the bedroom, she pulled the white eyelet comforter back and caught her breath. A bouquet of forget-me-nots rested on the pillow. With a note from Scott beneath them.

Breena, couldn't get past the pit bulls (Murray and Nick) to see you, so I went to Lake Vermilion and brought back all your stuff. I cooked up a safe place for the log. Wish I was here to welcome you home, but I have to find my brother before he causes any more trouble. Hope you understand. Hope you believe how much I love you. See you soon. Yours, Scott.

It was difficult to believe that he'd go to so much trouble if his feelings were a lie, but she longed for him to return and tell her the past three days were all a bad dream. She set the flowers on the dresser and got into bed.

Flannaghan settled down with a thump on the braided rug next to her. Despite all her worries, exhaustion caught up and she slept, carried along on stormy dreams. She awoke sometime later and groped for her glasses and the clock. Two a.m. Flannaghan's tail beat a tattoo on the floor. A door closed. Breanna reached for the Beretta and flicked the safety off. She slid from bed and listened at the partially open door. Footsteps came closer. She heard her name called.

Flannaghan wriggled through the opening and bolted down the hallway. She heard a thump and a muffled laugh and eased the door wide open. "How can you be sure I won't blast your kneecaps off," she called out and flicked on the hall lights.

Flannaghan's paws were planted squarely on Scott's chest while the Irish Setter gave him a welcome home face washing.

"I'm not, sweetheart, but right now I'm more worried about suffocating." He ruffled Flannaghan's fur, then pushed the dog away and stood.

Doubt and hesitation were forgotten as Breanna flung herself into his arms. Amidst all the uncertainties, he'd come back and for the moment that was all that mattered.

He buried his face in her hair, holding her so tightly she could barely breathe. "I was afraid you wouldn't want to see me."

She drew back and studied his face. "Why?"

"I don't know what Nicholson or Belcastro told you, but I'm fairly certain none of it was good. And I'd feel a lot better if you'd get that gun out of my back."

"Sorry." Breanna moved away, went back into the bedroom and set the pistol on the nightstand. Scott hesitantly followed.

"Where'd you get that vicious looking thing?" He shoved his fists into his jacket pockets and leaned against the doorjamb.

"Nick. He said Grandmother's guns wouldn't be good in a crisis."

"For once I agree with Nick."

Breanna watched him shift his weight and was reminded of

years ago when he'd sneaked into her bedroom at the Alden's London Road estate. "What are you so nervous about?"

"You do know about Derek?"

She nodded.

He tugged on his earlobe and met her gaze. "Guess I'm afraid you'll toss me out before I can explain."

"You're only half right." She yawned and put her arms around his waist, resting her cheek against his chest. "Save the explanations for tomorrow. One more sleepless night would be more than I could handle right now. I'm going to go back to sleep while you shower." She wrinkled her nose and looked up at him. "No wonder Flannaghan was so glad to see you. You smell like fish."

Scott's ears turned pink, but he laughed. "Sorry. I've been out in the *Liquid Asset* for the past two days. I left my other jacket at Lake Vermilion and this one's apparently been in the hold too long. Breanna," he hesitated, "I guess I shouldn't push my luck, but why aren't you mad? Why don't you need to hear my side of the story about Derek?"

Tomorrow would be soon enough to hear what he had to say. She stood on tiptoe and pressed a soft kiss on his mouth. "Because I'm too damn tired, that's why. And you came back."

Chapter 27

Scott watched Breanna climb into the four-poster bed, her purple sleep shirt riding up to expose a length of shapely leg before she snuggled under the covers. He swallowed and clenched his fists. Better make the shower a cold one. He counted himself incredibly lucky she'd even let him stay.

"Goodnight, Scott," she mumbled and turned her back.

He stayed in the shower a long time, expecting she'd be asleep by the time he finished, disappointed just the same when she was. Silently, he felt his way in the darkened room to the far side of the bed, tripped on a pile of clothes and banged his knee on the footboard. Luckily, he hadn't wakened Breanna, because he hoped she didn't intend to relegate him back to the couch. She hadn't said, and he sure the hell wasn't going to ask. He left his boxer shorts on.

Showering hadn't eased the longing ache in the pit of his stomach, but it had made him sleepy. He carefully lifted an edge of the covers and crawled into bed. The faint scent of lilacs assailed his senses the moment he lay down. Suddenly wide awake, he realized if sleep was his objective, then the couch was the only way it would happen. But he couldn't bring himself to leave her, even if it meant a frustrating night. After all she'd been through, he couldn't wake her to satisfy his desire. It wouldn't be right.

Breanna stretched out her hand and brushed his chest. He tensed.

"You didn't kiss me goodnight," she murmured, her eyes still closed.

Leaning over, he gave her a light kiss. "Goodnight, sweetheart," he whispered. "I love you."

Her lips curved in a slight smile. Twining her arm around his neck, she pulled his face back down to hers.

"Tell me again," she said, kissing him. She nestled close. Smooth skin pressed against his chest and thighs. His breath caught in his throat as he realized she had taken her shirt off while he was in the shower.

He ran his hand down her bare arm, her side, over the curve of her hip. "Breanna, I love you, always have. Always will."

Lying on her back, she studied his face, shadowy in the dark, and felt herself fully waken as his fingertips explored her skin. In her dreams, it had always been like this. Dusky, quiet, their breathing the only sound in the room.

Outside, waves softly caressed the shore beneath the windows. Her hands sought the smooth expanse of his chest, his abdomen, then slipped inside his shorts. He groaned and shifted onto his back as she tugged the boxers down his hips.

He gathered her close, and she took him inside. His mouth captured hers while she moved above him with slow, languorous movements until she felt as if she were drowning in a pool of liquid heat. And dreams became one with reality.

Scott watched stars fade from the velvety sky as he held Breanna close against his side and listened to the soft rhythm of her breathing. Straining his ears, he heard the faint chirp of the kitchen phone. He eased away, hoping it wasn't the midnight intruder who had probably made her unplug the bedroom phone. Or Nick. Last thing he and Breanna needed was for that nosy jerk to catch him at her house at four o'clock in the morning.

Flannaghan bounded down the stairs where he'd apparently gone to hide in the study and padded along beside him. Scott picked up the phone. "Hello."

"Scott. It's Ernie." Kowalski spoke in a whisper, but Scott recognized his voice. "You said I should call you if I saw anything fishy."

Scott's senses immediately became alert. "What's going on?"

"I'm not sure. But look's like Derek's back. Desperate to find something, too."

Knowing the phone was tapped, Scott was reluctant to let the foreman say more. "Just sit tight, Ernie. I'll meet you like we planned." He hung up the phone and hurriedly dressed.

Breanna remained asleep. If he woke her, she'd only worry, and he'd probably be back before she missed him. He ruffled Flannaghan's fur. "Watch out for our lady. I won't be gone long."

He took the Suzuki from its hiding place alongside the garage and rolled it out to the street before he started it. Maybe the jeep would be safer, but he'd been worried about Nick seeing his car parked at Breanna's house. Besides, the bike gave him greater maneuverability.

Ten minutes later, he sat in Ernie's beat-up pickup across the street from the fishery. The building looked dark and deserted, but after several minutes he distinguished a pencil of light in the high windows over the stairwell to Derek's office.

Scott glanced at the foreman. "How'd he get in?"

"Broke a pane out of the old skylight over the first floor, I think."

Scott gripped the door handle. "I'm going to see what he's up to."

Ernie grabbed his arm. "Got a gun?"

"No."

"Derek does. Think about that before you rush the building like the Green Hornet."

Scott sank into the seat. He'd forgotten about Derek's shoot-em-up at the warehouse two weeks ago almost as readily as he'd dismissed the fact that his brother would just as soon shoot Scott as let him take the heat for Derek's crimes. "Is he alone?"

"Think so."

"Okay, then this is what needs to happen. I'm going to wait until he leaves. Catch him off guard. You find a phone and call the police. The warehouse is off limits as government property, so just being inside ought to be enough to get the right people asking the right questions."

Scott waved Kowalski off and cautiously approached the building from the narrow alley. Footsteps scraped on the gravel-topped roof above his head. He flattened himself against the brick wall and shoved the top box off a stack of crates as Derek's feet groped the air beneath him. With a muffled curse, his brother landed hard on the pavement, a pistol clutched in his left hand.

Scott leaped on top of him and pinned his arms to the ground. "Find what you're looking for? Money, or that log book?"

"At least now I know who's got it."

Scott shook his head. "Not me. I suppose Brogan turned it over to the police."

Derek looked shocked and moistened his lips. "Just like I planned to."

An uneasy feeling settled in Scott's gut. Brogan. He hadn't bought his story from the first. "He's a Treasury agent, right?"

"And I'm the Pope," Derek recovered with a sneer.

"Give me the gun, Derek!"

"Not a chance, little brother. Dead men make great scape-goats. Just ask Lanier."

Alarmed, Scott tightened his grip slightly. "What do you mean? Why did you come back?"

"You think you're so smart, hotshot. Figure it out."

Scott smashed his fist against Derek's chin and thumped his gun hand against the pavement. Again. And again. Derek's grip loosened enough for Scott to swat the pistol from his grasp. It skittered along the pavement. "He's still alive, isn't he?"

Derek managed to smirk despite a cut lip. "If he is, your life ain't worth shit once he finds out you've been banging his old lady."

"You crude son-of-a-bitch—"

With a burst of strength, Derek struggled free and landed a blow to his ribs that knocked him aside. Scott started to rise. A crate cracked across the back of the head. Scott stumbled, fell to his knees and collapsed. Footsteps pounded the alley. An engine started and roared away.

Scott struggled to his feet. He touched the back of his head, winced and drew back fingers sticky with warm blood. Metal glinted several feet away under the dim streetlight. At least Derek hadn't picked up the gun. He pocketed the pistol, revved up the Suzuki and blasted down Lake Avenue. Early morning light streaked the sky, reflected off the rearview mirror of Derek's Samurai several blocks ahead.

Scott skittered over the railroad tracks and followed down Garfield Avenue. The Samurai picked up speed, bounced onto the interstate and veered left on the Highway 2 cutoff to Wisconsin.

The distant sound of sirens filled the air, but Scott didn't dare look back, intent on maintaining control despite the high wind that ripped the air over the St. Louis River.

Midway across the Bong Bridge, Derek accelerated and turned to glance over his shoulder. Moments later, the Samurai veered into the deflective concrete railing. Scott braked and slid sideways, painfully abrading his leg. Derek's jeep spun out of control, flipped over the median and skidded upside down in the oncoming lane.

Expansion joints rumbled from an approaching truck. Horrified, Scott stood as if grounded. Air brakes screeched simultaneously as a semi's front grill slammed into the jeep, crushing it. Metal scraped against metal. Glass scattered across the pavement, echoing discordantly in the early morning air.

Then silence hung ominously over the bridge. Scott leapt over the median and yanked open the door of the truck. He grabbed the driver's arm and pulled him out. Sick at heart, he knew it was already too late for his brother. The truck driver beside him, he ran for cover as flames erupted and the Samurai exploded into a ball of light.

Something breathed in her face. Breanna shrieked and jolted awake. Flannaghan's wet nose touched hers as he nuzzled her chin. Laughing, she reached on the other side for Scott and found empty space.

She put on her glasses and flopped back down on the pillows, reluctant to start the day. The house was quiet and void of the smell of brewing coffee. Flannaghan bunted her hand, pranced in a half crouch and spun around, ready to play.

"Must be nice to be a morning person, Flanny." She dug a robe from the closet and put the dog outside before she realized the house was also empty. By the time she reached the kitchen, the lingering sense of being loved had turned into a half-panicked feeling of unreality.

Scott was gone again and this time had not even left a note.

Water gushed over her hand as she filled the coffee carafe and momentarily drifted back into the night's events. She shook her head. He'd probably gone to pick up milk and would be back by the time she finished showering. She turned on the small television on the counter while she made coffee. The morning news program showed her leaving the courthouse yesterday afternoon as several reporters vied for attention and Wade Crandall offered glib non-answers.

Mesmerized, she stared at her image, unnerved by all that still lay ahead. The announcer's voice cut through her thoughts.

"Fire erupted this morning..."

Breanna shuddered and clicked the set off. How much more would she have to take before the nightmare would be over?

She showered, dressed and still received no word from Scott. Restless and uneasy, she searched for Marc's logbook. Scott had said he put it in a safe place and he must have. Thirty minutes later, she still hadn't found it.

Searching the upstairs bookcases only revealed several hundred dollars more of cash in Lillian's books.

Nick showed up at ten o'clock carrying a bag of Danish crispies. "I thought maybe you hadn't had breakfast."

Breanna smiled and shook her head. "Good guess."

He gave her an appraising grin. "You look like you had a good night."

She turned away to hide the blush she felt rising in her face. "Yes, thank you," she murmured. "Would you like coffee?"

He followed to the kitchen and poured himself a cup as she returned to her seat at the kitchen table. Flannaghan growled perfunctorily and settled down grumpily by Breanna's feet.

Nick leaned against the counter. "Any word from Edwards?"

She munched on the pastry and contemplated an answer that wouldn't be an outright lie. "No one's called this morning."

She darted a glance at Nick. He appeared on the verge of saying something, but he looked different this morning. Younger. Almost boyish. Then it hit her like a blast of lake wind. "You shaved off your moustache."

For a moment, she could have sworn he flushed before he took a large gulp of coffee. "Figured it was time for a change. Ready to do some target practice?"

"Only if you're going to insist."

Nick smiled and followed her out the door. "You bet I am."

At the gun range, Breanna's agitation returned as Nick used the situation as an excuse to have his hands on her arms, and his body close to hers. He persisted in showing her how to hold the Beretta, how to aim, how she should stand. She missed the target every time.

Frustrated, Breanna brought her elbow back hard into his ribs. She glanced over her shoulder and gave him a sweet smile. "Nicholson, if you don't quit standing on top of me, I'm going to shoot your goddamn foot off. Now move."

Muttering a protest and rubbing his side, he stepped back.

Breanna closed her eyes and took a deep breath. The Beretta weighed heavily in her hand. A serious gun she prayed she'd never need to use.

Grandmother's voice drifted through her mind as if it were only yesterday. "A woman has to be able to take care of herself. Sometimes the very ones you think you should trust are the ones who'll do you the most harm. You have to trust your instincts."

So far her instincts only brought more trouble. If she hadn't let Scott wander in and out of her bed last night, she might not be so worried about why he'd come back and where he was now. She wouldn't be wondering if he'd left for good. Or if he'd left because he wanted to, or because he had to.

As for Nick, although he'd given her a difficult time at first, he wouldn't be trying to protect her if he still thought she was guilty. At least she didn't think so. Keeping her eyes shut, she raised the Beretta and fired, shifted position and fired again. She opened her eyes, lowered the gun, spun around, and fired three times.

Nick stood behind her, arms crossed. "What the hell is it you're doing?"

"Practicing. You said I had to practice, so that's what I'm doing. My grandmother always said that if someone was after you, they weren't likely to stand around like a paper target waiting to get shot."

"Good point," he muttered. "Maybe I should take you to the police range. Or the carnival and you could shoot metal ducks."

She widened her eyes and pretended to consider the thought. "Great idea, Nick. Can we go right now?"

"Afraid not."

She laughed at his serious expression and stuffed the gun back into its case. "I was kidding. It's almost eleven thirty, and I'd like to go home."

"How about having lunch?"

She shrugged. "Sounds fine."

Nick's cell phone trilled as they got into the Mercedes. "Mind if I make a call?"

She shook her head and started the car. Nick punched in a number, and she tried to focus her attention away from his call as he spoke noncommittally into the phone. Twice he glanced speculatively at her as she drove.

Sunshine warmed her face. A perfect day. Maybe Scott had taken the boat out again.

Scott, Scott, Scott. Memories of the night before replayed in slow motion until she felt warm and lightheaded. She started at Nick's voice. He disconnected the call.

"I won't be able to take you to lunch after all. Any plans for the afternoon?"

"Just hang around the house, do a little unpacking, I guess. Who's the urgent caller?"

"You know there are things I can't tell you or I'd be risking my job." He studied her a moment before continuing. His fingers trailed down her bare arm. "Breanna, I'm trying to help you, and I won't give up or go back to Minneapolis until everything about this case is resolved."

Breanna was silent. Give up on what? This case? The words sounded far more clinical than Nick had acted in days, and she wondered exactly what his idea of a resolution was.

"What time did Edwards leave last night?"

"Last night?" She almost hit the huge oak at the foot of her driveway and knew there was no point denying what he said.

Nick's face was grave. "He got a phone call at your house early this morning. Then he left to meet Derek. Any idea of what he took with him?"

Chapter 28

Breanna froze, then got out of the Mercedes and slammed the door. "Nothing! He wouldn't steal anything from me." *Then where is the book, where is he,* her thoughts taunted.

Nick followed her to the front porch. "Take a good look around while I'm gone. Maybe there's something missing from those boxes you brought from the apartment. I'll stop by later."

She practically closed the door in his face. "I'll probably be at my uncle's."

Shaken, she checked the answering machine. A message from Murray, but none from Scott. Her mind mocked with a thousand possibilities and returned to one. He'd only come back for the logbook. She tried to push the doubts away, but they clamored like hungry gulls at the edges of her thoughts.

Maybe she had overlooked a clue about Marc amidst the junk she and Scott had hauled from the apartment. She dug through several cartons and found nothing unusual. Except for the new swimsuit she'd ordered a month ago. Marc said it made her look fat and told her she had to return it.

He couldn't tell her that now. She put on the suede string bikini and checked her reflection. Triangles of soft chamois tied at the hips and at the neck. Turquoise beaded fringe decorated the top and bottom, creating the illusion of being the only covering for bare skin. No way did she look fat, but she'd never dare wear the thing at the beach, either. But since she was alone, it didn't matter.

Tired and draggy from the days spent in jail, she sighed. It was too warm and sunny to waste sitting inside, waiting for something to happen or someone to call, digging through possessions she'd be better off trashing. She pulled a blanket from the closet, took the portable CD player and went out on the side patio. Flannaghan followed and flopped on the quilt as soon as she tried to lay a corner down.

"Okay, rascal, you asked for it." Breanna tugged on the blanket and rolled the Irish Setter inside. He thrashed and barked, finally wriggling free and knocking her to the ground.

Laughing, she cupped his head between her hands and let him lick the tip of her nose. The back of her neck prickled and for a moment, she couldn't move, too paralyzed with fright.

"Seems a shame to waste a suit like that on a stupid mutt."

Breanna gasped and glanced over her shoulder. Lucas Brogan stood at the edge of the patio wall, contemplating her as if she were dessert at a five star restaurant.

The trucker clamped a hand on Scott's shoulder as the air around them filled with sirens. "I believe you saved my life, son. What happened? Know who he is?"

Scott closed his eyes against shock deeper than pain. "He was my brother."

Squad cars arrived from both directions, the Wisconsin Highway Patrol initially taking charge until the place of impact was determined to be in Minnesota. Scott let a paramedic guide him to a waiting vehicle as fire trucks hosed down the semi-truck and the remains of Derek's jeep. How was he going to tell his father?

The hospital staff had to snip off his jeans to dress the abrasion that ran from hip to knee. Harvey Edwards shuffled into the emergency room carrying a cotton shirt and clean pair of trousers and surveyed Scott's bandaged hand.

"You left some clothes the other night. Thought maybe you could use these."

"Thanks, Dad. Who told you?"

Harvey stood awkwardly by the examining table. "Police came by. I asked them to bring me over. You were there?"

Scott's eyes burned, and he blinked. "I caused it."

"Now how do you figure that?" his father chided.

"I should have let him go. I should have waited for Kowalski to come back with the police. I should have—"

Harvey lightly tapped his arm. "Enough. You only did what

I asked you to. And I've been thinking a lot about Derek, ever since Brogan's visit last week. We lost your brother a long time ago. I really think that's why your mother left."

His mother. His father hadn't mentioned her in years. Scott's head snapped up, and he met his father's gaze.

Harvey's gray eyes were moist. "She tried to treat Derek like her own. She really did. But he was always a handful and it finally got to her."

"What are you saying, Dad?"

"I guess I should have told you before, but I didn't want there to be a difference between you and Derek. I was married before I met your mother. Derek's mother died when Derek was just a baby. Drove off the Arrowhead Bridge into the St. Louis River on the way home from a country tavern in Wisconsin."

Scott quietly contemplated what his father had just told him. He'd been nine when his own mother had disappeared which meant Derek had been sixteen. Rowdy, untamed and on probation for setting a fire at the high school. He rubbed his brow and remembered what Breanna had told him several times. *It wasn't your fault.* He took a small measure of comfort with the thought that maybe she was right.

Two police officers appeared to escort him to the station for questioning. Although Harvey wanted to go with him, Scott insisted his father go back home and rest. "It's just routine, Dad. Don't worry, and I'll stop and see you as soon as it's over." He hid his own uneasiness behind a smile and Harvey reluctantly left.

Nervous at first, Scott relaxed when the police seemed to be simply fact gathering about the accident. Then a deputy sheriff showed up to take him across the Civic Center Plaza to the St. Louis County Sheriff's Headquarters and his apprehension returned.

Scott sat at a narrow oak table and wondered if this was the same room where Breanna had been questioned. Small, windowless, and suffocating. Captain Belcastro was even less personable. No wonder Breanna had been so panicked.

Breanna. He hoped she was safe at home.

Breanna jumped to her feet. "What do you want?"

Brogan stepped over the low wall, but stopped short when Flannaghan emitted a low growl. "You have something I want."

Cold with fear, she hugged her arms until she realized the motion deepened her cleavage and made her breasts look as if they would tumble out from behind the tiny triangles of suede fabric. Brogan's blue eyes darkened. She moved back until she bumped the barbecue grill.

He flipped out a wallet and held it up for her inspection. Dressed in jeans, polo shirt and sport coat, he looked casually businesslike. A lock of blond hung across his tanned forehead.

"Take it easy, Breanna. I thought Scott or Nick had told you I'm with the IRS, Criminal Investigations Division. You took some papers from your husband's warehouse." He took her silence for agreement, though she remained frozen in place.

"I want them."

She moistened her lips. "I'd like to see your ID up close, please." Edging forward, she took the leather wallet and studied the picture and official looking badge. Having never seen one before, she knew she couldn't judge its legitimacy but something about the way Brogan's picture appeared superimposed on the card looked peculiar to her photographer's eye. "All I have are the insurance documents."

"What about the book? Might have looked something like a journal."

She started and silently cursed. Scott was right. She was no good at hiding the truth.

Brogan smiled. "I thought so. Will you get it for me, please?"

She edged closer to the door. "It's not here. But even if it were, before I turn anything over to anyone, I'm going to call my lawyer. Even the IRS must be required to have a subpoena."

Yanking on the French door, she darted inside and tried to pull the door shut on his foot. Flannaghan growled, leaped forward and received a heavy kick to his side that knocked the wind from him. Brogan shouldered through the opening and slammed the door. The Irish Setter went wild with barking as

Breanna dashed for the phone.

Brogan's hand covered hers as she started to dial. He took the receiver and replaced it on the cradle.

"Don't say I didn't try to be nice, but I'm sick and tired of games, and I'm running out of time. Give me the book."

She tried to swallow past the lump of fear in her throat. "I already told you I don't have it." Scott's note danced before her mind. *I cooked up a safe place for the log.*

Cooked up. Her eyes darted around the kitchen. Lillian's cookbooks lined the counter backsplash next to the refrigerator. A slim burgundy binder rested between the red Betty Crocker cookbook and Paul Prudhomes' Cajun Cookery.

Scott hadn't come back just for the book, just for one last fling. Which could only mean that something had happened to him.

Brogan's steely eyes bore into her, and she forced herself to return his gaze with a noncommittal shrug. Once he had the book, she'd lose any bargaining power. "My house has been burglarized and searched, so I had to find a safe place. It's not here, but I can tell you where it is."

"You'll show me."

The phone rang. Brogan's hand closed around her upper arm. "Let it ring."

"Lucas, it's probably my uncle. If I don't answer, he'll come storming over with the entire police force."

His callused hand trailed up her arm and circled her neck. "Then make it breezy. You've already seen my handiwork, and I can be long gone before anyone shows up to rescue you."

His handiwork. Nina Rogers stuffed into a packing crate at the warehouse, purple bruises circling her neck. "You killed Nina."

Cold metal jabbed her ribs. "Answer the phone."

She took a shaky breath and picked up the receiver. "Hello?"

"Breanna!" Murray's voice was filled with impatient concern. "I was about to hang up. Figured you might have gone to the jail."

"Why would I do that?"

"To see Scott. For Pete's sake, haven't you seen the news? Scott and Derek had a wreck on the Bong Bridge early this morning. Derek's dead and Scott's being held for questioning. Since I know you'll want to see him no matter what I say, I'll come pick you up, go with you for moral support."

"I don't think so, Murray." She knew her voice came out squeaky when Lucas poked her ribs again with a gun barrel. Swallowing hard, she rushed on. "I've decided to drive up to the ski lodge for a couple of days. Maybe I can get the kind of quiet I enjoyed at Lake Vermilion last weekend."

"For Christ's sake, Breanna," Murray's voice rose with incredulity. "The cops showed up and arrested you!"

"You're right. But it would be a welcome relief this time. Gotta go, Murr. Talk to you soon."

Brogan grabbed the phone and hung up. "Where'd you stash the book?"

"My parents had a place up at Lutsen. It's pretty remote. You have to know how to find it. That's where I hid the book. Once we're there, you'll practically be in Canada."

"*We'll* practically be in Canada. Now, let's get going. But first do something with your dog before he rips the door off."

One hand clutching a handful of her hair, the other holding the gun against her side, Brogan shoved her over to the French doors where Flannaghan barked and leapt, frantic to get in.

"No funny stuff. Remember I don't care who gets the first bullet, you or that stupid mutt."

Breanna gripped Flannaghan's collar, half dragged, half cajoled him to the utility room and pulled the door shut.

Brogan nodded, grabbed her by the elbow and propelled her toward the front door. "You're doing good. Now let's get going."

Time. She needed to buy time to let Murray figure out the message. Or get to the bedroom and get the Beretta. Breanna glanced down at the bikini. "Can't I please put some clothes on? And shoes?"

His smile was so malevolently lecherous, she shuddered. "I'd hate to think there'd be no time for fun when you're already undressed for it." He kept the gun on her, opened the hall closet and threw the first thing that he touched. Scott's sweatshirt jacket hit her in the chest. He kicked at the sandals she'd left by the door. "Put 'em on."

In the garage, he held the gun while she put the top up on the Mercedes. Then he bound her hands with a rope he produced from his pocket. The nylon cord bit into her wrists. He shoved her into the passenger seat, bumping her head against the doorframe. Tears stung her eyes.

"We'll take this as far as Grand Marais. Think I'll drive, but try anything stupid, and I'll find several ways to make you regret it. And none of them will involve anything as merciful as a bullet." He yanked her hair hard and pulled out of the driveway.

Breanna huddled in the seat as the convertible traveled along London Road toward the edge of town and the North Shore Highway.

Brogan switched the radio on and lit a cigarette. She edged closer to the door, placed her arms along the armrest and pressed the unlock button. Intent on the news broadcast, Brogan didn't glance at her.

She started as she felt his gaze crawl over her from behind his wrap around sunglasses. "Know what puzzles me?"

She shook her head.

"How you managed to get off that boat and look so damn sexy when your old man's fish bait."

She stared at him. "I didn't do it."

Brogan roared with laughter. "No shit, doll. Know why you don't have to convince me?"

Her eyes widened with horror. "Because you did? Why?"

Brogan's voice became icy. "I couldn't make him understand the way we do business in my port. He thought he could squeeze me out, but I used his greed to my advantage."

Breanna lapsed into silence. Her mind whirled. If Brogan had set the explosives, why had she been spared? If Marc was dead, who had attacked her in Montreal? "What about Gayle?"

Brogan pitched his cigarette out the window. "She was just a go-between for Marc and his brother. And a watchdog over you. Not that it matters. She won't be talking. Either that boyfriend of yours or Derek got to her in Montreal. Doesn't matter to me which one. Derek's dead and Scott's bound to get stuck with the blame."

Breanna shivered. She had to get away from him before they got past the city limits or she couldn't expect to find anyone to help her. Even bouncing out on the asphalt had to be preferable to what Brogan planned to do. Or would do when he discovered she was lying about the logbook.

An expansive view of Lake Superior appeared on her right. Lucas braked at the Lester River Bridge as the car in front slowed at the scenic overlook and Tourist Information Center. He leaned toward his side, peered out the side window and accelerated. Breanna reached over and yanked the steering wheel with all her strength.

Caught off guard, Brogan cursed as the tires skidded on the gravel on the edge of the road. Crouching on the far edge of the seat, Breanna swung her bound hands up, knocking his arm as he turned to grab her.

"You little bitch!" The Mercedes bounced, hit the three-foot boulders lining the roadway and stopped. Breanna's shoulder hit the door as her fingers frantically pulled on the handle. With a hiss, the air bag on the driver's side popped and expanded, momentarily trapping Brogan in place before it deflated. He cursed and clawed at his sunglasses. She fell from the car and landed on her knees. Gravel bit into her skin.

Scrambling to her feet, she ran.

Chapter 29

Gravel crunched beneath her feet. Breanna held her bound hands against her chest and ran toward the small building at the edge of the roadway. A hundred yards away. Endless miles.

Sirens shrieked, filling the air. Brogan roared her name. She glanced over her shoulder. Her leather sandals slipped on loose pebbles. She stumbled. A bullet whizzed past her shoulder. Diving for safety, she heard screams, saw the blinding approach of squad cars. Several shots rang out.

Someone shouted her name, but paralyzed with fear, she crouched against the tiny structure, gasping for breath. Footsteps crunched closer. Closer. She bit her lip, trying to slow her breathing, fighting panic, preparing to run. Then Nick's hands were on her arms, hauling her to her feet.

"Breanna. Thank God." His voice was husky as he cupped her face in his palms. Green eyes searched hers.

"I'm okay." She blinked back tears and collapsed against his chest. "How did you know?"

"The tap on your phone. And luckily, Murray also had the sense to call the police after you hung up, and he couldn't get you on your cell." He untied her hands and gently rubbed her chafed wrists. Arm around her, he slowly walked her to the circle of police and county sheriffs' cars.

Police led a handcuffed Brogan to a waiting police sedan. "Looks like you're going to be dry docked for a long, long time, Burkett." One of the officers chuckled and shoved him into the back seat.

Breanna shook her head. "His name is Lucas Brogan. He said he's a Treasury Agent."

Nick spoke up. "Lucas Brogan *was* a Treasury Agent. But this guy's Denny Burkett. He's got a long list of credentials of a different sort."

Nick held her at arms' length, checking her over, and frowned. "What the hell have you got on under that jacket?"

"Not much," she murmured, feeling self-conscious about the way she must look. The gray sweatshirt barely covered her bikini, and her hands and knees were scraped and bleeding. "When did you find out who he is?"

Nick wrapped an arm around her shoulder and helped her into the back seat of another police car. "This morning. Brogan's body surfaced near Barker's Island. He was doing undercover work when he stumbled onto what Derek and your husband were up to. Taking over what Burkett saw as his domain. Well, Brogan was after old Denny, too, so Denny got rid of Brogan. And none of the other dock workers were about to tell the police or anyone else what had happened."

Breanna shivered and looked at the lake, wishing she could lose herself on the calm waters. "What does all this mean?"

Nick took her hand in his. "Your husband is dead. So are Derek and Nina. Gayle's in a hospital in Montreal, in a coma from a gunshot wound, but the prognosis is good. The police suspect Derek, or—" he hesitated. "Scott. But it's over."

"Scott didn't do it!" Tears burned her eyes. She yanked her hand back and pulled the jacket tighter.

"Breanna," he began, in the tone one would use with an irrational teenager.

"I can prove it. And I won't give up until I do." She challenged him with her eyes.

Nick sighed and looked away. "You'll need to answer a lot of questions for the police. But first we'll get your car towed, and I'll take you home so you can get dressed. Lord help me, but you are one stubbornly loyal woman."

Murray was waiting at her house and greeted her with a rib-crunching hug. "Are you okay, kid?"

"Sure, Murray. You saved my life."

Murray scowled but his eyes twinkled. "Hey, I have to look after my favorite niece."

"I'm your only niece."

His eyes twinkled. "Well, yeah, but even if I had a dozen, you'd be my favorite. I promised your mother I'd take care of you. Any chance that I can give it up as a career?"

She punched him lightly on the arm and bent to pet Flannaghan and let him lick her face. "At least it keeps you out of the bars."

"Which in my case is bad for business," he pointed out and grinned.

Breanna changed into turquoise jeans and a striped knit shirt, then made a hurried phone call to Wade Crandall, who advised her to turn the logbook over to the Sheriff. Nick flipped through the journal.

"So why didn't you show this to me?" His tone was slightly accusatory.

She sighed. "To be honest, Nick, it's been hard to know if you were my friend or Belcastro's. And I wasn't sure it had any value."

"Had any value?" He looked astonished. "It's a gold mine."

"Burkett seemed to think so." She shuddered.

Nick moved closer as if to offer reassurance, but Murray intercepted him and squeezed her shoulders. "Hey, its over. How about if I go with you to the police station?"

She opened her mouth to accept, but Nick interrupted. "Why don't you get her car taken care of? I don't think it's totaled, but it's going to need some body work."

Murray ignored him and gazed intently at her. "What do you want me to do, Breanna?"

Good old Murray. She could always count on him to put her wishes above anyone else's. "See about getting my car fixed. Then meet me here for supper? We can order pizza."

"Sure thing, sweetie. I'll handle it. See you later."

After answering seemingly endless questions by the police, Breanna paced the lobby of the Sheriff's Headquarters and waited to see Captain Belcastro. She plunked coins into the paper vending machine and pulled out a copy of the Duluth *News Tribune*. The front page contained a story about her release from jail and a sketch of the earrings that had bought her freedom.

She threw down the paper in dismay. At least the reporter didn't know their true value. Now she'd have to keep them locked up. And then what was the point of owning them?

Belcastro stood and listened to her assertion that the caretaker at the estate in Lake Vermilion would verify Scott's alibi for the night Gayle was shot in Montreal.

He leaned against the table. "I'm sure you understand we'll have to ask him some questions. But if it checks out, your friend will be released tomorrow."

She sat forward. "Why can't he be released on bail?"

Belcastro stroked his chin. "Because I can't take the chance he'll disappear again. So, I've decided we'll hold him for the twenty-four hours the law allows." His eyes bored into hers. "And of course there's the matter of the two of you withholding evidence."

Breanna tightened her jaw. Damn him, but she supposed if she could stand two nights in jail, Scott would survive one. "Can I see him?"

The captain shook his head. "Visiting hours are over for the day. By the way, the Canadian authorities haven't been able to locate Gregory Lanier, or even verify he existed. We'll let you know what happens."

Breanna left the Sheriff's office, dazed and confused. If there was no Gregory Lanier, then who was Gayle's husband? Marc?

The thought of Marc being a bigamist in addition to everything else made her sick to her stomach.

Murray burned hamburgers for supper. Nick lifted the bun and tried to hide his distaste at the charcoaled lump of ground round. Breanna laughed. "Murray's burgers are best with lots of pickles, onions, and barbecue sauce. Lots and lots of barbecue sauce."

He leaned closer and whispered in her ear. "Want me to pick up a Sammy's shrimp and onion pizza after he leaves?"

She felt a start of surprise. "How did you know that's my absolute favorite?"

"Thought I told you I intended to find out everything about you."

Nick's gaze intensified until she felt compelled to turn

away. "So you did," she murmured and hurried out to the patio to join her uncle.

Nick helped with dishes but left before Murray. Breanna sensed her uncle wanted to make sure she was safely alone before he went on to close up the bar.

He kissed her forehead. "Goodnight. sweetie. Try to put it all out of your mind."

"I'll try. Thanks again for being here for me."

Put it out of your mind. Good advice she wished she could follow. She switched on the stereo to an Oldies station and immediately became swamped with longing for Scott as the Beach Boys sang the upbeat love song she remembered from her dreams the morning Scott rescued her from the lake.

Two and a half weeks ago. She felt she'd lived a lifetime since then. *Wouldn't It Be Nice.*

Flannaghan barked as the doorbell chimed. Nick stood on the porch, pizza box in one hand, a paper wrapped bottle in the other. He smiled. "Aren't you going to let me in?"

She stepped aside and closed the door, following him to the living room where he deposited the pizza on the coffee table.

"Are you as hungry as I am?"

She went to the bar to get glasses. "Probably not. I don't seem to have much of an appetite lately. But then, Marc always told me I could stand to lose ten pounds."

Nick looked at her. An amazed look creased his brow. "That just proves the man was nuts."

She shrugged and took a seat on the couch while Nick poured two glasses of white Zinfandel. Settling against the cushions, she took a tiny sip. Once again, her favorite, right down to the Beringer label. "Actually, Nick, I'm exhausted. I don't feel up to answering even one more question."

He sat next to her and stretched one arm along the back of the couch. "So don't. Besides, I figured it's your turn to do the asking."

She swirled her wineglass and contemplated the man next to her. Without his moustache, he looked younger than he had before. Light brown hair was neatly trimmed and styled. A sharp dresser, especially since the trip to Montreal.

Tonight he wore dark brown corduroys and a matching striped shirt with contrasting lines of forest green that deepened the color of his eyes to moss. She'd spent countless hours with him the past two weeks and yet knew nothing about him or his private life.

She decided to start at the first question she'd had about him. "Why don't you use your first name? What does N. J. stand for, anyway?"

"Norbert Jeremy."

Breanna laughed until she choked, and he had to pound on her back.

A slight flush stained his face. "It's not that funny."

"Oh, yes it is, Norbie." She giggled. "But only because it doesn't suit you even a tiny bit."

"Yeah, well if you tell a soul, I'll tickle the bottoms of your feet until you beg for mercy." He laid a hand on her ankle as if to carry out his threat. Breanna placed her hand on top of his to stop him. Nick hesitated, then leaned closer as if to kiss her.

She shifted around. "Maybe we should eat the pizza before it gets cold."

He drew back, his expression unreadable, then went to the kitchen for plates and napkins.

While they ate, Nick answered her questions about his family, how he'd grown up in St. Paul, but during his ten years of service with the FBI had lived in dozens of cities across the country, finally settling in Minneapolis and opening his own investigative services company three years earlier. But he again refused to explain why he'd left the government.

Afraid of his motivations for being there, Breanna insisted he leave as soon as the pizza and wine were gone. She couldn't handle it if he tried to get more than friendly with her. She was starting to like him, even if she didn't want *that* kind of attention from him. She walked him to the door.

Resting his hands on her shoulders, he looked intently into her eyes. "Breanna, I had no idea that I'd wind up feeling the way I do about you. I think you know what I'm about to say. But I have to tell you—"

Startled and confused, she placed her fingertips against his lips. "Don't. Please don't say anything."

"I think if you got to know me better, we'd discover something special."

"I like you, Nick, I really do and two weeks ago you terrified me. But I don't think I can feel anything more than friendship for you."

"Why not?"

She shrugged, looked away and forced herself to meet his eyes again. "No chemistry. I'm sorry, it's just not there."

He pulled her into a hug, released her and opened the door. "We'll see," he said. "I'll call you tomorrow."

Breanna spent a restless night, trying to reconcile the fears of the past three weeks with everyone's assurances that Marc was really dead. The Beretta rested in the nightstand, ready to fire as soon as the safety was released. Somehow, its presence allowed her to drift into uneasy dreams. She awoke several times, each time sleepily groping the space next to her and startling herself fully awake with its emptiness.

Her yearning for Scott was a physical ache. Although she wondered how they could patch a life together after all that had happened, it was what she wanted more than anything she'd ever longed for in her life.

She dreamed she was in Montreal. A dark man stared at her from the shadows, then moved closer, eyes burning like coals in the darkness. The sharp scent of Drakkar Noir tormented her senses. She screamed and bolted upright.

Flannaghan stood by the bedside, wagging his tail and whimpering. She fumbled for the phone and dialed the number for the Edgewater. The desk clerk put her through to Nick's room.

He answered on the second ring, as alert as if he'd been expecting a call. "What's wrong, Breanna."

"How can you and Belcastro be so sure Marc's dead and not Gregory Lanier?"

He sighed and patiently repeated the forensics involved in identifying a body. "So there's no way it wasn't your husband.

I'll take you over to the medical examiner's in the morning, if it will help. Would you feel safer if I came over?"

She would. Then again, remembering Nick's recent attentions, she wouldn't. She twisted the phone cord around her hand. "That's okay. I'll be all right. I'll call you in the morning." She hung up the phone and patted the bed. Flannaghan bounded up beside her and settled down with a contented noise. Turning off the light, she settled back against the pillows, but sleep eluded her for a long time.

She slept late. Bright sunlight streamed in the windows, but she awakened to Flannaghan bunting her arm, demanding attention. By the time Breanna showered, dressed and gulped down two cups of coffee, it was past noon.

Murray had arranged a loaner car for her with the Mercedes dealership. She backed the sedan out of the garage and remembered she'd forgotten to call Nick. He'd probably already be at the Sheriff's office, she consoled her twinge of guilt as she passed the Edgewater several miles later.

Besides, stopping at his motel might convey she'd changed her mind about what she'd said last night. Nick was a nice-looking guy, but lacked Scott's brown-eyed, blond appeal. Or chemistry. Or whatever it was that made her want him despite the time and distance of the past nine years.

The desk clerk at the Sheriff's office looked Breanna over, blue eyes bright with curiosity and informed her Scott had already been released. "Your picture was in the papers again this morning, Miss Alden. Did you want to speak with Captain Belcastro?"

Not if she could avoid it. Breanna murmured no thanks and stepped back out into the gray drizzle hanging over the city. Fog hung thickly over the harbor. She couldn't even see the Aerial Bridge, a mere half-mile away. She dug her cell phone from her purse and tried to call Scott, but there was no answer at his house.

Overwhelmed with loneliness, she felt a need to hold something of her parents. She got in the car and drove to the covered parking lot at the bank. She set up an appointment with Elliott Stenberg for the next morning to discuss the handling of her money and managed to wheedle the earrings from Albert Warren.

"Can I take them with me, Mr. Warren," she asked, holding the heavy antique gold to her ears and giving him her most persuasive smile.

"It's not in keeping with bank policy. I mean, we know you have the money to cover the loan, but—"

She felt a surge of determination but managed to smile sweetly. It was foolish to remove the earrings from the bank, she knew this. But they were the one thing which made her feel connected to her family. "Please?"

He held his hands out in a gesture of surrender. "Of course, Miss Alden. I wouldn't want you to think we can't accommodate you."

Another impulse made her stop at the florist for a flowering plant before driving to Scott's father's house. Pulling up in front of the small frame house, she surveyed the neighborhood and remembered the dire warnings both her father and Scott's had issued about insurmountable differences in their backgrounds.

Too bad. She buttoned her raincoat and pulled the hood up. If she and Scott could see beyond the money, why should it matter? Maybe they could find a way to help his father, too.

She rang the bell and waited. Then rang again before she heard slow footsteps approach the door. Harvey Edwards pushed open the battered screen and gave her a somber look.

She pushed the hood off and rushed to fill the awkward silence. "Hi, Mr. Edwards, remember me? Breanna Alden."

"I knew who you were. Mrs. Lanier."

Breanna felt heat flood her face. "Yes, well—"

"He's not here."

"That's okay, Mr. Edwards. I really stopped by to see you."

Bushy gray eyebrows shot up. "Me? What the hell for?"

She held the plant out to him, but he merely stared. Her arm felt like lead, and finally she set the basket on the porch. "I wanted to tell you how sorry I am about Derek."

A look of pain crossed his face, and his voice became gruffer. "Can't change the way things are meant to be, though sometimes we butt our heads against a brick wall trying."

She glanced away, then met his fierce expression. "If there's anything you need, anything I can do, please let me know."

"Leave Scott alone. That's all I ask," he said as he slowly closed the door. "You and your family have caused my son nothing but heartache."

Chapter 30

Breanna drove around for hours after she left the Edwards house. Harvey Edwards' words echoed in her mind, pounded her heart.

You and your family have caused my son nothing but heartache.

He was right. Scott had lost his brother, his business, been shot at, chased, and arrested.

All because of her.

She left a message for Nick at the Edgewater, telling him she was with Murray, in hopes he wouldn't stop by her house unexpectedly. If Scott decided he needed to see her, she wanted to be alone. Finally, she drove home, checked for messages and called her uncle.

"I think I'd like to be alone tonight, Murray. I'm beat and think I'll go to bed early."

He hesitated. "Are you sure? I'd be glad to come over."

"Thanks, but I'm sure. I'll call you in the morning." She hung up the phone.

Remembering the earrings, she took them from her purse and clipped the heavy gold on her ears. Tired and despondent, she stared at her reflection in the mirror. Blue glasses framed sapphire blue eyes. Dark hair hung sleekly to just past her chin. She swung her head, letting the earrings clunk against her neck. alexandrites, their color shifting from smoky purple to green, diamonds and antique gold gleamed in the soft light of the table lamp.

She knew she looked ridiculous, in violet satin pajamas, a fortune in her ears. But wearing the earrings cheered her.

She dialed Scott's number. No answer. She supposed he'd gone to be with his father. After her visit, there was no way she'd humiliate herself further by calling his house.

Scott sat on the worn couch and stretched out his legs. Why hadn't Breanna tried to see him? Or call? "Dad," he called out as his father moved slowly around the kitchen, determinedly heating soup and making sandwiches, "did Breanna Alden call here today?"

Harvey dropped a pot and swore. "Nope. Don't you think it's time to stop moping about that girl? Some things just ain't meant to be."

Maybe. Maybe not. Scott pondered his father's answer and glanced at the flowering plant on the bookcase. He strode into the kitchen. "Can I help you?"

His father waved a hand impatiently. "And have you fixing one of those jailhouse baloney sandwiches? Not on your life."

Scott crossed his arms, leaned against the door and watched as Harvey shuffled across the cracked vinyl floor. "She was here, wasn't she, Dad."

Harvey scowled. "So what if she was? It would be better for the both of you to let the past go. You were kids. Time to get on with your life."

Scott shook his head. "She *is* my life. And I'm sorry if you find that such a terrible thing."

Darkness fell early. Breanna sat on the living room couch and watched rain pelt the plate glass windows overlooking the lake. The foghorn sounded, eerie and melancholy.

Flannaghan curled at her feet. Flames danced in the fireplace. In her mind, she saw Scott asleep in the firelight. Scott, hair gleaming like gold, smiling sleepily at her. Scott loving her until her bones felt molten.

The phone rang. She grabbed the receiver and knocked it to the floor.

"Breanna! Everything okay?" Nick's anxious voice filled her ear.

"I'm fine. I bumped the phone off the table, that's all," she said trying to hide her disappointment at talking to Nick instead of Scott.

"Are you alone?"

She felt a twinge of irritation and sighed. "Just me and Flannaghan enjoying a fire."

"Want some company?" His voice had such a little boy lilt, she wanted to laugh and almost accepted. But encouraging him would only lead to other problems.

"That's okay. I'm planning on making it an early night. What did you find out today from the coroner?"

"If you're sure." He sounded disappointed, then launched into a grisly description of the medical examiner's report. "So you see, these guys can tell just about everything. Even more if we could use DNA, but that's not possible in this case. But I went over the reports myself. The dental records match perfectly. Right down to the gold crown on his wisdom tooth."

Gold crown. A cold ring of terror circled her heart. She sank back into the chair. Marc's perfect teeth had been his best feature, the one he'd been most proud of.

"Breanna? Do you understand? The records match exactly."

"Oh, God, no," she whispered. "Marc didn't have a gold crown."

He didn't answer.

"Nick," she shouted. "Didn't you hear what I said?" Silence. She depressed the switch hook. The line was dead. She scrambled to find her purse and her cell phone but it wasn't there.

No. In her blind anguish after leaving Scott's house, she'd left the cell phone in the car.

Scott finished supper and half-heartedly watched the Twins game. At least they were ahead by a run. He cleared up the dishes and wandered around the small house. Pulling the curtain aside on the living room windows, he peered out into the gloom. Usually he could see across to the Wisconsin shore, but fog rolled off the water in ghostly clouds, obscuring the lake. The foghorn sounded a mournful note.

Harvey put down the sports section of the newspaper. "For Christ's sake, call her and get it out of your system already."

Muttering beneath his breath, he continued reading.

"Good idea." Scott sprinted to the phone and dialed Breanna's number. He let it ring and ring, more keyed up with each electronic beep. She might be somewhere with Nick. The thought made him tighten his grip on the receiver until his knuckles turned white.

More likely with her uncle.

He relaxed and punched in the number for Murray's Bar. Murray's voice boomed over the clink of glasses. "Sorry, Scott. Breanna's not here. Said she was going to bed early. Didn't say where or with whom."

"Very funny, Murray." He hung up the phone and continued pacing around the living room. He dialed her number a second time. No answer.

Derek had never admitted Lanier was dead.

Dead men make great scapegoats. Just ask Lanier. Figure it out yourself, hotshot. He pulled his windbreaker from the closet.

For a moment, he considered calling Nick but decided he didn't want to share the discovery of Breanna up to her pretty neck in bubble bath. At least he prayed that's what he'd find. "I'm going out for awhile, Dad."

Harvey grunted. "What a surprise."

"I need a favor, though."

Harvey glanced up. "What?"

"I'm worried about Breanna. If I don't call within half an hour, send the police to Lillian Sullivan's house on London Road."

Breanna cautiously hung up the phone. Moving to the kitchen, she checked the other one.

Dead.

The weather. All the rain had affected the telephone line, that was all.

She was halfway to the bedroom to inspect the other phone when the lights went out. Flannaghan growled, low and throaty, and bounded after her. Shivering with fear, she ran into the bedroom and stumbled against the doorframe. A tremor of pain shot through her, but she hobbled to the night-stand and fumbled for the Beretta.

Releasing the safety and cocking the hammer, she took a deep breath and listened. Silence pressed against her ears, broken only by the solemn ticking of the grandfather clock, each minute an eternity.

She waited, remembering what Nick had said. *Someone breaks in, let them find you.* Sensible advice, but she couldn't stand in the bedroom till dawn. The muscles in her neck already ached.

She edged out into the hall. Flannaghan crept beside her, tense and sniffing as she stepped down to the sunken living room. The faint scent of spicy citrus assailed her senses.

Drakkar Noir.

It couldn't be. "Scott," she called out hopefully, knowing with terrifying certainty he wasn't there.

Satin moiré billowed at the French doors leading to the patio. She shivered. Flannaghan growled. The fire flared, revealing the outline of a man sitting in the wing back chair.

"Afraid not, Princess." Marc's voice carried across the room with deadly calm. "How disappointing your lover can't join us. I was looking forward to letting him watch what happens to bad little girls. Right before I cut his balls off."

A scream froze in her throat and for a moment she couldn't move, couldn't speak.

Marc chuckled. "Speechless with enthusiasm, like always. Care to share a bottle of wine? Only this time, be civilized and pour it into glasses. You really made a mess at the Four Seasons."

She stood frozen in place. He gestured impatiently toward the bar. "I said pour me a glass of wine, Breanna. Now do it!"

"No."

The fire partially illuminated his face. A muscle tensed in his jaw. "Grew a little backbone while I was gone, didn't you?"

"Why did you come back?" Her words emerged as an anguished wail.

He drummed an irritating rhythm on the arm of the chair.

"Why not? All my problems have been—disposed of. Besides, I couldn't let you try to spend seventy five million dollars by yourself. You'd probably do something stupid with it. The ASPCA maybe. Food for the homeless. Save the Children. You and Gregory. What a pair of gutless wonders."

"Gregory?" she squeaked.

"The stiff that washed up on shore. My late brother, savior of women and other dumb animals."

She gasped. "Gregory was on the yacht."

Logs shifted, sending up a shower of sparks. Flames roared up the chimney. Pictures of the night on the yacht played through her mind in slow motion.

Voices. *She wasn't supposed to be here, Marc.*

Strange hands on her, tugging on the red scarf, the flash of a knife blade as he freed her and tried to help her up.

Sick bastard.

Collapsing back against the bed. A strange voice murmuring in French. His fingers tugging the flimsy teddy in place, then buckling her into a life vest.

He may be a cold blooded killer, but I'm not.

Floating.

Marc's voice. *What the hell are you doing, Gregory?*

Shivering with cold. The buzz and thump of a bullet. Motors whining. A flicker of light as a seaplane lifted toward the velvet sky. Engines droning, becoming faint. Cold darkness. Then a deafening blast. Fire. She covered her ears with her hands.

"You tried to kill me." Her vision blurred. "You left him to die. Your own brother!"

He shrugged. "Expendable." He rose, a demon returned from hell in the firelight.

Flannaghan growled and stood poised, ready to spring. "Give me the gun, Princess." His voice softened, cajoled. "I promise I won't hurt you. I just want what's mine. You, dearest wife."

She laughed, a shrill sound that echoed off the paneled walls. "You hate me."

He shrugged and took a step closer. "How perceptive you've

become. But I do want you, Breanna. It's my curse. You're so charmingly—pliable. Then there's those lovely earrings you're wearing. And of course, the money."

"The money?" Fingers clenching the pistol, she pretended to consider him and edged around the room toward the foyer. Flannaghan hovered vigilantly beside her. "Now that does create a problem. I only get the money if you're dead." She raised and pointed the gun. "I guess I will have to kill you after all."

Marc hooted. "You don't have the nerve."

Her chest rose and fell with each painful breath. "Don't I? You always said I should learn to seize the moment. This one's mine."

"You're trembling, darling. Something you never did from lovemaking."

She kept the gun level with his chest. "How would you know? Your ideas of sex range from mediocrity to abuse."

"Cold blooded bitch."

Something scraped at the front door. She heard her name called and glanced over her shoulder. Marc vaulted over the sofa. She staggered backward up to the foyer, barely eluding his grasp. Flannaghan's growl intensified to a roar.

Metal gleamed. The dog leapt and knocked her aside. A shot rang out. Flannaghan collapsed in a heap of burnished fur. Marc lunged toward her.

Panic exploded into mindless rage. Screaming, she squeezed the trigger. Again. And again. A dark stain spread across the front of Marc's light colored shirt.

With a shower of glass, the front door burst open. Shots echoed, shattering the ginger jar lamp. Marc crashed over the step and fell to the hardwood floor at her feet. His hand stretched toward her, then stilled.

She stared at his motionless form. The gun slipped from her fingers, and she sank to her knees as Scott and Nick rushed to her side.

Scott dashed in beside Nick to where Breanna huddled on

the floor. In the dim light, her eyes were huge in her white face. Her fingers dug into his arm. "Is he dead?"

Gun drawn, Nick strode through the house while Scott checked Lanier's body for a pulse. "No question about it this time."

"Oh, my God, I killed him. I killed him." She wrapped her arms around herself and sobbed.

Flannaghan whimpered. Scott bent and examined the Irish Setter, then gave him a gentle pat. "Easy, boy. We'll get help."

Sirens swelled through the ominous quiet. Nick returned to the foyer and stood surveying the scene.

"Shit. This is the last thing she needs." He hesitated for a heartbeat, set his Beretta on the floor next to Breanna's and methodically wiped her gun with a linen handkerchief. Then he placed her 9mm in his shoulder holster. He nudged his handgun toward her. "Did you have to use your gun, Breanna?"

Her face was full of confusion as she picked up Nick's pistol, turned it over in her hand and dropped it as if it were a live rodent. "I killed him!" she wailed. "I killed him!"

"No, you didn't. I did."

Incredulous, Scott stared at the detective as Nick removed her glasses and slipped them into his pocket. His voice was hypnotically calm.

"You didn't have time to put your glasses on. It was dark. You couldn't see."

"Dark," she murmured. "So cold."

"She's in shock." Scott hunkered down next to Breanna, took her hands in his and tried to rub some warmth into her fingers. She buried her face against his jacket and sobbed his name. His arm went around her. "What the hell are you doing, Nicholson?"

"What's best for Breanna." Nick touched a lock of her hair. His eyes met Scott's, and he withdrew his hand. "Isn't that all we both want?"

Scott stared at the detective, the niggling jealousy he had turning into a grudging respect. He held Breanna closer, stroking her hair, rubbing her back. The urge to protect her grew even stronger. "You're right. That's what this whole thing has been about, from the beginning. Thanks, Nick."

Chapter 31

Breanna walked along the beach in front of Murray's house on Park Point, scuffed her toes in cold, wet sand and watched a fiery sunrise over the lake.

A week had passed, the formalities of Marc's death were settled, and still she felt as cold and amorphous as the water swirling around her ankles.

She had to stop hiding at Murray's and rebuild her life.

Starting today.

Murray, dressed in black jeans and pullover shirt strolled over, hair in morning disarray.

Breanna looked at her uncle in surprise. "What are you doing up so early?"

He pretended to scowl. "Just because you've been my house guest the past week, doesn't mean you know my schedule. Just finished going over the books for the bar. I thought Spencer had been a little heavy handed with the whisky lately, but actually business is better than usual. All that free publicity. Fed by him, unfortunately."

"I'm sorry about that, Murray."

He shrugged. "Spencer didn't mean to hurt you, he just saw a way to be a big shot."

Breanna hugged her arms. "Duluth's newest tourist attraction. See the uncle of the heiress accused of killing her husband."

Murray touched her arm. "Thanks to Nick, that's no longer what the papers are saying."

She shrugged and continued walking. "I've given up on the studio. All the speculation destroyed my business. Who wants to have their little darling photographed by a suspected murderess?"

"I never thought that's what you really wanted to be doing,

anyway." Murray's sneakers squished on the wet sand. He tucked her hand in the crook of his arm. "What have you decided?"

She turned to him in surprise. "How did you know I'd decided anything?"

He shrugged, eyes twinkling. "Some things you just know. You've got that determined tilt to your chin, for one thing."

"I'm going to call Mariette Marcel, the gallery owner in Montreal. See if the showing sparked any interest in my other work. Either way, I'll be leaving town for a while. Would you feel badly if I got rid of the big house?"

"Depends. If you're planning on torching it, yeah. If you've thought of something more suitable, probably not."

She stopped walking and faced him, marshaling her arguments. "Murray, you know no one will ever buy that house. It's an anachronism." She hesitated, then rushed on. "I want to donate it for a shelter for abused women and their children." She searched his eyes anxiously for several moments. "I really feel like I need your approval on this, Murray. I know the house went to my mother and now to me, but after all, you grew up there, too. What do you think?"

Murray looked thoughtful, then bent and kissed her cheek. "I think that's fitting. And I believe it's what Lillian would have wanted. People just don't live like that anymore. I don't want to. Neither do you. Will you keep Lillian's house?"

"Probably. I want to have someplace to come home to."

Murray's brow furrowed. "What about *someone* to come home to? Who's it gonna be, Breanna, Nick or Scott? Or better yet, someone whose motives you could be sure of."

She dug her hands in her pockets and walked down the quiet beach, the Aerial Bridge silvery in the early morning light. "Can you ever be sure of anyone?"

"Look at the facts, then trust your instincts. And whoever you end up with, make sure they've got love in their eyes. Not dollar signs."

Breanna stood on the porch at Lillian's small house

clutching the key in her hand. Scott had replaced the front door and matched the leaded glass inset so well no one would ever guess what had happened seven days earlier. She took a deep breath, turned the key in the lock and went inside.

Mingled scents of pine cleaner and wax tickled her nose. The hardwood floor in the entry gleamed. Scott and Nick had done a good job of cleaning up and setting everything to rights after the police concluded their investigation. Right down to the new ginger jar lamp on the living room end table.

She walked through the house amazed at the sense of home she felt and wondered if it would be this easy after dark. Pausing at the wingback chair, she shivered, then picked up the phone and dialed the Salvation Army. Keeping the chair was just a little too much. She went to the bedroom to pack.

Nick arrived as two men, dressed in khaki coveralls, hauled the chair up to a waiting truck parked in the street.

"Stopped by Murray's. He said you'd gone home." He looked her over, an anxious look in his eyes. "What's with the chair?"

"I decided I'd never feel comfortable sitting in it."

"I don't blame you. Are you okay?"

"Sure." She smiled. "I'm packing, getting ready to go to the lake house. I'll make coffee, if you'd like."

"No, thanks." He shifted his weight. "Talked to the life insurance company this morning. You should be getting a settlement soon. The marine insurance company said they'd mailed a check to your bank. Guess that's a relief."

Breanna laced her fingers together. "I've already given my banker instructions to give the money to charity. One third to a homeless shelter in Montreal, one third to the Humane Society, and the rest to a children's hospital."

She stared at her hands, wishing she had her family instead of the money. "I'd like to give it all away." She looked up. "What's going to happen with you?"

"Crandall said the grand jury hearing is just a formality. Lanier got no less than what he deserved. Guess we'll never know for certain when he switched the dental records, but it doesn't matter. It's over."

She shuddered. Something didn't ring true about that night. What she thought she remembered.

What Nick and Scott had said. "About that night,"

He touched his hand to her cheek. "You asked me once about why I left the Bureau."

She nodded. What did that have to do with her question now? "I admit, I've been curious."

"We were in the middle of busting up a smuggling ring. Going to take out an arms dealer in Chicago. Somehow one of the main players kidnapped my wife."

"Oh, Nick, I'm sorry. You don't have to say anything more."

"She managed to turn the tables on him. Got his gun away and fatally shot him."

"Oh, my God."

He looked off as if seeing things he didn't want to remember. "People always spout off about taking out the bad guy. Living with it afterwards isn't as easy as they think. Pamela couldn't take the questions, the insinuations. Knowing that she'd ended somebody else's life, even if everyone else figured he deserved it. She took her own before the Grand Jury finished their investigation."

Not able to bear the look of anguish on his face, she threw her arms around him. A tear trickled down her cheek. "I'm sorry," she whispered.

His arms tightened around her. "All you need to remember is that Marc Lanier wanted to kill you. He had to be stopped. And it was my gun that did."

Hazy memories flickered in her mind. Marc rising from the wingback chair. Flannaghan hovering by her side. Marc's jeering laughter, the flash of a gun. Someone calling her name.

The sense of falling into darkness.

Neither Nick nor Scott could or would tell her more than they already had. Maybe Nick was right. Time to let it all go. Silence stretched between them. She eased away.

He squeezed her shoulder. "What about you, Breanna? What will you do?"

She sighed and looked up. "I'm not sure."

"Murray said you were giving up the studio." He took her

hand, his eyes intent on her face. "I'm going back to Minneapolis this afternoon. Come with me."

Her heart fluttered, then steadied into a calm rhythm with the knowledge of what she needed to say. "I can't do that," she said softly. "Please understand. I like you, Nick. I appreciate everything you've done for me. But—"

"But you think you're still in love with Edwards."

She glanced down, avoiding the hurt in his face. "I just know I can't walk away this time and pretend he never happened."

"I'm going to miss you," he said slowly, releasing her hand and pressing a business card into her palm. "That has all my numbers on it. Office, home, beeper, cell. If you ever need anything—" He touched her cheek with the tips of his fingers and turned to go.

"Nick,"

He stopped, a faint flicker of hope in his green eyes.

Fighting tears, Breanna threw her arms around him and hugged him. "Thank you for giving me my life back," she whispered. "I'll never forget you."

Scott stood at the top of the steps leading down to Breanna's house, and hesitated, one hand on Flannaghan's collar. The past week had been full of family business to attend to, doctoring Flannaghan, fleeting moments with Breanna. But now everything had been taken care of.

Except for what mattered most, and his stomach tied into knots about what she would do. Too much had happened in the past month. Too little had been settled. And not once had she said she still loved him.

Flannaghan wriggled away, woofed, and cautiously picked his way down the steps. Scott followed. Breanna stepped back from Nick, slipped a card into the pocket of her jeans and knelt to pet and cuddle the Irish Setter.

Silence hung awkwardly for a moment. "I didn't mean to interrupt," Scott began.

"That's okay, I was just leaving." Nick held out his hand. "See you around, Scott. Goodbye, Breanna."

"Bye." Breanna fussed over Flannaghan for a few minutes, then stood and went into the house. She glanced over her shoulder. "Thanks for taking care of my dog."

"*Our* dog." Scott followed her into the bedroom. A suitcase lay on the bed, half full of clothes. His heart lurched, and he leaned against the doorframe. "Planning a trip?"

"Yes." She folded a sweater and placed it in the suitcase. "I'll probably be gone a few weeks." She waited for his response, peeking over at him from beneath lowered lashes.

Scott was silent. What could he say to change her mind?

"What's going to happen to the fishery?"

He crossed his arms. "Despite the fact that Brogan a.k.a. Burkett had no authority to seize the business, Derek screwed things up so thoroughly, it will take quite a bit of legal maneuvering before it's back in operation. I've just about convinced Dad to sell it to the employees."

Breanna scooped cosmetics into a small bag and tossed it on top of her clothes. "What will you do?"

"Depends on what other offers I get."

Warm breath tickled the back of her neck as she realized he had moved to stand behind her. Breanna clutched a hairbrush to her chest and squeezed her eyes shut. "I'm afraid to ask you," she whispered.

His hands rested on her shoulders. "Why?"

"I'm afraid you'll say no. Then I'm afraid you'll say yes, and I'll wonder why."

"It's up to you, Breanna," he murmured. "Take a chance."

Silence stretched interminably between them. As panicked as she was about what would happen next, she couldn't bear the thought of him leaving.

She took a deep breath. "Scott," she began hesitantly, then rushed on. "Do you want to come with me to Lake Vermilion?"

"Want to?" He turned her to face him and pulled her into a fierce hug. "Lady, I thought you'd never ask, but I must have been hoping because my gear's already packed and in the jeep."

By the time they reached Lake Vermilion several hours later, the sky shone like a brilliant orange ball across the peninsula. Breanna bounded up the steps to the deck and held out her arms, breathing in the scent of towering pines.

At last, someplace that really felt like home. A place with happy memories.

Scott took the key from her fingers and unlocked the door. Flannaghan brushed past and disappeared into the darkness.

Scooping Breanna up, Scott carried her inside despite her giggles of protest, and lay her down on the nest of quilts in front of the fireplace. He turned on the gas jets and touched a match to the logs piled in the fireplace.

Breanna looked up at him, a slow smile stealing across her face. "What are you doing?"

Scott peeled off his jacket and stretched out beside her. He grinned lazily as his fingers moved slowly, unbuttoning her cotton shirt. "Picking up where we left off, sweetheart. Now," he murmured, "where were we when we were so rudely interrupted?"

He pressed a kiss to her bare breast. "Close enough. I love you, Breanna."

She caught her lower lip between her teeth and brushed a lock of blond hair off his forehead. This was what she had been waiting for, all those lonely years.

"I love you, too, Scott. And right now, that's all I'm asking for."

The End

RAINY DAY RAPTURE
By
Breanna Alden

Wind chimes, flirting with a breeze,
tremble, anticipating
Stormy winds ripple across the water,
whisper round the eaves,
and bring you to me.
My heart pounding,
I feel your kisses
softly brush my skin
I am electrified,
so flooded with longing
fantasy obliterates reality.
You take my hand,
lead me away from unformed words,
to float on desire's turbulent sea
Raindrops play a rhapsody
on steamy glass,
the storm besieged with completion
till Lightning surrenders into Sunshine
and thunder's force recedes,
awed by our passion.
Joyfully, we shelter together,
seeking warmth,
finding love.

About the Author

Carolee Joy Bertrand, writing as CAROLEE JOY, balances her passion for writing with her position as a vice-president in the trust tax department at one of the largest banks in the U.S. She is a member of Romance Writers of America and the North Texas Professional Writers' Association. The author of six published novels and three short story anthologies, her many writing awards include:

Golden Quill, winner, best romantic suspense, (SECRET LEGACY)

Golden Quill, finalist, best short contemporary, (WILD ANGEL) and best first book, (SECRET LEGACY)

KOD, Daphne du Maurier awards, honorable mention, (BY AN ELDRITCH SEA)

Bookseller's Best, finalist, (WILD ANGEL)

Notable New Author Award, finalist, (SECRET LEGACY)

Rising Star Award, 2nd place (WILD ANGEL)

RWA Golden Heart Finalist, (BY AN ELDRITCH SEA)

Other books published by Dream Street Prose:

LOVE TRIUMPHS

"Guaranteed to touch your heart!"
~Aimee McLeod, MIDWEST BOOK REVIEW

"...warmhearted and charming." Three stars
~Jill M. Smith, ROMANTIC TIMES

LOVE MYSTIFIES

...(an) "excellent collection of stories for anyone who loves a romance with a bit of a twist." Four and ½ stars
~Susan Mobley, ROMANTIC TIMES

LOVE SIZZLES

"Within these pages are 21 wonderfully delightful tales of romance. Six talented authors have come together in this interesting variety of sweet and sensual love stories. ... a treasure trove of gems for a fleeting visit to places where love always has a happily-ever-after." Four stars
~Susan Mobley, ROMANTIC TIMES

HOUSE OF HEARTS

"A fast-paced and exciting story." Three stars
~Susan Mobley, ROMANTIC TIMES

SECOND THURSDAY CIRCLE

"Ms. Burn's Maggie Gilpin is everything a good wife should be, but widowhood fills her life with surprises."
~Elaine Moore, Author, DARK DESIRE

CAPTURED ANGEL

"This captivating story touched my heart and had me reaching for the tissues." Four stars
~Kathy Boswell, ROMANTIC TIMES

Printed in the United States
80095LV00002B/178-225

9 781928 704256